MONTARO CAINE

SPIEGEL & GRAU   NEW YORK

MONTARO CAINE

A NOVEL

SIDNEY POITIER

Published in the United States by Spiegel & Grau, an imprint of The Random House Publishing Group, a division of Random House, Inc., New York.

SPIEGEL & GRAU and design is a registered trademark of Random House, Inc.

Library of Congress Cataloging-in-Publication Data
Poitier, Sidney.
Montaro Caine : a novel / Sidney Poitier.
p. cm.
ISBN 978-0-385-53111-5—ISBN 978-0-385-53112-2 (ebook)
1. Coins—Fiction.   2. Chief executive officers—Fiction.   3. Consolidation and merger of corporations—Fiction.   I. Title.
PS3616.O547M66 2013
813'.6—dc23
2012025095

Printed in the United States of America on acid-free paper

www.spiegelandgrau.com

2 4 6 8 9 7 5 3 1

First Edition

Book design by Liz Cosgrove

To my mother, Evelyn Poitier,
whose knowledge of the universe
was instinctual.
She could barely read or write, but she knew . . .
and
to Carl Sagan
for introducing me to his many books
about the cosmos, the Milky Way galaxy,
and the universe at large.

I am looking forward to seeing them again,
in places yet unknown.

MONTARO CAINE

1

FOR A MAN WHOSE ADULT LIFE WOULD COME TO BE MARKED BY SO many strange and miraculous events, Montaro Caine had a comparatively unremarkable childhood. In fact, during the times when Montaro would look back upon his earliest years—before his father died, before the arrival of the Seventh Ship, before a deformed black boy only a few years older than Montaro himself would make him a gift that would change Montaro's life forever—he would remember his youth as if it had taken place in some distant galaxy light-years away. He was born in Hyde Park, a Kansas City neighborhood that was home to many academics such as his father, Robert, a professor of mathematics at the University of Missouri. Back then, the neighborhood was one of spacious front porches and vast backyards, just an easy bike ride away from frog-filled creeks and thrillingly perilous ravines.

To Montaro, childhood was a time of endless summers, a time when the things he loved most were close at hand—baseball, the end of school, staying up late to watch the stars with his father, the annual Ozark Mountains hiking trip with his dad and granddad Philip, and most of all, the time he spent with his Kansas City pals. Fueled by seemingly unlimited energy, his wild pack of friends would race across each priceless day in search of adventure, mischief, and fun, until hunger, exhaustion, or weather drove Montaro home, where his mother, Sarah, would always be there to feed him or order him to take a nap or read a book.

But that idyllic childhood would end suddenly and far too early, in fact not long after he turned eight. For Montaro, life would forever be divided between the time before his father arrived home from a meeting of his university's personnel committee bearing an important letter, and everything that happened afterward.

The odd part about the letter and all that it would come to represent to Montaro for his entire life was that it seemed to promise good news.

"Sarah?" Montaro heard his father call out upon entering his family's sprawling ranch house on that Monday afternoon; in Montaro's memory, his father's voice always seemed to echo throughout the house, but this time it sounded uncharacteristically cheerful. "Where are you, honey?" he asked.

Dr. Robert Caine was a gentle yet intimidating man, stocky and handsome. He was the son of Jewish immigrants from Austria and he counted both bankers and mathematicians like himself among his ancestors. The family name had once been Cohen, until Robert's father, Philip, who left Europe not long before the outbreak of World War II, had changed it at Ellis Island. Though at eight years old Montaro was too young to understand the true nature of his father's brilliance or the fact that he himself would inherit his father's scientific mind, he was always aware on some level of his father's great knowledge and kind authority.

"In here, Robert," Sarah Caine replied from the kitchen where she was cooking dinner—roast chicken with apples, which was both Montaro and his father's favorite. Sarah was a graceful woman—beautiful, warmhearted, and generous; to Montaro, she was the personification of love, which seemed to radiate from her, casting its glow everywhere, yet most directly upon her husband and son.

Robert Caine entered the kitchen, embraced his wife, and then presented the letter. "It arrived today. Out of the blue," he said.

"What is it?" She was already able to detect an unusual enthusiasm coming from a man who usually tried hard to downplay his emotions.

The letter was handwritten on Columbia-Presbyterian Hospital stationery and signed by a Dr. Andrew Banks. Though Sarah Caine had not completed college after she became pregnant with Montaro, she was aware of Dr. Banks's reputation. On many occasions, she had heard her husband speaking of the renowned behavioral scientist. Banks was known primarily for his studies of individuals who were afflicted with varying degrees of mental retardation but were inexplicably gifted in a single area, in some cases to the point of genius. Banks's work had revolutionized the thinking on mental deficiencies. This topic was also of great interest to Robert Caine, who had referenced Banks's studies in some of his own papers. Now, according to the letter he was showing his wife, Robert was being invited to join Dr. Banks's research group for a few days in New York as a member of an observation team consisting of about half a dozen professors to see how autistic patients processed mathematical equations.

"This is wonderful, darling; I'm so happy for you," Sarah said, then called to her son, "Montaro, dinnertime!" When Montaro entered the kitchen, he saw that his mother was beaming, and so was his father, who seemed almost stunned by his good fortune. Yes, to young Montaro, this all seemed like good news.

——

On his first day at Columbia-Presbyterian in New York, Robert Caine finally got to meet Dr. Andrew Banks, who turned out to be a tall, angular Gary Cooper look-alike. In a mostly empty examination room, Banks introduced Robert and his fellow observers, four men and one woman, all professors, to an autistic man who was said to have astonishing math skills. The man was named Tom Lund, and Banks referred to him as an "idiot savant."

Lund was a blond, wiry, sharp-featured fellow with hooded green eyes, and he appeared to be in his early thirties, about the same age as Caine himself. He was seated on a metal folding chair in the center of the examination room, and he acknowledged the introductions with a lazy nod of his head while avoiding eye contact with anybody present. Dr. Banks and the members of his research team each sat on metal chairs that were arranged in a semicircle around their subject, while

Dr. Caine and the other visiting professors seated themselves in a row of chairs behind the researchers.

Lund was consumed by nervous energy that drove his impatient left foot up and down in an anxious rhythm. He seemed to want to get this show on the road for yet another group of spectators hoping to gain some new understanding of his abilities. Even so, when Dr. Banks posed questions to him, Lund was unable to completely conceal how much he enjoyed being a star subject.

Banks began by presenting Lund with relatively simple problems, but those problems grew increasingly complex as he proceeded. The more Robert Caine observed, the more he became enthralled. In theory, he should not have been surprised that Lund was able to arrive at correct solutions to the questions that Banks posed. Having read Banks's work, Robert knew that individuals such as Tom Lund would most probably be able to calculate the sum of the first one hundred integers as 500,500 or know that the hundredth prime was 541. But what amazed him was the computer-like swiftness of Lund's calculations. Later that day, when Caine held his first one-on-one interview with Lund, he became only more awed by the man's genius, which seemed almost otherworldly. Caine recorded in his notebook, "A stunning experience," then added that there was always so much more to the world than what one initially perceived. The casual observer would have had no sense of all that existed beyond Lund's nervous demeanor and those hooded green eyes; the world was much like Lund, he wrote, so full of unexpected depths, so full of mysteries for men of math and science to solve. Science and education—those were the two subjects that Robert Caine valued above all others; these were the two subjects, he wrote in his notebook, that he hoped would be part of Montaro's future as well.

In New York, Caine spent the next three days interviewing Tom Lund and consulting with Dr. Banks in preparation for a paper he planned to write about his experiences at the hospital. The exchanges with Lund were exceedingly productive, at least according to what Caine wrote in his notes. He appreciated learning from a revered behavioral scientist such as Andrew Banks, and Dr. Banks, too, seemed to benefit from the insights offered by this comparatively young professor of mathematics.

After Caine's final one-on-one interview with Lund, conducted on his third day at Columbia-Presbyterian, Caine participated in an hour-long discussion in Dr. Banks's office with his fellow researchers regarding their observations and findings. Even though he knew he had to rush to get to Idlewild Airport to catch his plane back to Kansas City, he kept asking questions, holding the microphone of his Dictaphone close to Dr. Banks's face. And even afterward, while he hurried down a long corridor alongside Banks, Robert Caine still wanted to know everything the scientist could tell him about Tom Lund.

Robert Caine was heading with Dr. Banks toward the hospital's exit when he noticed a patient stepping into the corridor. The patient was a black boy with a twisted chin and a withered right leg, which caused a severe sideways tilt to his body motion as he limped forward. The boy was dressed in a faded gray T-shirt and a pair of old jeans that were much too large for him. He moved toward Robert Caine with an unsettling look of determination in his haunted, unblinking gray eyes. The youngster's face looked deformed—his bottom jaw seemed to swing severely to the left of the rest of his face. Both Caine and Banks tried to alter their course to move around him, but the boy blocked their way.

"This is Luther," Dr. Banks told Caine. "Luther, this is Dr. Caine. Now step aside, Luther."

But the boy interrupted by reaching out to Robert Caine. In his hands was a sleek black circular object that resembled a woman's compact. Caine, still holding his Dictaphone, pointed his microphone at the child. "For me?" he asked with a smile, looking down at the boy.

"Son," the boy corrected in a garbled, guttural voice that was not easy for Robert Caine to understand.

"The sun?" repeated Caine, gesturing up toward the ceiling.

"I think he means your 'son,'" Banks explained. Then Banks asked Robert, "You do have a son, don't you?"

"Oh yes," said Caine, looking at the boy with surprise, wondering how Luther could have known. "I do have a son, and this is for him?"

The boy nodded.

"That's very nice of you," said Caine, examining the item. "And this is very nice, too. What is it?"

"It's a ship," Luther said in his halting speech, which sounded as if it arrived after passing through a mouth filled with marbles.

"Aha. It's a very nice-looking ship," Caine said, though the object didn't bear even the slightest resemblance to a ship. He turned it over, rubbing his fingers along its smooth surface, then held it to his ear and gave it a gentle shake; the compact seemed to have a hollow interior, and Robert made a gesture toward prying it open.

"You're not supposed to open it," the boy said firmly.

"Oh, I'm sorry," said Robert. "But I think I hear something inside."

"Yes, but it's not delivering anything to you. It's coming to get something."

"And what's that?"

"Information," the boy stated.

"What kind of information?"

"It's a secret."

"I see." Caine thought for a moment, then smiled. "But suppose my son wants to know. What do I tell him?"

"I'll tell him when he comes to see me."

"When will that be?"

"When he's older."

"Has it got a name, this ship?" Caine asked. He felt awkward and didn't know what else to say to the physically afflicted child.

Dr. Banks stepped forward. "All right, Luther, Dr. Caine has to be off. He has a plane to catch."

"Thank you, Luther," Caine said as he and Dr. Banks proceeded down the hall.

"It's called the Seventh Ship," Luther shouted.

After a brief look over his shoulder at the small lone figure standing in the hallway, Caine, making sure that the boy was out of earshot, asked Banks, "What's his situation?"

"He makes objects out of wood," replied Banks as they continued to walk.

"He made this compact?" Caine asked.

"To him it's a ship," Banks corrected with a playful smile.

"Whatever it is, he made it?"

"Yes."

"From wood?"

"Yes."

"The finish is remarkable. It's beautiful—as a compact, that is," he added with a chuckle.

"Oh that's nothing," replied Dr. Banks. "He can sculpt." Banks slowed his pace and pointed as they approached a door near the exit. "His room is right here. Why don't we just peek in for a second?"

Luther's tiny, windowless room was surprisingly well ordered. Everywhere were carvings of toys, buildings, cars, animals, and birds, all astonishingly realistic.

"The hospital allows some of his work to be shown at two art galleries in the city, and in several others around the state," said Banks. "His situation is the same as Tom Lund's and the others in our study—all the classic signs of retardation, except in the one area where they are exceptional."

"How old is Luther?"

"Fourteen."

To Caine, the boy had seemed much younger, perhaps because he was so short, only around four-and-a-half feet tall.

"What's his last name?"

"He doesn't have one," said Banks. "He was abandoned when he was two or three years old. Because 'Luther' was all he could tell them at the agency when he was first taken there, they called him Luther John Doe. They never learned anything about his background, so now he's just 'Luther.' Come, I think you'd better be off."

As they exited Luther's room, Banks continued, "On your next visit, after you see Tom Lund, maybe you'd like to spend a little time going over our findings on Luther."

"I certainly would," said Robert Caine. "But let me ask you something."

"Yes?" asked Dr. Banks.

"Did you ever tell him I had a son?"

Banks shook his head.

"Then how could he possibly know?"

"I have no idea," said Banks. "Probably he just guessed."

On the flight back to Kansas City, Robert Caine made numerous entries in his diary, worked on the file he had already started on Tom Lund, and contemplated how he might expand his studies to include Luther John Doe who, he wrote, intrigued him. The private one-hour sessions he had conducted with Lund, exploring the abilities of the young man's brain, were among the most fascinating hours Caine had ever experienced, and he sensed that sessions with Luther would prove to be just as enlightening. Lund's brain was one that had difficulty with some of the most elementary problems of everyday living, and yet in certain areas of mathematics, he could astound the most knowledgeable in the field.

Caine hoped to have at least six more sessions with Lund before the end of the year, plus another six with Luther, after which he planned to present his paper to Dr. Banks for his approval before submitting it for publication. But Dr. Caine's plane never reached Kansas City. Ten miles from the runway at Mid-Continent International Airport, it crashed, killing everyone on board.

2

MONTARO CAINE, STILL EIGHT YEARS OLD YET FEELING AS though he had aged a lifetime in the past few days, stood trembling in his family's kitchen, gazing out at the long, dimly lit hallway that led to his late father's study. He was surrounded by his father's friends and by the relatives and colleagues who had gathered to mourn the passing of Robert Caine. And yet Montaro couldn't recall a time when he had ever felt more alone. From behind him, he could hear the voice of his grandfather P. L. Caine. Montaro's mother and his grandfather had brought his father's remains home. An open casket was not part of the tradition in which P.L. had been raised, but he liked the sense of closure that arose from such ceremonies that he had attended in America. Now, Robert Caine's body was lying on view for a last farewell, and P.L. thought it would be best for Montaro to be alone when he said his final good-bye to his father.

"Go on," Montaro heard his grandfather say. But Montaro held tight to his mother.

Sarah Caine took her son's hand in hers. "No, Sarah, you stay here," P. L. Caine told his daughter-in-law. "Let the boy say his good-bye in private."

His mother let go of his hand and Montaro walked forward. He felt terrified by the thought of being alone with what would surely be a terrible sight—the dead, mangled body of his father. His mother gave his hand one more squeeze, then ran her fingers through his hair. "It's all right," she said. "We'll be here."

Montaro looked up into his mother's eyes for reassurance, then turned to face his grandfather. The child took some strength from the tears that rolled down the old man's cheeks. "The difficulties of life can lick a man or they can strengthen him. It's the man's choice," P. L. Caine told his grandson now. Montaro understood his grandfather's words, especially his use of the word "man" instead of "boy"; the choices he would have to make now were the choices that men had to make.

Montaro looked up at his mother once more before he turned and walked out of the kitchen. "A man has to stand up to hard times, no matter what," he heard his grandfather say. This time, P. L. Caine was speaking to the others around him in the kitchen, but his words were still clearly meant for his grandson's ears.

The boy walked down the hallway, past his own room, past the guest room where his mother's brother Uncle Jim and Jim's wife, Aunt Carol, were staying, then across the living room toward his parents' wing of the house. He wondered if it would be possible for him to scare himself so badly that he would die like his dad. Die of fear. And now as he reached the massive mahogany door that led to his father's study, a sudden bombardment of horrible images of what he might find in the coffin exploded inside his head. He felt petrified, unable to move; he stood staring at the forbidding entrance beyond which unspeakable nightmares no doubt awaited.

He could turn back, he thought as he stood before the door. He didn't have to face his father's body alone; the choice was his. But then how would he face his grandfather afterward? "It's the man's choice," P. L. Caine had said. And now Montaro asked himself, *what would a man do?* He weighed his fears against his grandfather's wishes until deep down inside himself he decided on the course that he had to take even if it would kill him. There was no escape; he could not disappoint his grandfather.

Montaro took a deep breath and rushed the door, which flew open from the forward thrust and threw him into the room. His father's open coffin stood in the center of the study surrounded by pink and white flowers. Montaro shut his eyes tight and put his hands to his face to cover them. Then slowly, hesitantly, he squinted and peeked at the body through the openings between his fingers.

Montaro was surprised and relieved to find that his father looked alive. There was no blood. Robert Caine was wearing his blue suit with matching tie—he just seemed to be sleeping, Montaro thought as he moved a cautious step closer. His fears gradually subsided, allowing room for his grief to emerge. Montaro wished he could do something to wake his father up, make him breathe again, but he understood that he had lost him forever, that Robert Caine had passed from this world into another.

Now that he was no longer quite so afraid, Montaro became ashamed of the fear he had felt. He hoped that wherever his dad was, he would never know how frightened he had been. He made a silent vow to himself that he would never feel such fear again, that from now on, he would face every challenge life presented him like the man Robert Caine had wanted him to grow up to be, like the man his grandfather knew he was already becoming. "The difficulties of life can lick a man or they can strengthen him," his grandfather had told him, and no, Montaro Caine would not let himself be licked.

Three weeks later, at his grandfather's insistence, Montaro found himself with his mother and grandfather seated around the desk in his father's study. On top of the desk was his father's black leather briefcase. It had survived the plane crash intact, with only telltale scars from the impact. Montaro's mother, who had wanted to wait until more time had passed before dealing with such matters, had raised a timid objection to her father-in-law, but the man had forcefully overruled her. He knew that the locked briefcase might well hold substantial evidence as to how his only son had spent his last three days of life, and he said further that he didn't want to open the briefcase alone.

Montaro watched his grandfather unsuccessfully attempt to crack the lock, first with a screwdriver and then with pliers, while Sarah Caine began to cry softly. Hearing his mother's stifled sobs caused Montaro's eyes to cloud up in spite of his effort to tough it out. Montaro held his mother close—he felt that comforting her had now become his responsibility. Finally, using the screwdriver as one would a crowbar, P. L. Caine popped the latches on the battered case.

Inside the case, along with other personal effects, was Robert Caine's Dictaphone and two medium-size leather-bound journals containing the notes that Robert had written while he was in New York. There were comments on his trip, mathematical equations, calculations, projections, conclusions he had reached, and drafts of paragraphs for the paper he planned to write. There were also extensive notes about both Tom Lund and Luther John Doe. Sarah Caine took one of the notebooks, and, frequently interrupted by her own sobs, read some of her husband's notes aloud to her son and his grandfather. Through it all, P. L. Caine sat quietly, his face a wrinkled mask of sadness.

After Sarah had finished reading, the three of them began to listen to the tapes. Sarah wept openly while hearing her husband's voice, but Montaro was already learning to control such outward expressions of emotion the same way his father had and the way his grandfather still did, even at this very moment.

As Montaro listened to the recordings, he saw images in his mind of the way his father had spent his last day less than a month earlier. He could hear the urgent footsteps of his father and Dr. Andrew Banks pacing briskly along the corridor of the hospital in New York City. And he could hear the voices on the tape, speaking to him now, almost as if they were coming from another world.

"You do have a son, don't you?" he heard Dr. Banks say.

"Oh yes." His father's voice sounded distant, as if speaking from a faraway past. "I do have a son, and this is for him? That's very nice of you. And this is very nice, too. What is it?"

And then, Montaro heard the voice of a young man. The voice sounded slightly garbled, and yet he had little difficulty making out what it was saying.

"It's a ship," Montaro heard Luther John Doe say.

Montaro's mother couldn't bear to hear any more of the tape. She asked her father-in-law to turn it off and to dispose of the briefcase and send the relevant contents to Dr. Banks. A look at his brokenhearted daughter-in-law evoked a tender promise from P. L. Caine. "I will take care of it, don't worry," he said, then shut off the tape.

But P.L. would not return the tapes and notebooks to Dr. Banks. He would keep them; after all, he thought, his son's professional notes and personal diary might one day be of value to his grandson, particularly if the boy decided to follow in his father's footsteps. The boy was already showing signs of having a fine scientific mind.

Now P. L. Caine carefully lifted from the battered briefcase the carving mentioned in his dead son's notes, a present that had apparently been sent to his grandson by a little black boy whose name was Luther John Doe. The boy had spoken of a gift for Montaro; apparently, this was it.

"Here," P. L. Caine said. "Later in life, who knows? This might provide you with fond memories of your father." He placed the carving in Montaro's hands. Montaro had no idea what the carving was or what it might be for; he would be an adult before he would learn.

———

Nearly fifty years had passed. It was a summer afternoon in the departure lounge of the crowded Delta terminal at LaGuardia Airport, where a good-looking young couple sat among the many passengers milling about, waiting for their flights. Amid the cacophony of flight announcements and cable news broadcasts, of passengers texting and speaking on their cell phones or typing on their laptops, this couple was remarkable for their stillness as they sat together in the bustling waiting area.

Finally came the announcement they were waiting for: "Flight 674 to Atlanta is now ready for boarding."

Cordiss Krinkle and Victor Lambert squeezed each other's hands, then rose from their seats. They were within hours of taking a giant step closer to their goal. Their aim was deadly, their focus sharp, and their unsuspecting targets, Whitney and Franklyn Walker, were eagerly awaiting their arrival.

Weeks earlier, Cordiss had called Whitney Walker at her home in Atlanta. The two had met when Cordiss had worked as a receptionist for Whitney's doctor, Howard Mozelle. Whitney and Cordiss had had a friendly relationship, and Whitney had told Cordiss to give her a call if she ever found herself in Atlanta. During the course of Whitney and Cordiss's phone conversation, there had been the usual chatter and catching up. Cordiss made more than a few allusions to the fact that she and her boyfriend Victor had come into some good fortune and were doing quite well for themselves—something to do with real estate and health clinics, she said, but she didn't want to talk about all that over the phone; she hoped she could tell Whitney and Franklyn the whole story in person. She said that she and Victor would be traveling together on business to Atlanta; could the four of them get together for dinner while they were in town?

"We would love it," said Whitney. "But you're gonna be in our neck of the woods, girl; and down here you'll have dinner in our home. So get your butts down here and you've got a deal. I'm looking forward to seeing you and finally getting a chance to meet that rascal Victor of yours."

"Terrific. And I may have a surprise for you," Cordiss said quietly.

"What?" Whitney asked her.

"Just you wait," said Cordiss. "We'll see you soon."

———

Whitney and Franklyn Walker lived in a small two-bedroom apartment in the Buckhead section of Atlanta, but the dinner Whitney had prepared for Cordiss and Victor was far from modest. Since Whitney and Franklyn had moved south, they had had few visitors, and Whitney was thrilled to entertain guests from New York. She prepared Southern fried chicken, black-eyed peas, rice, and collard greens. For dessert, there would be vanilla ice cream and peach cobbler, the smell of which drew murmurs of anticipation from both Cordiss and Victor the moment they entered the apartment.

"It feels like coming home," Cordiss said with a smile. She and Victor embraced.

Cordiss then shook hands with Franklyn, who eyed the stylish couple with guarded enthusiasm.

In the Walkers' little kitchen, Whitney finished preparing dinner while Franklyn made cocktails, which everyone but Whitney drank. Cordiss and Victor discussed their new business ventures, which ranged from selling real estate to setting up affordable health-care clinics in impoverished nations. Meanwhile, Whitney and Franklyn spoke of the difficulty the two of them had had in finding decent-paying work ever since they had gotten to Atlanta.

"We thought we'd have it better down here. But the economy's tough everywhere these days," Franklyn said. "And we've been having a lot of bad luck."

"Well, maybe we can help you turn that luck around," Cordiss said once they had sat down to dinner and started passing around the collard greens and the chicken.

"What do you mean by that?" Franklyn asked, at which point Cordiss offered the surprise that she had mentioned to Whitney on the phone.

"We want you as our partners," Cordiss said.

Several seconds passed in silence. Cordiss shifted her eyes from Whitney to Franklyn across the dinner table. Franklyn's mouth was open in surprise, while Whitney seemed stunned, as if unable to speak.

"Our partners," Cordiss repeated.

Franklyn Walker's eyes narrowed quizzically. His usual winning smile, framed by a bushy mustache, had left his face, which remained neutral except for a questioning stare. Victor flashed a smile and a wink at Cordiss, who proceeded to enumerate some of the work they thought Franklyn and Whitney could assist them with in setting up medical clinics in Africa.

"We need what you both can bring to this venture," Cordiss said. "We have all the financing necessary for the first stage. After the program's approved, all other financing will be provided by the host country. When that government green-lights the project, then contracts can be signed between them and us. As our partners, you'll be twenty percent owners in the venture, and in all future projects in other countries. Victor and I have done a great deal of research on the commercial viability of the idea and there's lots more to do; but believe me, from any angle you approach this thing, it's a good, solid deal all around."

"How much are you talking about up front?" asked Franklyn. Something was fishy here, but he wasn't sure what. True, he had a degree in finance, but his wife's background was in literature and he didn't see how either of them was qualified to work in setting up health-care clinics anywhere, let alone in Africa. Plus, they barely knew this couple—as far as Franklyn knew, Cordiss's only work experience was as a receptionist in a doctor's office. And he had no idea what Victor did.

"Fifty thousand," said Cordiss. "I hope that sounds okay."

Whitney remained silent. She was thinking of the baby that she and Franklyn were expecting. The number fifty thousand was still echoing in her head as Cordiss pressed on. "And of course, we'll pay your expenses for the three-month period it will take to get our proposal shaped into a final draft," she said.

Whitney jerked her attention back to the table. "Cordiss! Are you serious?" she asked.

"Never been more so in my life. Tell her, Victor."

"She's serious, all right. We are both serious," said Victor.

"And make no mistake," Cordiss continued, "we're talking about a soundly conceived, soundly set up, soundly operated business."

"Bottom line," Victor interrupted, "it has to be a profit-driven entity from start to finish. This is no Peace Corps or missionary effort we're talking about."

"Absolutely not," Cordiss added. "Government-subsidized health clinics efficiently, professionally, and cost-effectively operated. The whole continent of Africa is ripe for something like this. We set them up, we operate them for ten years, then the government takes over."

Franklyn exploded into laughter. "You've got to be kidding. Us? Come on! Why us?"

"Why not you?" Cordiss responded. "You both have all the qualifications necessary."

"Yeah, Cordiss. Girl, come on!" giggled Whitney. "Shoot! Africa? I wish! Even if you were serious, your timing is wrong." Whitney looked down at her ballooned stomach. Her hands gently massaged her precious bump as she continued. "It will be just a few months before this little person here is ready to make an appearance."

Cordiss looked on sympathetically until a twinge of envy made her move on. "I know, but the baby won't interfere with anything, the way we see it," she said. "There's so much more research and paperwork yet to be done for the draft proposal. You'll be sitting on your fannies reading in libraries and typing at home till your eyes fall out. No, the baby won't be a problem."

"Think of it as a three-month vacation, with pay, before the real work starts," Victor said.

"Victor is right. That's virtually what it amounts to. Three months' vacation with pay. After that, who knows? We may all be Albert Schweitzers—with pay."

Both couples laughed. But as the chuckles subsided, Franklyn wondered what was really going on behind Victor's dark brooding eyes. Was he truly serious? And if he was, how smart was he? What had he accomplished? Did he have what it would take to carry out the grand vision they had just described? And why had he chosen to invite them of all people to join their venture? In his mind, he was developing a theory, but he didn't give voice to it just yet.

"If you don't mind my asking, Victor, what's your background in health care?" he asked.

"My background is in business, Franklyn, primarily real estate in New York. Cordiss is the one with the experience in health care."

"Victor brings management skills. He also provides all the financing the venture will need to get off the ground," said Cordiss. "Look, we've given you a lot to think about, so we won't say any more about it. Just know that Victor and I very much want you along on this." She leaned back in her chair. "It's an opportunity for us to bring in friends we can trust." She smiled at them, then glanced at Victor.

"But surely you have friends who could be of more help to you. We've got no money, no background in health care. We've got nothing to offer," Franklyn said.

Cordiss sprang forward. "You have a great deal to offer."

"Like what?" Franklyn asked.

Cordiss hesitated. "We'll get into that tomorrow. Enough for to-night. Let's talk about something else."

"No, I'd like to hear it now," Franklyn insisted.

Cordiss pursed her lips. "Well, first, I have known Whitney for years, and I trust her. Second, you're both very well educated, and I think you're willing to go the extra mile to move ahead in life. You're about to have a baby, so we figured you could use the extra money. And, most important of all, you're black."

Cordiss and Franklyn held each other's gaze. Then Franklyn turned to Victor and said, "I kinda thought so."

Cordiss smiled inwardly. That was exactly what she and Victor wanted them to think—that they needed black partners to showcase their project in a black country. But according to the plan that she and Victor had devised, Whitney and Franklyn would never see Africa. Where Cordiss and Victor planned to take them, no one would be able to find them until it was too late.

3

MONTARO CAINE WAS NOW FIFTY-FOUR YEARS OLD. HE WAS CEO of the Fitzer Chemical Corporation, a multinational mining company based in New York, and he had lived nearly two decades longer than his father had. As he stopped to glance in a mirror in the apartment he kept in The Carlyle hotel and studied his lined face, besieged with the events of the past weeks, he could see few traces of the boy he had been back in Kansas City, save perhaps for his sandy hair and his late mother's pale blue eyes.

Caine was on his way out of his apartment in the Upper East Side hotel where he stayed on nights when he had to work late enough that there was no sense in making the commute back to his home in Connecticut. He was meeting his old buddy Larry Buchanan, an attorney with whom he had attended the University of Chicago, at the "21" Club. Larry had told him he had an important matter to discuss in person. But before he left the apartment, Montaro needed one more drink. He poured himself a generous glass of Glenfiddich, gulped it down, and felt it sear its way into his stomach. He waited for the whiskey to relax him, to slow his heartbeat as it usually did. But he sensed that no amount of alcohol could defuse the explosion of thoughts still going off in his mind like a Chinese fireworks display.

The past two weeks had marked the worst period of Montaro's

career—there had been a collapse in Fitzer Corporation's Utah mine, which had trapped sixteen miners; then, three days later, there had been an even more devastating collapse, causing further damage to the already weakened chamber. Rescue of the trapped miners had proved to be futile, and some of the rescue workers had been unable to escape. *"Thirty-six Dead"* read the newspaper headlines. In strictly business terms, Caine understood better than anyone that without skilled and imaginative damage control the physical disaster could trigger a financial disaster. But no amount of damage control could ever undo the tragic loss to the families of those who had been entombed in the mine.

To compound Montaro's anguish and anxiety, the tragedy was emboldening his enemies, who had long been conspiring to wrest his company's chairmanship from him; before the first memorial service for the miners had been held, they were already launching attacks against him, questioning his judgment, his leadership skills, his fitness as a man of science to lead the company in this time of trial; what was needed was not a scientist but a businessman, Fitzer's manager of operations, Alan Rothman, had said. In Montaro's thoughts, the lines between the human tragedy, the economic setback, and his own personal plight had all become blurred.

Now, there were the inevitable takeover rumors. Mystery raiders were said to be rallying their forces; lesser players were positioning themselves in anticipation of a day, perhaps soon, when Fitzer's corporate bones would be ceremoniously picked: predators all, with an eye on a place at the table for that imminent feast.

To compound Montaro's difficulties, Carlos T. Wallace, senior vice president of finance at Fitzer had, without warning, switched allegiance from Montaro, his CEO, to Alan Rothman. Rothman, a formidably energetic man driven by fierce ambition, was now determined to destroy the career of the man who stood in his way. Rothman's recruitment of Wallace had been a critical victory. *A smooth move, no waves, no hints,* Caine had thought. And Wallace, the bastard, had stayed downwind the whole time, giving Caine nothing to go on. Carlos's raw betrayal was a painful bit of history that had been indelibly tattooed on Montaro's psyche.

Montaro was a realist, who had long sought the infusion of cash to finance the growth that market analysts had deemed essential. But under the current circumstances, even that cash infusion would now not be nearly enough to steady the company. Now nothing would help short of a new, bold, imaginative program, designed specifically to see the company through the dark days ahead in the short term, but whose long-term goal would be what it had always been—to maintain and strengthen Fitzer's independence. Montaro knew that finding the massive amount of cash that didn't mean death by merger or takeover by a hostile raider would be the most difficult challenge of his entire career. He had no bold, imaginative program, only the hope that one might materialize. And he would have hardly expected a potential solution to his predicament to arrive in the figure of Larry Buchanan.

Larry was a braggart and a loudmouth, had been ever since he and Montaro met back when both were undergraduates at the U of C. But tonight, when they met at Montaro's usual back table at the "21" Club, Larry skipped the small talk and went straight to the topic he wanted to discuss. Two of his law firm's clients wanted to meet with Montaro.

"Heavyweight investors. I tell you, Montaro, these folks are bona fide, triple-A players. Mega, mega bucks." Buchanan hoisted his eyebrows for emphasis. "With genuine interest," he added in a confidential whisper.

Buchanan was a junior partner in Hargrove, Hastings and Dundas, one of the city's most prestigious law firms. Their client roster included names long attached to old family fortunes, among them the Steven Phelps clan from the tobacco empire; the Vanderbilt family; the Bishops, whose fortunes had been made in automobiles; even rock stars. It was a client roster rich and powerful enough to camouflage any number of mysterious corporate raiders, Caine speculated.

Caine listened suspiciously to Larry, who sounded as though he were narrating a PowerPoint presentation.

"Finance is Carlos Wallace's department. You know that," Caine said.

"I know. I told them Wallace was their man," said Larry. "But, well—they know that things are sticky right now between you and Wallace, so they think you're the one they should talk to."

"Who are 'they'?" asked Caine.

Buchanan hesitated, reached for his drink, and inhaled deeply. "I don't know. The senior partners are handling this thing." Twice he slid his index finger around the rim of his Bloody Mary glass, then looked up at Caine. "Whoever they are, they're important clients. One of the seniors would've got ahold of you, maybe even old man Hargrove himself, except they know that you and I are friends from school days, so here I am."

For a long time, Caine said nothing, while holding Larry in an expressionless stare. Something about Larry's story didn't sit right with Caine—he sensed that there was either considerably more to it or considerably less. Most probably, Larry was unwittingly setting him up to meet with corporate raiders. He looked away. "I've got my hands full," he said.

"Please, buddy," Buchanan interrupted with a note of sincerity that signaled an uncharacteristic vulnerability from the typically cocksure lawyer. "Being a junior in a sea of seniors has its disadvantages. Half an hour, no more. And I'll owe you one."

Caine looked at Buchanan and remembered how irritating his friend had been throughout their time together in college. Unbearable. Plus, Larry was also a shithead in other ways, particularly where women were concerned.

"Do you, at least, know their names?" Montaro asked.

Larry's face brightened. "Herman Freich and Colette Beekman. Thanks, old buddy." Buchanan patted Caine's arm appreciatively.

Later that night, on West 52nd Street in front of the "21" Club, Caine watched Larry dart about in the middle of traffic trying to flag a taxi to Grand Central for his commuter train, then saw him suddenly race two elderly ladies in a sprint for an empty taxi, which he unashamedly commandeered after beating them to it.

"Just you and the clients, O.K.?" Larry shouted before he got into the cab and it sped away.

Hour by hour, over the following three days, Montaro's mood darkened until it matched the threatening overcast skies that had blanketed the city for as many days with no relief in sight. The steady downpour that beat against Montaro's office windows at Fitzer distorted his view of the sprawling panorama of Manhattan, which stretched out before him all the way to the East River and beyond into Queens. To the right, in the distance, at the southernmost point of Manhattan Island, the empty space where the twin towers of the World Trade Center once stood was barely visible through the drenching rain. Montaro had seen those towers fall, had watched them helplessly through these windows and on TV. Watching that disaster, he felt as though he were witnessing a recurring nightmare, one that he used to have for years after his father's death—Robert Caine's jet exploding before it reached the runway in Kansas City.

Montaro knew that he was steadily losing ground. By the late morning of the day when he would have to make good on his promise to Larry to meet his firm's clients, he became aware of signs that suggested his behavior was beginning to resemble that of a man under siege. He was drinking more; he was sleeping less. His troubles were enormous—why hadn't he seen them coming? *There must have been a sign*, he thought. What had happened to his gut feelings? Hadn't he always been able to detect even the subtlest of shifts in an opponent's position?

"People don't always mean what they want you to think they mean," his grandfather, still living in retirement in Carmel, California, and fast approaching the age of 100, had told him when he was just a boy. "So you have to listen for something else."

"What, Grandpa?" the then six-year-old had asked, looking up at his protector and teacher. Philip L. Caine had brushed away his grandson's tears as the child cuddled in his arms, wounded by a playmate's unkept promise to exchange toys.

Montaro would never forget his grandfather's answer to that simple question. It would have a profound effect on his life from that moment on:

"If you listen hard enough, your ears will begin to see things. And one day you will be able to listen to someone and see their real meaning hidden underneath their words. And sometimes you will even find those meanings sitting right on top of their words, as bold as ever, because a lot of people won't know that your ears can see the truth."

Yes, there had been signs, Caine could now admit to himself, too many for a good ear to miss. Had his instincts shut down suddenly? His grandfather had taught him to search for the meanings that could be lurking underneath his own thoughts. Searching, he realized that he himself was the real object of his anger and not Carlos Wallace, Alan Rothman, or anyone else at Fitzer.

Unprepared. Damn it. I was unprepared, Montaro thought. Though he was alone in his office, his body stood tense and coiled as if in readiness for the next assault. So lost was he in his thoughts, Montaro didn't notice when the summer sun unexpectedly blasted through the stubborn layer of clouds that had been hanging ominously over the city, sending floods of light crashing, splashing, and ricocheting everywhere at once through the canyons of Manhattan. Nor did he notice that the long, greenish-gray tinted window that ran the length of his well-appointed forty-first-floor office suddenly glowed with a golden haze that brightened the room.

"Mr. Caine, should I be with you at your eleven a.m. appointment?"

Caine spun away from the window to find his assistant, Jeffrey Mason, standing in front of his desk. Jeffrey, a slight, red-haired man in his midforties, had entered Caine's office through an interconnecting door from his own adjacent office. Jeffrey had waited several seconds before speaking. Usually, Caine would have felt his presence. This time he hadn't; his instincts were still eluding him.

"Oh, Jeffrey," Caine mumbled.

"It's 10:56. They should be here any minute," Jeffrey reminded his boss.

"Who should be here any minute?"

"Colette Beekman and Herman Freich. Do you want me to be here with you?"

As Jeffrey Mason stood before him, Caine fidgeted with objects on his desk; he twisted paper clips a fraction this way, a quarter of an inch that way, and absentmindedly rubbed a small, smooth, sculpted object that resembled a woman's compact, an object whose significance Montaro had long since forgotten.

Jeffrey stood quietly, waiting. He had observed Caine's nervous rituals over many years and knew that whenever his boss fiddled with objects on his desk, the man was shifting gears. Sometimes he was shifting up, from casual preoccupation with run-of-the-mill concerns to more critical matters: sometimes down, from a honed, focused concentration. There was much that Jeffrey admired about his boss, but nothing as much as his reflexes in crucial situations.

"No, I won't need you here. I'll handle it alone," Caine said.

"Mr. Caine, Mr. Freich, and Miss Beekman are here now," a voice breezed through the intercom.

"Show them in, Nancy," responded Caine.

Caine spun the smooth dark object on his desk counterclockwise; then, his index finger teased the blade of a letter opener from east to west. Finally, his thumb glided to the upper-left-hand corner of a neat stack of correspondence to nudge a paper clip from a vertical to an angled position. The ritual completed, he moved around his desk toward the door as Jeffrey exited Caine's office, making way for Nancy MacDonald, Caine's longtime secretary. Nancy's fifty-two years were clearly etched on her face, but she struggled furiously, through creative use of makeup, hairstyle, and affordable, up-to-the-minute fashion, to stay the hand of time. Following Nancy into Caine's office was a tall, middle-aged man and a stunning young woman with a sense of poise to match her beauty.

"Miss Colette Beekman and Mr. Herman Freich," was Nancy's brief introduction.

"Good morning, Ms. Beekman," said Caine, flashing a businesslike smile.

"Good morning, Mr. Caine," Colette Beekman returned warmly. She extended her hand in a manner, he felt, meant to put him on notice of some kind. Her handshake was firm, and it seemed to hold within it a promise or a threat.

"Mr. Freich," said Caine, looking into the somber, sunken eyes of the nattily dressed man as they pumped hands.

"Thanks for seeing us," Freich said.

Caine politely gestured toward the couches and armchairs in front of his desk and beckoned Freich and Beekman to sit down.

"Need anything else, Mr. Caine?" Nancy asked.

"I'm O.K., Nancy," he said, which was his code to his secretary not to let his appointment run even one second over the half hour he had promised Buchanan. Nancy nodded to her boss before she left the room.

Colette Beekman sat on the couch next to Herman Freich. She had already cast an appraising eye over the decor of Caine's office, which had a modern motif interrupted here and there by vagabond pieces of arresting antiques. She admired the Fitzer emblem embossed on the face of the immense crystal tabletop that rested in a sculpted, wrought-iron frame, giving the impression that the company's emblem was floating free.

Whenever Colette walked into someone's office, it was her habit to look for clues. Her experiences had already taught her that to really know a man one must first find out what he's afraid of. A man's office, even more than his home, usually revealed the best clues.

Two portraits, each of a different, beautiful raven-haired woman with classic features stared out at Colette from the wall behind Caine—or was it a woman and a girl? She took into account the bronze sculptures on pedestals, the designer plants in a corner, and the well-stocked bar—the bottle of scotch was nearly empty. Caine was a good man at a crossroads, one that was far from a run-of-the-mill midlife crisis, she figured.

While Colette Beekman examined Montaro Caine's office, Montaro examined Colette, reminding himself that corporate raiders could come in all sizes, shapes, and forms, including the stunningly beautiful. Though Caine's life had seen its share of temptations, he had never strayed from his twenty-year marriage to Cecilia except in his mind, such as now when he gazed upon Colette. Caine guessed her to be about twenty-six years old. *And God, what lovely eyes,* he thought; they actually sparkled.

Colette placed her briefcase on the table, then looked up at Caine and flashed a smile. Their eyes locked. When Colette felt satisfied that she had held the look between them a beat too long, she let her eyes fall slowly to her briefcase.

"Mr. Caine," Herman Freich began, "we represent an investor whose resources are considerable and whose holdings are quite diverse. However, we've come to see you for reasons over and above any interests we may have concerning investments in Fitzer."

This information was both surprising and extremely disappointing to Caine. He should have known not to trust Larry Buchanan. "What are those reasons?" he interrupted.

The lock on Colette's case sprang open as if in response to his question. With a slight hand movement, Freich deferred to Colette and her briefcase. She removed a monogrammed leather folder with a pearl latch, then leafed through its contents and extracted a standard-size white envelope, slightly yellowed with age. The young woman focused on the envelope for a long beat, tapping it against the up-turned fingers of her left hand.

Caine watched her. Herman Freich watched Caine. When the tapping subsided, Colette looked up, smiled at Caine, and held the envelope toward him faceup. "To Professor Walmeyer" was handwritten across it in large letters. She turned the envelope over, "M.I.T. Department of Metallurgy" was written on the flap.

"Richard Walmeyer," Caine read aloud. "I'll be damned."

"You recognize the envelope, Mr. Caine?"

"I certainly recognize the name printed on it," said Caine.

"And the handwriting?"

Not yet ready to acknowledge the handwriting as his own, Caine hesitated, glanced at Freich, and wondered if Colette Beekman was his lawyer, his employer, or his daughter. "It's not Richard Walmeyer's," he said evasively, as he searched Freich's face for a physical resemblance to Colette Beekman. He saw none. Freich was fiftyish with thinning gray hair, sunken cheeks, and thin, taut lips. On the whole, Caine thought, Freich's was a stern, cheerless face; laughter did not seem to be the man's recreational sport. Caine didn't really figure that Colette was a lawyer because she was behaving too much like one. Unlikely as it seemed, Colette Beekman had to be Freich's boss, he concluded. *But how does Professor Walmeyer connect to whatever it is they're up to,* he wondered. Pointing to the envelope, he asked, "So, what's in it?"

"A memo." Colette lifted the flap and pulled a paper from the envelope. Holding it delicately between thumb and forefinger, she extended her arms, giving him a closer look. It was a signed memo on M.I.T. stationery.

"Might that be your signature?"

Again, yes and no.

"Might it be a copy of your signature?"

"It might be."

"Please read it, if you don't mind." She handed the memo to him. Amusement crinkled the corners of Caine's mouth as he took the page from her, wondering why she had chosen this dramatic approach. *Whatever the hell Herman Freich does, I'll bet he's good at it,* Caine thought. At that same moment, Colette crossed her legs, distracting him. Great legs, he judged. To Caine, the discreet angle at which Colette held her lovely legs spoke of an extremely cultivated background. He was quite intrigued and cautioned himself not to become more so.

At first glance, the folded memo appeared to be not unlike scores of others Caine had written to his old professor. Near the top border of the page was a symbol over which was printed "Massachusetts Institute of Technology Metallurgy Department." But scanning it quickly, he knew exactly what it was.

In his third year of graduate work at M.I.T., Montaro had worked as an assistant to the feisty, diminutive, and brilliant Professor Richard Walmeyer, then head of Metallurgy. On a busy, cold morning in early December, a few hours before Professor Walmeyer was scheduled to leave for a conference in Spain, Caine had been summoned to his professor's office and introduced to Michael Chasman, a tall, middle-aged man who was said to be an old friend of the professor's.

"Dr. Chasman needs to have a workup done for a friend, as quickly as possible, Montaro. I want you to put everything aside and get to it," Walmeyer had said.

"Sorry about this mad rush, Richard," Dr. Chasman had apologized.

"Nonsense, Michael, I would do it for you myself if I didn't have to catch a plane." Casting a stern look in Montaro's direction, he continued, "I'll be back in five or six days. If you finish before the weekend, leave your report with my secretary, Linda, and I'll see that Dr. Chasman gets it first thing Monday morning."

Caine nodded curiously.

"Here," Professor Walmeyer said, picking up a small coinlike object that had been lying on his desk unnoticed by Caine. He placed the coin in Caine's hand. "Be careful; we don't want it disfigured in any way."

Caine had studied the object carefully; in some ways, it resembled a coin, but in other ways it did not. Dark gray in color, it was somewhere between the size of a nickel and a quarter. The surface on one face was sprinkled irregularly with dots of different sizes. Off to one side, one dot was considerably larger than the rest. In some ways, the dots seemed to suggest an arrangement of planets and constellations. The other side of the object was flat and smooth with no markings whatsoever.

Now at his office in Fitzer Corporation headquarters, Caine read the memo that he had written twenty-six years earlier and his heart began to thump violently in his chest. He knew that this particular memo was dynamite. Every word he had written seemed to ignite in his memory. In the memo, Caine told his professor about the extraordinary strength and durability of the materials that he had found upon analyzing the coin.

"To Professor Walmeyer," Caine had written. "Sir, after repeated analysis, I have been able to separate and identify only four of the seven compound elements that make up the object. So far, the three remaining ones do not conform to any available information we have. Individual analysis was run on each one, isolated from the others, with negative results.

"I could learn nothing from studying the elements in various combinations. The four known compounds make up approximately eighty percent of the coin's mass, which, in itself, is highly unusual, since these particular four elements have seldom, if ever, been used in the minting process of any coins or metal objects from any culture we know of. The remaining twenty percent of the object's mass, represented by the three unknown elements, exerts enormous influence on the behavior of the known properties."

As he sat behind his desk in his office, Caine kept his gaze fixed on the memo. The cold scientific language he had used while writing the memo had not expressed the fascination he had felt while examining the object. He remembered the ambivalence that had gripped him at the typewriter in Professor Walmeyer's lab that winter afternoon. On the one hand, he felt sure that he had disappointed his mentor by having failed in the lab to break down and explain a simple mass consisting of as few as seven elements. On the other hand, he had the strong feeling that he was on the verge of some sort of discovery. He felt certain that he had isolated three—not one, but three—previously unknown materials.

"They give every indication of being impervious to heat far above the temperature I was able to expose them to," he had written.

Professor Walmeyer's approval was hard to come by. Still, despite his apprehensions, Caine was not unmindful of the potential benefits to industrial America if, he fantasized, his "discovery" could be cost-effectively reproduced. But two weeks would pass before Walmeyer would offer any response at all. And when he did, he had only a grudging word of praise for Caine's workup. Walmeyer acknowledged that he was fascinated by the presence of the unknown elements that Caine had apparently discovered and said he wanted to subject them to more in-depth examinations. But neither Professor Walmeyer nor Montaro would see the coin again. They tried repeatedly, with the help of Dr. Michael Chasman, to persuade the mysterious owner of the object to submit it for a more scientifically thorough analysis.

"I'm embarrassed to hell," Dr. Chasman told Richard Walmeyer and Montaro after the owner turned down his last request. "He appreciates and respects your interest but, 'no, not at this time,' he says. He says it would be inappropriate for reasons he would rather keep to himself. Frankly, I'm baffled by his reaction. It's not at all like him. I'm sorry, gentlemen. That's all I can say."

Montaro Caine now looked up from the old memo into the radiant face of Colette Beekman, whose eyes seemed to dance with anticipation as he handed the document back to her. She took it and waited, expecting Caine to comment. As several moments passed in silence, her tongue glided across her already moist lower lip, betraying something of her own internal excitement.

Your move, honey, he thought, challenging her with his eyes before turning to Herman Freich, wondering if this austere man before him could have been the owner of the coin.

"Do you remember much about that object, Mr. Caine?" Colette asked with a forced casualness that recaptured his attention. "Given, of course, that it was you who wrote the original memo."

Aha, Caine thought, *no more cat and mouse—bottom line at last.* "Yes, I remember it," he answered in a controlled voice.

"Mr. Caine, may I call you Montaro?"

Montaro nodded.

"Montaro," she pressed on, "since so much time has passed and there have been so many new innovations in the analytic process of metals, we wondered if you would consider conducting another workup of the object with more sophisticated equipment."

My God, they've got it. They've got it! Montaro screamed inside his head while he struggled to keep his expression neutral. *How incredible. After years of speculating about the fate of that coin, these two walk in and they've got it—possibly right there in her briefcase. But easy now, easy. Not so fast,* he cautioned himself. *Who are these people?* He forced his imagination not to run wild with the endless possibilities he believed might be locked away in those unknown elements: exciting possibilities for industry, the military, the country, Fitzer Corporation too, perhaps even the solution to the problems he was facing. He swore not to let the coin's secrets evade him again. He reminded himself to remain alert, to stay a beat ahead until he could find out who these people were and what they really wanted. He smiled now as he thought of how suspicious he'd been when Larry had first told him of Freich and Beekman. He absentmindedly stroked his tie. Then he leaned forward in his seat with his head hanging down. He spoke as if addressing his shoes.

"What exactly are you interested in? The object or what it's made of?"

"Both," Freich said.

"This person you represent, how long has he had the coin?"

"Why do you assume it's not a she who has it, Montaro?" Colette asked simply. With the barest of nods, Montaro acknowledged her point.

"Long enough," said Freich obliquely in reply to Caine's question.

"Am I interested in having another look at it?" Caine replied. "Maybe. Providing my schedule permits. What time frame do you have in mind?"

"Tomorrow," Colette answered.

"That's rather fast," said Caine.

"But it can be done, can't it?"

He knew they knew it could, though not without some difficulty. He had planned to use much of the next day to prepare for an emergency board meeting that would be followed by a meeting of Fitzer's regional managers. "I have a very busy work schedule, Ms. Beekman . . . or Colette, if I may, and I would be hard put to accommodate something that doesn't have anything to do directly with the business of Fitzer Corporation. I'm sure you can appreciate that."

He wondered what their hurry was.

"We would of course compensate you for your inconvenience, Montaro," said Colette.

"Let me look into it," said Caine. "Where can I call you after lunch?"

"Waldorf Towers, Suite 2943," Freich answered.

Well, Montaro thought, *whoever Freich and Beekman are, they are certainly not New Yorkers.* The choice of the Waldorf-Astoria proved that.

"Good," Caine said. Then, after deliberately allowing a pause to grow awkward, he spoke again. "Larry Buchanan was under the impression that there was some urgency to your interest in Fitzer from an investment point of view. The impression is incorrect, I gather?"

"Not completely, Montaro," Freich replied. "We are genuinely interested in Fitzer, but we are more interested, at the moment, in an up-to-date analysis of the object in question."

Colette stood and thrust her hand toward Caine. "Thank you for your time. We will be waiting to hear from you, Montaro."

"You're welcome, Colette," he said.

They shook hands firmly. Caine was impressed to find that her hand was dry—there was no sign of nerves. *She's cool, this one. A clever dealer, sharp beyond her years,* he thought, then steered his visitors to the door.

"Montaro, if you find you can accommodate us tomorrow, we

would appreciate it if you would make the procedure a private affair, limited to just the three of us," Freich said before Caine opened the door into the reception area.

Caine stood staring at the door long after his visitors had disappeared into the main hallway. Nancy MacDonald hovered quietly by.

"Get ahold of Michen Borceau in Research. Tell him I'll be coming into the lab tomorrow for a few hours," Caine finally told her. "Cancel everything for tomorrow."

"Everything?" she asked.

"Everything."

"But, Mr. Caine, you have half a dozen meetings tomorrow."

"Reschedule all of them," Montaro said. "Then, get busy with Borceau. I want to know when he can make the lab available tomorrow. Then, call Freich and Beekman to set up the time. They're at the Waldorf Towers, Suite 2943."

"Mr. Caine?"

"Nancy, please, just do as I ask," he said, and then he closed his door.

4

THE STUDY OF MONTARO CAINE'S HUNDRED-YEAR-OLD COLO-
nial in Westport, Connecticut, was as well appointed as that of
any belonging to his neighbors, who included investment bankers,
doctors, lawyers, and CEOs like Montaro himself. A portable bar was
set up in front of a bay window that overlooked the patio and Cecilia
Caine's lovingly tended garden. But today, all these exquisite trap-
pings provided little comfort to Montaro as he sat in a black leather
Eames sofa beside his wife and daughter, listening to the harsh words
spoken by his family's bespectacled, nearly bald lawyer, Gordon
Whitcombe. Montaro's professional life at Fitzer Corporation was
nearly shattered, he was meeting with Herman Freich and Colette
Beekman the following morning about a mysterious coinlike object,
and now there was this.

"I have to know everything that the chief of police knows," Whitcombe was saying, leaning forward in his chair and repeatedly stab-
bing a finger at seventeen-year-old Priscilla Caine for added emphasis.
"And everything the dean knows. Then, I gotta know some things they
don't know." He tugged at his tie, stretched his collar with an index
finger, and stared intimidatingly at Priscilla, a tall, slender young
woman who had inherited her father's self-assurance but not yet his
capacity for making smart decisions.

Montaro's weary, expressionless face offered little sympathy for his daughter, so Priscilla cast a pleading glance at her mother while Whitcombe relentlessly probed her for information. He said he wanted to know all about Priscilla's life at Mt. Herman, the boarding school where she had been threatened with expulsion and possible criminal charges for supposedly dealing marijuana and cocaine. Priscilla cast her gaze down toward a dainty, wrinkled handkerchief—white and embroidered with strawberries—which had been severely stressed by her nervous fingers.

Priscilla said nothing. Montaro felt his wife stiffen next to him as tears welled up in her eyes and began slowly rolling down her cheeks. He saw Cecilia's lips begin to tremble as she watched Gordon Whitcombe stripping away Priscilla's defenses.

"Now," Whitcombe continued, "how many times per week did you use?"

"I told you," Priscilla mumbled.

"No, you didn't. You said more than once. Exactly how many times is more than once?"

"I'm not an addict."

"I know you're not, Prissy," Whitcombe monotoned.

"Then stop treating me like one."

Cecilia Caine made as if to change positions on the couch so that she could sit next to her daughter and comfort her, but Montaro's arm restrained her. "No. Stay out of it," he said, recalling a time when he had been a boy and his grandfather had stopped his mother from comforting him. Montaro had had to make adult decisions from the time he was eight years old, and he knew that, at seventeen, Priscilla was more than old enough.

"Let me go, damn it," Cecilia told her husband in a sharp whisper.

"I said stay out of it," said Montaro. "She's a big girl now. And she's going to have to deal with this without you."

Cecilia gave in to her husband's hold and slumped back into the sofa. For his part, Whitcombe seemed to pay no attention to the little drama that had just flared up between Priscilla's parents. Instead, he got up and ambled toward the portable bar, the contents of which represented Montaro's own drug of choice. Montaro could have used a scotch at this very moment, but given the topic of their discussion, this hardly seemed to be an appropriate time.

"I know I'm pushing hard, Cecilia, but first and foremost we've got to head off the criminal charges, no matter what. This is serious business," said Whitcombe. "When I talk to the police and the dean next week, I have to know all the facts. Montaro, why don't you and Cecilia go for a little walk and let Prissy and me have another ten, fifteen minutes alone?"

Priscilla looked apprehensively at Whitcombe, wishing desperately for her mother to veto his suggestion. She knew that her father liked Gordon Whitcombe, but that her mother never had. Even so, Cecilia rose and smiled reassuringly at her daughter. "Come to the kitchen when you're finished, Prissy," she said. "I'll have some hot milk and cookies for you." Then, Montaro led her from the room.

Priscilla sat quietly as her parents' footsteps faded down the hall. When she could no longer hear them, she spread her handkerchief on her thigh, ironed it several times with the palm of her hand, then waited for Whitcombe's inquisition to continue.

Strolling slowly, hands stuffed deep in the pockets of his pants, the lawyer half-circled the room before stopping directly in front of Priscilla and staring down at the teenager. Priscilla stared defiantly back, waiting for the attack, but the man's tone was gentler than she had expected.

"You know, the damage to you and the embarrassment to your parents will be considerable if this thing gets out of hand," Whitcombe told her. "I don't need to remind you about your father's situation; I'm sure you read the newspapers and I'm sure your parents talk to you about it, too. This problem of yours could wind up affecting your old man, too. There are some people who work with your father who would very much like to see him fall, and this information about you would only help their cause. So, help me to help you. We've got to convince the police up there that you never sold drugs to anyone. Think we can do that?"

"No."

"So, you were dealing drugs on campus?"

"Yes."

"Look," said Whitcombe. "Whatever you do in your private life should be none of my business, but..."

"It *is* none of your business," Priscilla interrupted.

"Understand me," said Whitcombe. "I am not interested, at this time, in the names of your friends or fellow students who might be buying, selling, or using. So"—he paused and stared at her before continuing—"you can relax about the other thing."

"What other thing?" She glanced up suspiciously.

"What you're most afraid of."

"What's that?"

"Let me put it this way, Prissy. Who you neck with at the drive-in, the beach, or wherever you and your boyfriend go to do whatever you do, is strictly between you and him."

"What's that supposed to mean?"

"It means that if you cooperate with me, intimate aspects of your private life can remain private."

"You think we're having sex orgies up there?" Priscilla asked. "Getting stoned and fucking, right?"

"That's pretty salty language for a young girl of your upbringing, Priscilla."

"But that's what you're thinking?"

"Orgies?" Whitcombe pretended to ponder for a moment. "No. Getting stoned? A definite yes. My only question is how often and on what. As for the rest, my guess is that you are no longer a virgin, and you're afraid that your father will find out."

"My father doesn't care," said Priscilla.

"He does," said Whitcombe. "More than he'd ever let you know. But you'd better start facing the facts. Here's the story the way I'd like to tell it—you never sold drugs to anyone."

"Yes, I have," she replied emphatically. But Whitcombe continued, ignoring Priscilla's objections.

"You have used, yes, and a great deal more than your parents, or at least your mother, probably imagine, but you have not sold any drugs to anyone."

"Yes, I did. Lots of times."

"My God, Prissy, is he so important to you that you're willing to throw your life away for him?"

Priscilla rolled her eyes toward the ceiling in exasperation. Turning away from Whitcombe, she addressed her attention to the handkerchief on her thigh. "I don't know what you're talking about," she said.

"Yes, you do. I'm talking about the boyfriend you haven't told your parents about. The one you've been seeing at Mt. Herman, the one who's about to graduate."

"Leave him out of it, O.K.?" she shouted.

"I can't do that, Prissy," he shouted back at her.

"Then I don't want to talk about this anymore."

"That's fine, but you leave me no other choice; I'll have to turn over the information I have to your parents."

Priscilla glared at Whitcombe. "What information?"

"I've had an investigator doing some interviews in that area for a couple of days."

Priscilla knew that Whitcombe was not bluffing. Her father had long admired the man's straightforward approach, his refusal to tell clients what they wanted to hear.

"You mean you've been spying?" she asked.

"Call it what you like," Whitcombe said. "I was just hoping that you would level with your parents and me. It would be better if they heard it from you, but if they don't, they'll hear it from me."

"I think you're despicable, Mr. Whitcombe," said Priscilla.

"I'll have to manage to live with that, my dear," Whitcombe said.

In the kitchen, Cecilia was warming milk in a small pot over a low flame when the phone rang. She glanced across the kitchen to the breakfast nook where her husband was seated in front of the dish of cookies she had set out for Priscilla.

The phone kept jingling, but Montaro made no move to answer it. As Cecilia reached for the phone, Montaro shook his head. Cecilia turned back to the stove and adjusted the flame slightly. Then, she took a seat next to her husband but said nothing until the ringing stopped. "Finally," she said. But then, the ringing started again.

Over the past few weeks, practically everyone she knew had called, including some friends she hadn't heard from in years. They were all calling for the same reason, but only Bette Grayson, Cecilia's tart-tongued friend since high school, had come right out and asked: "What's going on at your husband's company? Should Nelson and I sell our Fitzer stock? Give it to me straight, Cece, what the fuck is happening?"

Like everyone else who had called, Bette had read *The Wall Street Journal* and *The New York Times,* both of which had run articles suggesting that, in the aftermath of the Utah mining disaster, unknown suitors were planning to make a strong takeover bid for Fitzer, and Montaro's position was in jeopardy.

"It's been jumping off the hook all afternoon, the private line and my cell too," Cecilia said, indicating the phone that had momentarily fallen silent. Montaro responded with a detached nod.

"I hope this won't get in the way of any of our summer plans," said Cecilia. "We can't miss P.L.'s birthday. And we've already paid for the rental of the beach house in Southampton for August."

"I don't think we'll have to undo anything. At least not yet," Caine said. His thoughts had shifted from Priscilla to the business with Herman Freich, Colette Beekman, and the reappearance of the coin from his past. He hadn't yet told Cecilia about all that he had discussed with Freich and Beekman and the memories that discussion had conjured up. Cecilia was a woman of strong emotions, much like his mother; he worried that she would get unrealistically hopeful if he told her about the coin, then disappointed if things didn't work out.

"Fine," said Cecilia. "But whatever happens, P.L.'s birthday is a must. We have to be there."

"Of course," Montaro said. Philip L. Caine, Montaro's childhood protector, would turn ninety-nine this year, and Montaro knew what his grandfather's loss would mean to his wife as well as to him. Death had come often to Cecilia in her forty-four years. Her father, mother, older brother, her mother's sister, Dolly, and Dolly's husband, Jake—Cecilia had no one left from the family she was born into. When she was decorating her husband's office, she had hung the portraits of her mother and Dolly on his walls, two raven-haired women who closely resembled Cecilia, as if to remind her husband that he could take nothing for granted. It was no secret to Montaro that his wife's huge appetite for life was born out of her fear of death. And he understood, too, that this was part of the reason she clung so protectively to Priscilla and those remaining few on his side of the family—she had not learned the art of letting go, a talent he had perfected when he was just a boy.

"Don't worry, honey, we'll go," he told his wife. He put his arms around her and drew her near.

Once again, the phone exploded in the quiet kitchen. And once again, both Montaro and Cecilia glanced at it, then looked away. A few seconds later, a door slammed shut upstairs. Assuming Priscilla and Whitcombe were on their way, Cecilia kissed her husband, then moved to the stove to ready her daughter's warm milk.

Gordon Whitcombe entered the room alone and sat across the table from Montaro.

"Isn't Prissy coming?" Cecilia asked accusingly.

"No, she's not."

"Why not?"

"She said she doesn't feel like it."

"What did you do to her?"

"Nothing, Cecilia." The phones droned on. Though Whitcombe didn't say much, his weary appearance indicated that he and Priscilla had had a difficult exchange.

"She's all right," Whitcombe said quickly. "Just hold your horses, Cecilia." Turning to Montaro, he continued. "She's a lot like you; she's tough, that kid—mind of her own. I still don't have it all clear, but what I do have is not good. In fact, it's a hell of a lot rougher than either of you probably think."

Cecilia turned away from the two men, pretending to concentrate on the stove.

"Get to it," Caine told Whitcombe.

"She's in with a bad crowd up there," the lawyer began. "Casual drug use. Some evidence of dealing; but, that's just for openers." Whitcombe stole a glance at Cecilia, then sighed heavily.

"Go on," urged Caine.

"There's a personal relationship you don't know about."

Montaro seemed to take this information in stride, but Cecilia tensed. She waited, listening to the lawyer's asthmatic breathing until she heard her husband's question.

"Personal as in sexual?"

"I'm afraid so," replied Whitcombe.

"Who is he?"

"A student."

"Is she pregnant? Is that what you're saying?"

"I strongly recommend you check that out."

"What's this kid's name?"

"Nick Corcell."

"What's he like?"

"Bad news," said Whitcombe. "He's the root of the problem; but she's holding the bag, if you know what I mean. He's smart, cunning, manipulative, and apparently cold-blooded. I strongly recommend we come down on him hard and quick. It's the only thing that can save her, as I see it."

Cecilia poured the hot milk from the pot into a pitcher, and placed it on a tray along with an empty cup and the dish of cookies. Then, tray in hand, she walked briskly from the kitchen. As Caine followed her with his eyes, the phones stopped ringing, leaving the two men in heavy silence.

Caine took a breath, turned to Whitcombe, and gave voice to the pragmatic philosophy that ruled his personal and professional lives, both of which seemed to be on the verge of collapse. "We will do what we have to," he said, thus releasing Whitcombe to plan the downfall of Nick Corcell.

5

THE FOLLOWING MORNING, MONTARO ARRIVED WELL IN AD-
vance of his scheduled meeting with Herman Freich and Colette
Beekman at the Fitzer Lab, proceeding directly to the office of his
research director, Michen Borceau. The lab was located where it had
been since the company's founding, in lower Manhattan, despite the
long-standing advice of Montaro's colleagues, particularly Alan Rothman and Carlos Wallace, to move it out of the city to a location—
perhaps Stamford, Connecticut—where space was cheaper. Montaro
knew that his attachment to the Manhattan location had provided
much fodder for Rothman and Wallace, both of whom had accused
Montaro of intransigence and foolhardy sentimentality. But Montaro
still loved the lab's connection to Fitzer's nearly century-old history;
the place reminded him of the laboratories at M.I.T. where he had
trained, and more so than even his office, his Westport home, or his
apartment in The Carlyle, the Fitzer Lab provided him with a sense
of comfort, optimism, and satisfaction with his life's work. And the
truth was, as he had explained countless times to any person who felt
the need to question him, the science his business required had not
changed so significantly over the past fifty years as to warrant a move
to larger or more purportedly modern quarters.

Shortly after entering Michen Borceau's office, where his research director was awaiting him, Montaro announced that no member of the laboratory staff, not even Borceau himself, would be allowed to take part in the analysis he had scheduled to begin shortly after his guests arrived. The portly, Lyon-born chemist was instantly miffed; his brooding eyes glared from under bushy eyebrows and his smooth, ruddy cheeks blushed redder than usual, but he knew that Montaro must have had a good reason for the unusual protocol. Never once, in all their years of association, had Caine slighted him in any way. Never had Caine questioned any of Borceau's or his staff's procedures. Further, Borceau was sensitive and savvy enough to understand that delicate political concerns shrouded all human relationships in the world of big business. He was careful to display no sign of his annoyance, yet both his professional and personal curiosity were further piqued when his secretary, Gina Lao, led Colette Beekman and Herman Freich into his office.

"Welcome," Borceau said directly to Colette. "I am Michen Borceau, Director of Research." He looked from Freich to Colette. Though he was aware that Caine was waiting for him to depart, he was a man who had difficulty containing his appetites, and he could barely keep his eyes off the confident young woman in their midst.

"Thank you," said Colette, all too aware of Borceau's gaze.

As Beekman and Freich introduced themselves to Borceau, Caine addressed himself somewhat brusquely to Gina Lao, a woman whom he knew Borceau had hired more for her looks than for her efficiency or her trustworthiness. Caine had never openly questioned Borceau's decision to hire Gina, but he had thought many times that the lab could be run more efficiently if Borceau had hired someone more like his own reliable, but far from glamorous secretary, Nancy MacDonald.

"Gina," Caine said, "I don't want to be disturbed under any circumstances. Do you understand that?"

"Yes, sir," Gina replied. She prepared to leave, though her boss was making no move to do so.

"Well, I do hope you enjoy your visit with us," Borceau said awkwardly, still staring at Colette.

"Coffee, anyone?" asked Gina Lao, attempting to break the contact with Colette that Borceau had locked himself into. "Ms. Beekman?"

"No, I've had mine," Colette said. She finally turned away from Borceau.

"If you change your mind, buzz me," Gina added as she exited.

A long pause swelled before Borceau reluctantly turned from Colette, looked at Montaro, smiled at Freich, then followed his secretary out, closing the door behind him.

Colette laid her briefcase on Borceau's desk, opened it, reached in among its well-ordered contents, removed a folded dark velvet cloth, then turned to face Caine. After a moment's hesitation, she handed the packet to him. Caine felt a small box wrapped inside the soft material. Beekman and Freich seated themselves in the chairs before Borceau's desk and focused their attention on Caine, who moved behind the desk.

Caine sat and unfolded the cloth to reveal a small gray jeweler's box. He opened the box slowly. When he saw the contents of the box, his disappointment was instant, yet so was his confusion. Still, he tried not to reveal the slightest reaction. Yes, the object looked similar to the one he remembered—same size, same color—but the configuration of dots upon its face was not quite the same. He wondered if Freich and Beekman knew that the object was different from the one that he had analyzed at M.I.T.

Caine removed the coin from the box. He held it up for a long, close look at its face before turning the smooth, flat, reverse side upward toward the light. Had they brought him a fake?

"Well, let's go to the lab," he said, knowing that the spectrometer's results would say all that needed to be said.

In the wonderfully musty laboratory, Montaro attempted to couch his apprehensions by preparing the coin for its compositional analysis. As he gently polished the coin, he described to Freich and Colette the workings of the spectrometer, which resembled a hefty old-fashioned office Xerox machine, and he offered a rudimentary explanation of the sort of wavelength readings that the spectrometer would provide. He explained that though this form of analysis had been around since World War II, it remained the most reliable and, further, it would do the least amount of damage to the object. He continued his lecture, knowing that Freich and Colette would stay with him for however long the procedure would last, and that they would not let him or the coin out of their sight. He disliked the arrangement, but it was the one he had agreed to. So, with his guests watching his every move, he fired up the machine and waited.

As the results of the analysis began to reveal themselves, Montaro was surprised and increasingly heartened to discover that this object's toughness and resilience to heat were of the same remarkable level as that of the original coin. Throughout the workup, he remained careful to conceal his growing elation. What was the history of the coin, he wondered, and what was its connection to the other object he had once held? But no matter how many times his clients asked him and no matter how many times he analyzed, reanalyzed, checked and rechecked, he was not yet ready to tell his clients what the spectrometer was telling him. Yes, he had found elements that were not only unknown, but ones that he was fairly certain were not even contained in the makeup of the first coin.

All three of them remained silent when they returned to Borceau's office. When he was finally seated behind Borceau's desk, he placed the tiny coin back into the jewel box and snapped the lid shut.

"This isn't the same coin," he said at last. Freich and Beekman did not appear surprised.

"It isn't?" asked Freich evenly.

"It isn't," repeated Caine. He watched their faces carefully.

"I don't understand, Montaro. What do you mean?" Colette asked.

Caine stood up, leaned forward on Borceau's desk, and looked from Freich to Beekman before speaking in a clear, firm voice. "I remember every detail. This is not the coin I worked on at M.I.T. It is not the coin we discussed yesterday in my office."

Freich and Beekman exchanged looks. "Are you sure?" Colette asked.

"I'm certain of it, and so are you. So, no games please. Now, please tell me, what is the point of all this?"

Colette's only reply was an enigmatic smile before she looked down, pulling Caine's attention to Freich. "Bottom line, Herman," Caine said. "Get right to it or let's call it a day. I'm a busy man; let's not waste each other's time."

Freich stood up and took a step toward Caine. "Our apologies for misleading you. It is not the same coin," he said.

"Where's the other one, if you don't mind my asking?" Caine asked.

"First, Montaro," Colette interrupted, "can you tell us if there is a relationship between the composition of the two coins?"

Montaro disliked having a question answered by a question. He weighed his answer before he spoke.

"Yes," he said.

"Are they of the same nature?" Colette asked.

"In terms of their strength, yes," said Caine.

"Are they of two different compositions?" Colette pressed further.

"Both contain some elements that are in the other," Caine responded, trying to keep his answer as vague as he could.

"Then both are composed of some additional elements that are not to be found in the other?" Freich asked.

"Where is the first one?" asked Caine. He, too, could play the game of answering a question with a question.

"In a minute," said Freich. "One last question—given your expertise as a scientist and given what you wrote in your memo twenty-six years ago, do you know of any civilization in which these objects could have been constructed?"

"I don't," Caine replied. He thought he caught Freich's eyes dancing for a moment.

"Which is not to say that such a civilization did not exist, does it?" Freich continued. For emphasis, he shifted his body weight to his right foot, moving him inches nearer to Caine.

Caine remained silent until Colette interrupted his thoughts. "Is it possible they could have been made by a culture that might have existed some time in human history of which we presently have no knowledge?" she asked.

"Maybe. A very, very long time ago," Caine answered as he took a seat.

"Thank you, Montaro," Colette said with a smile.

"So, what about the other one?" Caine asked. "Do you mind telling me about it?"

With a glance, Colette referred the question to Freich.

"It's in America someplace," he said.

Caine was taken aback by the tone of crisp finality in this answer. "Come now, you can do better than that," he pressed.

"Afraid not. All we know is that it is somewhere here in America. Exactly where and in whose possession, we actually do not know."

Was that all they were after, Caine wondered, *a confirmation that the second coin was no less authentic than the first? Or was that simply the impression they wanted to give him? Who the hell were these two and what was their game?* He tried to keep himself from feeling both devastated and enraged. He felt as though he had been used—by Colette, Freich, even by Larry Buchanan.

"Are there more than two coins that you are aware of?" Caine inquired, attempting to plant doubt in their minds and to keep the conversation going. He theorized that Beekman and Freich might be collectors of some sort.

"Not to our knowledge," Colette answered with a slight frown.

"It would seem likely," Caine said, softly nudging the doubt along.

"But then again, they could be the only two of their kind in the entire world," said Freich.

"In that event, they would have to be considered among the rarest objects on Earth," said Caine. "Making this," he added, picking up the jewel box from the desk, "a true objet d'art."

Freich nodded noncommittally. "Would it be asking too much for you to jot your conclusions down in a letter, Montaro? We could have it picked up at your office some time next week, if you would be so kind."

Caine's mind reeled. Apparently, he had been had. He had given far more than he had intended and had received far less than he had expected. The compensation Freich and Beekman were going to give him was irrelevant, and so was their vague interest in Fitzer, which now struck him as little more than a con; he still knew nothing that he needed to know. Beekman and Freich had awakened a curiosity in him that had lain dormant all these years; it would distract and nag at him, and yet he still had no way to resolve it.

Colette raised her palm to Caine, who transferred the jewel box to her outstretched hand. Touching her soft, warm hand distracted him momentarily. The physical exchange, to both their surprise, somehow turned into a prolonged, tender handshake. "Thank you again, Montaro. It was good of you to take the time away from your busy schedule to help us," she said. "You can send the invoice to our attention at the Waldorf. They'll forward it to us."

Caine made no reply.

Turning, Colette moved toward the door where Freich waited.

"Good-bye, Montaro," Freich said, with a wave of his hand.

Caine nodded. He kept his eyes on Beekman's legs as she moved through the outer office.

When Freich closed Borceau's office door behind him, Montaro buzzed Gina Lao, and over the intercom ordered her to find her boss as soon as possible. Within minutes, Borceau arrived out of breath. Without skipping a beat, Caine ushered him into the laboratory, where he showed him a few minuscule fragments of the coin he had purposely set aside, slivers containing the unknown elements.

"I want to know everything you can tell me about these," said Caine. He made no mention to Borceau of the coin or the other elements, of what he was looking for, or of what he thought Borceau might find.

Caine then returned to Borceau's office, where he immediately got on the intercom with Gina again. "Get me Dr. Michael Chasman's office at M.I.T.," he told her. A few moments later, Caine was put through to Dr. Chasman's secretary, Madeline Pitcar.

"Hello, Madeline. How are you?" Caine said into the phone. As he spoke, he tried to envision the flirtatious, bleached-blond secretary of his former mentor; she had to be pushing sixty by now.

"Hello, I'm fine. How are you?" Madeline responded uncertainly.

"I'm O.K., but I'd feel a lot better if I was sure you hadn't forgotten me. It's Monty Caine—Montaro Caine."

"Oh my, Monty, forgive me," she said. "What a pleasant surprise, but Dr. Chasman is not here."

"I've got to talk to him. It's urgent," Caine said.

"I'm sorry, I don't know where he is. He's away."

"It's absolutely critical, Madeline."

"I don't know what to tell you, Monty. He's out of town; I just don't know where. He said something about Europe."

"I've got to track him down. Does anyone else know where he is? His wife?"

"She passed. Long time ago."

"I'm sorry to hear that. Does he have a travel agent?"

"No, his agency went out of business years ago. I usually set up his plans, but this time, he didn't ask me, so I have no idea where he is other than what I told you. When I hear from him, I will tell him that you called and ask him to get in touch with you right away."

"Madeline, listen," Montaro said. "You don't have to respond, just listen. Throw your mind back twenty-six years. I'm sure you'll recall that winter when Professor Walmeyer and I made such nuisances of ourselves regarding a rare coin. Do you remember how we pestered Dr. Chasman to get the owner of that coin to let us have a second look at it? No matter how hard we tried, Dr. Chasman would not let us know who the owner was.

"Now, I know you know who that person is," Montaro continued. "I'm sure you know, too, that I analyzed that object for Professor Walmeyer. Assuming the owner is still alive and has retained possession of the coin, I want you to call him and tell him this—I have just seen and done a workup on a second object that is almost identical to his, but not quite. It is certainly as authentic and, in my professional opinion, I would say their origin is probably the same. In other words, I found almost all the unusual characteristics of that first coin in the one I examined today. If he still owns the first coin, or even if he doesn't, please give him my number. Do you understand?"

Madeline swallowed audibly before speaking softly into the phone. "As soon as I hear from Dr. Chasman, Monty, I will let him know that you have tried to reach him. Thank you."

Gina Lao made sure that both lines had disengaged before she quietly replaced the receiver she had been listening in on, while in her boss's office, Montaro Caine placed a call to Lawrence Aikens, Fitzer's head of security.

6

"MORNING, CHIEF," LAWRENCE AIKENS SAID AS HE PICKED UP his phone. He had been listening to a report from his security officer Curly Bennett when he saw Montaro Caine's name appear on his caller ID. At that very moment, he told Curly that his report would have to wait. When Montaro called him directly, Aikens knew that there was an important matter he had to attend to immediately. Not only was Montaro his boss, but Aikens was a Nebraska Cornhusker, and Montaro came from Kansas City, and Aikens felt that, in New York, men from the Great Plains needed to stick together.

"Hi, Lawrence," Caine said. "How's the family?"

"Oh, everybody's fine, chief," Aikens said. Then, alluding to Fitzer's internal situation, he asked, "How goes it with you?"

"We do what we have to do," Caine said. "Speaking of which..."

"What can I do for you, chief?"

"I need some information."

"You got it."

Caine had first met Aikens sixteen years earlier, when Caine was manager of operations at Mosko Chemicals, a pint-size chemical company where Aikens was head of security. Over the years, Aikens had become both a good friend and a strong ally. And Caine, who valued Aikens's loyalty, his honesty, and his plainspoken Nebraska ways, had brought him to Fitzer. Caine appreciated the straightforward nature of his security officer, a profession that seemed to attract a fair number of men more interested in throwing their weight around than actually solving problems. Even now, despite all the turmoil and turf wars going on at Fitzer, Aikens was one man who Montaro trusted completely.

"I need to find out everything I can about a man named Herman Freich," Caine said. Aikens listened, jotting down pertinent information. "He's about fifty, fifty-five years old—and a woman, maybe twenty-six, answers to Colette Beekman.

"I want to know who they are," said Caine. "I want to know where they're from, where they go when they leave Suite 2943 at the Waldorf Towers, what they do for a living, and who they work for. Get me a business and a financial sheet and anything else you can come up with."

"How fast do you need it?"

"This afternoon."

"I'll do my best. Just hold on for a second."

Aikens finished scribbling on his memo pad, then looked up at Curly Bennett, who was waiting to resume his report. Aikens had chosen Curly as his personal assistant over several other candidates, all with more experience, because he recognized Bennett's instincts as those of a born investigator. In less than two years at his post, the young man had exceeded all of Aikens's expectations.

"Curly," he said, "Sorry about this. But everything else will have to wait. There's an emergency situation and I need you to get on it right away." Aikens ripped the top sheet from his pad and handed over the information. "The CEO needs this info in a hurry. Put as much manpower on it as you think necessary and get back to me—yesterday."

Curly stood quietly studying what his boss had written.

"Get to it, kid," Aikens said.

"Yes, sir," the young man replied with a smile as he dashed out of Aikens's office.

"I need it in hand by this afternoon," Aikens called after him. When Curly was gone, Aikens returned to Caine, who was still waiting on the other end of the phone. "I'll have something for you in a couple of hours, chief," he said.

7

ALAN ROTHMAN, FITZER CORPORATION'S FINANCE MANAGER, drove across town in his black, S-class hybrid Mercedes sedan until he reached the garage of The Brougham Arms Apartments, an impressive upscale rental complex in the mid-Seventies overlooking the East River. The Brougham Arms represented an ideal location, providing both the privacy and convenience Rothman required whenever he made his ever-more-frequent visits to a certain penthouse apartment on the building's twenty-ninth floor. Rothman left his car with the garage attendant, handed the man a crisp twenty, then walked to the self-service elevator. He moved through the garage almost as smoothly and as silently as his Mercedes.

All in all, Rothman thought as he stood alone in semidarkness waiting for the elevator doors to open, he had had an eventful and productive day. First, his CEO, Montaro Caine, had abruptly postponed two critical meetings regarding the continuing fallout from the Utah mining disaster and the persistent bad press and takeover rumors in order to have a confidential meeting with Michen Borceau at the Fitzer Lab. Then, there had been a rushed, rescheduled board meeting in which Caine had defended his increasingly rash decision-making process but refused to reveal what he had been doing at the lab or why it had necessitated postponing the meeting. Both Rothman and operations manager Carlos Wallace had argued heatedly with Caine, demanding to know what he was up to. Afterward, the two men had circulated a memo expressing outrage at Caine's behavior. "His shooting from the hip at such a delicate time for the company is disruptive and can't help but be damaging to all concerned," they had written. But Wallace's and Rothman's anger was mostly for show; they felt that Caine was proving their point that he was no longer up to his job. Now, Rothman had to meet with his associates to reassure them that his instincts were correct.

The elevator doors opened, and Rothman stepped in. He fingered the button for his destination and rode the elevator upward. Eyes alert, he stepped out onto the twenty-seventh floor, and, making sure that he had not been observed, he opened the door to an exit stairwell. He jogged up two additional flights to the twenty-ninth floor. Perhaps this was an unnecessary precaution, a bit more James Bond than the situation warranted, but he took it nonetheless, finding his way to apartment 2901 where Verna Fontaine, a stylish, well-built blond woman in her late forties, greeted him warmly. Verna was a senior vice president at Nevan, an international cosmetics firm that had recently been acquired by Colcour, a conglomerate owned by Richard Davis, the billionaire businessman who had started in oil and wound up in everything else.

"Are they here?" Rothman asked, stepping past Verna.

"They are." She closed the door behind him, then led him to the dining room where Richard Davis, a wiry man of sixty-two, was seated between his lieutenants, Bob Wildenmiller and Thomas Bolton. Davis was intent on a takeover of Fitzer, and he had selected and cultivated Rothman to be his man on the inside. Over the past eighteen months they had spent in their secret association, Davis had found Rothman to be bright, tough, ambitious, and hungry for power—a combination that perfectly fit Davis's plan for the restructuring of Fitzer Corporation after it was drawn into his orbit.

"Heya, Alan," Davis called out as Rothman entered the living room. "How are ya?"

"Fine," Rothman returned. "And how are you?"

"Good, good." While Verna set out a silver tray arranged with soft drinks, coffee, and cookies in the middle of the dining room table, Davis rose from his seat to shake hands with Rothman. Wildenmiller and Bolton also stood to shake Rothman's hand, then Davis got straight to the point. "So, what the hell's going on with our situation?" he asked.

"Everything's on schedule, Richard," said Rothman. "Nothing to worry about."

"Yeah?"

"Guaranteed."

"You seem confident of that."

"I am."

Davis took his seat. Bob Wildenmiller, Thomas Bolton, and Verna Fontaine did the same, while Rothman slid into a chair facing Davis.

"Caine, on the other hand, seems to have a different scenario in mind. Canceling meetings? Running off to the lab? Any idea what that's all about, Alan?"

"Blowing smoke," said Rothman.

"I wish I could be so sure," said Davis. "From the way he choreographed it, it looks to me as if he wants someone to think he's baiting a trap."

"I agree. That's what he wants us to think. But there's nothing to it. Believe me, I've been studying this guy; he is not above dealing in appearances. I know his style."

"Maybe," said Davis. "But he doesn't seem to be the kind of man who would be doing what he's doing without a damn good reason."

"I don't think he's got one, Richard."

"Then how do you explain his actions?"

"Nervous," said Rothman. "He's not a born businessman; that's what I've been saying all along. He's got too much to deal with and he's poking around in the dark. Everything's weighing on him and he doesn't know how to carry it all. Plus, there's a situation with his family. Frankly, all this sounds like a death rattle to me."

"Come now, Alan," said Davis. "The man is a tactician. You know that better than we do. Now, what the hell is he up to?"

"I really don't think there's anything to worry about," said Rothman. "But if there is, I guarantee you, I'll find out what it is."

Davis seemed to be satisfied with that response. He propped his elbows on the dining table, then resumed speaking. "Well," he said, "we're not as sure of his motives, or lack thereof, as you seem to be, so we'll give him the benefit of the doubt and let you find out what you can. And in the meanwhile, we have concluded that cutting him off at the knees would be the best counter." He paused for a moment, then continued. "We've decided it's time to move, Alan," he said. "First, we begin with a gradual buy-up of as much of the stock as we can before we make our intentions public." Davis then began to outline his plan to take over Fitzer.

An hour later, when Rothman rode the elevator alone down to the garage, he was smiling. Richard Davis was in a class by himself, no doubt about that; soon, Alan Rothman thought, he would find himself in that class too, and he would stop at nothing to get there.

8

THE CROWD AT THE "21" CLUB WAS THINNING OUT AS THE LUNCH hour drew to a close. In front of Montaro Caine was a plank of salmon he hadn't touched and a tumbler of scotch he had touched far too much of. His wife had been telling him that he needed to eat more and drink less. Every day at about this time, a text message from Cecilia would pop up on his phone—"Have you eaten yet?" "What're you having for lunch, Monty?" Given the stress he was experiencing on all fronts, Montaro knew that Cecilia was right to worry. Yet, the facts remained before him in the forms of a full plate and an empty glass.

Larry Buchanan's appetite, however, seemed to be faring just fine. When Larry was nervous, he ate; he was finishing off the last of his French fries while Montaro continued to press him for information about Colette Beekman and Herman Freich.

"I need you to tell me everything you can about those two," Montaro said.

"I don't know any more than I've already told you, Monty," said Larry, but Montaro knew that his old college buddy wasn't telling him the whole story.

"Tell me, where are they now?" Montaro asked.

"At the Waldorf, I guess."

"No, they're not," said Montaro. "They checked out yesterday morning before they came to see me."

"How did that go, by the way?"

Montaro glowered, irritated by Larry's obvious diversionary tactic, the one he had been using ever since the two men were freshmen at the U of C and Larry relied on Montaro to get him out of trouble with girls. "Who are they, Larry?" he pressed.

"They're investors, Montaro. Honest to God, that's all I know."

"How did they come to you? Do you know who pays their hotel bill?"

"No, I don't."

"Well, I do," said Montaro. "Have you ever heard of a company called Socoloux Limited?"

"Can't say that I have."

"They don't let you in on much over there at that office, do they, Larry?"

"That's a dirty crack, Monty. For Christ's sake, will you get to the point?"

"The only known address for Socoloux is in care of your law firm."

"No shit!"

"No shit, buddy. No shit. I put my best man on it and that's all he could come up with. Now, who the hell are Beekman and Freich? What do they do? I mean, *really do*? I've got to know and I'm leaning on you, Larry."

"Jesus, I can't," said Larry. "I told you before—being a junior in a sea of seniors has its disadvantages."

"You're gonna have to do better than that," said Montaro. "I'm gonna need you to give me some answers."

Larry looked away. "I just can't do it," he said.

"Yes you can." Caine stared unblinkingly at Larry. "Which one of the seniors handles them personally?"

Larry turned back to face Caine. He hesitated before answering. "Hargrove," he said.

"The head man?"

Larry nodded. "Yes, Monty," he said. "But look, if you're thinking..."

"Yes, you know exactly what I'm thinking," said Caine. "Goddamn it, I did you the favor of meeting with Beekman and Freich and I've got nothing to show for it. Now, you're going to do me the favor of finding out everything you can about them."

As the two men stared at each other, Larry began to sweat. He looked down at his plate in search of some comfort, but there was no food left on it.

9

Dr. Howard Mozelle was an obstetrician who operated the Mozelle Women's Health Center on East 67th Street near the Sloan-Kettering Cancer Center and had done so for nearly forty years. He was a good-hearted man of considerable integrity, a throwback, many said, to a previous age. He rarely ever refused a patient regardless of their insurance status or their ability to pay. His idealistic approach was perhaps not particularly beneficial to his bank account, but it was not all that dissimilar from that of his wife of forty-one years, Dr. Elsen Mozelle, a professor of European history at Columbia University; she had passed up dozens of think tank and consultancy positions rather than abandon the teaching job she loved.

As was nearly always the case, Dr. Mozelle had been working later than he had planned to and was just getting ready to close down his office for the night when the phone rang. His receptionist had already left, so Mozelle picked up the phone himself before his service could answer. Though he immediately recognized the voice on the other end, he was stunned to hear it; he hadn't heard it in years.

"I hope I didn't act incorrectly in calling you," Madeline Pitcar told him. She spoke rapidly and Mozelle had trouble grasping everything she was saying, though he did understand her to say that there was a man who wanted very much to get in touch with him. "His name is Montaro Caine," she said. "I didn't let on that I knew anything about you. But, since I can't reach Dr. Chasman, and since Mr. Caine said it was of the utmost importance, I wrote down what he said." At which point, Pitcar repeated the story that Caine had begged her to pass on to the owner of the coin he had seen twenty-six years earlier at M.I.T. And the more Dr. Mozelle listened to that story, the more trouble he had believing his ears.

When Madeline Pitcar was through telling Mozelle what Caine had told her, Dr. Mozelle thanked her, then hung up and called his wife, who was at her office at Columbia, also working late. Then he called Anna Hilburn, who had run his office for thirty years before arthritis had forced her into semiretirement, reducing her on-the-job time to only a few hours per week. He asked both women if they could try to meet him at his office as soon as they could.

"It's about the coin; I think something may be happening," he told both of them, and neither had to ask what he was talking about.

Dr. Mozelle's office had a spectacular easterly view, but he kept his blinds drawn and his door closed while he and Elsen spoke with Anna Hilburn about the strange phone call he had received from Madeline Pitcar. The call reawakened memories of events that had occurred more than twenty-five years ago when the odd and seemingly miraculous discovery of a mysterious coin had put him in contact with both Michael Chasman and Richard Walmeyer, whose young assistant Montaro Caine had found that coin to have seemingly otherworldly properties. A girl named Whitney Carson had played a crucial role in the story as well.

"Have you heard from Whitney lately?" Mozelle asked Anna Hilburn now as she sat in his office.

Anna shrugged. "Not lately," she said. "And I'm pretty sure she's overdue for her checkup this year."

"I need you to try to get in touch with her and find out what her current situation is. Can you do that?"

Anna Hilburn nodded, then rose unsteadily to her feet. Mrs. Mozelle reached out and patted Anna on the arm. After Anna had exited the room, Elsen turned to her husband. "What do you think about this guy Caine?" she asked. "How do you think we should handle him?"

"We'll hear what he has to say," Mozelle said.

Elsen took a short, tight breath. "You're not going to show it to him, are you, Howard?" she asked.

"I honestly don't know," he said. "We'll have to see."

When Anna Hilburn returned to Dr. Mozelle's office, she looked dazed and bewildered, and both the doctor and his wife immediately understood that something was amiss. In Anna's three decades of working for the Mozelle Women's Health Center, she had always been a model of calm and efficiency, rarely allowing emotions to get in the way of her work.

"What's the matter?" Howard Mozelle asked.

Anna took a deep breath, then let it out. "I just got off the phone with Whitney," she said. "She couldn't talk long because she was at the airport and had to get on a flight."

"And?" asked Mozelle.

"And she said she got married," Anna said.

Howard Mozelle looked momentarily pleased. Then, he looked stunned. And then he looked worried. "When?" he asked. But before Anna could answer, he was on her with more questions, each one more emphatic than the one that preceded it. "Did you speak with Whitney herself? Who did you say she married?"

"She said her husband's name is Franklyn Walker," said Anna. "She sounded happy."

"Well, can she come in for her checkup?" Mozelle asked.

Anna shook her head. "She moved," she said.

"Moved? Where to?" he asked.

"Atlanta. And she's traveling anyway."

"Traveling where?"

"Abroad."

"How didn't we know about this?" asked Mozelle. "Why didn't she tell us?"

"I don't know what could have happened," said Anna. "She said that she was in touch with the office and that she sent word."

"In touch with whom? What does that mean? 'Sent word'?"

"She said she was in town to pack up her apartment and dropped by to say hello and have her annual checkup, but it was when you were on vacation."

"Damn it," said Dr. Mozelle, remembering the most recent trip he and Elsen had taken to Budapest, for one of his wife's academic conferences. "Who did she say saw her?"

"Dr. Chambers," said Anna. "I saw the record of the appointment in his files. But here's the strange thing—I didn't see any record of it in Whitney's chart."

"Shouldn't you have known she was here?" Mozelle demanded, even as his wife touched him lightly on the arm in an attempt to calm him.

"Must have been on a day when Cordiss was here by herself," Anna said. She was referring to Cordiss Krinkle, one of Mozelle's former employees who had left her position abruptly and apparently not long after Whitney had her appointment.

"Cordiss didn't tell you Whitney was here?" he asked.

"No, she didn't."

"And Chambers's nurse didn't mention it to you?"

"Neither she nor Dr. Chambers knew that we were monitoring Whitney," Anna said.

"Well, Cordiss Krinkle sure as hell knew, didn't she?"

"She must have," said Anna. "But Cordiss is long gone."

"Where is she?" Mozelle asked, his face now crimson. "There's no way Whitney could have had an examination in these offices without Cordiss knowing about it. We need to get in touch with her. Do you know where she is?"

"I have no idea," said Anna. "She said she was going to California. But she didn't leave any number or forwarding address. We sent her her final check, but it was returned. Her email address is dead. I tried finding her, but I couldn't, so I just gave up."

Elsen Mozelle took a step closer to Anna and spoke to her in a gentle voice. "You're sure now, Anna? Cordiss never mentioned anything to you about Whitney, you're absolutely sure?"

"I've got arthritis, not Alzheimer's. I'm sure, Elsen. She never mentioned anything."

"Married? And we missed it?" Elsen said in disbelief.

"The boy she married, what did she say about him?" asked Dr. Mozelle. And then, as his eyes met Anna Hilburn's, he felt as if he understood everything, and the knowledge terrified him. "Is she pregnant, Anna? Has she had a child?"

"I don't know, Dr. Mozelle," said Anna. "She didn't say."

"Get her back on the phone," the doctor told her. "We need to find out."

This time, Anna took out her cell phone and redialed Whitney's number, but the call went straight to voicemail.

"She said she was about to board the plane," said Anna. "She's probably already on it."

"Where's she going?"

"She didn't say."

"Leave her a message. Tell her to call us as soon as she can."

As Anna left that message on Whitney's voice mail, Elsen Mozelle stroked the lapel of her husband's jacket, then took his hand in hers and held it close to her chest.

"Something's going on here," Howard Mozelle said after Anna hung up her phone. "Somebody must have found out."

"But how could they?" asked Anna. "The three of us are the only ones who know what happened. I've never spoken to anyone about it. Not one word in twenty-six years. You're not thinking that Cordiss found out, are you?"

But that was, in fact, exactly what Dr. Mozelle was beginning to think. "Well, Elsen and I haven't spoken about it to anyone, obviously," he said. "This Montaro Caine couldn't know anything. He saw the coin, analyzed it, and made a report. He never had a clue about its background. I didn't even tell Dr. Chasman. To this day, he knows nothing, and so Caine knows no more than he does, except he now says there's another coin."

"Which is in the hands of someone in this city," Anna reminded him.

"Oh God," Mrs. Mozelle suddenly gasped, and at the exact moment, she, her husband, and Anna Hilburn all had the same thought.

"The safe," Elsen Mozelle said.

Though Dr. Mozelle had two bad hips, he sprinted out of his office, then through the corridor to a narrow hallway at the rear of the building while the two women struggled to keep pace. Just past the laboratory, he turned left and entered a small, windowless room. Forty-five years earlier, when the building had served as headquarters for a wholesale furrier, the safe had been a walk-in storage vault. When the doctor became the new tenant, it became a repository for medical and financial records.

Dr. Mozelle stopped at a steel door only to realize that he had not been here for so long he could no longer recall the vault's combination. When Anna, helped along by Mrs. Mozelle, arrived at the door, Dr. Mozelle pointed at the lock and impatiently gestured for her to apply the combination. Once inside, they wove their way around boxes of outdated paperwork, stacks of charts, medical books, pamphlets, and a few stray pieces of office furniture. When the women reached an old wooden file cabinet in a corner against the wall, Anna Hilburn forced her arm into the narrow space between the cabinet and the wall until her fingers reached a small key hanging on a nail embedded in the wall. With the key, she unlocked the bottom drawer of the cabinet, then stepped to one side.

Dr. Mozelle kneeled quickly, slid the drawer open, plunged both hands to the bottom, and after several forceful jerks, he surfaced with a manila folder. He opened it, then shuffled frantically through many sheets of paper. He turned to his wife in horror.

"All my notes are still here, but the coin is gone. Stolen," he said. He looked to Anna Hilburn.

"Call Montaro Caine," he told her. "Call him now."

10

Traffic was heavy on Manhattan's East Side, so Montaro Caine handed a twenty-dollar bill to his taxi driver and told him that he would cover the rest of the distance to the Mozelle Women's Health Center on foot. Anna Hilburn had left Howard Mozelle's name, address, and a simple message with Caine's secretary: "Tell Mr. Caine that we are ready to discuss the matter he expressed an interest in." Caine had already scheduled a Fitzer board meeting as well as a phone conference with his lawyer Gordon Whitcombe for the morning to discuss his daughter's situation at Mt. Herman. But when he received the message from Anna Hilburn, he told Nancy MacDonald that she would have to reschedule everything again.

Caine moved east along 67th Street with a quick stride that every now and then exploded into a jog. He was overanxious and he knew it; he reminded himself to calm down before arriving at Mozelle's office. It seemed strange—for twenty-six years, he had imagined the owner of the coin to be a wealthy collector of rare objects who lived somewhere in the Boston area not far from M.I.T., when in fact the coin's owner was apparently right here in Manhattan, just ten minutes away from Fitzer.

When Caine entered the office of Howard Mozelle and introduced himself to the doctor, his wife, and Anna Hilburn, who were already seated, awaiting his arrival, he sensed a pronounced uneasiness among his hosts. Perhaps it was just the clinical office setting that made Montaro feel that he was about to undergo some sort of invasive exam. Handshakes were loose and smiles seemed forced. Dr. Mozelle stared at Caine for several awkward moments, studying his features.

"I've seen your name in the newspapers and on the society and financial pages, but your face is unfamiliar. I don't think we've ever met. Have we?"

"No, we haven't, I'm afraid," said Caine with a smile. He was not surprised that Mozelle did not recognize him; his managerial style had always been to stay out of public view as much as possible in favor of focusing on the business of his company. Even after the recent mining accident, he preferred to let his spokespeople talk to the press.

"Through no fault of yours, as I recall," Dr. Mozelle said by way of an apology for his refusal twenty-six years earlier to let Montaro and Richard Walmeyer reexamine the coin. "Yes, well, that was a long time ago," he added. "Anyway, I recall that your interest in the coin was primarily in the composition of various elements, some of which were intriguing to you and my good friend Dr. Chasman."

"Yes," said Caine. "We were fascinated and wanted very much to do a follow-up analysis. Some of those elements were strikingly unusual. I'd never seen anything like them before or since—until this week, that is."

Dr. Mozelle's face turned serious. "How sure are you about what you saw? I mean, twenty-six years is a long time. Could what you saw possibly have been the same object you saw at M.I.T.?"

"No, they're different," said Montaro. "They're alike in many ways, but they are different objects. Absolutely."

"How can you be so sure of that?"

"Chemicals and metals are my profession, Doctor."

"You were interested in commercial exploitation back then. Would it be fair to say that this is still true?"

"I am interested in its potential value, yes," said Caine. "But over and above that, I must admit to a healthy curiosity about the object itself."

Dr. Mozelle liked Caine's forthright and accommodating manner of speaking. He had been expecting a much more aggressive man. Mozelle's eyes shifted to his wife and his elderly secretary; then he gestured for Caine to have a seat.

As Caine sat in the armchair in front of Mozelle's desk, the doctor spoke. "We wanted to talk with Dr. Chasman before we saw you, but, as you have no doubt found out yourself, his secretary hasn't been able to reach him. Have you kept in touch with him throughout the years?"

"Three or four times in the last five years, I would say."

"Well," said Dr. Mozelle, "since he isn't here, and since time is of the essence, I'm going to tell you a story, one I very much wish he was here to listen to. Have you ever heard the name Hattie Sinclair?"

Montaro shook his head. "I haven't," he said.

Dr. Mozelle's eyes seemed to glaze over and to focus on something beyond Caine. He rose slowly to his feet, took a deep breath, and then began pacing the floor as he went on to tell a story that, to Montaro, seemed almost as strange and wondrous as the coins themselves. For him, the story that Howard Mozelle related brought to mind not only the experience of encountering the coin when he was a young man at M.I.T., but also the lesson that he had learned as a child—that there is a great deal more to this world than we can perceive with our eyes. When Montaro began listening to Mozelle's story, he had never heard the name Hattie Sinclair; when Mozelle was through, he knew that he would never forget it.

11

Dr. Mozelle stopped pacing and stood behind his desk to face Montaro Caine. Then he began the story Elsen and Anna Hilburn knew so well but had rarely spoken of in the past two-and-a-half decades. "About twenty-six years ago in the spring—on April seventeenth, to be exact—Elsen was diagnosed as having a quite fatal disease, a type of cancer that is usually unforgiving. To be brief, we explored every option open to us: cancer specialists, the usual institutions, the unusual ones as well. We even made ourselves available for experimental procedures, as long as they held out the slightest glimmer of hope."

Howard Mozelle said that he had already received three pessimistic opinions about his wife's prognosis when he arrived at the office of famed cancer specialist Dr. Rudolf Kempler. At first, Dr. Kempler's prognosis was hardly different from the others that Howard and Elsen had heard from the previous physicians; the cancer had spread too far to respond to treatment, and the only option was palliative care.

"And you see no chance?" Mozelle asked. "None?"

"Early diagnosis is the key to what few victories we've had," Kempler said apologetically.

"Dr. Kempler," he asked. "Is there any research going on anywhere? Here? In Europe? Anywhere at all?"

"There is nothing that I know of that would reverse what I would characterize as a terminal situation," said Kempler. "There is, of course, the Hattie Sinclair case, but there has been no scientific verification for the treatment she was supposed to have received, so that case remains little more than an intriguing dilemma."

"What case was that?"

At first, Dr. Kempler seemed reluctant to tell Howard Mozelle the story of Hattie Sinclair, for fear that it might give the doctor and his wife unreasonable cause for hope. But after Mozelle pressed him, he told the story.

"Hattie Sinclair's case was an intriguing dilemma out of which we have learned nothing, regretfully," said Kempler.

"What intriguing dilemma?" asked Mozelle.

"She was cured."

"How?"

"It's a very bizarre story, Dr. Mozelle. I wrote a paper on it. It might be interesting for you to read. But again, I assure you, nothing about it can be applied to your wife's situation."

"Still, I'd like to hear about it if you don't mind."

The story Dr. Kempler told began in this way: Earlier in his career, Kempler had worked as a physician for a family named Gulkievaugh in Great Neck, Long Island, who employed a maid named Hattie Sinclair. Sinclair came from New Providence, one of the hundreds of islands that make up the Bahama Islands, and the seat of the Bahamian government. Sinclair's family was typically poor and semiliterate and, at the age of seventeen, Hattie had come to New York and found her job as a maid with the Gulkievaugh family for whom she worked for fourteen years. She had ignored all the early warning signs of her disease, and when she finally did seek help, she went to an outpatient clinic at a local hospital where she was misdiagnosed. By the time the family brought her to see Kempler, she was terminal.

When Hattie finally understood that nothing could be done, she went back to her family to die. The Gulkievaugh family received a couple of letters following her departure, and from the contents of those letters, they understood that her condition was rapidly deteriorating. They heard no more from her and assumed that she had died.

But a year later, they received a phone call from Hattie. She said that she was in New York, she was cured, and she wondered if she could have her job back. The family couldn't believe it. They were delighted, though shocked. They brought her to Kempler to examine her. He was unable to find any trace of the disease.

Sinclair maintained that she had been treated down in the Bahamas by a man with no formal medical training and none of the equipment necessary to ascertain the facts of her condition. The man lived on a virtually primitive island with a population of 150, and no running water or electricity. The only thing resembling modern accommodations on the island was a small tourist hotel in a remote fishing village. This particular gentleman lived a few miles away from that hotel in an isolated hut at the top of a hill.

One day after the terminal diagnosis Hattie had received from Dr. Kempler, her father had called and said he had made contact with this gentleman who would try to help her. Some family members were opposed to the idea because it would entail moving her to be near the stranger, but her father insisted and eventually took her to the island himself on a native sailboat, and left her there.

As Sinclair later described her treatment, the man, whose name was Matthew Perch, had boiled a variety of roots, leaves, and bark into a brew and fed it to her three times a day. Each feeding was a combination of different roots, leaves, and barks, which was all she ingested for three months. After that, he added solid foods to her diet, in addition to reduced portions of the brew for another two months. At the end of five months, she returned to her family in New Providence. They took her to a local hospital where she was examined and found to be free of the disease.

Baffled but intrigued, Dr. Kempler and some of his colleagues traveled to the Bahamas, hoping to meet with the man, but he refused to see them. Hattie Sinclair's father interceded on their behalf, telling Perch that the doctors wanted only to talk to him. He refused nonetheless. The government was very supportive of Dr. Kempler's efforts, but they were unable to provide any help. Finally, Kempler and his colleagues went to the island on their own, checked into the hotel in the fishing village, and found their way to the hut on the hill where the man lived. They waited for four-and-a-half hours and were about to return to the hotel when he suddenly appeared, stepping out of the woods into a clearing to stare at them. As the doctors started toward him, he began backing into the woods.

"We're doctors," they called after him. "We only want to talk about Hattie Sinclair."

But with a shake of his head, the man refused. The doctors begged him, tried to tell him of the importance of what he had done. Perch just turned and walked back into the woods. That was the last they saw of him. Kempler returned the next day and the day after that. But the man never reappeared.

Kempler later learned from Hattie Sinclair that Matthew Perch had been born and raised on that little island. His family history could be traced back as long as records had been kept on his island, which was not all that long, and the records were probably not all that accurate. He had attended a makeshift one-room school until he was twelve years old, at which time he went to work with his father farming tomatoes, root vegetables, corn, and peas. Apparently, a knowledge of root medicine ran in the Perch family; Matthew's father dabbled in it and so had his grandfather.

Over the years, news of Matthew Perch's gift of healing spread. Rumor had it that every sick person on Perch's island wanted to be treated by him, but he nearly always refused. He had treated only eight people aside from Hattie Sinclair over the course of fifteen years, and he had treated each with a method different from the one he had used on Sinclair.

Kempler persuaded Sinclair to accompany him to the Bahamas one more time, with a list of questions for Perch, hoping that the man would answer if she were the one to pose those questions. In fact, Perch did see her, but he did not respond to any of the questions, and Kempler never learned anything further.

"It's unfortunate that we were not able to obtain his cooperation because there might have been something we could have learned about in that combination of roots, leaves, and barks he used," Dr. Kempler told Howard Mozelle shortly before he called an end to their meeting. "Or it could have been something in the solid food diet he put her on, or the water, or her faith, or hell, even his personality or his attitude. It's hard to say. Well, as I told you, it is a fascinating story. Not a very helpful one for you, though. I'm truly sorry about that."

"But he did see eight people, even though it was over a period of fifteen years. He did see them, right?" Mozelle asked.

"Yes, he did."

"And whatever their problems were, they're still alive as far as you know, right?"

"We don't know anything about them. But there's no reason not to think so."

The two men looked at each other in silence for nearly half a minute before Dr. Mozelle stood up and extended his hand to Dr. Kempler. "You're right; it's truly a fascinating story," he said.

12

When Dr. Mozelle began relating his story to Montaro Caine, he tried to maintain a sense of calm detachment. But as he spoke of the first time his eyes met those of Hattie Sinclair, he couldn't help but grow more excited. He had called Sinclair at the Long Island residence of her employer—finding her was not difficult, for there were few Gulkievaughs in the phone book. On the phone, she sounded cautious, but she finally agreed to come to his office.

"She walked into this room," Howard Mozelle told Caine. "She was a tall, majestic-looking woman. About thirty years old, though she seemed older."

Mozelle told Sinclair about his wife's illness, and she said that she was sorry. But even after he pleaded with her to help him try to save his wife's life, she said, "I just don't think it would do no good, sir. That man never said one word to Dr. Kempler or any of the other people. Even when I went down there with them, he wouldn't see them. If it weren't for my daddy knowing his daddy, he wouldn't have seen me either. Honestly, I'm truly sorry about your wife, and if there were something I could do, I would do it. I wanted Mr. Perch's medicine to help other people too, but he's a peculiar, stubborn man. The way he treated Dr. Kempler and the others was uncalled for, but that's the way he is and nothing's going to change him."

Still, Howard Mozelle was unwilling to give up. "But Dr. Kempler and his colleagues wanted his secrets," he told Sinclair. "I don't. All those doctors and government officials must have seemed like the modern world coming to rob him of a sacred tradition. All I want is for a dying woman to benefit from that tradition. Please, Ms. Sinclair, I'd like you to meet my wife."

Mozelle walked over to the door that led to the adjoining room, opened it, and beckoned for Elsen, who had been seated in a chair trying to read a magazine.

Elsen Mozelle had once been a strong, vibrant professor, but the woman who appeared before Hattie Sinclair looked emaciated and exhausted. Hattie gently took Elsen's hand, and the two women sat quietly, looking at each other.

"Your husband tells me you're sick like I was," Hattie said. "I wish there was some way I could help you, ma'am."

"You can," Elsen said, her breaths short. "There is no guarantee that he will see me. I know that. And if, by chance, he would, there is no guarantee that he would be able to make me well, I know that, too. But I do want to live, and as small as this chance is, it is all that is left to me."

"What is it you have in mind?" she asked quietly.

Little more than a week later, Hattie Sinclair was standing beside Howard and Elsen Mozelle on the bow of a rickety sixty-foot motorboat that chugged among various islands in the Bahamas hauling cargo and mail.

The sky was a deep blue, without a single cloud in it. The little fishing village appeared to glisten in the bright sunshine as the boat approached the makeshift wharf on Perch's island. During the course of her journey to the Bahamas, Mrs. Mozelle had grown noticeably weaker, though her face did radiate with a glimmer of hope. Dr. Mozelle watched over his wife, very much aware of how deeply he loved her and how much he feared losing her. Hattie Sinclair remained quiet on the trip; Mozelle assumed she was recalling her own boat ride to the island when she first met the elusive Perch.

The two women left the doctor behind and took a taxi from the hotel, driving along a dirt road into the interior of the island.

"Let us out at the sapodilla tree around the next bend," Hattie instructed the perspiring, heavyset, middle-aged driver, who had subjected the women to very close scrutiny from the moment he had picked them up in front of the hotel, constantly observing them in his rearview mirror. He had seen Hattie Sinclair before. The first time she had been forty-six pounds lighter and near death. Now she had come in the company of a white woman, and from the looks of her, she may have brought her too late.

As instructed, the driver parked in the shade of the sapodilla tree and waited as the two women continued on foot around the bend to the bottom of the hill on top of which sat the secluded home of Matthew Perch. The walk was no more than two hundred yards, but the blazing sun, the humidity, and the stress of the trip were telling noticeably on Elsen. There was no human activity anywhere in sight, just the singing of birds and the humming of insects.

Hattie Sinclair had sent word to Matthew Perch through her family, saying she had to see him as quickly as possible, but she had no idea if he had gotten her message. She had made no mention of the other person she was bringing with her, and she worried about how Perch would react to the frail white woman standing beside her. She hoped he wouldn't just walk off into the woods without speaking, though she feared that was exactly what would happen.

Slowly Hattie led Elsen Mozelle up the hill. She could remember just about every tree, every stone, every twig. At the summit, they stopped in front of the adobe hut with its thatched palm leaf roof.

They stood there breathing hard, but before they could catch their breath, the door opened and Matthew Perch stepped out. He was a tall black man of about sixty, with stern, serious eyes in a lean, granite-like face. He had full lips, set jaw, and a short, salt-and-pepper beard that matched his eyebrows. His trousers were faded and worn, patched with different fabrics. His jacket had seen more wear than his trousers or the rumpled denim shirt. The women were startled speechless by the man's sudden appearance.

Hattie Sinclair had never gotten used to Perch's imposing presence. Now she couldn't find her tongue. Perch stared back unblinkingly until Hattie blurted out, "I'm sorry, Matthew, I had to come. She's not like the others, I swear to you. She's just like I was—very, very sick. All she wants is to live, like I did. You know I'll always be grateful to you, and I'm sorry to disturb your peace again. But this lady broke my heart, Matthew. Forgive me, Matthew. Please don't be angry."

Perch continued to stare silently at the two women who waited for a response. None came. Hattie was apprehensive. Perch was an explosive, complex man. During the course of her treatment, he could take her head off one minute and comfort her the next with a reassuring touch of his hand.

Finally, Hattie filled the void. "This lady is..." she began.

"I know who she is," interrupted Perch.

Elsen felt a jolt travel through her body. She was too afraid to ask Perch what he might mean.

After a long pause, Perch spoke again. "Where is the man?" he asked.

"My—my husband?" asked Elsen.

"Three of you came," said Matthew.

"He's at the hotel," said Elsen.

Matthew turned to Hattie. "Why did you not bring him?"

Elsen spoke instead. "We didn't want to risk upsetting you with too many people. Also, my husband is a doctor. He cannot help me, and none of the doctors that he knows can help me. He thinks that maybe you can. He will not interfere, I promise."

Matthew looked intently at Elsen Mozelle, shifting his gaze from her eyes to her lips, her ears, her hair, and finally to her hands.

"Go away," he said to them. Then he turned and started toward the door of his hut. "Come tomorrow. Bring the man," he continued without turning back. "Not you, Hattie. Good-bye." Then, he closed the door.

The women stood frozen in place. Then, smiling cautiously, they turned to each other. Hattie took Elsen by the arm and slowly guided her back down the hill and around the bend, where the driver and his taxi were still waiting by the sapodilla tree.

"What do you think, Hattie?" Elsen asked when they were back in the car.

Hattie Sinclair was certain of only one thing. The way in which

Matthew Perch had examined the sick woman was exactly the way he had looked at her when they had first met. She knew that he had diagnosed the frail white woman and that he knew all he needed to know about her condition. But Hattie believed it would be wise for her to keep that thought to herself. "I don't want to speak too soon about what I think. I'm just gonna pray hard for you for tomorrow," she said, putting her arm around Elsen.

Elsen reached up and patted Hattie's hand while their taxi rumbled on.

The next morning, when Matthew Perch opened his door, a perspiring white couple was breathing deeply before him. Holding each other, they squinted through the blazing sunlight at the silhouetted figure of the black man standing in the darkened hut.

"Hello," said Elsen, managing to smile through her exhaustion. "This is my husband, Dr. Howard Mozelle."

"Pleased to meet you, Mr. Perch, and thank you for seeing us." Howard Mozelle extended his hand.

Perch remained silent but stepped to one side of the door, clearing the entrance while ignoring the doctor's gesture. The Mozelles hesitated, not sure that they had received an invitation to enter. Perch waited. Finally, Howard Mozelle led his wife into the hut.

Perch closed the door and remained standing by it like a sentry. Moments passed before the Mozelles' eyes adjusted to the semi-darkness. The large one-room interior was plain and sparse: There was a bed, two chairs, one table, all handmade from native wood, and in one corner a chest of drawers from which most of the varnish had long since peeled away. In another corner stood an old, battered steamship trunk. Beneath a window at the southern end of the hut was an open fireplace with piles of wood neatly stacked beside it. On the other side were several rows of shelves on which could be found tin plates, spoons, a few tin cups, clay jars, and a box of matches. Underneath the shelves were a variety of inexpensive cooking utensils. But what caught Howard Mozelle's attention most were the two-foot-square pieces of artwork that were suspended on the hut's east and west walls. Each piece was attached to the wall by a string that hung on a nail driven into the mud plaster.

Dr. Mozelle guessed that Perch had made the hangings; though he himself was a man trained in the science of medicine, for years he had relieved the stress of his profession through sculpting and painting. How intriguing, he thought—their worlds seemed to be light-years apart from each other's, and yet he may not have been all that different from Matthew Perch; they were both physicians of one kind or another, healing themselves through art. He was trying to determine whether he was looking at abstract carvings or sculptures when Perch spoke again and interrupted his thoughts.

"She must eat here, sleep here, live here with me in this room night and day. You cannot," Perch said directly to Howard Mozelle. "She will relieve herself in the woods. She will wash herself in the stream. If she is unable to wash herself, I will wash her. You may come in the afternoons at three and leave at four. No one else must ever come; and you may bring only clothing, toothpaste, and soap as she needs them. You may leave now. Tomorrow, bring her sleeping clothes, toothpaste, and soap. Good day."

13

THE HIGH-PITCHED WAIL OF FIRE ENGINE SIRENS ALONG 67TH Street invaded Dr. Mozelle's office, forcing him to pause while the monster machines rumbled past. Rising from the couch where she sat with Anna Hilburn, Elsen Mozelle stepped toward Caine. "Mr. Caine, would you care for some coffee or some water?"

"No, thank you."

"Coke? Diet Coke?"

"Thank you, no."

When the sound of the sirens had faded, Dr. Mozelle directed his attention back to Montaro, who waited eagerly for the doctor's story to continue.

"As I was saying," Mozelle began. "Matthew Perch, from what we can gather, treated my wife in much the same manner as he did Hattie Sinclair," Mozelle said. "She drank all sorts of different brews. Sometimes they were thick and pulpy. Sometimes they were thin and clear. Sometimes they were in between. They were all pitch-black in color, like ink, and at first, all of them were equally revolting."

After about four weeks of treatment, according to Dr. Mozelle, his wife became accustomed to the treatment. Still, there was no discernible sign of improvement in her condition. In fact, by the end of the second month, she took a turn for the worse.

"I must tell you, it was a dramatic turn," Dr. Mozelle told Caine. "She couldn't hold anything in her stomach. She retched for days on end, couldn't lift her head. She was so weak, and she remained that way for fifteen days. I didn't think she could lose any more weight, but she did. I was afraid that dehydration and malnutrition would kill her. Her pain seemed so terrible that I finally asked if she wanted to stop. She said no. I begged Matthew Perch to allow me to stay with her at night. He refused. I began to think we had made a mistake."

During the eleventh week of Elsen Mozelle's treatment, however, her condition stabilized and she began to show slight signs of improvement. By the end of the twelfth week, she was able to leave her bed and walk around Perch's hut. Four weeks later, she felt well enough that her husband began taking trips to New York so he could begin reviving his dormant medical practice. Still, when he was in New York, he never discussed his wife's progress with anyone, partly because he had no way of knowing the extent of Elsen's recovery, and partly because he felt that he owed Matthew Perch his absolute discretion.

And then, one day, during the fifth month of treatment, as Howard Mozelle was leaving the hut after one of his afternoon visits, Perch, who had not said much more than hello or good day to him in all that time, told the doctor in a most matter-of-fact way, "You can have her back tomorrow." Then he walked off abruptly toward the rear of his hut.

"The next day, when I arrived, Perch was sitting under a tree a short distance from the hut," Mozelle told Caine. "I waved to him; he didn't wave back. But I didn't mind because I had grown quite used to his ways. I entered the hut with the overnight bag I had brought to pack Elsen's things. I had a camera with me and when Elsen saw it, she asked me to take some shots of her in the hut so that she could always remember it. I snapped about half a dozen pictures, and then, for reasons I don't fully understand, I stepped over to the artwork on the west wall and took a picture of it. I did the same with the piece on the east wall. Then, I took out an envelope from my jacket pocket with ten thousand dollars in it and laid it on the table. Perch had never mentioned money, but we wanted him to have it."

When the Mozelles stepped out of the hut into the sunlight, Matthew Perch got up from the shade of the calico tree and walked toward them. The doctor thanked Perch. Elsen asked if she might visit him again sometime. Perch just shook his head. Then, Elsen reached up and kissed him on the cheek. He looked down at her, first into her eyes, then, in turn, at her ears, her hair, her nose, her cheeks, her lips. Knowing what he was doing, she smiled, raised her hands in front of her face to show him her palms first, then the backs of both hands. Perch smiled and nodded his head slightly. It was at that particular moment that Elsen knew he understood that she had been completely cured.

Dr. Mozelle held out his hand to Perch, and this time the man took it. As they said good-bye, the strong, calloused hand of Matthew Perch gave Dr. Mozelle's hand an extra squeeze before he disengaged his grip, turned away, entered his hut, and closed the door behind him. Mozelle and his wife started down the hill, but a few moments later, they heard a shout—Perch was rushing down the hill toward them with the envelope of money in his hands. He stopped when he reached the Mozelles.

"Take this," he said quietly.

Mozelle took the envelope, feeling deeply sorry that they might have offended him. "We just wanted to do something to thank you," Mozelle said apologetically. Perch didn't respond directly; he stared intently into Dr. Mozelle's eyes, then into Elsen's, then into the doctor's again.

"To thank me?" Perch asked.

Howard Mozelle nodded, whereupon Perch made a statement that was as intriguing as it was baffling, a statement that both Elsen and Howard Mozelle had been puzzling over ever since.

"Then remember this," Perch told them, speaking each word slowly and carefully.

"After the two have been joined together, the son shall hold the coins, and he will bring them to their destination."

Howard and Elsen tried to ask Matthew Perch what he meant, but the man only repeated what he had already said—*After the two have been joined together, the son shall hold the coins, and he will bring them to their destination.* Then, he turned and walked away.

Back in New York, Elsen was examined and pronounced cured by Dr. Kempler, who agreed to respect the promise they had made to Matthew Perch not to disturb his peace.

"After that, I went back to my practice," Mozelle told Caine now. "Elsen went back to teaching history at Columbia, a new person in many ways. Life was wonderful again."

Dr. Mozelle paused and took a deep breath before looking over to his wife and the elderly nurse; the doctor seemed to be seeking their permission to continue. The two women gazed back at the doctor, who curled his lips between his teeth and nodded to the women before turning back to face Caine.

"Mr. Caine, during that same year, I delivered a baby to one of my patients, a healthy baby girl. The baby's left hand was folded like this"—Mozelle made his left hand into a ball. "Anna and I were the only ones present. We opened those tiny fingers, and in them was an object. I want you to understand what I'm saying. In the baby's left hand was an object that looked like a coin. It was not attached to the hand. We picked it up. It was firm and had the consistency of a stone. I walked to an overhead light to examine it more closely. The first side I looked at was smooth and blank, but then I turned it over. It was at that moment, Mr. Caine, that I realized that the configuration on the face of the object seemed to be an exact miniaturized replica of the artwork on one of the walls of Matthew Perch's hut. I was dumbfounded. Anna did not understand its significance; she was simply bowled over by the fact that we had discovered an object in the baby's hand. She couldn't believe it, and neither could I.

"I asked Anna not to tell the mother about what we had found until we had a chance to have the object examined, to find out what it was made of, and to check it against the photographs I had taken of the objects on Perch's walls. I discovered that I was correct; one side of the object was exactly like the piece of artwork that hung on the east wall of the hut. I did not tell the child's mother what I had found in her baby's hand. I have wrestled with the ethics of that decision from time to time over the years. Later, I justified my actions with 'Science should come first,' and with Perch's strange prophecy to me, which seemed to justify my role in the coins' fate.

"And now, Mr. Caine, here is where you came in. The configuration on that artwork in Matthew Perch's hut resembled a portion of the night sky: a sprinkling of stars. That was my impression the very first time I saw them on his walls. I wondered about the significance of such a sprinkling of stars. The next day, I flew to Boston to see an astronomer friend of mine."

"Dr. Chasman," said Caine.

"Yes, but I wasn't honest with him either. The time wasn't right, I thought, to turn the scientific community loose on such little facts as we had. I told Michael that the object was a coin from an ancient civilization, and that it belonged to a friend of mine who wanted to have it analyzed by a top metallurgist. I asked him to intercede on behalf of my friend with Dr. Walmeyer at M.I.T. After he agreed, I asked him what he made of the configuration on the face of the coin."

"What did he say?" asked Caine.

"He said that it brought to mind a familiar grouping of stars that includes portions of two different constellations," said Mozelle. "He asked me who the owner was. I told him he was a dealer in rare objects who preferred to remain anonymous. That afternoon, after I returned to New York, he went to your old professor in the Metallurgy Department and asked him to do the workup. As you know, the professor had to leave for a conference the next day, so he turned the job over to you.

"Until now, Elsen, Anna, and myself were the only people in the world who knew what I've just told you. The girl never met her father; he was out of the picture. But the mother and child remained patients of our clinic. In fact, we did our utmost to maintain a doctor/patient relationship with the family and did so for many years. During that time, we closely monitored mother and child. The child was normal in every way—perhaps a bit above average in intelligence, but not strikingly so. Nothing unusual appeared anywhere in the mother's chart. Then the mother died fifteen years ago, and the child went to live with her uncle in Brooklyn."

"What were you looking for, specifically, when you examined the woman and her daughter?" asked Caine.

"Explanations," said Mozelle. "Any explanation. There were so many questions that we wanted answers to. The object was found in the hand of a newborn baby, and it seemed to be an exact image of something hanging on the wall in a Caribbean hut. Why had this happened? What did it mean? Had such a thing ever happened before? Why was the object from the child's hand not an exact image of both pieces of art? It was a carbon copy of one, but the other side was blank. What about Matthew Perch? Was he the one who had made those pieces on his wall? If not, who did? We didn't know what we were looking for. I kept thinking about those last words Perch had spoken to us—*The son shall hold the coins.*

"We began to quietly research everyone in the mother's family— her brothers, sisters, parents, grandparents. We did the same with the husband and his family. We came up with nothing. I made sure that the girl was examined in our clinic, and when she was older, I saw her myself for regular appointments, but we found nothing extraordinary about her either. There were no unusual signs in her blood work or development, nothing unusual in her behavior.

"That's the way everything stood for years, until you called us. A tragedy has taken place, Mr. Caine. From the beginning, we kept the coin you analyzed here in a safe in these offices. Today, we discovered that it's been stolen."

"When?" Caine asked, stunned by the news yet riveted by the story.

"We can't say for sure—it could have been any time over the last few years. After we heard your message, we checked to make sure it was still there. It wasn't. If the coin you saw this morning is indeed different, we will not be surprised if it turns out to match the other object on the west wall of Matthew Perch's hut."

"But where did it come from, that second coin?" asked Caine. "The girl's husband maybe? Her boyfriend? Someone in his family? In hers? Do you have any idea?"

But Dr. Mozelle remained silent.

"Or...did she have a baby?" Caine asked. "A son?"

"We're not sure yet," Dr. Mozelle said. "All I can say is that for years Anna, Elsen, and myself have all had the same theory—that when that girl has a baby, whenever that might be, something momentous will occur."

"Another coin, you mean?" asked Caine.

"Coins," said Mozelle. "Perch said 'coins.' But for now, we must find the coins that we already know to exist; I feel that it's our duty to do so. They must be preserved for science, your branch and mine, and Matthew Perch's, whose involvement, I suspect, might be far more significant than we can presently imagine. The person who went into my safe and stole the coin also had access to my notes. Whoever has that coin probably knows just about everything I've told you. I hope your interest is sufficiently high, Mr. Caine, to want to help us with this situation."

"How do you see me helping?" asked Caine.

"We must get hold of those coins."

"That may be extremely difficult, Doctor."

"Difficult, but not impossible, particularly for a man as influential and resourceful as yourself."

"It actually may be impossible."

"But you do know where the second coin is? I mean, who has it? The people who brought it to you this morning?"

"Hold on, Doctor," said Caine. "The first questions we have to tackle are: Who stole the *first* coin from your safe, and where is that item now? Whoever has it won't just hand it over to anyone just for the asking."

"You're right about that. Of course we have to find out who has it," said Dr. Mozelle with stubborn determination. With his hands on his knees for support, he bent over closer to Caine and asked in a low, confidential tone, "Can we pursue this together, Mr. Caine?"

Caine shook his head at the strangeness of the situation. "First, please call me Montaro. And second, I would like nothing more," he said.

14

MONTARO HAD SPOKEN BRIEFLY TO HIS WIFE, WHO HAD ADvised him to stay in the city and get some rest. He was in his apartment in The Carlyle and though it was only nine o'clock was, in fact, about to pop an Ambien so that he might enjoy a few hours of peaceful sleep when his cell phone rang. He was expecting Howard Mozelle might be calling, but when he looked down at his cell phone display, he saw the name Larry Buchanan.

Caine answered the phone. "What's up, Larry?" he asked.

"You at the hotel, Monty?"

Larry's casual tone sounded cocky and self-satisfied, which made Caine fairly hopeful that his friend might be calling him with news about Herman Freich and Colette Beekman.

"You got something for me?" Montaro asked.

"Think I do," said Larry. "Come over to Sam's and let me buy you a drink." With a modicum of regret, Montaro put the Ambien back into the medicine cabinet.

When Caine arrived at Sam's, the usual noisy crowd ringed the circular bar near the entrance. Sam Vogel, a practicing attorney and former college football star who frequently doubled as maître d', was, next to the food, the most important reason his pub had become a popular watering hole. Sam was busy arguing with a party of six whose members were complaining that Sam hadn't placed them in the back room. To be seated in the back room, one had to be a very special customer or a close friend of Sam Vogel's, which was why Montaro Caine, an impressive CEO, and Larry Buchanan, who racked up impressive bar tabs, got to sit there.

Caine crossed behind the group of six that was still arguing and paused long enough to get Sam's attention. Sam waved a greeting and pointed to the back room, then escorted him through the packed dining room through an archway covered with flowers to the booth where Larry was waiting. As Caine slid in across from Larry, Sam placed a menu on the table and left.

"Want a drink?" asked Larry.

"No, thanks," Caine replied.

"Did you know that being scared shitless cleanses the psyche in some deep, dark sort of way?" asked Larry.

"Rough time?"

"You could say that."

"Tell me about it."

"What's to tell? Anyway, it sure as hell can rattle your marbles. And I'm not sure I didn't enjoy it in some fucked-up way." Larry pushed his empty Bloody Mary glass to one side of the table before bending closer to Caine. "Socoloux is an investment company," he said. "The names Beekman and Freich didn't show up on anything I saw."

"Why were their bills paid by Socoloux?" asked Caine.

"My guess is that those two work for one of Socoloux's clients."

"Who're their clients?"

"Companies, corporations, trust accounts, insurance outfits, manufacturing concerns, banks headquartered in Europe, Tokyo, and Hong Kong."

"No individuals listed?" Caine asked.

"Not a one," said Larry. "Old Man Hargrove is a meticulous son of a gun. I only hope I'll be that good when I get that old. I went through everything I could, and let me tell you, there's a lot locked away that no one can get to. But what I did see, which was plenty, looked pretty clean. Nothing out of place. His tracks are covered; the firm is covered."

"Who does Socoloux's accounting?"

"It's done in-house by our own people. But I couldn't find a thing there either. Socoloux is paying Freich and Beekman's hotel bills, but there's no record of where those costs will be passed on to. Old Hargrove designed a system that delivers every morsel of privacy permissible under U.S. law."

Montaro scowled. "So what you're saying is, you dragged me out here and you got nothing for me?"

"On the contrary, partner," said Larry, who was grinning widely. "The lady is traveling on an Argentinean passport issued to one Colette Beekman, which may or may not be her real name. The guy, Freich, is Austrian, or that's what his passport says. As we speak, they're finishing dinner at Hargrove's house in Chappaqua, New York. That's where they went after they left you this morning. From there, they will head for Sheltair Aviation at LaGuardia and a private jet back to Switzerland. Scheduled to take off at eleven-thirty tonight. Haven't yet found out if they own the plane, a Gulfstream II, by the way, or if it's a rental. Either way, the answer to that one will tell you a lot about Freich and Beekman."

"That's a pretty good score." Caine was smiling now. "For a moment there, I thought you'd struck out."

"I did at first. I tried the old man's office, his secretary's files, accounting, and the computer; I got zip. But I did get an idea from the computer when it showed that Socoloux was paying their hotel bills. If these clients were important people from out of town, I figured they wouldn't be running around the city in a taxi. I figured right."

"Limo?" Caine asked.

"That's right. Our firm has used the same service for years. Two or three of their chauffeurs do most of the work because the old man likes their manners. I called the company, didn't tell them who I was, just said I was from the accounting department of Hargrove, Hastings and Dundas and I needed some information. That's how I learned they'd gone to Hargrove's house. The rest was easy. I called the airport, told them I was from the D.A.'s office and needed to verify a couple of passport numbers. The guy on the other end of the phone was suspicious as hell until I threatened him with obstruction." Buchanan nodded his head in quick jerks to punctuate his remarks. He was still grinning at Caine, waiting for his friend to show some sign of approval.

Caine obliged with half a smile before reaching into his jacket pocket to take out his phone. "Registration number?" he asked, poised to key in the number.

"What registration number?"

"Of the plane. You got it, didn't you?"

Buchanan grimaced and spanked his forehead with his palm.

"Oh shit. I didn't think of that. Of course. How else would you check ownership?"

"It would make it a lot easier."

"Damn it. Type and manufacturer, that's all I asked for. Shit! I'll call them back."

Caine stopped him. "No, they're already suspicious and they'll probably give you the runaround this time. We know where the plane is; let's take a look ourselves."

Caine saw a flicker of doubt in Larry's eyes—he was nervous about missing the last train home that evening. He had already told his wife he would be late and that she should feed the kids but hold dinner for him. Going along with Caine's idea meant he would probably not make it home at all that night. At the same time, he didn't want to refuse Caine.

"Ahh, what the hell," Larry said. "LaGuardia's only twenty minutes away. Let's go."

A light rain was falling as Caine smoothly maneuvered his car over the Triborough Bridge and Larry looked out at New York City. When they were young men together at the U of C, Montaro had told Larry something his grandfather had told him—if you listen close enough, you can see things; and if you look long enough, you can hear things. And, as he did from time to time, Larry tried to listen carefully with the ear of his inner consciousness; sometimes, if he did so, particularly if he had drunk a triple Bloody Mary as he had tonight at Sam's, he could hear human hearts breaking. Tonight, he could hear the soundless screams of a nameless brigade trying to find its way out of a concrete jungle of unrealized dreams.

What a massive, unpredictable, neurotic giant of a city this was, Larry thought as Montaro steered his Mercedes, what a multitude of worlds existed within this one world. And what an undeniable majesty shone from within this tattered queen of all the world's cities. To Larry, New York was like no other place. At heart, he still counted himself as one of the many—probably millions—who squared off against themselves first thing every morning in the never-ending struggle against the enemy within.

That terrible struggle, that most personal of battles, thought Larry, was what fueled the routine of living and dying here. Secretly, he viewed himself as one destined to bear witness to the emotional rampage of his eight million neighbors. He knew, firsthand, how some of them hammered, clawed, struggled, and scratched in the often-punishing search for success, knowing all the while that failure's dark shadow was spreading over their lives faster than their best efforts could outrun it. He knew others who strained relentlessly each day simply to avoid pain. Or to capture a little joy. But best of all, he knew those kindred spirits, those peculiar, disturbing all-or-nothing shooters for whom winning was life—a place above the crowd—and losing was death, to have come and gone with no sign of their having passed this way. Alas, he also knew that each of those people would, in time, discover that he or she had lived out their lives in the unbearable in-between, exactly where destiny had anchored them. Larry, however, was determined to be one of those inevitable exceptions to that rule, one who would rise to the top, even if he had to struggle a little more than his pal Montaro did to get there.

Montaro passed through the guard gate, where his Mercedes was well known. Then, he drove along the private road that led to La-Guardia's Sheltair Aviation terminal, where private planes took off and landed. Montaro parked his car in the fixed base operators' lot so that he and Larry could have an unobstructed view of both the terminal and the airfield. Dozens of parked planes stood row after row in dark silence. Peering through the windshield of his car into the semi-darkness, Caine managed to isolate the familiar lines of four Gulfstream II aircrafts sitting like mother hens among the mostly smaller planes.

Caine ripped a fistful of tissues from a Kleenex box resting between the front seats of his Mercedes. He arched forward over the steering wheel and wiped away the moisture that had fogged the windshield. Suddenly, a pair of headlights attracted both Caine's and Buchanan's attention. The two men locked their eyes on a vehicle that was moving through the hazy blackness toward the terminal building. Not until the Holiday Inn courtesy van pulled into the pool of light that spilled out from the terminal's window could they see that it was not a limousine.

Two men carrying overnight bags stepped leisurely from the van and waved their thanks to the driver, who gunned the van back into the darkness as his passengers strolled toward the Sheltair lobby. Pilots, Caine guessed. He jammed the soggy Kleenex into his Mercedes's ashtray.

"Thanks, Larry. Really appreciate this," Caine said, thinking that now was as good a time as any to say it.

"Don't mention it."

"I know you're dying to ask some questions," said Caine.

"That I am," Larry said, brightening.

"Don't. Not now. It's complicated. For now, let me owe you some answers."

Larry wanted desperately to know what was going on. There had to be some reason why his friend was being turned upside down, inside out, and tied up in knots, trying to read numbers off the tail of some plane as rain and fog wrestled for control of the night. Less than a mile away, the intermittent drone of takeoffs and landings from La-Guardia's main terminals rumbled through the night air, sending out sound waves strong enough to make the Mercedes vibrate. For several minutes, neither man spoke. They sat quietly staring into darkness until they saw the headlights of a limousine.

"That must be them," Caine said. Larry narrowed his eyes for a better view. Caine turned the ignition key, then twisted the stem beside the steering wheel, sending the wipers sweeping back and forth across the glass to swoosh away the mist on the windshield. Larry absentmindedly cracked the knuckles of both hands while he watched the headlights drawing nearer.

When the car stopped, the chauffeur leaped out of the limo and moved briskly around the front of the car toward a passenger door.

"It *is* them," Larry said, bobbing his head back and forth. "That's one of Hargrove's drivers."

The chauffeur extended his hand to assist Colette Beekman from the massive automobile. Close behind her came a stocky older man, then Freich. The older man looked familiar to Caine. The three headed for the terminal entrance, leaving the chauffeur to gather the luggage from the trunk. Freich swung the front door of the terminal wide and held it open for Beekman and the stocky stranger. The man bore a striking resemblance to Dr. Chasman, thought Caine. But it couldn't be Chasman; he was supposed to be in Europe.

Armed with curiosity and determination, Montaro burst from the car and moved quietly through the darkness toward the fence that separated the parking area from the terminal itself.

"What's up, buddy?" Larry asked, then followed Caine to the fence, through which they could view a side window of the terminal. Yes, Caine thought as he looked, the third person was indeed Dr. Chasman.

Peeking over Caine's shoulder, Larry whistled softly at the sight of Colette Beekman. "Which one is Freich?" he asked.

"The tall, thin one. Keep an eye on them and let's get the number of that plane. It should pass close enough for us to see it. I'm gonna make a call," Caine said.

Montaro took out his cell phone and keyed in Howard Mozelle's number.

"May I help you?" a woman's voice asked. It was an answering service.

"This is an emergency. I must speak with Dr. Mozelle immediately," said Caine.

"Would you tell me the nature of the emergency, sir?"

"My name is Montaro Caine and I need to talk to him. Get that message to Dr. Mozelle."

A half-minute later, Mozelle was on the phone with Montaro.

"Yes, Montaro?"

"I need you to answer a question for me."

"What is it?"

"The person who stole the original coin from your safe, do you have any evidence or even any suspicions as to who it was?"

"Why is that important right now?"

"Look, I think I'm on to something," said Montaro. "But I've got to move right away. Right now. You asked for my help, and now I need you to help me."

"Well, we don't have any hard evidence, but everything points to one of my former employees, a receptionist named Cordiss Krinkle who worked for me for about six years," replied Dr. Mozelle, then spelled Cordiss's name.

"But it could have been any number of people, couldn't it?" asked Caine. "Me even, or a burglar, or a cleaning woman, or some patient in your office?"

"It could be, but it wasn't," said Mozelle. "The circumstantial evidence is too overwhelming."

"Howard," said Caine. "I'm going to have a man call you tonight. He is an investigator. He represents me. His name is Lawrence Aikens. I want you, your wife, and Anna to give him all the information you can about Cordiss Krinkle. I would like to locate her within the next six hours."

"Six hours?" asked Dr. Mozelle.

"Yes. Before a certain airplane lands in Switzerland."

Caine quickly called Aikens to update him while Larry continued to stare through the fence at the plane. They watched the shadowy outlines of Beekman, Freich, and Chasman on the other side of the fence. A dispatch officer was leading the three of them along a corridor between parked airplanes. The Gulfstream II sat at the far end of the field with its lights on and its motor humming. Caine was weighing two possibilities: one, that Chasman was merely escorting Beekman and Freich to their plane; and two, that he himself might also be a passenger.

An electric golf cart departed the terminal; Caine could make out a pile of luggage stacked on the seat next to the driver. He glanced back at the plane to see the blur of images silhouetted against the light spilling out of the G-II's interior. The passengers were about to board.

It was nearly eleven-thirty now. Takeoff was probably only five or six minutes away.

Caine's thoughts leaped back to the limousine that was still parked in front of the terminal. *If it's waiting for Dr. Chasman,* he thought, *then the doctor is only seeing Beekman and Freich off. Do I approach him when he returns to the limo, and if so, what do I say? Was Chasman at Hargrove's estate in Chappaqua? Was he in Chappaqua because he knew Beekman and Freich were coming to see me, or doesn't he know that they came to see me? Was Chasman somehow involved in the disappearance of the original coin?*

Caine heard the thundering whine of the jet engines; then the plane moved slowly forward, and the limousine pulled away into the darkness, heading back to the city. Caine's attention settled on the baggage cart, which was returning to the terminal. Two figures got out of the cart and entered the building—the baggage handler and the dispatcher. *So, Chasman's leaving for Switzerland,* Caine thought. *I'll be damned.*

Larry stood ready with pen and notepad in hand, expecting to see the numbers on the G-II's tail pass right by where he and Caine were standing. But the plane was too far away to make out the numbers, and now it was turning and moving farther away.

"Damn it," Caine said.

Larry looked at Caine, confused. "I didn't see a thing. I thought it was coming this way," he said.

"Wind conditions," said Caine. "They're heading over to runway two. We're screwed."

"No, we're not, buddy," said Larry, and before Montaro could ask what his friend meant, Larry was running along the length of the fence, shouting something at some of the uniformed men who were standing near the terminal building.

Montaro let Larry go about his business while he watched the jet roll toward its takeoff position. This place was no stranger to Caine, who had taken off dozens of times from here in the Fitzer Corporation jet. He knew exactly where the taxiing jet was heading. He kept looking at its running lights flashing through the misty night before the jet swiveled around its front landing gear until its nose faced east.

When Larry returned ten minutes later, he was grinning. "You owe me two now, buddy," he said. He flashed a scrap of paper on which he had scribbled the plane's registration number.

"How'd you get it?" Montaro asked.

"Couple of the line guys," said Larry. "They don't get paid much more than minimum wage. Fifty bucks got 'em talking real quick."

Montaro began to reach for his wallet, but Larry shook his head. "I'll put it on your tab," he said.

Once the men were back in Montaro's car and headed for the Grand Central Parkway, Larry said that by the time they got back to the city, it would be past midnight—too late for him to catch the last train home.

"Got a spare bedroom at The Carlyle, buddy," Montaro said, knowing full well that Larry could get home if that's what he really wanted to do. "I can put you up there for the night. It'll be like college all over again."

Larry smiled, but then he shook his head.

"Take me to the Wyndham," he said.

"You sure about that?"

Larry nodded.

When they pulled to a stop in front of the Wyndham Hotel on West 58th Street, Caine stabbed his hand at Larry, who slapped his palm against Caine's. They held a firm handshake before Larry stepped out onto the curb, slammed the door, and leaned back through the open window smiling at Caine.

"This has been one hell of an evening, buddy. Thank you."

"Thank *you*," Caine countered with genuine appreciation. "Sure you don't want to try the extra bedroom?"

Larry shook his head and Montaro knew why—no doubt Larry would be prowling the bars of the nearby deluxe hotels looking for action. Whenever Larry spent a night alone in the city, the Larry of old, temporarily smothered into submission underneath a three-piece suit, came bursting out. As he looked at his friend, Montaro paused to wonder how his life would be different if he lived according to Larry's code of ethics. His mind drifted quickly to the face and figure of Co-lette Beekman, but then, just as quickly, it drifted back to his wife, his daughter, his home, and his room at The Carlyle, where he hoped that he would finally be able to get some sleep.

"Naw, thanks anyway," Larry answered. "You know, if you want the information about that plane's registration, it'd be pretty easy for me to get it at my office, if you'd like me to handle it."

"I'd appreciate it," Caine told him before driving off.

Montaro had been sleeping in his room at The Carlyle for a little over three hours when he was jarred awake by the sound of his phone.

"I don't have a hell of a lot for you," Lawrence Aikens began the moment he heard Caine's voice. "We'll have to wait till morning to go any deeper, but for now, here's where it stands. Cordiss Krinkle has completely erased herself from everywhere one would expect to find her, starting about a couple of months ago. She told people that she went to California, but she never did. She's from Nebraska, but she didn't go there either. Her father died, her mother is still there, so are some distant relatives, but the girl hasn't kept in touch with them. Before she vanished, she and a boyfriend named Victor Lambert sublet their apartment here in New York to complete strangers."

"Who's Victor Lambert?" Montaro asked.

"As we understand it, he's a handsome, street-smart jack-of-all-trades," said Aikens. "He was in the restaurant business for a while. He dabbled in construction. But he disappeared about the same time Krinkle did. Word around Hell's Kitchen is that he owed a loan shark fifteen grand, so he took a powder. That wasn't quite the case, though. He owed the money all right, but he paid it back before he and Krinkle dropped out of sight. I'm gonna keep digging here, but for now that's about it."

"Good work. Keep digging," Caine said before he hung up.

Caine was now wide-awake again. It was too early in the morning to call his wife and it was too late to take another sleeping pill. He sat in a chair next to the window thinking about the strange turns his life had been taking of late, until he could see that dawn was breaking.

15

D R. MICHAEL CHASMAN STOOD NEAR THE BACK OF THE TOUR-
ists' and visitors' line in the customs and immigration area of
Geneva International Airport where he watched his hosts, Colette
Beekman and Herman Freich, approach the front of the line for citizens and resident foreigners. He didn't know whether it was his jet lag,
his bittersweet memories of having traveled to Switzerland with his
late wife, Lena, or the sheer strangeness of recent events that was
making him feel so out of sorts.

Just three days earlier, he had received a call from a brusque and
authoritative lawyer named Julius Hargrove, senior partner of Hargrove, Hastings and Dundas, urgently requesting his presence for a
consulting matter that would necessitate a two-day trip to Geneva.
When Chasman said he wanted to know more, Hargrove swiftly arranged to bring the doctor to the Hargrove family home in Chappaqua, New York, where he was introduced to Freich and Beekman.
There, Freich had explained to Chasman that the people responsible
for the invitation Hargrove had extended to him wanted very much
for him to consult on a sensitive matter that related specifically to his
area of expertise.

Chasman felt uneasy about agreeing to take the trip, since he had never met these individuals before and knew nothing about them. But when Freich mentioned that they would be meeting the esteemed astronomers Johann Flugle and Gertz Welbocht in Switzerland, Chasman became intrigued.

"Obviously," Colette had told Chasman, "since we are not trained astronomers, it would be impossible for me, Mr. Freich, or Mr. Hargrove to explain in detail why your services are needed, but Flugle and Welbocht would very much like your assistance."

"We are prepared," Hargrove said, "to pay whatever fee you deem appropriate, of course, and to fly you to Geneva and back. One or two days is all it will take."

Dr. Chasman spoke directly to Freich. "But you've given me no information at all about the nature of the project. Assistance pertaining to what? The field of astronomy is as wide as the cosmos itself. And, forgive me, but you speak as if my expertise covers it all." Still, Chasman's curiosity had already been whetted.

Now, as he stood in Geneva in the customs line waiting to be processed, Dr. Chasman watched Colette Beekman, who was being greeted by an adoring smile from the tall, blond-haired customs agent who had processed her many times before. The young man had rescued her on numerous occasions from the backs of long, slow lines and Colette paid him well in warm smiles and, occasionally, with flattery.

After Dr. Chasman finally made his own way through the line, he joined Beekman and Freich, who led him out of the terminal building to the pickup area, where two black sedans awaited, their drivers standing like statues by the vehicles' open doors.

"Hello, Charles," Colette greeted her driver as she approached the car.

"Welcome home, Mademoiselle," he replied cheerily.

"Thank you," she added, and turned to face Dr. Chasman, offering her hand. "I hope you enjoy Lausanne. It's lovely this time of year."

"I'm sure I will." He watched Colette step into her sedan before he got into the back of the second car with Herman Freich.

In the front sedan, which was heading toward Colette Beekman's family estate, Colette felt comfortably reassured, the way she always felt when she returned home. But as he sat beside Herman Freich in the back of the vehicle that was headed toward Johann Flugle's home, Michael Chasman's emotions were more complicated. He could not help but recall the last time he had come here with Lena; though she had already fallen ill, he had never allowed himself to consider that it would be the last time the two of them would travel together, and he never would have been able to imagine that he would return here without her.

As the car sped toward Lausanne, Chasman tried to linger on the most romantic of his recollections, partly for the comfort they brought him and partly to make sure they were still vivid and bright. As long as his memories kept the good times in focus, he hoped he would be able to continue staving off a sense of having been cheated by life.

Johann Flugle, doctor of astronomy and astrophysics at the University of Geneva, lived in a modest cottage situated next to a small vineyard on the outskirts of Lausanne. Chasman and Freich were greeted by Johann Flugle and Flugle's German colleague Dr. Gertz Welbocht, doctor of astronomy at the University of Heidelberg. Flugle, in his early seventies, was tall and slender and looked as though he had been a playboy in years past. Welbocht was the younger man and yet he looked older—what was left of his hair was gray and his stomach hung over his belt.

"It was good of you to come, Doctor," said Flugle, while Gertz Welbocht's analytical eyes measured the American astronomer with a steady gaze. "Both Gertz and I are greatly honored by your presence. Come." Flugle gestured with his arm as he moved toward the house. "Let's get you settled, give you time to freshen up a bit, and then we'll have lunch. Were you able to sleep well on the plane?"

"Not too badly. I don't require as much as I used to," said Chasman, falling into step beside his host.

"Yes," Flugle chuckled. "For some of us, that goes for a hell of a lot more than sleep, I'm afraid. Though I sometimes wonder, is it that we really don't require it, or is it that we've simply developed the habit of doing without it?" Then, over his shoulder to Freich, who was walking a few steps behind with Welbocht, he asked, "What do you say to that, Herman?"

"I think the body speaks to itself about its own needs, and sleep is no exception," responded Freich.

"Which is to say, you don't have a list of what you no longer require much of," said Flugle with a wry smile.

"Correct. But which is also not to say that time and gravity won't eventually force its own list on those of us who are reluctant to bow prudently to the irrefutable fact that we grow old and die," said Freich.

"Only if we're lucky do we grow old and die," said Gertz Welbocht. "Only if we're lucky."

A splendid lunch was served in the garden; one, Chasman surmised, that was meant to put him at ease, for no mention at all was made of the reasons he had been asked to come all the way to Switzerland. Conversation was wide-ranging and included the tennis prowess of Roger Federer, the dangers of nuclear weapons development in Iran, and famine and unrest in northern Africa. Indeed, it seemed to Dr. Chasman that astronomy was the only subject that his hosts were specifically avoiding.

Once lunch was over, the men moved inside to Flugle's cozy study and settled themselves comfortably around a table that had been dressed for the occasion: notepads, pencils, carafes of spring water, glasses, ashtrays, and, for Dr. Flugle's sweet tooth, a bowl of individually wrapped chocolate-covered caramels. Flugle ate a pair of candies, washed them down with half a glass of water, then cleared his throat.

"Michael," Flugle began, speaking in a soft, serious voice and looking steadily into Chasman's eyes. "Let me get right to the point. Twenty-six years ago, you happened to come into contact with a very unusual object—a coin that appeared to predate even the oldest known civilizations. On the face of that coin was a remarkable configuration of the star Sirius, its companion star, and other nearby stars. Each star or configuration was fixed precisely where modern astronomy has confirmed it to be, with one distinct exception. Assuming you can recall the coin after such a long time, we would like—first of all—for you to comment, if you will, on that one distinct exception."

Chasman was caught off guard. How did these men know about

the coin, he wondered. Were these the mysterious owners his friend Howard Mozelle had never told him about? And if so, why, after all these years, had they come into the open? And why had they called him and not Mozelle?

Flugle, Freich, and Welbocht sat patiently, awaiting the American's response.

Chasman removed his glasses, closed his eyes, and pinched the bridge of his nose with thumb and forefinger, as if trying to pull a faded image back to memory. A heavy, palpable quiet hung in the room until Chasman asked, "Is this in some way related to the project we're here to discuss?"

"It is," replied Flugle.

"Well, that's news. I take it you have proof that this coin, or whatever it is, actually exists?"

"We have."

"Can you tell me under what circumstances it was supposed to have first been brought to my attention?"

"We won't ask you to betray confidences, Doctor. But we know beyond question that the coin exists. Our knowledge of the coin goes far beyond its mere existence."

Flugle looked away from Chasman to Freich and made a beckoning motion with his head. Freich reached for the briefcase he had placed on the floor next to his chair and lifted it onto the table. Not until Freich opened the case did Chasman realize that Freich had been carrying Colette Beekman's briefcase since they had left the plane. He found it strange that Freich should have it now when it had never left Beekman's side at Chappaqua or on the plane.

Freich lifted a small velvet box from the case, passed it to Flugle, then closed the case again. Suddenly, in spite of himself, Chasman flushed with excitement.

Welbocht edged forward in his chair as Dr. Flugle lifted the lid of the tiny box. Flugle then turned the box in the palm of his hand until it faced Dr. Chasman. He tilted it slowly forward, inviting his guest to examine more closely the object that lay on the maroon satin cushion. Dr. Chasman fumbled in his breast pocket for his reading glasses.

It was not the same coin; Chasman knew that immediately. Nevertheless, he studied the face of the object thoroughly to make absolutely sure.

"It's very similar," said Chasman. "But there is, to use your phrase, 'one distinct exception.'"

"You're certain of that?" asked Flugle.

Chasman looked down again. He matched the face of the coin to the one in his memory. Then he picked up the coin and lifted it as close to his own face as his bifocals would allow. One by one, arresting similarities drew his attention, but the dissimilarity piqued his interest even more. In the first coin, a moon seemed to be orbiting the star Sirius, a moon that, as far as he was aware, had never been detected by modern science. On this coin, however, no such moon was present.

"No question," answered Chasman. "If you were under the impression that this was the same coin that was brought to me, I'm sorry to disappoint you."

"My apologies, Doctor," said Flugle. "I did not mean to question your recollection."

"Similar, yes," Chasman said. "Identical in some ways, if you allow for subtle differences such as the position of Reigel and Balustrade to the star Sirius. In this configuration, both Reigel and Balustrade are each found where the other should be—as they would appear looking back at them from deep space. Up close, though, as you know, such subtle differences become cosmic divergences of massive proportions. However, to answer your question, I am certain this coin is not the one I saw."

Chasman passed the coin back to Flugle, and as he did, he wondered why these men had really asked him to come. It seemed unlikely that he had been summoned to simply comment on that "one distinct exception" on the face of the original coin. Surely, Flugle and Welbocht knew as much as he did about the strangeness of the moon that orbited Sirius on the first coin and its absence on this one. Assuming they hadn't brought him all this way to discuss a fake coin, the object here must bear some genuine relation to the original, he thought, possibly even to the point of also having unknown elements in its composition. The coins were probably companion pieces, de-signed and created as a unit: two halves of a single whole.

Herman Freich interrupted Chasman's thoughts by abruptly reaching into Beekman's briefcase for a large manila envelope, which he then slid across the table to Flugle.

Flugle, with gentle deliberation, pulled out three eight-by-ten-inch photographs and laid them before Chasman as if he were expos-ing cards in a poker game. Chasman's eyes widened. The face of the original coin, magnified approximately one hundred times, stared up at him. He could see the moon orbiting Sirius, big as a coin.

Now Chasman knew why he had been invited here—his hosts wanted to be sure, beyond all doubt, that they were not being drawn into some elaborate hoax, that these were, in fact, photos of the coin he had held twenty-six years earlier. He looked up speechless at the three men in turn, then looked back down to focus on detail after de-tail of the images before him.

Chasman reached across the table toward the velvet box. "May I?" he asked.

"Of course," Flugle said.

Chasman picked up the box, held it close to the pictures, and looked repeatedly from the small coin to each of the photos. He was surprised at how exactly he had retained those details in his memory over so many years. "Oh my, oh my," was all he could say; his hand trembled so much that he finally set the box back on the table.

Then Chasman spoke. "This coin was brought to me by a friend whose name I am not at liberty to divulge, though I would venture you already know it," he said. "In any case, my friend was representing someone who preferred to remain anonymous. My friend thought I could be instrumental in having the object analyzed. I took it to an-other friend, a metallurgist, whose assistant did the actual workup. That young man discovered some extraordinary and puzzling facts about the object. I returned the object to my friend, who presumably passed it on to the owner. In the meantime, my metallurgist friend and his assistant were so intrigued by their findings that they asked if I could arrange for them to have a second, more in-depth encounter with the coin. I tried, but the owner refused.

"That, in a nutshell, gentlemen, is the history of my contact with the item. I never discovered who the owner was, and I don't know where the coin is now." With a mischievous glint in his eyes, Chasman looked at Flugle, then at Welbocht. "Do you?" He was greeted with silence.

"At present, we are much more interested in your conclusions about the design on the face of this object," Flugle said, pointing to one of the photographs.

Chasman raised his right hand under his chin and rubbed his fingers back and forth. Then, after studying Flugle for a moment, he spoke. "I'm not sure I know any more than you do. But in my opinion, whenever and however this coin was created, the markings on its face are, either by accident or design, an exact miniaturization of Sirius and the local group of stars around it, with the sole exception of this unexplained object here that appears to be a moon. But I believe you are aware of that as well. I can also say that the coin seems to be older than any civilization we know of that might have had the technical capabilities to produce it. That's about all I can say."

"We would very much appreciate it, Doctor, if you would consider incorporating your opinions in a formal, written statement," said Flugle.

"I will consider it," Chasman said, though the more he thought about it, the more he realized that he had no intention of doing so. He was a cautious man, unwilling to attest to something that, as of now, was little more than conjecture.

Later that day, on the pretext of wanting to visit with an old friend in Lausanne, Chasman approached Flugle to ask if he could arrange for a rental car.

"A car will be here within the hour," promised Flugle, adding, "Can we expect you back for dinner by nine?"

"If lunch was an indication of what dinner will be like, wild horses couldn't keep me away," Chasman replied.

Johann Flugle stood in his foyer and watched the American astronomer head upstairs to his room for a nap until the car arrived; he wondered whom the astronomer would call first after he had gotten into his rental car: Montaro Caine or Howard Mozelle.

After Chasman had closed the door to his room, Flugle, accompanied by Gertz Welbocht, escorted Herman Freich outside to a waiting limousine.

"Well," Freich asked the men as they walked, "what do you think?"

Freich wanted quick answers, but Flugle and Welbocht had both been trained in a scientific discipline that abhorred jumping to conclusions. The two astronomers stared at each other, each pondering whether they had thoroughly covered all the points they had agreed were necessary before confirming the authenticity of the coin.

"Time is of the essence," Freich told the men. "We have to move or not move before the day is out. What's your verdict? What do I tell Mr. Fritzbrauner?"

Flugle spoke first. "Well, as outrageous, as bizarre, as hard to believe as the history of those coins may seem to any rational person, the evidence so far, though not conclusive, is hard to ignore."

"And you?" Freich turned to Welbocht as the three men arrived at the limousine.

"I'm inclined to agree," Welbocht replied to Freich, adding, "Going on the assumption that Chasman hasn't seen Dr. Mozelle's notes and knows nothing about them, then he has practically confirmed that the history of the coins, as outlined in those notes, is authentic."

"So as scientists and rational individuals, your assessment is that the coins themselves are authentic?" asked Freich.

Silence lingered before Flugle spoke again. "As a rational person, I feel Mozelle's notes are to be believed, as irrational as they sound. As a scientist, I don't think that we should be on record on this matter. I'm sure Mr. Fritzbrauner will understand."

Freich cocked his head toward Flugle. "If you are hesitant about putting your candid, scientific appraisal on the record, what do you think about Dr. Chasman's promise to consider putting his remarks in writing?"

"I doubt very much if you will get that from him any more easily than you would from us," Flugle said. "He is, after all, a scientist, as are we."

"Good day, gentlemen, see you at dinner," said Freich, as he got into the limousine.

———

Threading his rental car along the road past the shadowy vineyards, Dr. Chasman, whose habit was to avoid night driving as much as possible due to his weakened eyes, began to fret when darkness caught him still following strands of precious memories through a distant Lausanne of long ago as he mulled over the events of the previous two days. Time had slipped away while he retraced his path by the light of happier times. Then, before turning back to return to Flugle's estate, he pulled his car over to the side of the road, took out his cell phone, and called his secretary in Massachusetts. Before she could fill him in on what had taken place in his absence, he instructed her to connect him with Dr. Mozelle and added, "Do you remember that chap Montaro Caine?"

"Yes!" she blurted out.

"I want you to locate him, too."

"That's what I have to tell you," she said. "He called."

"He did?"

"Yes. He said it was an emergency, but I couldn't reach you."

"Emergency?"

"Something to do with a coin you once had examined by Dr. Walmeyer when Mr. Caine was his assistant."

"What did he say?"

She told him what Caine had asked her to do. "I didn't know what to do. I was frantic, so I called Dr. Mozelle. I hope I didn't make a mistake."

"My God!" Chasman exclaimed, dumbfounded by the speed of events. "Get me Howard on the phone first, then Caine."

When Chasman's secretary called back, she told him that Dr. Mozelle was not at his office and there was no answer at his home or at the hospital. Nor was she able to locate Caine.

"Keep trying," Chasman said. "When you do reach them, let them know I must see both of them as soon as I return."

"When will that be?"

"I'm not quite sure at the moment, a few days maybe. In any event, when I know, I'll text you the arrival time. I will go directly to Howard's office. When you get ahold of Caine, tell him to meet us there."

16

LARRY BUCHANAN WAS RUNNING LATE. HE HADN'T HAD TIME TO shave, and he was already feeling self-conscious about his slovenly appearance even before he arrived at the front desk of the Carlyle Hotel where he told the skinny and officious young desk clerk that he was on his way up to see Montaro Caine. Larry hated the way the desk clerk's eyes swept over him. Larry knew that he needed a clean shirt, but it was nine-twenty in the morning and Bloomingdale's didn't open until ten a.m. He waited for the string bean with a phone in his ear to grant him safe passage to the elevators across the hall.

"Yes, sir, right away," said the string bean into the phone before hanging up. "Mr. Caine is in 1709. Do you need me to show you the way?"

Larry shook his head. Of course he knew the way to Montaro's suite, even if he didn't exactly look like he belonged in the hotel.

When Larry arrived at the suite, Montaro was eager to hear his friend's report. But he had to wait until the slightly hungover Larry had demolished the cherry danish that Montaro ordered for him and washed it down with a large, freshly squeezed orange juice.

"Well, buddy, here's what I've got for you," Larry started. "The plane belongs to a company, okay?"

"What company?"

Larry held up an index finger signaling for Caine to hold on and let him finish. "And the company is owned by another company."

Caine knew that Larry's windy introductions usually led to substantial information, so he humored his friend. "Okay."

"Which is owned by a trust."

"Yeah, one of those," Caine said.

"Which is owned by another company, and so forth, and so on— the usual shit that leads to the usual dead end."

"I know the routine," said Caine.

Larry proceeded, paying little attention to Caine's impatient tone. He smiled broadly. "But because I'm suicidal and also smart, tenacious, and incapable of accepting 'dead end' as anything but an invitation, I got to the bottom of it. The real bottom."

Caine brightened. "Let's have it."

"And there at the bottom, I found a man named Fritzbrauner."

"Kritzman Fritzbrauner?"

"You know him?"

"I've heard the name."

"I'm sure you have. Piss pots full of dough. Lives in Switzerland. He's into oil, shipping, arms, heavy manufacturing, and pharmaceuticals. His net worth is just below ten billion dollars. He also has one of the world's most extensive collections of rare objects. I couldn't come up with anything that explained why he'd be interested in Fitzer Corporation, but that doesn't mean he's not."

Montaro smiled broadly at his friend, as if he were seeing a Larry he had never known.

"The girl, what's her connection?"

"Beekman? She's Fritzbrauner's daughter. Beekman was her mother's maiden name. She travels sometimes on a Swiss passport issued to Colette Fritzbrauner, other times on an Argentine passport issued to Colette Beekman—the mother's Argentinean. She left Fritzbrauner for a singer in Argentina and she's been living in Buenos Aires ever since."

"How about Herman Freich? Find out anything about him?"

"He's an assistant to Fritzbrauner."

"Fantastic. How'd you get all this?" Caine asked.

"Spent a little time snooping in Hargrove's office around five this morning."

"You what? Son of a bitch! Larry!"

"Yeah, I know. Jesus, I still can't believe I did it. It was fucking suicidal, I know it. But when my contact in Switzerland gave me all that stuff about companies and trusts owning each other and the plane, I had to dig out the names of as many of those companies and trusts as I could, and I knew the old man's office was the place to do it."

Suddenly Caine felt uncomfortable, but he wasn't sure why. Hadn't Larry just brought him more valuable information than he could have asked for? Caine thought briefly of Colette Beekman Fritzbrauner. He wondered if she was married. He considered asking Larry but didn't want his friend to get the wrong idea. Or was it not the wrong idea?

"So," said Larry, chuckling, "where the hell are we? You ready to fill me in?"

Caine stared at Larry with a troubled smile. He felt his breath catch in his throat. Larry had no personal investment in this case—he didn't even know what it was about. And yet he had risked his career to help a friend. At that moment, Caine understood his discomfort. Larry was now invested in this too, as much for his own sake as for Caine's. For Larry, it was all about being a winner, and he was willing to risk everything he had to finally become one. *Does a man run faster,* Caine wondered, *to avoid the loser's destiny or to embrace the winner's reward?*

Caine threw an arm around the shoulder of his friend and squeezed him affectionately. "No, not yet," he answered gently.

Larry's chuckle faded. "Look, buddy..." he began.

"Say it," Caine said.

Larry averted his eyes from Caine's, swallowed hard. He tried to crack his knuckles, but no sound came.

"Come on, I'm listening," Caine urged.

"What I want to say is..." Larry began haltingly. "Monty, if Fritzbrauner takes a meaningful position in Fitzer, one or two credit points for my helping to bring that about could move me up a notch. Sorry I have to put it that way, but I've been lost in that fucking firm for nine years now. I—I've just got to do something, Monty. I'm dying on the vine. You know what I mean?"

Caine was touched again by his friend's vulnerability, surprised to find it lurking so close to the surface.

"I hear you," he said, although he felt fairly certain that Kritzman Fritzbrauner, a collector of rare objects, was most probably a great deal more interested in a particular rare coin than he was in Fitzer Corporation.

Larry looked into Caine's eyes. "O.K. buddy," he said. "Your word is good enough for me." Larry started for the door. "I gotta dash. Stay in touch."

"You, too, and love at home," said Caine.

"Same," said Larry. "Love at home."

As Larry pulled the door shut behind him, those words echoed in Caine's mind—*Love at home.* He took out his phone to call Cecilia.

17

THE SUN WAS SINKING BEHIND THE MOUNTAINS OF THE SAVOY Alps beyond Lake Geneva as Herman Freich drove his black Mercedes to Kritzman Fritzbrauner's estate. He parked the car at the turnaround in front of the main house, grabbed Colette Beekman's briefcase from his front passenger seat, then stepped purposefully from the car and moved briskly past the butler, Marchand Gilot, who was standing at the door with a stiff smile.

"*Bienvenue*, Monsieur Freich," Marchand said with crisp formality.

"Thank you," Freich mumbled in English, still not quite used to being back on European soil. He hurried past Marchand into the estate.

Freich marched through the splendid seventeenth-century foyer. Though as Kritzman Fritzbrauner's most-trusted lieutenant he had been here countless times before, he still had a hard time believing that any human could actually live in this palatial setting, which resembled a grand château or museum. Wherever he looked, he saw a painting or sculpture that had been created by a master. Here, a Rembrandt; there, a Vermeer; at the top of a set of marble steps, a Bernini. At the far end of the foyer, he passed windows that looked out onto the garden and the terrace where Colette and the family chef were consulting with household staff members about a dinner for fifty that would be held here this evening. Freich had arrived an hour before the first guests were expected to arrive for cocktails on the terrace.

As Freich moved along the hallway en route to Fritzbrauner's study he made eye contact with Colette, who then leaned in toward the chef. *"Je m'excuse. Monsieur Freich est arrivé,"* she told him, then excused herself and headed into the house.

Meanwhile, in his dressing room, Kritzman Fritzbrauner was searching the racks in his closet for a tie more appropriate to his dark pinstripe suit than the one his valet had laid out for him. The intercom voice of the butler, Marchand Gilot, filled the room.

"Mr. Freich is on his way up, sir."

"Good," said Fritzbrauner as he held a red tie under his chin against his pale blue shirt. "Tell Colette to join us."

"She's already on her way."

Fritzbrauner lay the red tie against the leg of his pinstripe pants. He checked for a clash of colors, but saw none; the combination pleased him. Satisfied, he slid open the top drawer of his jewelry chest and reached for a pair of cuff links—a simple gold pair that his ex-wife had purchased for him many years earlier to mark their joyous first six weeks of married life. Fritzbrauner strode from his dressing area through his bedroom, across the sitting lounge of the suite to a door that opened into his study. Simultaneously, from the outer corridor, Freich and Colette let themselves in through a door on the study's opposite side.

"Hello, Herman," Fritzbrauner greeted him.

"Hello, Commander."

"Did you get some sleep?"

"A little."

"New York weather was steaming, eh?"

"Too much humidity," agreed Freich with a frown.

"You should go to the mountains next week," suggested Fritzbrauner. He lowered himself into the high-backed chair behind his desk while Freich remained standing.

"Maybe. We'll see," Freich said, then glanced at Colette, who knew what her father didn't: Freich hated the mountains. Freich opened the briefcase and took out the velvet jewel box containing the coin. He handed it to Fritzbrauner along with his four-page report.

"Well," said Fritzbrauner softly as he opened the box. "Let's see where we are." He gave the coin a perfunctory glance, then immediately centered his attention on the report. Meanwhile, Freich returned the briefcase to Colette along with her copy of the report. A few minutes of silence passed while father and daughter read what Freich had written. When they were finished, Fritzbrauner looked up at Freich.

"How satisfied are you that this Professor Chasman knows nothing about what Dr. Mozelle wrote in his notes?" Fritzbrauner asked.

"Reasonably sure. Mozelle kept him in the dark."

"And," said Colette, "in so doing, he also kept Professor Walmeyer and Montaro Caine in the dark."

"So whether we move ahead or not boils down to the integrity of Mozelle's notes?" Fritzbrauner asked.

"The dossier Hargrove put together was quite thorough," Colette said. "Mozelle appears to be a solid man held in esteem by his colleagues."

"Yes, but even men of great standing and character can be duped by fakes, scams, and shams," warned her father. Fritzbrauner looked to Freich for comment.

"I see it exactly as Colette does, Commander," Freich said.

"There's always a downside," said Colette. "Yes, we're risking our reputation. But if we're right and if everything in Mozelle's notes is true, if the coin was indeed found in a baby's hand and if it is truly made up of unknown metals from an unknown civilization, the upside will be considerable."

"So you say go?" Fritzbrauner looked at his daughter with both pride and some small regret—for better and worse, she was very much his daughter, ambitious to a fault.

"I do," Colette said evenly.

"Herman?" Fritzbrauner asked, turning to Freich.

"I'm inclined to agree with Colette, Commander."

"O.K., proceed." Fritzbrauner rose from his chair and moved

around his desk to shake hands with Freich. "As for Dr. Chasman, what are his plans?"

"To return home, I imagine," Freich answered.

"When?"

"Two or three days if we're done with him, and I think we are."

"I'm sure he's anxious to return home," Fritzbrauner said pensively.

Colette and Freich both sensed hesitancy in Fritzbrauner's voice. "You'd like to keep him here?" Colette asked.

"It might not be a bad idea. A few extra days, a week, maybe. Once he gets back to America, wheels will begin to turn. A delay, if it can be arranged, will be to our advantage."

"Leave it to me, sir," said Freich.

Fritzbrauner smiled, then turned to his daughter. "I'll be downstairs in a few minutes, dear." He kissed her on the cheek, then disappeared into his bedroom suite.

After her father had left, Colette looked at Freich. She could tell there had been a meeting of minds between Freich and her father. "If the gamble is worth the risk, why not go all the way?" they had seemed to tell each other.

She now understood that her father's real objective had become the same as her own—the outright, legal ownership of both coins.

18

A s she circled the floor of her room in the Tremont Hotel in Paris, awaiting a phone call that could conceivably be worth approximately ten million dollars to her and her boyfriend Victor, Cordiss Krinkle paused to consider how she had gotten here. In some way she could trace her arrival at this moment all the way back to her early Nebraska childhood, when she had rebelled against her strict Catholic upbringing and her repressively religious, admonishing mother. Cordiss briefly considered her early teenage years when she had first realized that her full and sensuous lips, her smoldering brown eyes, and her wild, unruly hair could compel men's second looks. Then, Cordiss thought about the years not so long afterward when she became aware of the fact that her good looks would never be enough to win her all she wanted. But if she had to pick one day that had led her to this particular moment, it would have been the one earlier this year, when Whitney Carson arrived for what would be her final checkup at the Mozelle Women's Health Center.

On that fateful morning, Cordiss had been working for the clinic as a receptionist, office manager, and general all-around helper for approximately six years. She had been drowning in a sea of paperwork, too preoccupied to notice the entrance of the young black woman until she heard someone clearing her throat.

When Cordiss looked up she saw the attractive, soft-spoken Whitney standing before her, a sheepish smile on her face, as if she had been trying to keep a secret but was not doing a very good job of it.

"Whitney Carson. Well, what a nice surprise," Cordiss blurted out. "Sorry, my mind was off somewhere in Medicare land."

"Hi, Cordiss, how are you?"

"Fine. But never mind me, how the hell are you? Where've you been?"

"Around."

Cordiss searched her appointment book, looking unsuccessfully for Whitney's name. "I don't see you down in our book," she said.

"I just wanted to stop by and say hi to everybody," said Whitney.

"But why haven't we seen you for such a long time?" Cordiss pretended to scold Whitney, but she truly did want to know the answer to her question.

"What can I tell you?" Whitney said. "Things get hectic sometimes. I'm sure you know how it is."

"From that grin you're wearing, it couldn't have been all bad."

"As a matter of fact, it's not."

"Aha! Tell me, tell me."

"In a minute. Let me just peek in and say hello to Dr. M. first," said Whitney, turning toward the doctor's office.

"Oh, honey, he's not in."

"Aw, shoot. What about Anna?"

"No, she's not here either. The doc's on vacation and Anna's under the weather. Her arthritis is pulling her down."

"Oh damn," Whitney said.

"Yeah. You're overdue for a checkup, and the doctor's gonna be pissed when he hears he missed you. Let me see"—she reached for her book—"you better come in next week. He'll be back then," she murmured as she leafed through the pages.

"I can't next week. Won't be able to for a while," said Whitney.

"What do you mean? What about your checkup? I told you you're due for one."

"Some other time."

"You want to get me fired, right?"

Whitney laughed. But Cordiss's flip remark was heartfelt; the doctor always took very special care of Whitney, and Cordiss sensed that part of her job description involved according the same special treatment to this patient.

"You know what?" said Cordiss. "Since you're here, I think we should let Dr. Chambers examine you. Let me see if I can get his nurse to slip you in before he goes to lunch." She pointed Whitney down the long corridor. "Last door on the right. I'll be there in a jiffy with your chart."

A half-hour later, Whitney reentered the reception area from Dr. Chambers's office.

"So, you were saying?" Cordiss asked, picking up the conversation where they had left off.

"Well, you remember that I graduated CUNY about four years ago?"

"Yes. Dr. Mozelle and Anna went to the graduation," Cordiss said. She had found it unusual that both the doctor and Anna seemed to act as if Whitney was their own daughter, even though she knew that Whitney was not related to either of them.

"Right. Well, those first years out of school were a complete mess."

"Happens to most of us," said Cordiss.

"Yeah, I moved out on my own—and that was a trip. It's a whole different world out there when you're responsible for yourself, and that took some getting used to. My uncle didn't want me to leave Brooklyn, but I had to earn my own living and all that. Then, because I was lonely or scared, I spent some time with my cousins down in Cleveland. *Eight months.* Then back to Brooklyn. Aaaa-nd," she stopped and another sheepish grin alit on her face.

"And what?" Cordiss prompted with an expectant smile.

"I met a very special guy," Whitney said.

"Now it's getting good." Cordiss moved closer.

"Well, it gets a lot better," Whitney teased.

"Uh-oh." Cordiss moved even closer.

"We got married," Whitney whispered.

"You're kidding."

"No, really."

"Oh. Wow." Cordiss sighed, then recovered. "Congratulations! That's great news." She sprung up from her chair, then stepped around her desk to hug Whitney. As they embraced, Cordiss laughed and said, "So that's what you've been up to, you lucky girl." She kissed Whitney on the cheek, then led her to a couch in the center of the empty waiting room, where they both sat down. "So, Mrs....?" prompted Cordiss.

"Mrs. Walker. Mrs. Franklyn Walker," Whitney said.

"I like it. Mrs. Walker! So, go on, go on. Where did you meet him?"

"Uptown. At the planetarium."

"Stargazing?" asked Cordiss.

"We didn't spend much time looking at the sky," said Whitney with a coy smile.

"And it was love at first sight? Just like in the movies?"

"Pretty close to that."

"And you had this big wedding and you didn't invite me or Anna or the doctor?"

"Well, we didn't invite anybody; we eloped."

"Eloped? Oh, how romantic!" The two women giggled like school-girls. "But why?" Cordiss asked. "Were there *problems*?"

"No, just a spur of the moment impulse." Whitney spoke at length about how refreshingly honest, direct, and unpretentious her husband was. She described how they felt destined to be together, almost as if some otherworldly force had drawn them to each other. She spoke of how desperately she wished her mother could be with her now, in this time of her greatest happiness, that without her mother to see her through the wedding, eloping had seemed like the right idea.

"Jesus," Whitney said when she was done, "I haven't seen Dr. Mozelle and Anna in over a year. I'm so disappointed they aren't here." As she stood and slowly ambled toward the door, she added, "Give them my love. Tell them I stopped by and that I'll be in touch soon."

"I will," said Cordiss.

"Also, tell them that my uncle Frederick sends them his best regards. And" —she paused for a moment—"If Dr. Chambers doesn't mention it to them, tell them I'm pregnant."

Cordiss tried to hide the complex emotions that were hurtling through her brain all at once. *"What?"* she asked, desperate for Whitney not to leave just yet, at least not until she had learned all she could. "You saved the best for last! Pregnant! Oh, Whitney, you're gonna make me cry. When're you due?"

"About six months or so, give or take."

"Did Dr. Chambers just tell you?"

"No. He just confirmed what I already knew. That's what I dropped by to tell Dr. Mozelle and Anna."

"Ooooh," Cordiss cooed, opening her arms. "It's so wonderful. Really wonderful."

"Thank you, I think so too. But we haven't had a chance to talk about what's going on in your life."

"Oh, no, forget it," said Cordiss. "With Victor and me it's always the same. Nothing new. Next time I'll bring you up to speed with all the glorious details. Meanwhile Victor is Victor, my saving grace. But I haven't woken up to find a little gold ring on my finger yet."

"You will, honey, I know. It's written somewhere."

"From your lips to God's ears," Cordiss said, adding, "I just can't help myself; I love that rascal."

As she turned to the door, Whitney did not notice the glazed look that had come over the receptionist's face as Cordiss Krinkle's thoughts switched to a private track.

"By the way, where did you say you're living now?" Cordiss asked nonchalantly. She reached for a notepad and a pencil.

"Atlanta."

"Atlanta?" Cordiss frowned.

"I gave up my apartment here. Packed and shipped everything yesterday. Franklyn comes from Georgia, so we thought we'd try it down there for a while, see if we have any better luck finding work."

"So we won't be seeing you?" asked Cordiss, her pencil poised.

"Not for a bit. But I'll stay in touch, I promise." She then dictated her new address and phone number to Cordiss.

"Was your husband born right in Atlanta?" Cordiss asked, affecting the casual disinterest of a medical interviewer as she jotted down the information.

"No, about a hundred and fifty miles away, in Augusta."

"Is he a Pisces like you?" Cordiss maintained the same monotone voice.

"Aries."

"Aries? My dad's an Aries," Cordiss lied. "What date?"

"April eighteenth."

"No, my dad's the eighth." Cordiss smiled before returning her attention to the notepad. "Let's see, Franklyn Walker, born April eigtheenth, 19...?" she looked up questioningly at Whitney.

"1984," Whitney responded. "I even know the time—10:56 in the morning."

"I bet you even know which hospital," Cordiss said, teasing.

"Yep, I do. County. With a midwife," Whitney said with a laugh.

"You are hopelessly in love, honey," said Cordiss.

"You got that right," Whitney said. "Nice seeing you, Cordiss, take care."

Cordiss told Whitney that she hoped to see her soon—she added that Victor frequently traveled to Atlanta on business and that perhaps the four of them could get together sometime.

"I'd love it," Whitney said. "I don't have too many friends down there yet. I'd even cook you dinner."

"You've got a date," said Cordiss.

Then Cordiss said good-bye with a wave of a hand and Whitney Carson Walker was gone. But long after Whitney had left, Cordiss continued to think about her. She thought back to her second year on the job to one evening when she was working after hours, and she had overheard Dr. Mozelle and Anna Hilburn discussing the circumstances of Whitney's birth. Cordiss could hardly believe her ears when she heard them mention a coin they'd found in Whitney's hand at her birth, how shocked they had been and how curious, afraid to mention the strange circumstance to anyone, lest they be ridiculed. They had said they didn't want Whitney's mother, a young woman they had cared for since she was a teenager, to become some freakish attraction just at a moment when she would need peace and quiet alone with her baby. She heard the doctor and Anna speculate about where the coin might have come from, what materials it might have been made of, whether there might be a second coin somewhere, one that had appeared in the hands of Whitney's future husband, what might happen if and when Whitney became pregnant and had a child. All this explained the doctor's unusual interest in Whitney. In the following months, Cordiss took every opportunity to dig into the doctor's old files to track down as much information as she could about Whitney. During the course of all this snooping, Cordiss also discovered a key hanging on a nail between the old wooden file cabinet and a wall in the cluttered safe that office personnel used as a storeroom. She knew exactly where Howard Mozelle and Anna kept the coin.

Now Cordiss also knew information that Dr. Mozelle and Anna had not yet learned—that Whitney had gotten married, that she was pregnant, that her husband's name was Franklyn Walker, and that he had been born at the county hospital in Augusta in April 1984 with a midwife in attendance. With this information, Cordiss spent hours online scouring birth records, genealogical websites, and other Web resources to learn all she could about Whitney's husband Franklyn and the circumstances surrounding his birth. If Dr. Mozelle and Anna's theories proved true, with a little luck, those theories could lead to Cordiss Krinkle's salvation. Whitney had described her relationship with Franklyn as if it had been somehow fated—she had used the words "otherworldly force" to describe their meeting. Perhaps Whitney was some kind of messianic figure, Cordiss wondered. And yet, she had never noticed anything remarkable about the pleasant young woman who came into the office every year for her checkup.

Over the following week and a half, Cordiss made a series of phone calls and sent a flurry of e-mails—to the Bureau of Vital Statistics in Augusta, Georgia, to the county hospital, to each of the local elementary schools, and finally to the aged minister of an A.M.E. Church in the town's black section, which was now known as the Laney-Walker Historic District. The minister Cordiss spoke with mentioned a midwife named Carrie Pittman. "If you're looking for someone who was born at the county hospital round about that time, chances are good Ms. Pittman was there or knew about it," said the minister. "Of course, she retired years ago and moved to Kansas City, but I'll bet she's still alive."

Carrie Pittman was surprised when a caller with a pleasant voice introduced herself as the curator of the Augusta Richmond County Historical Society, which, the caller claimed, was preparing an exhibit on the history of midwifery in Georgia. The caller went on to make polite inquiries about the birth of a certain baby the midwife may have delivered early in her career.

"We here at the Historical Society understand that you were the midwife in attendance on April 18, 1984, when Franklyn Walker was born," Cordiss Krinkle said.

"Yes...I suppose so...Franklyn Walker...Yes..." The midwife chuckled at her next thought. "'Course you know they run into the hundreds, all the babies I pulled into this life," she said.

"Well," Cordiss continued, "our information also tells us that something unusual and dramatic occurred during that particular birth. You brought Franklyn Walker into life with something special in the palm of his hand."

The name itself had been one Pittman had never forgotten, even as her memory had begun to fade. But now she was stunned into silence. The old midwife's thoughts raced backward, but only fragmentary flashes from the past danced across her mind. She could not recall having mentioned this incident to anyone, not even to her sister. *Dear God,* she thought, *did I tell someone? How could I have told someone and not remember?*

"Who told y'all about that?" Carrie Pittman asked, haltingly.

"It was some time ago," Cordiss continued in a soothing tone. "The information reached someone connected to our museum, but no one acted upon it. Now that that someone is no longer with us, it was recently brought to my attention. Frankly, I thought the discovery you made that morning was much more than just a wonderful human-interest story. I think the object should be a part of our exhibit. Something that might, in time, prove useful for history and science. It should be properly preserved."

From the silence at the other end of the line, Cordiss sensed Pittman's anxiousness. She continued to reassure the woman before she pushed her luck.

"Do you still have the coin?" she asked.

The old woman hesitated before answering. "Yes, yes, I think I do have it somewhere."

Cordiss gulped, but quickly pressed on. "We would be willing to purchase it from you for a reasonable sum."

"You want to buy it?"

"Yes, if you agree." The thought had never occurred to her that she would find the coin so quickly, and she hadn't considered what sum to offer. "Ten thousand dollars," Cordiss stated.

There was a long pause. "I don't know," the elderly woman finally said. "I'll have to think about it and talk about it with my sister. I don't know right now."

The change in the old woman's voice told Cordiss she should let things rest for a while. "All right, you think about it, and I'll call you again in a couple of weeks."

Cordiss was ecstatic when she hung up the phone. The coin existed, and aside from the old woman, she was the only one who knew. Mozelle didn't know. Anna Hilburn didn't know. It appeared that Franklyn Walker didn't even know. Her plan might just work.

While she waited patiently for her next conversation with Pittman, Cordiss force-fed herself a diet of information about rare art collectors. She was coached by her streetwise boyfriend of five years, Victor Lambert, who was a product of Hell's Kitchen, where even now, survival depended, more often than not, on highly honed instincts and the ability, so said Victor, to "piss ice water."

With Victor's help, Cordiss selected as their first choice a man named Roland Gabler. Unlike some of the other top collectors, Gabler had not been born into wealth. A native of Needles, Nebraska, he had worked at the Brixton Hardware Store throughout his teenage years. He had charmed and manipulated store owner Ed Brixton to such an extent that the man had remembered Gabler in his will, which had provided Gabler with the money to put himself through Columbia University. Cordiss had recognized something of Victor's and her own stories and backgrounds in Gabler's biography and thought he might be a man with whom they could do business.

When she finally succeeded in getting Gabler on the phone, she calmly let drop the information that she had access to an item so rare that it would, unquestionably, be the number one prize in the entire world for the collector lucky enough to possess it.

Of course, Roland Gabler had heard such talk before, hundreds of times, in fact; but on the off chance that one in a thousand such calls might yield something of substance, he usually had an assistant check them out. In the past thirty years, only once or twice had there been anything worth pursuing. This time, Gabler's assistant came back with a simple message inviting him to a private viewing of what the caller claimed was the most astounding discovery in human history. So Gabler agreed to see Cordiss in person and asked her to send his assistant some photographs and corroborating documents regarding the object she was preparing to sell.

Then Victor Lambert boarded a plane with fifteen thousand dollars in cash that he and Cordiss had borrowed from a loan shark and flew to Kansas City to meet Carrie Pittman, who had told Cordiss that she was willing to do business with the Historical Society.

19

"Mr. Voekle will be right with you, Miss," Roland Gabler's slim, gray-haired butler told Cordiss Krinkle before he withdrew down a side hallway.

Cordiss stood in the entrance hall of Gabler's Park Avenue apartment. She had never been in the presence of so much wealth. The marble floor under her feet was buffed to a polish so high that it threw back reflections of Gabler's beautiful antique furnishings—elegant French tables, ornate benches, magnificent tapestries, paintings Cordiss had seen only in books. Cordiss felt awestruck and out of place until she remembered something she'd read in a recent copy of *Fine Art Connoisseur Magazine*: "Things are always as they should be when money has been wisely spent." At one point in his life, Gabler's circumstances had been as modest as Cordiss's own, she reminded herself, and there was no reason to think that she couldn't get as far as he had gotten.

"Good afternoon, Miss Krinkle."

Cordiss stopped admiring the artwork and turned to see a broad-faced, well-dressed man moving aggressively toward her. "I'm Jerome Voekle, an associate of Mr. Gabler's." They shook hands. "Would you please follow me?"

As Cordiss followed Voekle through the formal, reserved beauty of the sprawling apartment, she felt ready; she had done her home-work. She knew that in the highly competitive world of rare-art col-lecting, Roland Gabler was a star, a Grand Marshal in the inner circle referred to as The Ten. He was a longtime survivor of this game in which the coolest head, the steadiest hand, and the strongest nerves nearly always prevailed. And yet he had begun his professional life working in a hardware store.

But Gabler's presence was so strong that it seemed to vacuum up Cordiss's attention the moment she laid eyes on him. Jerome Voekle stepped to one side of the door as they entered. "Miss Krinkle, sir," he told his employer flatly, cueing Cordiss across the room toward Ga-bler, who stood on the far side of his study, between the fireplace and an oblong seventeenth-century oak table. He was taller and bulkier than she had imagined he would be, with the broad, high chest of a weightlifter. His thick gray hair was conservatively trimmed, and his piercing green eyes were set deep in a lined but still handsome face.

Cordiss was fully aware that Gabler's green eyes had already locked on to her and were scanning her attire, her stride, her posture, and, above all, her face as if he were examining a rare object that he wasn't yet sure he would purchase. She assumed he was a good reader of faces. And she was not unmindful of the cold eyes of Jerome Voekle on her back. In her brain, she heard Victor's voice coaching her: *Stay within yourself, don't move too fast. Show your strength. And always hang on to your cool. Make him think you piss ice water.*

"Miss Krinkle?"

"Mr. Gabler."

They pumped hands. "Welcome," he said, motioning for her to be seated.

"Thank you." She sat herself at the desk directly across from him.

In her six years of working at the Mozelle Women's Health Cen-ter, Cordiss had learned to pinpoint apprehension, fear, joy, relief, anxiety, or exhilaration in the eyes of the patients who passed her on their way into and out of Dr. Mozelle's office. But Roland Gabler's eyes told her nothing at all.

Hold his gaze no matter what, Victor's voice coached her.

Gabler drew a chair close to the desk and sat, crossing his legs while his eyes continued to bore into her. She stared back as if this were a contest, then decided that she should let him win the first round. "What a beautiful apartment," she offered.

"I'm glad you like it," Gabler responded, then fell back into silence. He seemed to be waiting for her to explain why she was there.

"You've seen the photographs of the object?" Cordiss asked.

"Yes, I have," responded Gabler.

"And the documents as well?"

"Yes. So, let's get right to it. Questions will come later."

Jerome Voekle laid before Gabler the photographs and papers Cordiss had sent him earlier. Voekle also placed on the table instruments of the trade for examining small items—magnifiers, light-scopes, jewelers' loupes, and the like. Then Voekle maneuvered a chair into a position that allowed him to sit at his employer's left elbow. Both men's eyes fixed on Cordiss as she withdrew from her shoulder bag a clear plastic pill container, unscrewed its top, and tilted the container to a careful angle. The coin slid gently onto the tabletop. Cordiss glanced up at the two men, hoping for a reaction; even the slightest flutter could tell her something. But their faces remained unchanged.

Voekle carefully clamped the coin between the arms of a jeweler's caliper and raised it to Roland Gabler's eye level, while Gabler wedged a loupe in place around his eye. Taking the caliper from his assistant's hand, Gabler examined the coin for a long time, referring occasionally to the photographs and documents on the desk. The Xerox copy that Cordiss had made of Montaro Caine's twenty-six-year-old report to Dr. Chasman commanded more of his attention than did Dr. Mozelle's notes on the coin's history. Gradually, Gabler's concentration deepened until he appeared to be submerged in a private world in which only the collector inside him could dwell.

Cordiss found herself speculating about the workings of such a mind. The chance to examine the coin had to be fascinating—if not historic—to someone consumed with possessing the sufficiently rare, the distinctively artistic, the aesthetically priceless, or, as in the case of the coin, the outrageously unique. "If this guy's got an ego, and what man doesn't, we'll definitely do a deal," Victor had told her.

Gabler continued to murmur softly to Voekle in abrupt phrases that apparently were not meant for Cordiss's cocked ear.

Voekle's notebook flew open as if on reflex, and the assistant began scribbling. Cordiss listened hard, but most of what Gabler seemed to be saying consisted of technical terms or trade references she didn't understand. She suspected that he was purposely making his comments obtuse to stump her. She let her eyes roam about the study, startled by the variety of objects elegantly mounted in tall, glass showcases—pre-Colombian clay figures, Egyptian artifacts, African carvings, Native American masks, Chinese pottery, Fabergé eggs, ancient daggers, and other unusual items whose shapes, sizes, and colors offered no clues as to what they might be. *God! What a treasure this place is,* she thought.

On a shelf, all by itself, in a showcase near the fireplace, sat a human skull glistening in a white beam of light. Cordiss tried to imagine whether the skull had belonged to a woman or a child. A beheaded queen maybe, or a young prince, or perhaps a Biblical figure from the time of Christ. *One thing for sure,* she thought. *To wind up on a shelf in Roland Gabler's study, whoever it was had to have lived a spectacular life and likely died an unnatural death.*

As she continued to survey the scene, Cordiss recognized several pieces from descriptions she had read in articles about Gabler. She searched the shelves in vain for the seventeenth-century Hungarian music box for which, according to an article in *American Art Collector,* he was reputed to have paid more than ten million dollars. Nor could she find any sign of the legendary rainbow pearl whose existence was strongly hinted at in the book *The World of the Private Art Collectors,* which she and Victor had recently devoured. Rumor had it that the pearl, the only one of its kind ever found, had been discovered in the South Seas by a native diver who had plunged to a seemingly impossible depth in order to avoid sharks. Although no one knowledgeable in the trade publicly admitted to having seen it, there was general agreement that the pearl did exist in someone's private collection, and there was very little doubt in anyone's mind that that someone was Roland Gabler. Of all Cordiss had read about Gabler's collection, the pearl intrigued her most. And surely, the coin was more extraordinary than a pearl, she thought.

Jerome Voekle chuckled in response to a comment made by Gabler, and Cordiss's attention swung back to focus on her host.

Gabler lowered the coin to the desk, then released it from the caliper. It bounced harmlessly and quivered to stillness while he removed the loupe from his eye. Then he looked up at Cordiss. Instinctively, she tried to sit taller; she threw her head back and engaged his expressionless stare.

"Is it six years that you have worked for the doctor?" Gabler asked.

"Yes, thereabouts," she responded.

Without moving his eyes from Cordiss, he extended his left arm toward Voekle. The assistant pulled several pages from the folder on the table and laid them in Gabler's hand. As Gabler stared unblinkingly at Cordiss, he waved the pages in her face.

"Your background, Miss Krinkle," he began in a mocking monotone. "Nowhere in it do we find anything that remotely suggests that you are in any way qualified to engage in an undertaking such as the one you have suggested to us. Your proposal is preposterous, young lady, if I may be blunt. You are obviously not the true owner of this . . . object. Your credentials? May I ask where they are? Or do you think credentials are not necessary for transactions such as the one you propose? Well, let me inform you, they are. Therefore, we find no basis for any discussion along the lines you have suggested."

For a moment, Cordiss wondered why Gabler was speaking as if an active tape recorder were hidden somewhere in the room. Then, a flash of intuition told her that Gabler was taking a necessary and understandable precaution. "If we are wrong, and this biographical material we have here"—he shook the pages in his hand—"is incorrect or incomplete, you will have the opportunity to set us straight. Let me ask you some questions about your background, if you don't mind."

With a nod, Cordiss indicated that he should proceed.

Gabler fired a barrage of questions, most of which concerned the biographical material he held in his hand, which described Cordiss's place of birth, family history, educational background, employment history, credit rating, and personal ambitions. She assumed that he was making sure she was who she said she was, though Cordiss noticed that he also managed to slip in a few inquiries about Dr. Mozelle, his practice, Anna Hilburn, Mrs. Mozelle, and, finally, the child mentioned in Dr. Mozelle's notes.

"And the baby in this bizarre tale in whose hand this thing"—he pointed scornfully at the coin lying on the desk—"is supposed to have been found, where is he or she now?"

"Around," said Cordiss, trying to sound vague yet tantalizing. By then, she knew that Gabler, no matter how harshly he was speaking to her, was hooked. His assistant's behavior had given his boss away—Voekle had glanced at her while taking notes, then back at his notes, then seconds later, back at Gabler. Not once did he look at the coin. Cordiss figured that Voekle was trying not to bring undue attention to the object, and was making an extreme effort to appear so disinterested.

After Gabler seemed satisfied that the answers Cordiss gave matched the facts contained in the personal history he had been consulting, a smile of disdain creased the corners of his lips.

"Now, would you mind telling me exactly how you came to be in possession of this item?" he asked, his elbow on his right knee and his chin resting on his fist.

Cordiss smiled, leaned back in her seat, and said with a twinkle in her eye, "Exactly how I came upon it would take a very long time. All that should really matter is the fact that I have it."

"Well," Gabler said, "however you acquired it, I can tell you right now that there's no way in hell anyone in his right mind would purchase it without the rightful owner signing a bill of sale. That is, assuming it has any value at all."

Taking her cue from what she thought was the first crack in his façade, Cordiss offered a carefully worded suggestion that it would be easy enough for her to forge Dr. Mozelle's signature. She felt sure that this was precisely what the art dealer was implying. But in words not so carefully chosen, Gabler berated her for making such an outrageous suggestion. Never in his professional dealings had there been a signature that could not be authenticated, he said. "So you see, young lady," he added, "since you obviously have no chance of delivering the signature of a legitimate owner, along with his consent for you to act as his representative, we have nothing to discuss."

A long pause followed. *Anna Hilburn,* Cordiss thought. Gabler would definitely be less reluctant if she could present him with documents that identified Anna as the legitimate owner. How simple it would be to get Anna's signature on a document without her knowing what she was signing. In the clinic, Anna always seemed to be signing dozens of papers while barely even looking at them. But Cordiss's thoughts were interrupted when Gabler abruptly called the meeting to an end. "Now I have another appointment, Miss Krinkle. Jerome will show you out," he announced.

Cordiss picked up the coin from the table, then secured it in the pill container before returning it to her shoulder bag.

"May I come see you again on this matter?" she asked Gabler.

"I don't see why—unless, of course, you come with the proper documents with the signature of the rightful owner, and permission in writing from that person declaring you as that person's representative. I hope I have made my position clear. Good day, Miss Krinkle."

"Good day, Mr. Gabler," she said.

Voeckle said a polite good-bye in the foyer, and as she moved toward the elevator, Cordiss listened for the front door to click closed behind her. When no click came, she knew that he was still standing there with cold eyes on her back. Not until she had entered the elevator did she hear the door click shut.

Cordiss emerged exhilarated from the exquisite Park Avenue building into the sunshine. Neither the oppressive summer heat nor the dreadful humidity could dull the heady, tingling sensation of a new excitement laced with danger. Cordiss had gotten her first whiff of the power game; she liked it, and she now knew she had an instinct for it.

That evening, Victor returned from Kansas City with the second coin in his possession, along with the remaining $1,500 from the juice loan he had taken out, plus a hard-earned lesson on the dangers of underestimating wise old black women—before Victor could take the seat the elderly midwife and her sister had offered him in their kitchen, the shrewd sister had raised the price to $15,000, then ultimately settled on $13,500. As for Cordiss, she had little difficulty in getting Anna Hilburn to sign her name to yet another document.

A week later, Cordiss called Jerome Voekle to inform him that she was ready for a second meeting with Gabler. At first he seemed reluctant. But after she told him that she had the requisite documents and signature, a meeting was arranged. During that second meeting, Cordiss introduced the idea of the possible existence of a second coin. She divulged very little beyond what she deemed to be the one piece of information necessary to further whet his appetite: "Other dealers," whom Cordiss said she would not name, were interested in the coin he had seen, but Gabler was the only dealer so far who knew about the second coin.

Cordiss told Gabler that this "companion piece" had come into the world in the hand of a child born to a different family some twenty-six years earlier—just as had happened with the birth of the girl at about the same time. And someone who had participated in that delivery had kept the object. She had the requisite documents from that person as well. Cordiss wanted to tempt Gabler, but she and Victor had already agreed that they would not sell both coins to the same buyer—when there was competition, prices would surely rise.

Gabler betrayed no reaction, yet as he sat, he recalled every facet of Dr. Mozelle's notes, every element the doctor had focused on in his search for such a second coin. In a moment of uncharacteristic sentiment, Gabler allowed himself to wonder about the babies. What would they look like now at twenty-six? Were they still alive? Were they destined to meet? Or had they already met? He wondered just how much of this whole incredible story about the coins was truth and how much was fiction.

Interrupting his thoughts, Cordiss tried to press upon Gabler her belief that the person who purchased the first coin would have a better chance of obtaining the second. At this suggestion, a tiny smile appeared on Gabler's face. He felt amused by this upstart's attempt to manipulate him, yet he also felt an unlikely bubble of admiration for the spunky novice seated before him, green as an apple, still miles from being a true con artist. She certainly had the flair and maybe the talent, and she reminded him a bit of what he had been like as a teenager worlds away back in Nebraska.

"So," Cordiss began, her voice even. "Are you prepared to make an offer on the object I showed you?"

"How much do you want for it?"

That response had come more quickly than Cordiss had expected. "Twelve million," she said. Cordiss and Victor had based their asking price on the ten million Gabler had reputedly paid for the Hungarian music box. The coin, in their view, was considerably more exciting than a music box.

Gabler didn't bat an eye. She hadn't expected him to.

"Another coin, eh?" Gabler muttered softly. "That makes two. Well, in my business there is a saying: Two of anything has only half the value of one of a kind. What guarantees can you make that there are not three of a kind, or four?"

"There are only two," Cordiss assured him. "Dr. Mozelle has searched for twenty-five years, without any results. You've read his notes. You've seen the photographs, and you're familiar with his theories about a second coin."

"Yes, I've read the notes, I'm familiar with his theories, all of them; but the fact is, he didn't find it after all these years, correct?"

"Correct."

"Yet you tell me it exists. If he hasn't found it, and if, in fact, it does exist, who did find it? And where is it at present?"

"I'm not at liberty to tell you that right now."

"At any rate, twelve million is out of the question," said Gabler. "You've been seeing too many movies, my dear. If that is your last word—then, good-bye." He challenged her with a stare. She challenged back; her nerves were steady. He waited. She continued to sit. Not a hair moved that he could see. "On the other hand," he said. "I will be prepared to tell you how much I will pay after I've had a chance to consider everything carefully. Say a week from today. Would that be reasonable?"

"I don't know," said Cordiss crisply. "For me, it might be. But I may have other commitments to honor. I'll call you back this afternoon, after I've consulted with my partner."

Later that afternoon, Cordiss and Victor argued about the wisdom of allowing Gabler the week to make up his mind. Victor was against it, but Cordiss said they would be showing weakness if they did not agree to the delay.

"Maybe give 'em two days, or three. We don't have that much time to play with," said Victor.

"He's looking to test our strength," Cordiss said.

"He's looking to fuck us," said Victor.

"We're so close, honey, let's play it out. I told you, he wants it bad."

In the end, Cordiss prevailed. She and Victor wound up making love before she phoned Jerome Voekle to tell him the week's delay would be acceptable.

Still, during the course of the week that Gabler bought himself to try to learn more about Cordiss and the alleged second coin, Gabler learned nothing more of substance. The week came and went leaving him no alternative but to enter an offer for the first coin without knowing the whereabouts of the second, if it existed, or, more important, who among his competitors might already have it or be preparing to buy it. Gabler offered Cordiss $750,000 for the coin, and after prolonged negotiation, a deal was struck calling for two million dollars to be delivered to Cordiss in an account in Europe.

Shortly thereafter, Cordiss Krinkle quit her job. She was burned out, she claimed. "I need a break from this town. Too hard on my nerves; I need to find a quiet place and clear my head. Maybe I'll look around in California," she told Anna Hilburn. "You've been great to work with. And, of course, I'll stay until the doctor finds someone he feels comfortable with," she added with bogus conviction.

As soon as they learned that the deposit into their new account had been confirmed, Cordiss and Victor left for Europe. In the quaint municipality of Liechtenstein, they checked in to an elegant room at the Schatzmann Hotel, an easy drive from the private bank where Cordiss had scheduled an appointment for the following day. They ate their first European meal—grilled monkfish and white asparagus accompanied by a chilled Grüner Veltliner white wine—in the hotel's dining room, seated by a window that looked out onto the Eastern Alps.

The following morning, Cordiss entered a bank that closely resembled the graciously understated lobby of a Manhattan brownstone. There were no tellers, no cages, and no lines. Only two other customers were in evidence.

"Good morning, Miss Krinkle," said a middle-aged man with gray hair and a prominent gray mustache as he approached Cordiss. "Welcome. My name is Peter Fourneaux." The man led her to his desk and handed her a folder. "Here are the documents we need you to sign. This is a necessary procedure that allows us to provide you with the privacy of a numbered account."

Cordiss liked the sense of importance she felt during her meeting with Mr. Fourneaux. *Money surely has a language of its own,* she thought, and she appreciated the fact that she was learning how to speak it.

For a full week, she and Victor slept late, made love, strolled hand in hand along the trails of the Ruggeller Riet national park and along the Rhine River. They sipped cappuccino in romantic backstreet bistros, toured the castles of Liechtenstein and the municipality's *Kunstmuseum*, and attended an open-air performance of *Fidelio.* In short, they submerged themselves in a weeklong binge on European culture and continental food, most of which, according to Victor, failed to live up to the food that was readily available in Hell's Kitchen. But these were far from the most important items on Victor and Cordiss's agenda; those were Switzerland, Kritzman Fritzbrauner, and the next seven-figure transaction they hoped to make. They wanted another target, and they had chosen Fritzbrauner from the lofty Ten to be the next dealer they contacted. Their decision was based less on the obvious influence and power his ten-billion-dollar conglomerate generated than on the crude psychological profile that emerged from their extensive research, which suggested a man whose tastes tilted toward the mysterious.

The young couple settled comfortably in a suite at the Geneva Hilton, which became their headquarters for what turned out to be ten frustrating days of fruitless effort. Each day's attempt at arranging a meeting with Fritzbrauner, or any of his representatives, ended in disappointment. On the morning of the eleventh day, however, Cordiss received a call from a man named Anatole Ziffren, who invited her to lunch.

The luncheon at Le Cygne, a restaurant with an arresting view of the Alps, set in motion a series of stressful events that included interrogations, probes, background checks, legal threats, and psychological intimidation. But though Cordiss felt she had handled herself well under the stress, she was not granted an audience with Fritzbrauner. After she faced Herman Freich, and later Colette Beekman, she realized that they were probably as close as she would ever get to Fritzbrauner.

Throughout her meetings with Freich and Beekman, during which she allowed them to examine her Xerox copies of the documents pertaining to the first coin, and, finally, the second coin itself, Cordiss did not mention the asking price for the object. Then, toward the end of the third meeting, held again at Le Cygne, she introduced the subject without warning.

"The price, you understand, is ten million dollars," she announced.

An impatient frown clouded Freich's face. "It's premature to discuss money," he stated. Then he softened slightly and asked if she would consider releasing the coin for the period of time necessary so that he could have it examined by someone whose scientific expertise they were willing to trust. Cordiss, taking his request to mean that her price was not out of the question, agreed.

During the time that Herman Freich busied himself with consulting such individuals as Johann Flugle, Michael Chasman, and Gertz Welbocht, Cordiss received no communication from any of Fritzbrauner's people. Not a word. Victor and Cordiss fought the urge to call Freich's office. During that time, they flew to Atlanta where they had dinner with Whitney and Franklyn Walker to discuss the possibility of working together on a plan involving health care clinics in Africa. Then, after securing the Walkers' unwitting cooperation, they arranged for a secluded, off-the-grid dwelling in Spain where they could keep close watch on the young couple until their child was born, a coin or coins appeared, and Gabler and hopefully Fritzbrauner would bid against each other for them. But as the days wore on, uneasiness pervaded Cordiss's and Victor's moods. They grew increasingly tense, each unable to shed the gnawing fear that the decision of allowing Freich to take the coin with him had been imprudent.

But then a call arrived from Anatole Ziffren. "Mr. Freich is away on business," he told Cordiss. "But he has asked me to relay this message. In four days you will be advised of our intentions as to whether or not we wish to discuss your proposal further. Someone will call you at eight p.m. on Thursday."

"Four more days of not knowing which way they're gonna come down will drive me up a fucking wall," Victor said. "Let's go somewhere. Do something. Anything. Get our minds off it."

Cordiss, who now felt herself to be an expert in the ways of the wealthy, suggested a few days in Paris. There, they checked in to the Tremont Hotel, which had been recommended by the concierge at the Geneva Hilton, whereupon they lunged headlong into a love affair with the City of Lights and all that they could now afford in it. Enchantment scooped the couple into her net by the end of their first evening on the town; and, after two days of roaming around like smitten teenagers, Cordiss called Freich's office in Geneva to say that they would remain in Paris and await his call there on Thursday at the appointed time.

On the Thursday in question, as the late afternoon folded gradually into night, Victor was walking back from the Arc de Triomphe for the third time in an hour as he tried to keep his anxiety within manageable range. Meanwhile, Cordiss paced their hotel suite, considering and reconsidering the lucky chain of events and coincidences that had brought her to this moment. These thoughts were interrupted at precisely eight o'clock by the sound of a telephone.

Cordiss jumped. Both hands flew to her mouth as the phone splintered the silence. She stared down at the phone, momentarily paralyzed.

The phone continued to ring.

She inhaled deeply, crossed the fingers of her left hand for luck, then snatched the receiver from its cradle with her right. "Hello?"

"Miss Krinkle?" a male voice asked.

"Yes," Cordiss answered, recognizing the voice. "How are you, Mr. Freich?"

"Very well, thank you. Are you enjoying your stay in Paris?" Freich inquired with little apparent interest in her answer.

"Yes, very much," she replied, biting the nail on the pinkie of the hand that held the phone.

"Miss Krinkle?"

"Yes, Mr. Freich?"

"Could you return to Geneva tomorrow?"

Cordiss gasped. Her head swirled a little. "Of course," she managed shakily.

"At the Union Bank of Switzerland at one p.m.?"

Oh my God, she thought. *Oh my God.* But all she said was "One p.m., yes."

"Ask for Mr. Helmont Zurber. There will be a few questions we need to address. Once that is done, we hope to be able to conclude our transaction."

Cordiss felt her whole body flush with excitement. A light-headed feeling flowed over her. She reached for a pen with a trembling hand and instantly tightened her grip on it to steady herself. "Mr. Helmont Zurber," she repeated with as much calm as she could muster, jotting down the name.

"You are booked out of Orly, eleven a.m., Swiss International Flight 86," said Freich. "A car will meet you, drop you by your hotel so you can freshen up if you would like, and then bring you to the bank. Have a pleasant trip, Miss Krinkle."

"Thank you, Mr. Fr—." Then, the phone went dead. He had hung up before she could thank him. Gingerly, she replaced the receiver. She gazed curiously at her shaking hand, then raised it to the level of her face and showed it to the reflection in the mirror. Cordiss and her image smiled broadly at each other. Then she lifted her other trembling hand and snapped both hands into clenched fists. Cordiss spun from the mirror, then strode once more around the suite. This time, her thoughts were audible. "It's gonna happen, son of a bitch, I knew it! I knew it! Way to go! Way to go!" She jabbed the air with her

clenched fists for punctuation. Just then, her thoughts were interrupted by the click of a key in the door lock. The door burst open and
Victor hurtled in. He stopped in his tracks when he saw Cordiss
standing in the center of the room wearing a radiant smile.

Victor's eyes brightened. "Yes? Yes? Yes?"

"Yes, baby. Yes, yes, yes," she gushed.

Cordiss opened her arms wide. Victor rushed over, swept her off
her feet, and twirled her around in a victory dance while Cordiss
laughed and laughed.

20

THE RECEPTION SALON OF HELMONT ZURBER'S OFFICE, ON THE
uppermost floor of the UBS's main headquarters, offered a grand
view of the city, Lake Geneva, and the mountains beyond. But Cordiss had little interest in sightseeing as she was promptly ushered
along a stately hall toward Herman Freich, who stood waiting just
inside the doorway of Zurber's private chambers.

"Miss Krinkle, you've had a pleasant flight, I hope?" Freich greeted
her.

"I did."

"This is Mr. Helmont Zurber. He represents Mr. Fritzbrauner's
interest in this matter."

Standing before her, Helmont Zurber seemed younger than
Freich, but not by much. Cordiss had not been able to scare up much
information about him on the Internet, but she had learned that, in
financial matters, he was a member of the six-person watchdog committee made up of European bankers who kept Fritzbrauner's world-
wide holdings under constant review. To Cordiss, Zurber's skinny
body, broad chin, bull-like neck, overscrubbed complexion, thick
spectacles, fat hands, and concave chest seemed a mixture of contra-
dictions.

"Pleasure meeting you, Mr. Zurber," she almost purred as she took his hand.

"No, mine, my dear lady, mine indeed," he charmed back, bowing slightly from the waist.

"Please have a seat, Miss Krinkle," Zurber offered, gesturing Cordiss toward a chair at the table near the window. Standing politely behind her, Freich assisted Cordiss as she sat. "I do hope you've been enjoying our city."

"I have," she said, smiling warmly, sensing that this was neither the time nor the place to mention the fact that she preferred Paris. To her, Geneva seemed to be a place where you gathered wealth; Paris, on the other hand, was where you spent it.

"Geneva is especially beautiful this time of year," Zurber said, turning to the window for a glance at the view he had never grown tired of.

"Yes, especially the mountains," said Freich, with a sly smile.

Zurber and Freich joined Cordiss at the table where Zurber turned his attention to the paperwork in front of him, all of which bore directly on the coin. He thumbed through one page and then another. Then, without warning, he looked up at her with a hardened expression.

"We're not prepared to offer you ten million dollars. I've been instructed to offer you one price and only one price. You will give me a yes or no answer. The price is three million."

Cordiss was taken aback by the abrupt, harsh tone. *What is he up to?* she wondered. Then she heard herself say coolly, "That's not quite what I had in mind."

"I take it that is a no?" Zurber said.

Cordiss tried to return the man's intense stare while she searched for a way to respond. *Was there to be no discussion at all?* Cordiss glanced at Freich, who glanced back for only the barest moment. This is Zurber's show, not mine, he seemed to say to her before he turned to look out the window at the mountains, which he did loathe up close but did not mind admiring from this distance.

Cordiss's eyes returned to Zurber. He had her and knew it. He had pushed the right button when she least expected it and he could see the doubt on her face. Shaken, Cordiss leaned back in the chair while Zurber abruptly stood and extended his hand. "Sorry you have refused our offer. We wish you the best of luck. Good day, Miss Krinkle."

Cordiss felt herself thrown off balance with no possible way to recover. She smiled at Zurber as if admitting defeat. "I accept your offer, Mr. Zurber," she said humbly.

Seconds after the words had passed her lips, Cordiss saw the corners of Zurber's mouth curl into a faint smile before he shot a triumphant glance at Freich. When he turned back to face her, he seemed almost to be gloating. *You sneaky son of a bitch, you tricked me,* she thought. It had dawned on her too late that Zurber's instructions must have been to pay the full price—only if he had to.

Cordiss struggled to calm herself, to remind herself that either way, she stood to collect more money than she had ever seen in her life, that she would never have to go home to the States or work as a receptionist ever again. Nevertheless, she felt blood racing through her veins and she knew that her cheeks had reddened. *If it is the last thing I ever do, I will teach myself to piss ice water,* she thought.

"There is of course a caveat, Miss Krinkle," Zurber said.

"Oh? A caveat?" Cordiss muttered, still lost in her own thoughts.

"Yes. Our price is dependent upon your giving us the name of the person or persons who now hold the first coin."

Cordiss tried to think of a way to hold the line. She and Victor had planned that such information would play an important role later and should therefore be held in reserve. It was a bargaining chip of considerable power and could not be squandered now, she thought.

But Cordiss was too close to a done deal to play brinksmanship with this barracuda banker. She took comfort in the thought that, when this deal was successfully put to bed, the way would be cleared for the third and most lucrative act of her scheme, one in which Whitney Carson and Franklyn Walker, currently living in a safe house in Alcala de Henarés, Spain, and generating useless spreadsheets for imaginary health clinics, would play a key role.

"You may have that information," she told the banker.

"Good," said Zurber.

"However, I have my own caveat."

"Oh?" Zurber said. "And what may that be?"

"You may have it at the moment your check clears my bank."

"I'm sorry, that is not satisfactory," he said.

Cordiss suppressed an explosive urge to lash out. *You prick,* she fumed inwardly. *Sexist bastard.* Then, remembering the costly lesson she had only just learned, she decided there could never be a better time to piss ice water. "I'm sorry, too, Mr. Zurber. Good day, sir." She turned to Freich. "May I have the merchandise back, please?" She stood, extending her palm.

Freich was not quick enough. She had knocked him off his cool. "I'm afraid I don't have it here at the moment," he said.

"Where is it?" she asked. "I no longer want to do business here. I must have it back this afternoon. I have a flight at five-thirty."

"It can be arranged." He started across the room. "Let me make a phone call. Excuse me a moment." He disappeared into an adjacent office.

Cordiss sensed that Freich was calling Fritzbrauner for instructions. Zurber, in the meantime, stared at her disdainfully. But the uncertainty in his eyes told her she had him by the balls. She liked pissing ice water. And hell, if she turned out to be wrong and the deal fell through, there were still eight other names from The Ten on her list of potential customers.

"Heading back to New York, are you, Miss Krinkle?" inquired the barracuda banker, apparently hoping to signal that she should not mislead herself into thinking she had scored some kind of victory.

"Not yet. We have meetings in London and Paris," she said.

When Freich returned from his phone call in the next room, he nodded to Zurber, who responded with a displeased look at Cordiss before he walked to his desk and pulled open a drawer. He hesitated, then shot Cordiss another cold look before fishing in the drawer for a folder.

"We accept your condition, Miss Krinkle," Freich told Cordiss.

"But you have not heard my condition, Mr. Freich. My price is once again ten million. That is my condition if we are to do business. Otherwise I will return for the merchandise this afternoon."

Freich smiled, but for a long time he said nothing. Then, turning to Zurber, his smile disappeared. He gave the banker a curt nod before his stern eyes shifted back to Cordiss. "When our check clears, you will tell us what we want to know," he said. Taking her by the arm he led her over to Zurber's desk. From his folder, Zurber reluctantly removed the paperwork needed to complete the deal. Cordiss read the pages carefully, then signed. When she finished, Zurber gave her a glare and an envelope. She lifted its flap and pulled out a check made out to her for ten million dollars. In light of the wild exhilaration that had just been let loose inside her, she was proud of her cool, controlled appearance.

"My bank in Liechtenstein has a branch here in Geneva," she began before Freich interrupted her.

"Therefore, your check should clear by tomorrow at noon," he said.

"Then you should hear from me no later than two." With that, Cordiss Krinkle, now a multimillionaire, turned and walked out of Helmont Zurber's office. She had made quite a payday for herself with only two little coins, plus a lifetime's worth of preparation. In addition, she now knew how to piss ice water.

21

Montaro Caine had endured a sleepless night and a distracted day before arriving at the Mozelle Women's Health Center to meet with Howard and Elsen Mozelle, Anna Hilburn, and Michael Chasman. *The New York Times* and *The Wall Street Journal* had been refreshingly free of stories speculating about Fitzer Corporation's future, but that didn't necessarily mean good news. In the all-too-smooth exchanges he'd had earlier in the day at his office with Carlos Wallace and Alan Rothman, he sensed that they were concocting a plot against him, although he couldn't say for certain what that plot might be. Later, he had tried without success to get hold of Gordon Whitcombe to see if he could glean any new information about Priscilla's case, but this didn't necessarily mean bad news; Whitcombe was a perfectionist and generally did not like to speak until he had brought matters to a successful resolution.

On the taxi ride to Mozelle's office, Caine made what he judged to be a tactical error by telling his wife more than he intended to when he called to tell her that he would be coming home late, if at all. Feeling guilty about spending so many nights in the city, he began to tell Cecilia the story about the coins and what he hoped might come out of the meeting with Mozelle, then had to stop midway through when he realized that he couldn't answer half the questions his wife was asking him. *What coins? How much are they worth? How can they be used? Wait, what?*

Dr. Michael Chasman was the last to arrive at the meeting. His return flight from Geneva had touched down at 2:15 p.m. at JFK Airport. Two hours later, he rushed into Howard Mozelle's office, where he found the doctor, Mrs. Mozelle, Anna Hilburn, and Montaro Caine seated expectantly.

Chasman felt energized yet exhausted from his trip, and he spoke before he had a chance to take the chair that Dr. Mozelle had offered him. "I know we have a lot to discuss," Chasman said breathlessly. "I can certainly assure you, from my end, that the past few days have been astonishing. But I think you should first bring me up to speed on what's been going on here. I've obviously been operating under some erroneous impressions over the last twenty-six years." He turned to Dr. Mozelle. "Is that a fair assessment?"

Dr. Mozelle nodded. "Yes, apologies for that, old friend. But please, make yourself comfortable." He once again gestured for Chasman to take a seat. "There's a lot to discuss, and most of it is more astonishing than you already think."

An hour later, Dr. Chasman sat spellbound by the strangest story he had ever heard. It began with the story of Elsen Mozelle's illness and concluded with the tale of Cordiss Krinkle, whose phone records had been obtained by Montaro's investigators, leading them to find out all that she had learned while researching Whitney and Franklyn Walker's births. Then, it was Chasman's turn to tell the others about the phone call he had received from Julius Hargrove; his meeting in Chappaqua with Herman Freich and Colette Beekman; the private jet to Geneva; his ride to Lausanne for the meeting with Johann Flugle and Gertz Welbocht; and finally, his fruitless trip to Berlin, where he had been asked to comment on a seemingly endless number of outdated astronomical charts. He said that he had come to believe the Berlin trip had simply been intended to delay his return, though he had been paid handsomely for his troubles. When Chasman finished, the others remained silent until Montaro spoke, addressing everyone in the room.

"Am I correct in assuming, since all of us in this room have a stake in this concern, that we are all interested in the exact whereabouts of both coins?" he asked.

"Absolutely," Dr. Mozelle said.

"O.K.," said Caine. "But beyond that desire, which we all have in common, our individual interests come into play. Those interests differ from one another in varying degrees and could be the source of misunderstandings down the line." Caine faced Chasman directly. "Therefore, I think each of us should state now, before we go any further, what it is we want"—Caine pivoted back toward Dr. Mozelle— "over and above the return of stolen property to the rightful owner."

Dr. Mozelle leaned forward, peering over his glasses at Caine. "Fair enough," he replied. Briefly, his eyes slid away from Caine to stare out the window overlooking 67th Street and the afternoon traffic that was beginning to clog the streets. Then, he turned his attention back to Caine. "First of all," he began. "There's the question of ownership. Anna and I never told Whitney or her mother about the coin. I've tried to justify that decision to myself in several ways—if word got out, her life would no longer be private; no one would believe me and I would be ridiculed. And then, once we started to learn more about the coins, I didn't know what the next step to take might be.

"Most of all," he continued, "I'd like answers. I believe we are dealing with more than science here, much more, something beyond us and beyond Whitney. Twenty-six years ago, Whitney Carson was born with a tiny object in her hand. Why? And why, less than two months later, fifty-six days later to be precise as we have now learned, was Franklyn Walker born in Georgia, with an object in *his* tiny hand? They grew up in different parts of the country, but still they found each other. They fell in love, they got married, and now they are having a baby." Mozelle glanced, in turn, at Caine, Chasman, his wife, and, finally, at Anna Hilburn.

"It is my strong feeling that we have to think a great deal about what will happen when that baby is born," Dr. Mozelle said. He paced back and forth across the room a few times before he spoke again. "As to the question of the return of stolen property to its rightful owner, yes, I would very much like to have the coin returned to me. But again, I can't claim to be the rightful owner in any true sense. If such a claim can be made on behalf of anyone, then the coins are the property of Whitney and her husband. What I want are answers about the coins, and I think we need to do our best to have those answers as quickly as we can and hopefully before that baby is born. What about you, Montaro?"

"My interests are in the materials the coins are made of," Caine said plainly. He rose from his chair, rammed his hands deep into the pockets of his trousers, and cocked his head at an odd angle toward the ceiling as he searched for the right words. "I confess to being truly fascinated by the strange way in which the coins came into existence—who wouldn't be, after all—and my curiosity has been at fever pitch ever since you first took me into your confidence. I don't want to overstate the case, but if a way could be found to synthetically reproduce the materials in these coins, it could revolutionize my industry, just about every industry in fact. Think about it—a metal stronger than any we have ever seen, impervious to heat. I'm sure I haven't allowed myself to imagine all the possibilities and implications. My overriding desire is to be able to conduct an in-depth, laboratory examination of each coin, when and if we manage to obtain them. That is the basis on which I am willing to work with you."

Dr. Mozelle glanced at his wife and Anna before turning back to Caine. "We three have had twenty-six years in which to develop interests far beyond those of fascination and scientific curiosity," he said. "Though my wife, myself, and, I believe I speak for our friend Anna, have different interests from yours, they are in no way incompatible. You will have no resistance from us, as long as your work does not destroy or disfigure the coins."

The room turned to Chasman. "My interest is solely scientific at this point," the astronomer said, "and I see no reason, from what I've heard here, for any conflict down the line."

"Well," said Dr. Mozelle, "with that settled, we must now put our minds to finding where the coins are and who controls them."

"The coin I saw in Switzerland," Chasman quickly broke in, "is controlled by whomever that man Freich and my colleagues Flugle and Welbocht were representing."

"Kritzman Fritzbrauner," Caine said. "You're right. If he bought it, it's in Switzerland. But what if he didn't?"

"In that case," Dr. Mozelle said, "it would still be with Cordiss, who would probably be busy right now searching for another customer." He turned to Caine. "Have you had any luck in tracking her down?"

"Her phone's gone dead, but we're on top of it as well as we can be," Caine said. "By the end of the day, we should have a fix on her. Certainly no later than tomorrow."

"And then?" asked Dr. Chasman.

"Then someone will have to pay her a visit," said Caine.

Howard Mozelle's face grew alive. His wife reached out to Anna Hilburn and squeezed her hand while Caine looked long and hard at each of them. How much like children they were, he thought. Dr. Mozelle was brilliant beyond question; the two women were highly accomplished in their areas of expertise. As a student at M.I.T., Montaro had been a lot like them, he thought. And yet, as the CEO of Fitzer Corporation, he understood that they were all extremely naive about what went on in the trenches of the real world he had to inhabit on a daily basis. In his world, he rode the bulls of chance and fate, cunning and greed. Dog ate dog, and the mighty crushed only each other, since the weak had long been accorded the ultimate indignity of not being worth the fight.

"If I'm going to carry the ball, which I am happy to do, I should let you understand what I think we're up against," said Caine. "To begin with, we're fighting the clock. A hot item cannot be kept secret for very long. Every day the circle widens. If both coins are already in the hands of people like Fritzbrauner, our job starts out about as tough as can be. I've never met a collector yet who wasn't a hard-nosed businessman first. By now, a man like Fritzbrauner will have gathered every bit of information there is about the coins, beyond the notes stolen from your safe. You can bet he has imagined a variety of scenarios, each of which will lead him to the pregnancy of Whitney Carson Walker." At this point, a thought occurred to Caine. He whipped around to face Dr. Mozelle. "Howard? In your notes on the history of the first coin, did you ever mention Whitney or any member of her family by name?"

Mozelle closed his eyes and gently massaged them, as if trying to call forth mental images of his note pages. He slowly shook his head. "No, we didn't," he said. He shot a glance at Anna as he often did when he felt unsure. Anna nodded her agreement. "No," Mozelle continued, more confidently. "We specifically left her name out of it. At the time, I thought it might be an unnecessary precaution, but now I don't believe it was. Why do you ask?"

Caine ignored the doctor's question. "I want you to pull Whitney's chart and all references to her and her mother from any of your active files in this office. If you have records online, trash them. Do it today; and, instruct everyone with access to those files to report to you any inquiries of any kind about Whitney or her parents."

"I don't understand," said Dr. Mozelle.

"If there is no reference to Whitney by name in your notes, and if Cordiss Krinkle is as smart as I think she is, she will withhold all that information from her buyers."

"Why would she withhold it?" asked Chasman.

"Because if Whitney is going to have a baby, information about her pregnancy and her whereabouts could bring a handsome price. My sense is that Miss Krinkle will first sell the coins to two interested parties; later, when the time is right, she will sell the information about the pregnancy and have those parties bidding against each other."

"But," interrupted Anna, "wouldn't whoever she has sold the coins to insist on having that information?"

"Not if there is no indication of it in the notes. My guess is that Miss Krinkle will claim to have no knowledge of Whitney's whereabouts, and she will not, under any circumstances, divulge what she knows about the pregnancy until she can sell that information. In any event, time is of the essence."

When Caine emerged from Dr. Mozelle's office into what intermittent sunshine was left, the Friday afternoon getaway traffic to Long Island had all but strangled the exit routes from the city. The bumper-to-bumper parade of vehicles on Park Avenue was barely crawling now. He'd have to walk to The Carlyle if he wanted to get there by nightfall, he thought. As he walked west, he wondered when he would ever get a decent night's sleep. He longed to be home—he needed the comfort of his wife's touch; his daughter needed him. He longed to hear both of their voices, not on the phone, but in person. Unfortunately, other matters beckoned.

When Caine reached The Carlyle, Michen Borceau was already waiting for him in the lobby, flushed with excitement. In one hand, he held the printout of the analysis that he had conducted on the coin slivers that Caine had provided him. The Frenchman's words began to come forth in a torrential flow, but Caine silenced him with a wave of his hand. Borceau talked too much—Caine had often cautioned him about this indiscretion—and, though he was as eager to hear Borceau's report as the man obviously was to deliver it, he would not let Borceau speak until they were alone in his apartment.

"I tell you, Montaro, the behavior of these elements is astounding," Borceau said once he had sat down in Montaro's living room, somewhat calmed by the Lillet that Montaro had poured him. "I mean, what is hinted at here is mind-boggling. Their influence on a number of common elements is dramatic. Am I allowed to ask what we're dealing with?" Caine didn't respond, so Borceau continued. "Never in all my experience have I seen elements like these. They're ... what I'm trying to say is ... "

"I think I know what you're saying."

"The damn things are so ... How can I say it? So *active* is what they are. *Organic*. Montaro, I don't know exactly what I mean by this, but this material behaves almost as if it's *alive*. Does that sound crazy to you?"

"Not at all," Montaro said. *That's exactly the word that came to my mind twenty-six years ago*, he thought.

By the time night had fallen, Montaro had long since abandoned any hope of returning home before morning. Though he had little appetite, he had, upon his wife's advice, forced himself to eat half his dinner of braised Alaskan halibut accompanied by green asparagus risotto. He was just placing his tray, along with the empty bottle of Lillet whose contents Michen Borceau had consumed, out in the hallway for the housekeeping staff to remove when he saw Lawrence Aikens walking down the hallway toward him in tandem with his assistant, Curly Bennett. He assumed that they were coming to inform him about whether or not they had been able to discover any information about Cordiss Krinkle. And, by the looks of their confident strides, Montaro figured they had.

"You got her?" Caine asked after the men had entered his living room.

"Think so," Aikens answered, pleased with himself. "That lady is damn impressive, let me tell you. She did a helluva job covering herself, but we got her."

"Where is she?"

"Europe. Six thousand miles from where she's supposed to be."

"Europe instead of California," said Caine. "Can I get you something?"

"Oh, something cold, maybe," said Aikens.

"Like what?"

"Like beer."

"You, Curly?"

"Same for me."

Caine took two beers out of the mini-refrigerator and handed them to the men before leading them to the couch.

"Well, according to our information," Aikens began, "she and her man friend have been on the move a lot lately. Right now they're either in Paris, where they've taken a small apartment under another name, or San Remo, Italy, where they might have the same setup. In any case, there was one 'T' she didn't cross; and, if my guts are reading her right, we'll have their exact addresses in a couple of hours."

"What 'T' didn't she cross?"

"Remember that loan shark they borrowed the fifteen grand from?" Caine nodded.

"Well, before they disappeared, they paid him back with a draft drawn on a Liechtenstein bank that was issued at a branch here in the city."

"An account in Liechtenstein," Caine mused.

"Yeah, and somehow or other," Aikens continued, "she managed to finagle herself a secret numbered account. My guess is there's probably a hell of a lot more in that account than a thirty-year-old reception's salary would explain. I couldn't get into the account—I tried but couldn't come close to cracking it before I had to back off. But I did learn that the bank in Liechtenstein is instructed to make monthly transfers to a bank in Paris and one in San Remo. I couldn't get the size of the transfers or the amount of her balance, though. Sorry 'bout that, chief, but I'm on it as best I can."

"And I appreciate it," said Caine.

Curly Bennett stared at the two other men in the room, feeling uneasy and even somewhat miffed. He had listened intently to Aikens describe detail after detail about Cordiss—her whereabouts, her finances, all information Curly had painstakingly assembled after long hours of persistent digging. Curly had been expecting a little credit: a mention, a pat on the back. Aikens was a good boss in many ways, and Curly knew that lots of men in Aikens's position would sometimes find it in their best interest not to give credit where credit was due. Still, he felt a little resentful toward his boss for not telling the CEO that it was Curly Bennett and only Curly Bennett who had done the actual work that Aikens was now accepting thanks for.

"Can't you tell us what this is all about?" Aikens asked Caine now.

"The most I can tell you," Caine offered, "is that Cordiss Krinkle may have stolen something, a very rare object."

Aikens looked at Caine, startled, then exchanged a glance with Bennett. "Son of a bitch," he said.

"What?" asked Caine.

"A rare object like...like...an antique or..." Aikens fumbled for the right word.

"Antique what?" Caine asked.

"Jewelry? Little statues or something?"

"Why do you ask?"

"Her apartment."

"What about it?"

"I was there." Curly shot Aikens a glance and his boss corrected himself. "*We* were there, me and Curly. For fifty bucks, her janitor let us look around her apartment while the couple she leased it to was out. There were some books there—only about two dozen in the whole place—and at least ten of those were about artifacts, antique coins, jewelry, collectors, that kind of stuff. I wondered if it was her hobby. The janitor didn't know. I thumbed through a couple of the books. Some pages were dog-eared, and there were scribbles here and there."

"Can you get those books?" Caine asked.

Aikens looked at Curly, who checked his watch, then nodded, but neither man moved.

"Can you start getting them now?" asked Caine.

Aikens rose, then spun toward the door with Curly at his heels. "I'm on it," he said, then correcting himself, he said, "*We're* on it." And with that, the two men were out the door.

22

Alan Rothman was getting ready to leave his office at Fitzer Corporation for the night when he felt his phone vibrating in his pocket. Assuming that his wife was calling to remind him once again not to be late to the Four Seasons, where they would be meeting her parents for dinner, Rothman figured he would let the call go straight to voice mail. But when he checked the caller display, he instantly answered the phone.

"What's up?" he asked, then heard a familiar female voice on the other end of the line.

"Are you free?"

"I've got a dinner with Lauren's folks at six-thirty," he said. "Why? What's up?"

"An important matter needs your attention."

"Important?" he asked. "How important?"

"Very important."

"Be there as quick as I can," Rothman said.

Less than half an hour later, Rothman used his own key to let himself into an apartment located above a used-record store in Greenwich Village. The apartment was small but tidy and well-insulated from the sounds of Thompson Street below.

"That you?" The same familiar voice called from the bedroom as Rothman shut the door behind him.

"Yeah, hon."

Michen Borceau's secretary, Gina Lao, had changed from her work outfit to the halter top and shorts she usually wore to the gym. She embraced Rothman and kissed him forcefully. When he had freed himself from Gina's arms, his tone became more businesslike. "So, what's up?" he asked.

"I think something major is happening," Gina said.

"How major?" asked Rothman.

"Major major," she said. "Want me to fix you a drink?"

Rothman shook his head. He had already been wondering how he might explain the aroma of Gina's lavender perfume on his jacket and he didn't want to explain the scent of alcohol as well. It wasn't like Gina to ask to see him outside of their usual rendezvous times, so he assumed that Gina had to discuss something that was related to Fitzer Corporation and, unlike his erratic boss Montaro Caine, he didn't feel he needed to drink while discussing business.

"This may sound crazy," said Gina. "But I think Caine has found a miracle material."

"What's that supposed to mean?" Rothman's tone was curt.

"I don't have all the pieces, so I can't give you the whole picture, but from what I can tell, it sounds like something amazing." Gina was more animated than Rothman had ever seen her as she went on to discuss all that she had overheard Borceau saying about the slivers of coins that Caine had asked him to analyze. Caine had warned Borceau to keep all aspects of the analysis secret. "Don't discuss this with any-one," he had said. But that hadn't kept Borceau from discussing the matter with himself out loud and at length and sometimes in French, a language Gina had studied in college.

Still, the more Gina told Rothman about what she had heard Borceau saying, the more skeptical he became. He furrowed his brow. Then, he chuckled.

"This material, have you actually seen it?" he asked Gina.

"No."

Rothman's chuckle grew into a hearty laugh.

"Alan!" Gina snapped sternly.

But Rothman couldn't help smiling. He could sense what he felt certain to be Caine's desperation, which would inevitably lead to what Rothman had been helping to plan for more than a year—Richard Davis's takeover of Fitzer with Rothman as his second in command. "What's that son of a bitch up to now?" Rothman wondered aloud.

"I don't think you should laugh this off, Alan," Gina said. "I heard exactly what Borceau was saying. He said 'miracle material.'"

"Miracle material?" Rothman laughed. "Out of where? Caine's desperate and your boss is a drunk. It's a diversion tactic, honey. I know how Caine's mind works. I've been studying it for years."

"Alan, yes, he's up to something, but it's not what you think. Just listen..."

"He's up to exactly what I've been saying all along. Games, playing for time."

"I don't think so." Gina sat Rothman down on her couch and told him about the man and woman who had visited Caine and Borceau.

"They shut themselves off in the lab, just the three of them," Gina said. "Michen wasn't even allowed in."

As Gina continued to talk, Rothman became increasingly curious. "This man and woman, who are they?" he asked.

"Their names are Herman Freich and Colette Beekman," said Gina.

"What's their business?"

"I've got no clue."

"Had Borceau ever seen them before?"

"No. Never."

"So, this 'material,'" Rothman asked, "where is it now?"

"It seems like the man and woman brought it with them when they came and took it with them when they left. But Caine kept some slivers of it for Michen to analyze."

"And your boss analyzed these microscopic slivers Caine conveniently left for him and found them to be made of miracle material?" Rothman asked.

Gina was growing irritated. For years, she had been attempting to plot ways to secure herself a more important position at Fitzer, which had a lot to do with why she had been sleeping with this smug married man for the past year. And now, this same man was dismissing all she had learned with his trademark smirk. "Stop jumping to conclusions," she told him. "Don't be so sure of yourself all the time. Something bizarre is happening and I think it's for real. Borceau has been in the lab working by himself night and day."

"You mean he's been drinking night and day," Rothman said, but Gina waved off the remark. "He won't let anybody in there," she said. "Before he went to meet Caine at his hotel, he seemed so fired up I thought he was going to explode. 'Miracle material,' he kept saying. *Miracle material.*"

"Well," said Rothman, "don't you think it's a little unusual for this miracle material to suddenly pop up and find its way into our lab just when Caine is hanging on by a thread?"

"It didn't just 'pop up.' He's known about it for twenty-six fucking years, Alan."

Gina's reply jerked Rothman to attention.

"Are you ready to listen now, hotshot?" she asked.

"All right," replied Rothman. Now, he found that he actually did need a drink. He got up to fix himself one in the kitchen before he sat down again beside Gina on the couch.

"So, okay, where did he find this material?" Rothman asked.

"In a coin," Gina told him.

"A coin?"

"Yes, a coin."

Rothman listened as Gina told him about the call Caine had asked her to make to Dr. Chasman. "Then, I called Nancy and asked her for a rundown of his appointments in case Michen wanted to reach him in a hurry, and she told me about his meeting with Dr. Mozelle," Gina said. "Mozelle's not Caine's regular doctor. In fact, Nancy had never heard of him."

"What about Freich and Beekman?" Rothman asked. "Are you sure Caine didn't know them?"

"Positive. They had to be strangers because he ordered Lawrence Aikens to dig up everything he could about them."

"Aikens?"

"I'm sure he's come up with something by now. We need to find out what it is."

"Aikens is a creature of Caine's. He won't tell us anything."

"I know," said Gina. "But if he has information you need, there might be other ways of getting it."

"I'm listening."

"Aikens has an assistant," said Gina.

"Right. Curly Bennett," said Rothman. "But he's Aikens's boy."

"Yes, but he's also very ambitious and he doesn't think Aikens appreciates him. And then there are other things."

"What are other things?"

"Like he's young and single and likes to hit on women at company parties."

Rothman was beginning to get the idea. "I see, and what else?"

"What else does there need to be?" Gina asked.

Rothman noticed the familiar curl at the corner of Gina's mouth, and from the sensuous movement of her lips he knew immediately what she had in mind. As Gina leaned into him, he felt his phone vibrating in his pocket, but he didn't stop to look to see who was calling him. He could be a little late to dinner tonight, he thought, to hell with his wife and her parents.

23

When Curly Bennett returned home to his one-bedroom apartment on East 37th Street, he felt pleased with himself, much the way he always felt after a fruitful day on the job. He and Aikens had, once again, greased the palm of the janitor to obtain the books they had seen at Cordiss Krinkle's subleased Manhattan apartment and had delivered them directly to Montaro Caine. The apartment was a mess and Curly doubted that the tenants would have noticed a few missing books. While Aikens had stayed with Caine to pore over the books, Curly went back to his office where he tracked down addresses for Cordiss in Paris and San Remo. All things considered, this had been the kind of day Curly liked. In the absence of any recognition from the executive suite, he stood ready to give himself a generous pat on the back.

The landline was ringing as he entered his living room. That phone rarely rang; he hoped there wasn't an emergency at the office; his plan was to nap for an hour before venturing across town for his weekly poker game. He snatched the receiver from its cradle.

"Curly Bennett here."

The voice on the other end of the phone startled him. "Hi there, Curly Bennett. Gina Lao here. Remember me?"

How could he forget? "Gina. Of course I remember you."

She had caught his eye the first time he'd seen her at Fitzer accompanied by Michen Borceau. He had wanted to talk to her then, but though they had crossed paths several times at company headquarters, no graceful opportunity had presented itself. The nature of his business had taught him to proceed cautiously in such matters with a fellow employee. He wasn't able to talk to Gina until six months later at a company party at the Hilton, where they were formally introduced.

At the party, Gina picked up his scent almost immediately, and with mild flirtatious glances, she let him know. Encouraged, he began to close in gently as the evening wore on. But soon he noticed that, with each step he took toward her, she drifted farther away. Finally, Curly labeled her a high-end tease and dismissed any thoughts of her. Now, rumor had it that she was dating Alan Rothman, a slick creep who made Curly even more dubious of Gina's character.

"Curly, I hope I haven't caught you at a bad time," Gina said now.

"Oh no, not at all."

"I'm so glad. I need your advice on something."

"Advice on what?"

"Well, the phone's so impersonal; I wonder if we could meet for a drink."

"Depends on when and where," Curly said. "I've got a poker game tonight."

"Oh my goodness. Curly, it won't take long—a half hour, forty-five minutes at the most. Would you mind coming to my apartment? I would really appreciate it."

Despite his cautious instincts, Curly felt an instant response in his groin, as if some involuntary message had been reflexively dispatched to his testicles.

"Do you still live in the Village?" he asked as he swallowed hard.

"I do," she said. And after she had given Curly the address and hung up her phone, she placed a call to Alan Rothman.

24

A LITTLE MORE THAN TWENTY YEARS EARLIER, DURING ONE long, tedious train ride home from her grandmother's house in Omaha, Nebraska, to her mother's apartment in Lincoln, seven-year-old Cordiss Krinkle had counted telephone poles as the flat, gray landscape streaked past her window seat. Then, when the telephone poles no longer interested her, she reached across to the seatback pocket in front of her and picked up a copy of a giveaway travel magazine. Browsing through it, Cordiss was quickly captivated by eight pages of color photographs of laughing children who were about the same age that she was—they were splashing each other on the beach, playing in parks, reaching out to a grinning ice cream vendor who was teasingly holding a bouquet of Popsicles before them. Cordiss studied the pictures enviously.

The article was entitled "San Remo, Jewel of the Mediterranean," and the city did appear to be a jewel; it seemed to contain everything that was missing from the world Cordiss knew—laughter, friendship, beauty, love. That moment, that day, on that train, her life was transformed forever. The children from those magazine pages became the friends Cordiss didn't have. One face in particular, that of a saucer-eyed boy with a turned-up nose and a mischievous half smile, drew her attention like a magnet. He became her secret friend in her faraway world. She confided in him, shared with him her innermost dreams. Even as a teenager, whenever she felt lonely or sad, her thoughts would return to that boy with the big, round, wondrous eyes.

Now, as she gazed out at the sun-drenched Mediterranean coast from the balcony of her San Remo apartment, Cordiss thought of that boy. Where was he now, she wondered, and how could he still hold such a special place in her heart? During the course of their relationship, Victor had never quite believed Cordiss when she told him that she was first attracted to him because of his eyes, which resembled those of an Italian boy she had once seen in a magazine. He didn't realize that she had been telling the truth until they arrived here in San Remo and Cordiss had said, "Finally, I'm home."

As Cordiss stood on the balcony, a buzzing sound snapped her head around. She looked first at the door, then over to Victor, who was watching a soccer match between AC Milan and Palermo on TV. Victor didn't know much about the teams or the players or even the sport itself, but he was a competitive man and he could relate to the players' vigor and their tenacity. He had gotten so involved in the action on the TV screen that he didn't notice the door buzzer the first time it sounded. Victor was still on the couch, hooting in approval as Milan's striker rammed a header past the Palermo goalie, when the buzzer sounded again. This time, Victor grudgingly got up from the couch, walked to the front door, and yanked it open. Two unfamiliar men, one slightly taller than the other, were standing shoulder to shoulder in the hallway, glaring at Victor from behind tinted sunglasses.

"*Buon' giorno,*" Victor said, smiling inquisitively.

"May we come in?" the taller of the two men asked.

Victor recognized the accent as American. His smile disappeared. "How can I help you?" he asked.

"We're here to see Cordiss Krinkle," the shorter man said politely.

"What about?" Victor asked.

"An important matter," replied the taller man.

"Who are you, and what is this very important matter?" Victor's tone was challenging and sarcastic.

"Something of great value to Miss Krinkle and to you, Victor."

Victor started slightly at the sound of his name. "Do you guys have names?" he asked, recovering his cool. Victor received no reply. He looked the two men up and down. Something about their conservative dress, dark shades, and quietly intimidating manner reminded him of the soldiers from the Carlino family whom he would see now and then in the Mafia-owned restaurants in Hell's Kitchen where he had worked as dishwasher, busboy, and waiter.

"Why don't you let us in?" the taller man asked.

Victor stood his ground. "First, tell me who you are and what you want."

"Inside," the shorter man said, nodding toward the living room.

"Bullshit, mister. Right here. And make it fast," Victor said.

"Look, Victor," the tall man began.

"Or fuck off," Victor interrupted, his voice rising.

"Stolen property, Victor," the shorter man said coldly. "That's one of the things we're here to discuss. Twenty years in prison is another."

Victor felt a hot flush at the back of his neck; then, the nerve endings came alive in the pit of his stomach.

"Dr. Howard Mozelle," continued the shorter man, "Anna Hilburn, Herman Freich, Colette Beekman, Montaro Caine, the coin or coins—you name it, we're here to talk about all of it."

Victor's heart galloped. "I don't know what the hell you're talking about, so you may as well just get lost." Whatever they wanted, Victor told himself, whatever had brought them here, he had faced far worse back in New York—some of his boyhood pals had served time on Rikers Island; he'd seen two mob hits in Hell's Kitchen; once, when he had borrowed money from one of his mentors, a man named Johnny, and hadn't paid it back on time, he'd wound up choking on a gun that Johnny shoved against the back of his throat. He comforted himself by noting that these men had not mentioned Franklyn and Whitney Walker—apparently, he and Cordiss had done a good job of hiding them away. Nevertheless, he could feel himself beginning to sweat.

Cordiss was the one pissing ice water now. She had drifted in from the balcony and was standing motionless in the center of the room. She was barefoot, wearing jeans, a white T-shirt with no bra underneath, and she hadn't put on any makeup, but she seemed completely unconcerned with her appearance—as if she were truly at home here, as if San Remo was where she had always belonged and the two men standing in her doorway were old friends.

"They're cops, Victor, let them in," she said. "We have nothing to hide."

Still, Victor, his fears hidden behind his belligerent façade, continued to stare the two men down.

"Not until I see some I.D.," he said.

The taller man gave a condescending smile, assessing Victor in his baggy Italian pants and sleeveless shirt as if he were some sort of gigolo or a Hollywood version of a blue-collar ladies' man. "We're not cops, Victor, but if you don't talk to us, the next people you talk to will be cops."

"Then who are you?"

The taller man spoke. His eyes were fierce and predatory. "My name is Alan Rothman. This gentleman is Carlos Wallace. We're businessmen."

"Come in, Mr. Rothman, Mr. Wallace," Cordiss said. Victor stepped aside while Cordiss moved to the TV and switched it off. Victor glanced longingly at the black TV screen, peeved that he wouldn't get to see the end of the game.

"Sit, gentlemen." Cordiss pointed Rothman and Wallace to the couch and took a seat across from them in an overstuffed chair. Victor sat on the edge of the table that served as a TV stand. *Stay cool*, he told himself, just as he had told Cordiss many times before. *Whatever happens, stay cool*. He wondered why Cordiss had become so much better at following his advice than he was.

"How did you track us down?" Cordiss asked.

Rothman smirked, thinking of how easy it had been for Gina Lao to get the information they needed from Curly Bennett. "You should've used a pseudonym at the airport," he said. "For a few bucks, people remember a name like Cordiss Krinkle."

Cordiss let Rothman's sarcasm wash over her. "Well," she began. "Since stolen property tops the list of items you wish to discuss, suppose we start there."

Rothman inched forward on the couch. "First, let me acquaint you with the underlying reason we are here. We represent a firm that may have become involved, rightly or wrongly, in this matter of the coins. It is our job to make sure that the integrity of that firm has not been compromised." Here, he paused to look at Victor, who hoisted his eyebrows and offered a cool, comical smile.

"What is the name of your firm?" asked Cordiss.

Rothman's stern gaze swiveled back to her. "We'll ask the questions," he said.

"Oh, I see," Cordiss said, letting the matter rest there for the moment.

"If we determine that the firm has not been compromised," Rothman went on, "then you have nothing to fear and we will be on our way. If we find that it has been, through no fault of your own, we will likewise be on our way, with apologies for the intrusion." He folded his arms across his chest as his ice-cold eyes slid back and forth between Cordiss and Victor.

Cordiss chewed her bottom lip, tilted her head upward in a manner suggesting serious contemplation, then stared at Rothman as sternly as he had stared at her. "Well, Mr. Rothman," she said. "I'm not aware of anything that might have been stolen from your firm, whatever its name, or from anywhere else for that matter." She turned to Victor. "Are you, Victor?"

"Sure as hell not."

Cordiss spread her hands out, palms down, to indicate they were done discussing this particular subject. "So we can move on to your next point, which was something about twenty years in prison. A threat, I gather, related to this 'stolen property,' which, if I understand you correctly, is a coin or coins. Right?"

"Right," said Rothman.

"Well, Mr. Rothman, let me be blunt. Whatever I may have sold either would have been mine to sell, and I would have the documents to prove it, or the rightful owner would have given me the legal authority to represent him or her. So your threat does not apply to me. None of the people you represent can make any legal claim of any kind against me that will stick. Therefore, neither they nor you can touch me. Legally"—she smiled confidently—"or otherwise." She leaned back in her chair, then bounced back to an upright position.

"As to whether the integrity of your firm has been violated, it is impossible for me to say, as I don't even know its name."

Wallace pulled an iPhone from his jacket and used an index finger to scroll to a particular page in a document. "Before leaving New York," he began, "you opened a secret account at a private bank in Liechtenstein," he said. "Two substantial deposits have been made into that account via Mr. Peter Fourneaux, assistant manager of new accounts. The money arrived there through a maze of companies, corporations, trusts, and names of nonexistent individuals as payment for items you will have to prove were not stolen."

Cordiss appeared unfazed, yet her mind was racing. How had they managed to pierce the secrecy of the banking system? Could they actually prove what he had just said? As if in answer to that unspoken question, Wallace opened his briefcase and pulled two copies of Cordiss's deposit slips from it and laid them before her.

Wallace continued, "Your next burden of proof will have to do with fraud and forgery. If you have behaved like a good U.S. citizen, close to half the amount in your Liechtenstein account has been sent or will be sent to the I.R.S. If you're thinking otherwise, that's tax evasion. Long time in jail. Unless you skip to one of those few places in the world that has no extradition treaty with the U.S. In short, you talk to us, tell us what we want to know, and this visit never happened. Refuse and you'll have more trouble than you can handle."

Cordiss leaned closer to the men with a smile that suggested that they had gotten all they were going to get. Wallace tried to wait her out through a long silence.

"Bullshit," Victor finally blurted out. "You guys are not here about the integrity of no fucking firm. Now spell it out. Specifics on the table. What the fuck is it you want?"

"We want to know everything you know about those coins," Rothman said. "What are they? What can they do? Where did they come from? Who had them? For how long? When and how did you get them? How much did you sell them for, and to whom?"

Cordiss burst into laughter. Rothman watched her warily, not understanding why she was laughing. Victor, too, wondered what the hell was going on in her mind. Soon, Cordiss's laughter subsided.

"These guys are big business, Victor. The circle is widening, new players are coming in. Soon, we'll be expendable; but for now, we're not. So, Mr. Rothman, you've told us what you want. How about what Victor and I want?"

"Which is what?"

"First, to be left alone."

"You can have that. It's up to you."

"Can you guarantee it?" she asked.

"Pretty much," Rothman answered.

Cordiss didn't believe him for an instant; nevertheless, she continued. "Next, that bullshit, as Victor puts it, about your firm's integrity is just that, bullshit." She paused, glanced at Victor, inhaled deeply, then deliberately examined her fingernails. "I know what you really want. And we want the same thing—a piece of the action down the line."

Rothman looked surprised—Cordiss was apparently far smarter than he had guessed she would be. He looked at her for a long time before answering. "Something could be worked out," he said.

"In writing—before we talk," said Cordiss.

"I'm sure we can arrive at something reasonable," Rothman said.

"Good, now let me see your passports."

"Why?" Rothman asked.

"Why not?" asked Cordiss.

Rothman briefly weighed the request, then produced his passport. Carlos Wallace followed suit. Cordiss examined the documents thoroughly before handing them back.

"Business cards, please, gentlemen?" Cordiss said.

Rothman reached into his vest pocket and pulled out a card from his Gucci card case. He was liking Cordiss less but respecting her more. Wallace handed Cordiss a business card, too.

Cordiss read from a card, "Alan Rothman, Manager of Operations, Fitzer Corporation." She looked up. "So, chemicals are what you're into." She burst into laughter once again. Then, after looking at Rothman and Wallace as if for the first time, she said, "You may find, to your surprise, that we are not such small potatoes as you may think. And, speaking of potatoes, have you gentlemen had lunch?"

"No we haven't," replied Rothman.

"Good, I'll rustle up something while we talk. Victor, open some wine."

Rothman and Wallace glanced at each other, somewhat uneasily. Meanwhile, Cordiss headed for the kitchen and Victor crossed to the dry bar in the far corner of the living room. Victor wondered if these men were underestimating Cordiss every bit as much as he once had.

25

WHEN MONTARO CAINE ARRIVED UNINVITED AT THE HOME OF Roland Gabler accompanied by Howard Mozelle, he knew there was a good chance he might seem either too eager or too desperate. Yet with both coins currently out of his control, and with Alan Rothman and Carlos Wallace out of the country for reasons he did not yet know, he understood that time was of the essence. Nancy MacDonald had tried without success to arrange a meeting with Gabler, leading Caine to understand that the collector was probably stalling. So now, Caine had taken matters into his own hands, showing up first thing in the morning. He was gambling that the collector's curiosity would overcome his sense of protocol and that Montaro's bold act would pique Gabler's interest. Apparently, he had gambled correctly, for no sooner had Gabler's assistant Jerome Voekle informed Caine and Mozelle that his employer was not inclined to see guests without an appointment, Gabler himself appeared, introduced himself, nodded at Caine, dismissed Voekle, and led the two visitors to his study.

Caine shook the man's hand. "Please forgive the intrusion," he said, and introduced himself and the doctor.

"Thanks for receiving us," Mozelle broke in, somewhat startled by the strength of Gabler's grip. The collector's rough, calloused hand reminded him of what he had read in one of the books Caine's investigators had gotten from Cordiss's apartment—that Gabler was an amateur weight lifter.

"Not at all, Doctor. It so happens I have a bit of time at the moment. Mr. Caine, of course I'm well aware of who you are. Sorry to hear about the state of affairs at Fitzer." Adopting the demeanor of a gracious host, the smiling Gabler gestured his guests toward the sitting area in front of his fireplace. "Be seated, please," he urged.

Caine and Mozelle sat on the couch in the spot where Cordiss Krinkle had sat during her first visit. As Gabler settled into his favorite chair across the table from his guests, he directed his questions to Dr. Mozelle. Caine understood the collector sensed his companion was a far less threatening presence than he himself was. Though he feigned no prior knowledge of Mozelle and claimed to know Caine only as the CEO of Fitzer, Caine suspected that he had learned far more than he was letting on from Cordiss Krinkle.

"So, gentlemen, how can I help you?" Gabler asked Mozelle.

"We're here to discuss something you have purchased recently," Caine responded before Mozelle had a chance to speak.

"My," said Gabler. "I've purchased many things recently."

Although they had barely begun to speak, Caine was already growing impatient with Gabler's coy, condescending tone and his games. "You purchased a coin from Cordiss Krinkle, and it was not hers to sell," Caine said plainly.

Gabler's brow knotted into a series of jagged lines, as if he was trying to make sense out of something unfamiliar. "Miss Krinkle?"

"Yes. Cordiss Krinkle. A former employee in my office," said Mozelle.

"She stole the coin from Dr. Mozelle, who owned it, and she sold it to you," Caine said, impatiently explaining what he now felt certain Gabler already knew.

"My goodness. Perhaps you gentlemen should talk to my lawyer," Gabler said, attempting to appear more amused than irritated.

"That wouldn't be a good idea," said Caine.

"But it would be proper procedure if I'm hearing you correctly," Gabler said. He stared into Caine's steady blue eyes.

"Yes," Caine said with a nod. "But even among the still small number of us who know about the coins, the situation is already at serious risk of becoming an open secret. If that happens too soon, we'll all lose."

"I have never purchased stolen property, if that's what you're suggesting," said Gabler.

Caine interrupted. "Whatever documents you have to verify legal purchase are false, Mr. Gabler," he said.

"I beg your pardon?"

"Whether or not you knew they were false when you contracted with Cordiss Krinkle is, indeed, a question for your lawyer and the courts to decide."

"Are you trying to frighten me?" Gabler asked. "I've bought many coins from many people whose faces and names I have long since forgotten. All I understand is that you have fallen just short of accusing me of misconduct in my business. Let me enlighten both of you. In my entire collection, there isn't one single piece that is not properly documented."

"Mr. Gabler, a court challenge at this time, to establish legal ownership, will tell the world about the coins," Mozelle said gently. "The moment that happens, you, Montaro, and I will lose any chance for control. No matter in whose favor the courts eventually decide, the interest of the world's scientific community will immediately overwhelm us—there will be pressure for access to those coins from the American Astronomical Society, the American Medical Association, and God knows who else."

"So let's get back to where we were," Caine said pointedly. "The name of the woman you purchased the coins from is Cordiss Krinkle."

"Krinkle? I'll have to check my files on that."

"Please save us both the time of feigning ignorance. You already know about Krinkle, much more than we do. You also know about me, about Dr. Mozelle, his wife, Dr. Chasman, and Dr. Walmeyer. You know the whole history from Dr. Mozelle's notes. There are, of course, a few things you don't know. For example, where the companion coin is, who Cordiss sold it to, at what price, and what she's planning to sell next."

Caine's remarks caused Gabler's jaw to tighten. "The information I have on you, Caine, does not include a penchant for rudeness," he snapped.

Mozelle quietly gave Caine a warning glance not to push so hard, but Caine knew that Mozelle didn't understand what had just happened. He and Gabler had just completed an intricate, preliminary skirmish during which they had taken each other's measure. They had listened and watched for telltale signs—fluctuations of voice level, word choice, eye movement, hand gestures, even the pauses between sentences. Now, the opening round was over, and each man was poised for serious talk.

"Mr. Caine," Gabler said. "Is it fair to say that your interest in these alleged coins is primarily commercial?"

"Primarily," Caine acknowledged.

"You wish to conduct research with an eye to how well the properties in these alleged coins can be reproduced for commercial exploitation. Am I correct?"

"You are correct."

"Let us, for the moment, assume for the sake of discussion that the items you are referring to do, in fact, exist; and that the research you're proposing proves successful, and the elements carry considerable opportunity for commercial exploitation. Who do you propose would have control of that information?"

"If we worked together, Mr. Gabler, we would, but only if we got there first."

"I see," said Gabler.

Dr. Mozelle leaned over the coffee table. "We cannot impress upon you strongly enough how important a factor time is in all of this."

Gabler moved forward in his chair as well and stared silently at Dr. Mozelle before asking his next question. "Why? Because the holder of the second coin could, by moving faster, beat you to those findings before the world at large gets any information about the coins' existence?"

"That's about it," Caine replied simply.

"How do we know they haven't beaten us to it already?"

Gabler's use of the word "us" heartened Mozelle.

Caine shook his head. "Because as of now, no one has gone to the U.S. Patent Office to register their findings about the coins; the sooner we have access to one or both of the coins, the sooner we can be certain we have the edge."

"And when you have that edge, you plan to let the holders of the second coin know?" asked Gabler.

"Yes," said Caine.

"If they know they can't beat us, they will be more inclined to join us," Dr. Mozelle added.

"Ideally, it is our wish," Caine continued, "to analyze both coins at the same time."

"And what role do you see for the owners of each coin in the control of your findings?" Gabler inquired.

"None," said Caine.

Gabler didn't bat an eye. "I see," he said.

"You will have a financial interest in the entity that has control of the findings, but you will have absolutely no control over that entity. The financial interest, however, will be a fair one."

Gabler nodded as if he had expected this answer and found it reasonable. "The second coin, who has it?" he asked.

"We will let you know in time," Caine said.

"How much did he or she pay?"

"A good deal more than you."

At this, Roland Gabler smiled.

"Mr. Gabler, how do you feel about what we are proposing?" asked Dr. Mozelle.

"I'll need some time to think about it. Suppose I call you in a few days."

———

In the privacy of the elevator heading down to the lobby of Gabler's building, Mozelle asked, "So, what do you think?"

"He'll come in," said Caine. "He needs us more than we need him."

With a disbelieving frown, Mozelle chuckled. "Explain that to me," he said.

Caine reminded himself of how much he liked the old doctor; he assumed that this was why the doctor's naïveté didn't annoy him.

"Underneath," Caine told his friend, "that man is all about money. We're a giant opportunity for him. Without us, the coin is all but worthless to him. No one can know of its properties, and therefore he can't even have bragging rights. I think he was already waiting for other players to seek him out, and he knew that eventually they would. Of course he was surprised when we showed up. We weren't what he expected."

"What was he expecting?" Mozelle asked.

"Gamblers like him," said Montaro.

"Really? I didn't get that at all." Mozelle scratched his temple. "In fact, I got just the opposite."

Caine smiled, recalling something his grandfather had often told him. "Sometimes what we hear isn't always what we see, Doctor," he said.

"I just hope you're right."

"So do I," Caine said with a sly smile.

Mozelle smiled back. "Where do we go from here?" he asked.

"Fritzbrauner."

"That's what I figured," said Mozelle. "When do we leave for Switzerland?"

26

WHEN ALAN ROTHMAN FINISHED SPEAKING, AN ELECTRIFYING quiet descended upon those seated around the oval table in the dining alcove of Verna Fontaine's condo. Each face registered some combination of astonishment and disbelief. With plaited fingers, Rothman's hands rested on the table in a pose that seemed almost religious. His gaze moved counterclockwise, taking in first Bob Wildenmiller, whose face wore a dumbstruck expression, next Thomas Bolton, Richard Davis's lieutenant. Bolton stared back at Rothman with a look that could have meant either hypnotic fascination or the assumption that Rothman had gone mad. Verna Fontaine wore the scowl of a skeptic; she stared off into empty space. Finally, Rothman's eyes settled on Richard C. Davis, the billionaire industrialist in whose hands his future rested. Davis's expression was inscrutable; his cold eyes offered no hint as to what thoughts were taking place behind them. Then, as if he knew that the younger man was growing uncomfortable, Davis lowered his eyes to the documents Rothman had laid before him as corroborating evidence for the improbable tale he had just reported upon his return from San Remo. Among the items scattered upon the table were copies of Dr. Howard Mozelle's notes, Caine's memo to his professor, and photographs of two coins.

Davis fingered several of the documents. Then, finally, he held up a page on which the names of the coins' purchasers were typed in boldface. He abruptly laid the document back on the table and turned to Bob Wildenmiller.

"Kritzman Fritzbrauner," Davis said.

Wildenmiller nodded slowly. He knew the name; both he and Davis had reckoned with it before.

Davis turned back to Rothman. "Alan, I'll be a son of a bitch if this isn't the damndest thing I've ever heard of."

"Richard, it struck me the same way, but I went through it step by step."

"It's a real attention getter all right," Davis said. "It's bizarre, it's off the wall, but I'm not convinced how genuine it all is. I've listened to what you said. I've examined these documents, but I've got to tell you, after sixty-two years of living, my better judgment tells me there's a hell of a catch hidden somewhere."

"I understand," Rothman began cautiously, "but what if there is no catch? Forgive my saying so, but what if you're wrong?"

"It wouldn't be the first time," chortled Davis, who liked to surround himself with people who had the guts to question him. "But if I am, and this fairy tale is for real, then Alan, I'll be the most flabbergasted son of a bitch you'll ever see."

"I know it sounds preposterous," Rothman continued. "But can we afford to simply ignore it? Particularly in the face of the opportunities that will fall in our laps if this whole thing turns out to be legit?"

"I think you're letting yourself be captured by the upside of this thing, Alan. It might have blurred your vision. I always say in any game," Davis continued, channeling the part of himself that had once played Division I football, "if you want to be an effective player, you've gotta see the ball clearly from every side."

Rothman glanced around the table to gauge how the others were reacting. "But we have a limited window of opportunity," he replied. "Two weeks down the line I don't want us to find out that there was no catch, and that Caine actually does have some kind of revolutionary formula. If that happens, all our efforts will be dead in the water."

Richard Davis sighed heavily, leaned back in his chair, folded his hands behind his neck, and pulled his head forward to stretch his spine.

"What do you think, Bob?"

Wildenmiller took his time in responding. He weighed sound judgment against gut reactions and searched his feelings. It was his nature to always anchor decisions in the concrete of hard evidence, yet he was now being asked to offer an answer that could only arise from intuition.

"I think we should hear what the girl has to say," Wildenmiller finally said.

"You do, eh?" said the billionaire. He then turned to Alan Rothman and signaled with a slight nod of his head. Bolton pulled out his cell phone and keyed in a number.

Downstairs, an air-conditioned limo was parked in front of the Brougham Arms Apartments. The chauffeur behind the wheel had been listening to the ball game on the radio. The Mets were playing the Pirates, the score was tied, and two men were on base with Angel Pagan coming up to the plate. But the moment his stern-faced passenger's cell phone rang, the chauffeur turned off the radio and waited quietly as he heard Thomas Bolton's voice on the passenger's speakerphone.

"Wallace?" Bolton asked.

"Here," Carlos said from the back of the limousine.

"Bring her up."

"Right away."

The chauffeur leaped from the car, then scrambled to open the curbside door. Cordiss Krinkle emerged from the backseat of the limo, followed by Wallace, then Victor.

"Hold it, Victor," Wallace said. "You stay here."

Wallace took Cordiss's arm and guided her into the Brougham Arms while Victor stood beside the limo, chewing on his bottom lip and muttering to himself as he watched the two disappear into the lobby. He thought of how satisfying it would be to punch Carlos Wallace in the mouth, even though he was most angered by Cordiss's refusal to insist that he join her. He could see Cordiss becoming a new woman. He allowed himself to wonder whether Cordiss's new money, new attitude, and tastes would mean she would soon be seeking a new man as well. He sulked as he got back into the limo, slightly consoled by the fact that at least he'd be able to listen to the rest of the Mets game.

When Cordiss arrived at Verna Fontaine's apartment, she and Carlos Wallace were greeted by Verna's broad smile. "Come in," Verna said, holding the door open for them. She trailed her guests across the living room into the alcove where Rothman introduced Cordiss to the others. Bob Wildenmiller directed Cordiss to an empty chair at their table while Carlos sat on the couch.

"Miss Krinkle, we understand you have information that would lend clarity and credence to the story Mr. Rothman has been telling us," Wildenmiller began.

"I hope I can help you," replied Cordiss.

"And what information might that be, my dear?"

Cordiss smiled at the condescension. "I would say that's the wrong question, Mr. Wildenmiller," she said.

"How so?"

"If you've read those documents, what you now know about the story is already very clear. What isn't clear to you, however, is what's going to happen next. That's the question you should be asking me."

"Because you can foretell the future?"

"Not all of it, certainly; but what I do know is vitally important."

"So," Wildenmiller began, "one thing you know is the name of the young woman in whose hand the coin was originally found. True?"

"That's true," Cordiss said.

"And the name of her husband, whose birth produced the second coin?"

"That's also true."

"Well," said Wildenmiller, "beyond that, we fail to see what other essential information may or may not be in your possession that might have escaped our attention. Please enlighten us."

"The whereabouts of the young couple in question, for one thing."

"And?" asked Wildenmiller.

"The fact that she may or may not be pregnant and preparing to give birth soon," responded Cordiss.

"That about it?" Wildenmiller asked.

"What more would you want?" asked Cordiss.

"You will have to do better than that, my dear. Your burden is to present us with reasons why any of this should interest us at all."

"The birth of that child will be an event," said Cordiss. "I know who the parents are, where they are, when the child is due, and, above all, what most likely will happen when that baby is born. We can control the circumstances of that birth; and, by doing so, we will be there at the right moment when an amazingly remunerative miracle might well occur. Do you need more information, Mr. Wildenmiler? Or," she concluded, parroting his own words back to him, "*is that about it?*"

There was silence in the room before Wildenmiller asked, "Who else knows about the pregnancy and the due date of the child?"

"Dr. Mozelle and possibly Caine," answered Cordiss.

"What about Fritzbrauner and Gabler?" asked Bolton.

"No."

"How can you be so sure?"

"Because I haven't told them and there is no one else who would."

"Who else knows the whereabouts of the couple?"

"Just me and Victor," said Cordiss.

The conversation fell into another pause, leaving the humming of the air conditioner to dominate the uneasy quiet in the room until Richard C. Davis finally spoke.

"Miss Krinkle, how do you envision controlling the circumstances of that birth, as you put it, without stepping into legal, and possibly ethical, quicksand? I would like to hear you translate what you are proposing into concrete detail. Take me through the specifics—steps one, two, three."

Though the name Richard Davis meant nothing to Cordiss, the way he took command impressed her. *Well, well, Mr. Davis*, Cordiss thought, *so you're the boss here.*

"I'm of course prepared to do that, but what I'm proposing is a sure thing. What's not sure yet is whether or not we're going to have an arrangement," said Cordiss. "May I have some Perrier, please?" Victor had been telling her that she had come back from Europe with new tastes, and designer water was one of them.

"Of course," said Verna Fontaine, rising.

Cordiss waited for the water to arrive, then took several sips before she spoke. "O.K.," she said. "Here's how I think we should proceed."

Downstairs, the Mets game was over. Victor had fallen asleep during the eighth inning and was dozing in the back of the limousine when Cordiss woke him, shouting playfully, "Wake up, wake up, sleepyhead."

Victor shook the sleep from his head and looked at Cordiss's wide grin. "Are we in business?" he asked.

"We are," said Cordiss.

"Yeah?"

"Honey," chuckled Cordiss. "Are we in business!" She pushed the button that raised the partition window to isolate the chauffeur.

"Did you talk numbers?" Victor asked.

"Nope."

"Why not?"

"Because ten million dollars here or there is nothing to these guys. Believe me, if this thing works out, we can jack our numbers way up."

"Shit, I wish I was up there with you."

"You were, honey, I was thinking about you all the time."

Cordiss lowered the partition. "Take us back to our hotel," she told the driver, and as the limo pulled into traffic, Victor wasn't sure what made him happier—all the money that he and Cordiss would be making or the fact that Cordiss still loved him and that they would be spending it together.

27

THE EXECUTIVE DINING LOUNGE OF DAVIS INDUSTRIES WAS LO-
cated on the tenth floor of the corporation's Park Avenue headquarters in one of the priciest zip codes in Manhattan. But what
Roland Gabler found most noteworthy when he arrived there for his
one p.m. meeting with Bob Wildenmiller and his associates was how
great the disparity could be between wealth and taste. There was an
impersonal, corporate sheen to these rooms—the long table and
chairs were undoubtedly expensive and yet were so lacking in distinc-
tive qualities that they might as well have been chosen from a whole-
salers' mail order catalog. In Gabler's domain, every objet d'art
possessed a fascinating and sometimes dangerous history; what passed
for artwork on these walls had probably been mass-produced on an
assembly line. When Wildenmiller had called to request a meeting,
Gabler had suggested that his own chef devise a menu; when Wildenmiller declined and Gabler agreed to meet at Davis headquarters, he
was still looking forward to the discussion, but not to what would be
served at lunch.

The dour individuals who greeted Gabler as he entered the
room—Carlos Wallace, Verna Fontaine, Alan Rothman, Thomas
Bolton, and Wildenmiller himself—made no greater impression on
Gabler than the lounge itself or the two platters of lukewarm chicken

Caesar salad set out on the conference table. Ice cubes were already melting in the pitchers of iced tea. These were sharpshooting businessmen; unlike some of the eccentric characters Gabler encountered in the collecting world, they didn't know much about style and were likely to dispense with small talk and get straight to the point. True to Gabler's expectations, it took barely more than a minute for Wildenmiller to say, "We're interested in a recent addition to your collection, Roland."

Gabler was used to taking his time in these sorts of discussions, engaging his potential adversaries in banter to take their measure. "What addition is that?" he asked.

"The one with what appears to be a very unusual history."

"Forgive the immodesty, gentlemen, but all of my objects have very unusual histories, otherwise I'd be in the junk business." Gabler laughed; the other men at the table did not.

"We would like to purchase it," Wildenmiller said flatly, at which point Gabler abandoned the pretense of friendly discussion; clearly, this was to be solely a business conversation—disappointing but ultimately fine with him.

"It's not for sale," he said.

Wildenmiller took a mouthful of lunch, washed it down with swallows of iced tea, then rested his fork gently on his plate before speaking again. "You will need enormous resources to take full advantage of the potential represented there, Roland."

Gabler kept his face blank while his eyes shifted about the table. "It sounds as if we're on two different tracks," he said. "To me, the real value of an object, such as the one you are discussing, is the extent to which it enhances my collection."

"I understand," Wildenmiller interrupted. "And fundamentally I agree with you. Rarity and beauty are, indeed, the object's true values, even for an old accountant like me. However, let's be practical. The chances of that coin remaining in your collection are very slim, given the likelihood of ownership disputes and the real possibility of public discovery. Therefore, secondary values of a more tangible nature than rarity and beauty might be all that will be left for you to hang on to. Your business is not equipped to take advantage of any of the possibilities that may be locked away in that rarity and beauty we all admire, while we, on the other hand, are fully equipped to exploit its potential."

Gabler tried not to betray the elation he felt on hearing Wildenmiller's words. "I don't know what to say, except that I don't agree with your assessment," he said carefully. "If we are both operating from the same set of facts, then one of us is interpreting them incorrectly."

"We have the same information as you have," Wildenmiller said, "but we also have information that you do not have. Information you will not be able to uncover in time to successfully pursue this thing alone, even if you had the capacity to do so. Trust me, Roland, our offer, which will represent a substantial profit to you, is the only way things can work out to our mutual benefit."

"Sorry, gentlemen, the item is not for sale."

"Not even for, say, ten million dollars?" asked Wildenmiller.

"It is a priceless item, Bob."

"For which you just paid two million dollars, if I'm not mistaken."

Gabler remained silent.

"And in a very short time it may have no value at all to any of us," Wildenmiller pressed on.

"You're asking me to rush to judgment, as if I were a common hustler of trinkets," said Gabler. "I assure you, I am not. Now, unless you can treat me with the respect I believe I deserve, there's no point in continuing this discussion."

"My apologies, if I've offended you," Wildenmiller replied. "We have simply offered what we feel to be a very fair price, all things considered."

"All things considered but not evenly balanced," said Gabler. "Forgive me for saying so, but I couldn't be less interested in your money, as unthinkable as that may sound to you. And I would like to disabuse you of the notion that no alternatives are open to me."

Wildenmiller's eyes lit up. "In that regard, Roland, I think it's fair to tell you that we already know we're not the only interested party."

"Meaning?" asked Gabler.

"Meaning that our investigators have already told us that you have met with Montaro Caine and Howard Mozelle," Wildenmiller said pointedly. "And I highly doubt that they offered you anything near the amount that we have offered you. We figure that they proposed some sort of partnership arrangement."

Alan Rothman passed his linen napkin across his mouth, removing the salad dressing that had gathered on his lips. "Roland," he said, "I think you should know that Caine and the doctor won't be able to make good on anything they've proposed. Soon, Caine will not be in a position to honor any deal; he will no longer have a company to cover it."

"No? Why not?" Gabler raised his eyebrows.

"The company will be changing hands shortly," Thomas Bolton chimed in.

Carlos Wallace cleared his throat twice, always a reliable indication that he was ready to speak. "Let's be candid," he told Gabler. "What you're really after is a better deal than the one they offered. Isn't that true?"

Gabler let the question pass.

"If no agreement is reached between us," said Wildenmiller, "let me repeat, your deal with Caine collapses the minute he is no longer CEO of Fitzer Corporation. So, with respect, I ask that you reconsider our offer."

"Your offer is not acceptable. The item is not for sale," Gabler repeated.

"At any price? Or at the price we have offered?" asked Wildenmiller.

Gabler hesitated. He searched their faces before he answered. "At that price," he said evenly.

"At what price can we do business?" Wildenmiller asked.

Gabler was ready. "At the same price you offered, in addition to the same partnership arrangement that Caine and Mozelle proposed. I will retain a small percentage of all income that arises commercially from the exploitation of the coin and any of the elements it's composed of."

Now that the posturing was over and there was an actual deal to negotiate, the others at the table awaited a cue from Wildenmiller. Finally, he broke the silence and attempted to lighten the mood with a question:

"Well, so what do you think of our chef?" he asked.

"No contest," answered Gabler. "Mine's better."

28

WHEN MONTARO CAINE AND HOWARD MOZELLE ARRIVED AT Kritzman Fritzbrauner's estate, they were greeted by Fritzbrauner himself, who had been standing on his patio as their chauffeured limousine pulled up. Dr. Mozelle was impressed that a man of Fritzbrauner's wealth and reputation would be greeting them personally. But Caine's experience as a CEO had taught him that men of Fritzbrauner's stature, particularly when they were truly interested in the people they were meeting, did not need to reassure themselves of their own importance by relying on underlings and intermediaries. He understood that in trying to avoid Caine, Roland Gabler was still trying to escape his Needles, Nebraska, upbringing. When Caine and Mozelle had requested a meeting with Fritzbrauner, the man's reply had been quick and affirmative.

Following formal introductions and warm handshakes, Fritzbrauner led his visitors to his drawing room, where he introduced them to Gertz Welbocht, doctor of astronomy at the University of Heidelberg, and Carl Spreight, dean of philosophy at the University of Heidelberg. Caine and Dr. Mozelle recalled Dr. Chasman's meeting with Welbocht, but Carl Spreight was a total stranger. Colette Beekman was here as well, though she was not quite a stranger to

Caine; in fact, the way she looked at him made him somewhat regret the fact that she wasn't more of a stranger and also that he hadn't mentioned her name when Cecilia had asked him whom he would be meeting in Switzerland.

In Fritzbrauner's opulent drawing room, after a round of cocktails and polite conversation about the weather and the difficulties of coping with transoceanic travel, Fritzbrauner turned his attention directly to Caine and Mozelle and addressed the matter that the men had journeyed all this way to discuss.

"Montaro," he asked, "have you heard of a legendary pearl that is widely thought to be in the collection of . . . "

Caine finished the sentence for him. "Roland Gabler," he said.

"Yes," said Fritzbrauner. "Are you familiar with the history of that pearl?"

"Not really," said Caine. "I've recently seen some books that mention it. But I've never had much interest in collecting."

"Have you ever seen any part of his collection?"

"Just the little that I saw in his apartment."

"Were you impressed?"

"As much as I could be." Caine looked Fritzbrauner straight in the eye. "He has the other coin," he added. "But you already know that." Nothing in Fritzbrauner's manner confirmed or denied Caine's statement.

"Have you seen it?" Fritzbrauner inquired finally.

"No."

"How do you know he still has it?"

"We're certain of it."

"Having not seen it, you're certain?" Fritzbrauner raised his eyebrows.

"Yes," said Caine. "One can know many things without necessarily seeing them up close; unfortunately, the same cannot be said of the coins. In order to understand them, we need to examine them. We're expecting Gabler's cooperation to help us solve many of the baffling questions that have been raised by the coins' existence."

"And how do you plan to go about solving such questions?"

"Mass spectrometry," said Caine.

"Sounds like big-time stuff." Fritzbrauner offered an amused but sincere smile.

"Afterward, we expect to have answers to much of the riddle of the coins."

"Answers? Such as?"

"The process by which they came into being, for instance. What they're made of. And maybe, just maybe, even the purpose behind their existence, if one exists. I'm sure you're intrigued by your own list of whys and hows, and we can try our best to discover the answers to those questions as well."

For Caine, his elusive host was not an easy read. Fritzbrauner was too experienced and sharp to telegraph his intentions. Caine's staff had researched Fritzbrauner and Caine had learned that the man had a fascination with metaphysics. All Caine could tell for sure right now was that Fritzbrauner was a man with an insatiable need for intellectual stimulation. For his part, Fritzbrauner liked the candid, straight-to-the-point manner of his guest. He looked at Caine silently for a moment, then asked, "But suppose that what surrounds the coins are mysteries for which there are no answers?"

"Logic and reason tell us there are always answers," Caine responded. "Even to mysteries for which there appear to be no answers."

"Not necessarily, Mr. Caine. The path of logic and reason sends one in search of cause and effect, which can sometimes lead one to discover only that one's riddle is much more of a riddle than one previously thought, and one might have to wait an eternity for an answer to it. I'm sure you would agree that there are some things in this world that logic and reason cannot measure."

"The combination of logic and reason is the route to inquiry, cause and effect, trial and error," said Caine. "All are part of a process that has proven, over time, to lead eventually to answers—save, of course, for the big questions—the existence of God for example, and the origin of life. Still, your point is taken."

The others in the drawing room detected the shift of tone in the exchange between Fritzbrauner and Caine. Their polite patter faded; they stopped sipping their cocktails, and before long, they had quietly circled the two men.

"What are the chances that we are all being stymied by something that we'll never have a satisfactory explanation for?" Fritzbrauner asked.

"I'd say fair to good," said Caine.

"Arriving at a dead-end conclusion would be a waste of time for all of us."

Caine frowned. "Time spent seeking answers to questions as profound as the ones we're addressing is rarely ever wasted," he said.

Dr. Mozelle raised a finger. "It could be that we're being stymied by something that is the result of a purposeful series of events that were designed and are being controlled by forces for which we have no frame of reference."

Fritzbrauner's eyes danced a little as he turned back to Caine. "Where would that leave logic and reason, Montaro?" he chided with a friendly chuckle.

"At a temporary disadvantage, I'm afraid," Caine responded laughing, pleased to see an edge of humor in the man.

Fritzbrauner spun back to face Mozelle. "Could you be more specific, Doctor?"

"Perhaps it is not outside the realm of possibility that we are all acting out predetermined behavior," said Mozelle. "Think of the odds of two coins being found in the hands of two babies who were destined to marry. That can hardly be a coincidence, but does it represent purposeful design? Who can say? We should, therefore, do everything we can to uncover whatever truth lies at the base of our riddle."

Fritzbrauner turned to Carl Spreight. "What do you make of all this, Carl?" he asked. "Have we succeeded in baffling you completely?"

"On the contrary," said Spreight. "It seems to me that, if this whole affair is not a random series of coincidences, it then stands to reason that a specific purpose does in fact lie behind it all. And if that is so, in my humble opinion you gentlemen should prepare yourselves to look beyond known science for answers, possibly into that realm where unknown dimensions lie. Or you might find yourself at the point where logic and reason break down and you will have to accept that your riddle yields no answers."

Fritzbrauner laughed. "Montaro, you have just witnessed a dean of philosophy give us his rendition of a cagey politician." As laughter greeted his remarks, Fritzbrauner threw his arm around Gertz Welbocht's shoulder.

"And you, Gertz, we all know that you would be a Protestant minister today if the Big Bang Theory hadn't messed up your plans." More laughter erupted. "Montaro, here is a man who can look back through the eyes of science to the very beginning of time. But all he has ever been able to see is an explosion. God has been watching this man and his friends, wondering when they are going to give Him credit for the fireworks. He's growing mighty upset with their refusal to acknowledge His work."

As she stood silently listening to the conversation, Colette Beekman tried to keep her attention focused on her charismatic father, so that she wouldn't spend her time staring at Caine. This man stirred something inside her; something about him reminded her of her father. Even when she shook hands with Caine, she felt a signal fire up within her. *A warning*, she thought, one strong enough to make her promise herself to keep her distance.

"Well," Gertz Welbocht began. "As a curious bystander, not as a scientist, you understand, my mind has settled on two aspects in this affair of the coins and stubbornly refuses to budge. First, I am overwhelmed by the astounding mechanics that must have been used to forge such material. Second, look back with me for a moment, if you will, to a time before the coins came into being. The same objects that now present us with our riddle were foreshadowed in the primitive artwork on the walls of one man's Caribbean hut. I have to wonder how he was inspired to create such prophetic images. It is my unprofessional opinion that a look at Matthew Perch could yield useful insights if not outright answers."

Fritzbrauner turned to the others, smiled broadly, and gestured toward Welbocht. "My friends, you have just seen a true phenomenon—a mystical Gertz Welbocht. But he begs you not to give him credit for his reckless observations for fear they may ruin his reputation."

"Ahh yes, Gertz," mused Caine. "I do thank you for mentioning the elusive Mr. Perch. We must consider his role in this mystery as well."

Dr. Mozelle quickly raised a cautioning finger once more. "Allow me to point out that Matthew Perch and the machinery that will study the properties of the coin can both be seen as symbols: one of mysticism, the other of science. I think we should try to avoid an either-or approach in our search for answers."

"Like opposite sides of the same coin," Fritzbrauner said with a smile. "We have been speaking of coins, haven't we?"

"Yes," said Mozelle. "Both sides should be explored."

"Your tilt toward Matthew Perch and his world of mysticism has not gone unnoticed, Doctor. Nor has Montaro's toward the science of mass spectrometry," said Fritzbrauner.

"And where are you, Kritzman, as of this moment?" asked Mozelle.

"Undecided."

"Good. An open mind generally allows for discovery."

"Does it?"

"Yes. Because it can accommodate surprise."

Colette moved forward into the circle, waving her hand. "Gentlemen, it's time for dinner," she said.

"Your timing could not be better," said Carl Spreight, following close behind Colette.

As Fritzbrauner led Caine toward his dining room, his voice took on a more confidential tone. "Have you anything in mind regarding this fellow Matthew Perch?" he asked.

"If possible, a visit," Caine replied, "after which we would decide, depending on what we come away with, whether or not it would be safe to do the workup we have planned for the coins. All of this, of course, assumes your cooperation."

"And Roland Gabler's, I presume."

"Yes."

"What kind of man did you find him to be?"

"Energetic. Smart."

"Trustworthy?"

Caine paused, then sighed. "I trust him to come to the conclusion that his interests are compatible with ours."

At the entrance to the dining room, Fritzbrauner fixed Caine with an intense stare. "Do you believe in God, Montaro?" he asked suddenly.

"Does dinner depend on my answer?"

"No."

"Does anything else?"

"No."

"Good. Then yes, I do."

"Then you must be perplexed."

"Perplexed? Why?"

"By the philosophical question Howard touched on earlier."

"Which was?"

"Predetermined behavior versus free will. Both of which claim responsibility for human destiny."

"Well, of course that question is inescapable in any serious contemplation of these unusual objects. But I'm not perplexed by it."

"Do you, then, believe that human destiny was already written before man was created, as the theory of predetermined behavior argues, or that free will is the force that fashions individual as well as collective destinies?"

Not since those intellectual free-for-alls during his college days at the U of C, where heated, passionate arguments raged through the night at Hitchcock Hall, could Montaro Caine remember making such a plunge into the weighty philosophical issues that were being discussed here at the Fritzbrauner estate.

"Do your questions get easier as the night wears on?" Caine asked as the two men walked into the dining room where the others were already gathering around the table, "or do I need to ask our dean of philosophy here to coach me through the evening?"

Carl Spreight had seemed focused more on blowing his nose into his handkerchief than on the conversation and spoke for the first time since he had entered the dining room. "I'm afraid I wouldn't be of much help as I've been chronically perplexed by that question since I was five years old," he said. "In fact, I'm beginning to think that the mere mention of it triggers my sinus allergies."

"Well," said Caine, addressing his words to Fritzbrauner, "let me answer you by saying that I'm not one of those people who believes in waiting for proof before choosing one side or another."

"Then, as I thought, for you it would be a matter of faith," Fritzbrauner said.

"Any judgment I would make in that regard would be based on another belief I hold, which states that anything the human mind can conceive is possible, however impossible it may appear to the rational mind."

"My goodness, Montaro," said Carl Spreight with a slight sniffle. "I think you're the guy to cure my sinus problems."

Fritzbrauner laughed appreciatively. Caine liked the man's laugh. By the time dinner was over, Caine was feeling more optimistic about the chance that Fritzbrauner would cooperate with him. The man's intellectual curiosity was too strong for him not to, he finally decided.

Two days later, however, Caine and Mozelle were dismayed to learn that they had misread Fritzbrauner. They were in a suite in the Four Seasons Hotel in Geneva, where Caine had been teleconferencing with the members of the Fitzer board regarding the revelation that Richard Davis had acquired a large block of the corporation's stock, when the phone in the room rang. The moment Caine picked up the phone and heard Herman Freich's voice, he understood that the news would be bad; if it were otherwise, he knew that Fritzbrauner would have been calling him directly.

"I'm calling on Kritzman's behalf to say that, after long and thoughtful consideration, he has decided to pass on your suggestion regarding the coin," Freich said. "He sends his regrets."

Long after Caine had hung up the phone, he and Mozelle sat in their living room picking at their breakfasts in glum silence while considering what could have happened. Had they said something to put Fritzbrauner off? Or was his decision a foregone conclusion? Had Fritzbrauner had a different scenario in mind from the beginning, one in which they were not meant to play a part? Was it all a game to Fritzbrauner? Was he more interested in winning than in doing what was right? Or had someone gotten to him first?

Caine called Roland Gabler in New York and was disappointed

but not surprised to receive a response that was just as shattering as Fritzbrauner's. Gabler would not accept the terms they had offered.

Caine was nearly ready to call Cecilia to tell her that he would be returning home earlier than expected when he received a call from Gina Lao.

"I have Michen Borceau on the line for you," she said. "Do you have time to speak with him?"

"Put him on," Caine said, hoping that Borceau would have something encouraging to say, but upon hearing Borceau's frantic voice, he understood that what his lab director was calling to tell him was even worse than anything he had heard from Fritzbrauner and Gabler. The normally jovial Frenchman sounded more deflated than Montaro had ever heard him.

"Montaro," Borceau said, his voice soft and shaky. "Do you remember the tiny particles of those strange coins you asked me to examine?" he asked.

"Yes," Caine said, fearing what Borceau would tell him next.

"The particles have disappeared. They've been stolen."

"Stolen? How?"

"I don't know." Borceau explained to Caine that ever since Colette Beekman and Herman Freich had left the Fitzer Lab, he had kept the slivers of the coins in a tiny plastic container in his safe at the lab. They had still been there that morning. But before he had left the lab, he had checked the safe once more, just to make sure the slivers were still there. He had found the plastic container exactly where he had left it; the particles inside, however, had vanished.

"I have no idea how this happened," said Borceau. "No one else knows the safe's combination. I haven't even told it to Gina. I didn't leave my desk all day. I didn't even leave for lunch."

"Objects can't just disappear," Caine said.

"I can't for the life of me figure out how someone could have gotten in here without my knowing."

After he hung up the phone, Caine slumped on a couch in the suite, dejected. For the first time in his adult life, he felt the self-pity his grandfather P. L. Caine always warned him against succumbing to, the helplessness that Montaro always counseled his own daughter against. He tried to slam the door on those feelings, and yet he could feel them trying to shove their way inside him. He tried to drink, but his heart wasn't in it; he tried to eat, but he had no appetite. His phone rang frequently. Cecilia called; so did Gordon Whitcombe and Nancy MacDonald. He avoided all of them; he didn't want to talk to anyone, not even to Howard.

Mozelle left Caine to take a walk through Geneva, and when he returned near sundown, Caine was still in the same nearly catatonic state, seated by a window, staring out at the gorgeous lake. Caine kept replaying in his mind the words that his grandfather had told him when he was just a boy—"The difficulties of life can lick a man or they can strengthen him; it's the man's choice"; "A man has to face hard times, no matter what"—but all those words sounded empty to him now. Everything seemed to be falling apart—his company, his family, all his quixotic hopes. Flawed judgment and wrong turns had brought him aground to flounder on the rocks of his mistakes. He thought of the conversations he had had at Kritzman Fritzbrauner's estate—purposeless coincidence versus purposeful design. The answer to that riddle seemed to be beside the point—life itself felt purposeless to him now.

Montaro's mind went back to the grim news he had received from Michen Borceau. "Objects don't just disappear," he had told Borceau. And yet now, as he considered the statement he had made, he recalled the first time he encountered the coin at M.I.T. He had thought that objects weren't supposed to behave the way this one did. And as Caine continued to ponder, an idea occurred to him, one that at first seemed absurd. But anything the human mind could conceive of was possible, he had often told himself, and so perhaps what he was beginning to think might not be so absurd after all.

Mozelle was packing his belongings in preparation for the trip back to New York. He had given up trying to buoy Caine's spirits, for it had become clear to Mozelle that Caine wasn't even listening to him; and besides, he, too, was feeling hopeless. Yet after the doctor finished packing his suitcases, he was surprised to see Caine standing in the bedroom doorway with an awed, almost otherworldly look on his face.

"I've had a thought," Caine said in a loud whisper.

"What?" asked Mozelle.

"We've got to go back," said Caine.

"Where?"

"To Fritzbrauner."

"Why?"

"Trust me."

29

With their plane scheduled to depart that night, Montaro Caine called Herman Freich on his cell phone to ask if Kritzman Fritzbrauner might agree to one more meeting before he and Mozelle left for the airport. When Freich called back to report that Fritzbrauner was willing and ready to meet with them, Caine and Mozelle hired a car to drive them back up the mountain to the Fritzbrauner estate. Herman Freich met the car in the driveway and escorted the men to the terrace where Fritzbrauner and Colette awaited them.

"The doctor and I came a long way to seek a partnership with you to explore the issues raised by the existence of these mysterious coins," Caine told his hosts after they were seated. "Needless to say, we are disappointed that you have decided not to join us and we still hope that one day, you will change your mind about that. But for now, we must live with your decision. We are here again only to ask one small favor. Would you allow me to just look at the coin? It would take no more than a minute."

"Why, Montaro?" Fritzbrauner asked, looking perplexed.

"I have reason to believe it will answer some questions for me."

But before Fritzbrauner could formulate a response, his daughter interrupted. "Show it to him," Colette said. She turned to Caine with a smile, but he acknowledged her intervention on his behalf with only a polite nod; his mind was stuck on the theory that had occurred to him the previous night.

In Fritzbrauner's study, Caine picked up a magnifying glass that had been lying near an open dictionary on the desk and examined the object. He took only fifteen seconds before he slid the coin across the desk back to Fritzbrauner.

"What did you see?" Colette asked him.

"I saw what I imagined I would see," said Caine quietly, his eyes filled with wonder. He took a step back from the desk so that he could direct his attention to Fritzbrauner. "Thank you for allowing me to take another look," he said.

Colette asked Caine what he had seen, but he demurred, unwilling to reveal more.

When they got back into the car, Mozelle looked at Caine curiously. "So now, are you ready to tell me what the heck's going on?" he asked.

"Not yet," Caine said. He looked more certain of himself than Mozelle had seen him; for the first time, the doctor could easily see how this man had climbed to the top of Fitzer Corporation and how, even now, he might remain there. Back at the hotel, Caine excused himself to place a call to Dr. Richard Walmeyer. When he finally returned to the suite, Mozelle was waiting at the door.

"So, tell me!" Mozelle said. "What sent you running back to look at the coin? I know you saw something when you looked at it."

"It was something out of the past," said Caine. He grabbed the animated hands of the excited older man and held them gently. "Listen to me, Howard. I was right. It's alive!"

"What is?"

"The coin. It's alive."

Mozelle smiled in disbelief. "Explain that to me," he said.

"Those tiny particles I set aside, the ones that Borceau was working on that disappeared, they're back in place on the coin. Back in the very same place I dislodged them from. Each and every sliver is back where it used to be."

"My God, that can't be true."

"It can't be true, but it is," said Caine. "Son of a bitch! It's true."

"My God, but how could it be?"

"I don't know."

Caine explained that his conversation with Professor Walmeyer had further confirmed his findings. Twenty-six years earlier at M.I.T., Walmeyer had also dislodged a small number of particles from the coin that was now in Roland Gabler's possession. "That original coin was sent back to Dr. Chasman, who, in turn, sent it on to you," Caine told Mozelle. "But we kept the dislodged particles in the lab for weeks until we decided that they were too small to have any further research value. Chasman put them back into his research files. When I called him today, I asked him to see if the particles were still there."

"Were they?"

"No. They've disappeared, too. My hunch is that they're back in place on the original coin that Roland Gabler has. If my hunch proves correct, we may have to pray for guidance, my friend."

"Why do you say that?"

"Because that would put us at the center of something so monumental we might wish we had never heard of the coins."

Mozelle's mouth hung open as if to speak, but no words came. His head bobbed back and forth in a rhythmic nod as if confirming what was in his mind. Yes, ever since he had first seen that coin in the hand of the newborn Whitney Carson, he had felt premonitions, signs of some unimaginable power lying in wait. *The son shall hold the coins*— he still had no idea what Matthew Perch's words might mean. He looked up to ask for some answers to all the questions that were swirling through his mind, but Caine was already heading for the bedroom; he was making another phone call, this time to the one person upon whom he had always relied when he needed the sort of guidance that no one else, not even his wife, could provide.

"Grandpa?" Montaro said after he heard P. L. Caine pick up the phone. "I need your help."

P. L. Caine, at nearly one hundred years old now, was living in Carmel, California, with Rosalind Twichell, a spry young woman of seventy-five. Though his mobility was severely reduced and he had lost a good deal of his hearing, his mind was still sharp and his advice was still sound. After Montaro had left home for Chicago to start college, he had maintained few contacts with his Kansas City past; now, P.L. was the only one who remained. Hearing the elderly man's voice filled Montaro with such a flood of memories and emotions that he had to struggle to keep his attention focused on the reason he was calling.

"What do you need my help with, son?" P. L. Caine asked now.

"I need you to remember something," Montaro said.

The old man heard the urgency in his grandson's words. "What is it?" he asked.

"I need the name of the New York hospital Dad was returning from when his plane crashed; and the name of the doctor who invited him to observe the research he was doing there."

A long pause ensued.

"I don't know that, son. I don't believe I'll be able to help you," P. L. Caine began, then added, "But I think I know someone who can."

"Who?" Montaro asked.

"Your dad," said P. L. Caine. He told his grandson that against his daughter-in-law's wishes, he had held on to his son's briefcase and all his tapes and his notes, suspecting that someday Montaro would want them.

Caine was stunned. "You kept them?"

"I did, my boy; I always knew this day would come," said P. L. Caine. "Where shall I send them?"

When Caine and Mozelle got back to New York, they went straight to Roland Gabler's apartment. Gabler was surprised to see them; he explained to them that he had a new "silent partner," whose involvement meant that he could no longer consider a deal with Caine. But Caine interrupted him.

"Our reason for coming is unrelated to any conditions, new or old," said Caine. "We're here for another matter."

"What matter might that be?" asked Gabler.

"A small favor," said Caine.

"Which is?"

Caine repeated the same request he had made of Fritzbrauner: "To see the coin."

"For what possible reason?" Gabler asked.

"Only to see the difference between this coin and the other," said Caine.

At first, Gabler appeared reluctant, but he could see no reason to deny the request; he always got a special thrill out of displaying the items in his collection, particularly when he was showing them to individuals whom he had outbid or outfoxed to get them. He left the room for a moment, then returned with the coin, which Caine examined briefly with a jeweler's loupe before handing it back to Gabler without revealing what, if anything, he had seen.

"Well?" Mozelle asked Caine once they were in the elevator heading down to the lobby.

"I was right. They're there. Back in place."

Mozelle shook his head. "Particles vanish in Boston and reappear in New York City. Others vanish in New York and reappear in Switzerland. What can it mean?"

"I don't know yet," said Caine. "But I'm hoping my grandfather was right."

"How do you mean?"

"I'm hoping my father will be able to help me."

Back at The Carlyle hotel, Robert Caine's briefcase was already waiting for Montaro. Mozelle sat with Montaro in the living room of his apartment as he examined its contents, but Montaro barely noticed the doctor's presence. He seemed to be in another world, one full of painful yet reassuring memories. He took out the objects one by one, slowly, carefully, holding each as if it were even more precious than the mysterious coins that had tantalized him for more than two decades. He studied his father's precise handwriting, both in his notebooks and on Robert Caine's Dictaphone cassette tapes, which his father had labeled "Dr. Andrew Banks," "Thomas Lund," and "Luther John Doe."

His hands trembling, Montaro placed the cassette labeled "Luther John Doe" into the Dictaphone and pressed play. P. L. Caine had put new batteries in the machine and it whirred to life. Montaro couldn't remember the last time he had shed tears and yet he could feel them welling up in his eyes the moment he heard his father's slightly speeded-up voice, so confident, so engaged, so young—Montaro had already lived nearly twenty years longer than Robert Caine had. As he listened to the tape of his father and Dr. Andrew Banks back at Columbia University, he could almost imagine his dad here in the room with him, speaking to him as if he had just arrived from some world beyond this one.

"I do have a son, and this is for him?"

Montaro swallowed hard as he listened to his father speak.

"That's very nice of you. And this is very nice, too. What is it?"

And then Montaro heard a voice he did not recognize. It was the voice of a boy, and though it sounded slightly garbled, Montaro could easily make out the words the boy was saying.

"It's a ship," the boy said.

When Montaro got hold of Dr. Andrew Banks, the former professor was living in a retirement community outside Key Largo, Florida.

"Oh, yes. I remember your father," Dr. Banks said over the phone. "Terrible accident that was. Loss of a good man, much too early. What can I do for you?"

"Do you remember Thomas Lund, the patient that you and your staff were studying? You had my dad and some other professors observe him."

"Ah yes, of course. Tom Lund. What about him?"

"I would like to try to find him, if he's still alive. And, Luther John Doe, too."

"I have no idea if either one is alive. But I can make a few calls and see what I come up with."

Less than an hour later, Dr. Banks reported to Caine that Tom Lund was living in a small town on the outskirts of Philadelphia and Luther John Doe was in a home for the elderly in Connecticut. When Caine was finished with the phone call, he spoke to Mozelle, who had been waiting patiently for him.

"I have to go to Connecticut to talk to somebody who might be able to help us," he said. "Care to join me?"

"I'm up for it," Mozelle assured Caine.

"I don't know how many answers we'll find," Caine told the doctor as they left the hotel. "Maybe more than we're ready for."

30

I T WAS QUITE LIKELY THAT THE SMALL WHITE-HAIRED MAN DID not hear them as they approached. He was a solitary figure, hunched over in his white lawn chair as he sat by an empty pine table; he seemed to be lost inside himself, somewhere between his mind's eye and his inner ear. He had the aspect of a man preoccupied with his own thoughts, out of touch with the reality surrounding him. As Montaro Caine and Dr. Howard Mozelle strode urgently toward him on the late summer grass, the aged man signaled no awareness of their advancing presence.

The sky was overcast and the air was muggy. Swirling rain clouds were randomly rearranging themselves into threatening configurations. The outdoor recreational area of the Oakville Estates retirement facility was otherwise deserted. Even the crickets in the nearby grass remained silent and still. As Mozelle and Caine approached the man with the twisted chin and withered right leg, they shared a quick, meaningful glance. Then, Montaro's firm voice shattered the silence.

"Hello, Luther," he said.

Startled, the old man wheeled to look up at the faces peering down at him. He squinted, but for a moment nothing seemed to register. He frowned, puzzled. A long, cautious moment passed. Then his eyes lit up. As his eyes roamed Caine's face, a smile began to gather slowly upon his weathered lips.

"Hello," he said in a garbled voice that Caine recognized instantly from the cassette tapes he had listened to. His smile broadened. Caine smiled back. Luther then shifted his gaze to the face of Caine's companion, where it lingered. Luther's smile grew even wider. He moved as if to rise, but Caine's arm shot out and rested on his shoulder with a gentle downward pressure, and Luther eased back into his chair.

Mozelle introduced himself to Luther, but the moment Caine began to say his own name, Luther interrupted.

"I know who you are," Luther said plainly. "You're his son."

Caine felt himself involuntarily gasp. He tried to maintain his poise as he and Howard Mozelle sat across from Luther at the table.

"I am," said Caine.

Luther's smile dissolved into an expression of quiet seriousness. He watched Caine pull out from a jacket pocket a small flannel bag with a drawstring. Caine loosened the drawstring, carefully turned the flannel bag upside down, and slid an object out into his hand. Luther's and Howard's eyes fixed upon the dark, round, shiny form that was nearly as large as the palm of Caine's hand. On one of the tapes, his father had said it looked like a compact, but Luther John Doe had called it a ship.

Caine placed the object gently on the table, then looked at Luther, who raised his eyes to meet Caine's.

"Tell me about it," Caine began.

"What do you want to know?"

"Why did you carve it?" Caine asked.

Luther looked down at the object. "Because I saw it."

"Where?"

"In my head." Luther's tone was matter-of-fact.

"Forty-eight years ago?"

"Forty-eight years and three months," said Luther.

"You mean you saw it in a dream?" asked Caine.

Luther looked up, one eyebrow arched. "No," he answered, almost as if Caine's suggestion offended him.

"You told my father you made it for me," Caine said. "Is that right?"

"Yes," Luther said. "For his son."

"But we had never met."

"I know." Once more, Luther stared into the steady blue eyes of the handsome, sandy-haired man seated across from him.

"Luther. You're sure we're not talking about a dream?"

"It was no dream, no sir." Luther spoke firmly.

"Why are you so sure it wasn't?"

"Because you're here now. And you're no dream, are you?" He tilted his head toward Howard Mozelle. "I saw him, too," he said. The weather-beaten face of the elderly doctor flushed and his body shivered slightly. "And I saw the ship, inside and out," Luther added.

"What is the ship called?" Caine asked.

"The Seventh Ship," said Luther. "It should be coming soon, now that you're here."

"Where is it coming from?"

Luther looked up and pointed toward the restless sky—the dark clouds above seemed to be fidgeting. "Out there," he said. Dr. Mozelle's pulse was racing, but he sat quietly as Caine continued to question Luther.

"Who are they, Luther? Who's coming on the Seventh Ship?"

Luther shrugged.

Caine's forehead knotted. "Think hard, Luther. Who or what is on that ship? What do they look like? You've seen the inside of the ship; you must know."

The bewilderment on Luther's face deepened. "I don't know," he said. "I never saw what they looked like. That would have been impossible."

Caine glanced at Mozelle, who appeared both intensely absorbed in what Luther was saying and also far away. He understood that Mozelle was reminded of another time in his life when he had allowed his faith to overcome his doubts about what was possible—when he and Elsen had traveled to an island in search of a man named Matthew Perch.

"You told my father the ship was coming to get information,"

Caine continued. "When he asked you what kind of information, you told him it was a secret and that you would tell me when I came to see you."

"That's right," said Luther.

"What is that secret information, Luther?" Caine asked kindly.

The little old man with the twisted chin and withered right leg had waited most of his life to answer this question. His chest swelled and his body seemed to straighten slightly, as if his answer would mark the most majestic moment of his life. "Everything," he said simply.

"What do you mean, everything?"

"Everything about them," he explained, his voice full of reverence.

"Them?"

"Yes. They are coming to get all the information there is about them. From the beginning to the end."

Howard Mozelle leaned across the pine table closer to Luther. "What does that mean?" Mozelle asked. "Help us to understand. Please. How did this secret, this information, whatever it is, come to be here?"

Luther leveled his eyes at the doctor and whispered. "They've stored it here."

Caine and Mozelle exchanged glances. "How did they store it here?" Caine asked.

"In people. In me, in you, in him," Luther whispered, pointing to Dr. Mozelle. "In lots of people. Most of them don't know anything about it." He smiled and added, "But I do."

"If you've never seen them, how do you know so much about them?" Caine asked.

"I don't know. I must have seen only what they wanted me to see. But I never saw what they looked like."

"Did you ever tell anyone else about them, or about the information?"

"No. It was meant only for you."

"How did you know you were only supposed to tell us?"

"I just knew." Luther shrugged. "I guess that's how they wanted it."

"Why did they choose you, Luther?" Caine asked. Then he added, "I mean, to let you hold their secret all these years, until today, for me?"

"I don't know. Maybe because they liked me," Luther replied.

"I'm sure they do. You seem like a very special person."

Luther smiled broadly. He liked the compliment and also the attention.

"Luther," Caine said, leaning closer for emphasis. "A very special, smart, and talented guy like you can help us figure this thing out. Of all the people in the world they picked you, me, and Howard, and some others; but why us? For what reason? They picked us for a purpose, Luther, and we have to know what that purpose is. I know you can help us with this. Will you?"

"I'll try," Luther murmured.

Caine massaged his chin and pulled at it as if to draw milk from his mind. "Judging from the size of the ship," he asked Luther, "how many of them would you guess are on board?"

"None," said Luther simply.

"None?"

"None are on any of the ships. They died a long time ago."

"Then who operates the ship?" Mozelle asked.

Luther turned to Mozelle. "It operates itself," he said, then spoke with greater enthusiasm. "That ship knows everything that was ever known, and can do everything that was ever done on that place that used to be. With the information that we have been keeping for them, the ship will take it and bring it someplace where they can be born again, and in turn, you can use the information it has brought here."

Luther leaned back and waited, giving Caine and Mozelle time to digest what he had just said.

"Tell me about the place where the Seventh Ship is coming from, Luther," Caine said.

"It's a place that isn't there anymore."

"Why isn't it there anymore?"

"Its sun died. Just as ours will," Luther stated plainly.

Caine's brain jammed as if it could not compute the appropriate imagery. He swallowed hard.

"How far away is the sun that died?" Caine asked.

"Thirty-three thousand years by light."

"And how long ago did it die?"

"It's been one hundred thousand years since the light stopped."

"The Seventh Ship left before the sun died. Is that what happened, Luther?"

"A long time before. All of them did."

"There were seven of them?"

"Yes."

"And they're all coming here?"

"No, only the Seventh Ship."

"What has happened to the others?"

"They have all been here and gone."

"Gone? Where to?"

"Each has gone in search of a sun that won't die soon."

"Will they stay here?" asked Caine. "Is this where they'll be reborn?"

Luther shook his head. "I doubt they'll stay," he said.

"Why not?" asked Caine.

"Because someday the people here will have to leave, too. Just like they did."

Caine gazed at Luther with wide-eyed fascination while Mozelle interjected. "Luther, do you know of a man named Matthew Perch?" he asked.

"No. Who is he?"

"Have you ever heard of a woman named Whitney Carson?"

"No."

"She is married to a man named Franklyn Walker. Have you heard of him?"

"No."

"Someday soon, Whitney and Franklyn will have a child. Do you know what will happen when that child is born?" Mozelle continued.

Luther shook his head. "I don't know. I don't know these people," he said. "Who are they?"

"People who, like you, have had something to do with the information you've given us," said Caine.

Howard mentioned the names Hattie Sinclair and Carrie Pittman, but Luther had not heard of them either.

"I'd say they must have something in common, though," said Luther.

"What would that be?" asked Caine.

Luther shrugged. "Maybe they're just honest people like you," he said. "Maybe they're people who have the capacity to believe."

"Luther," Caine asked. "Do you know how fast light travels?"

"One hundred and eighty-six thousand miles per second," answered Luther.

"And thirty-three thousand years by light would be how many miles?"

Luther smiled. "Five trillion, eight hundred and sixty-five billion, six hundred and ninety-six million, one hundred and seventy thousand."

Dr. Mozelle gasped.

"Where did you learn that?" asked Caine.

"From a friend of mine," answered Luther.

"Who?"

"His name is Tom Lund."

"Where is Tom now?" Caine asked.

"I don't know. Maybe dead by now."

"When did you last see him?"

"A long time ago."

"Where?"

"In the hospital in New York. When he was my friend."

"You haven't seen him since?"

"No."

"How much did Tom Lund know of what you've just told us?"

"Nothing. One day when I was carving the ship for you, he asked me what it was. I told him it was a ship, and we got to talking. I asked him how many miles away thirty-three thousand light-years was. He knew about things like that. He was smart with numbers. We got along good. But I didn't tell him anything about what I just told you."

Before Caine could ask anything else, a distant voice shouted,

"Sorry, gentlemen, we are starting to serve dinner now." The group looked up to see an approaching orderly dressed in white.

"It's time for Luther to join the others," she said as she neared the table.

"That's all right," Luther said. "We're done here."

Caine started to ask the orderly for more time, but Luther had already begun struggling to his feet; he now seemed more fragile than he had when they arrived. He tilted to his right side so severely that it seemed as if his spindly, withered leg would give way beneath him.

Luther picked up the carving of the Seventh Ship and passed it to Caine.

"Don't forget this." He placed the object gingerly in Caine's outstretched hand. It seemed to rattle slightly. Caine hadn't noticed that rattle before.

Raising the carving to his ear, Caine shook it lightly and heard the same faint rattle. "Is there something inside?" he asked.

"Yes," said Luther.

"What?"

"A surprise."

"Is there a way to open it?"

"You can't. It will open when it's time." Luther turned and walked away with the orderly. He looked satisfied and at peace.

"God bless you, Luther," said Mozelle. But Luther didn't hear him. Mozelle and Caine watched Luther hobble along across the lawn with the arm of the orderly supporting him. Finally, he disappeared into the main building of Oakville Estates. For a long time, Mozelle and Caine stood still, gazing upon the spot where Luther and the orderly had been swallowed up by the red brick building.

Mozelle looked dazed, as if struck by a traumatizing blow. "Oh my God," he said, quietly. "I hope we're not losing our minds."

Overhead, lightning ignited and thunder rolled. Then, silently, Caine and Mozelle turned and moved toward the parking lot where Caine's car was parked.

"Maybe we are," said Caine.

Once the men were back in the car, a light rain began to pepper the windshield. As Caine began to drive back toward Manhattan, both he and Mozelle sat silently, deep in thought.

Dr. Mozelle was thinking about the artwork on the walls of Matthew Perch's hut, the configurations of constellations that he had also seen on the coins, the strange moon or star that appeared on one coin but not on the other. Perhaps, he allowed himself to think, this was actually the star Luther had spoken of, the star that had died.

Caine was thinking of that long-ago day when his grandfather had handed him the carving of the Seventh Ship, a gift from a little black boy he had never met. "Later in life," his grandfather had told him, "who knows—this might provide you with fond memories of your father." *Yes*, he thought, *that indeed had been true.*

31

THE NEXT MORNING, WHEN CAINE PULLED TO A STOP IN FRONT of a modest house on a tree-lined street on the outskirts of Philadelphia, he was alone. As he approached the front door to the house, carrying a shoulder bag full of his father's old tapes and notebooks, the door opened and there stood Tom Lund, a slender man of medium height with a full head of salt-and-pepper hair, blue eyes, and a warm smile. He appeared to be in his midseventies.

"Thank you for agreeing to see me. I appreciate it," Caine said, extending his hand. He was surprised by Lund's firm handshake.

"Come in, Mr. Caine. Welcome, welcome."

Caine followed Lund into a comfortably appointed living room where both men sat, Lund in his favorite easy chair and Caine on the nearby sofa, setting his bag down on a plain wooden end table. Nothing in the humble room attested to Lund's mathematical genius—no framed diplomas, no awards, no photographs of academic ceremonies.

"So, how is Dr. Banks these days?" Lund asked.

"He sounded fine on the phone," Caine said. "He's retired now, of course, and living in Florida. You have fond memories of him?"

"He was O.K.," Lund said flatly.

"How long did you stay in his research program?"

"Fifteen years, four months, and seventeen days."

"That long, my goodness."

"Wasn't as bad as it sounds. I didn't mind it," said Lund. "But was it downright boring sometimes? Well, that depended on how smart the professors were who came to pump me. Your dad was special, though. I'm not blowing smoke at you. He was one of the best. I only sat with him three times, but I remember thinking I wanted to sit with him again. He was as much a professor of philosophy as he was a professor of mathematics. By the way, what you probably don't know about me is that I wasn't at the hospital full time like most of the others. I always lived with my folks here outside Philly. Early Friday mornings, I'd take the train into the city; Sunday nights, I'd take a train back home. I had a day job Monday through Thursday."

"Really?" said Caine. "You're right; I didn't know that."

Tom Lund chuckled. "How else do you think I made my living? I was crunching numbers, keeping books. Back then, Dr. Banks was only allowed to pay me forty dollars for three hours a day, three days a week. That was supposed to include train fare."

"You know," Caine said, "yesterday, I visited a friend of yours from those days, Luther John Doe."

"No! Really?" Lund's face displayed surprise and delight. "That little son of a gun! Well, I'll be damned. He's still alive?"

"He is."

"Can you beat that," Lund exclaimed. "How's he holding up?"

"Fairly well, given the degree to which age and deformities have taken their toll."

"Well—hey, that's the process of the journey, if you live long enough. There's not much you can do about that."

"He said you were his friend."

"Yeah, I was. And it was the other way around too. We just took to each other."

Touched by the tenderness in Lund's remark, Caine waited for the moment to run its course, then said, "When I was eight years old, he made a present for me. He asked my father to take it home with him even though he had never met my father before and couldn't have known he had a child. And my dad died in a plane crash on his way home that very night."

The two men slowly began drawing themselves into a meaningful quiet until Lund cleared his throat. "I was in the hallway that afternoon," he said. "I saw Luther give that carving to your father. He told your dad that the carving was a ship, but it didn't look anything like a ship. I remember how considerate your father was, how gracious. He tried to open it and couldn't. Luther said, 'It will open when it's time.'"

"Did you get the sense that Luther was mentally deficient? Like he was not all there?" Caine asked.

"Not at all. I thought he was exactly like me. He could carve ordinary wood into designs like no one I've ever seen. Just like I could crunch the hell out of numbers. But neither of us was ever much good at anything else. That's how it has always been for people like Luther and me. For whatever reason, that's how we were wired." Lund looked Caine in the eye and said, "I know you came to see me for a reason. And I've tried to imagine what that reason might be, but I can't pull it up. So you might as well just lay it out for me. If I can be of any help, you got it."

Caine paused for a moment, then asked, "Ever heard of a man named Matthew Perch?"

Lund's brow wrinkled. "Matthew Perch? No, I can't recall having heard that name. Who is he?"

"He's a mystery," Caine said.

"Oh," Lund responded, then leaned over to Caine and asked, "What does this 'mystery' fellow do?"

"Things that border on the impossible." Caine reached for his shoulder bag and pulled out a folder containing several pages of his father's notes. "Here are the questions my dad put to you forty-eight years ago, and your answers," he said. "May I read a few to you?"

Lund nodded.

Caine began reading: "In your lifetime and mine, two digits, a zero and a one, were recently introduced by innovators as revolutionary forces in the field of mathematics. These forces will be technologically applicable in countless ways never before imagined—in data processing, medicine, mechanics—and they will spawn new inventions that will bring abundant changes into the lives of people everywhere. These two digits may change the face of technology. Modern technology will be able to fashion, in a fraction of a second, endless multitudes of sequences out of just these two digits. Think of it, an endless alphabet of only two digits. My question to you, Tom, is, did you ever think you would see such a day in mathematics?"

As Montaro read these words, he could hear his father's voice. In flashes, Caine saw himself as a little boy; he saw his father alive, then later, his mother reading these notes that had survived the plane crash. As Tom Lund looked at Caine, he seemed to see both men before him—the father and the son.

Montaro looked up from his father's notes. "Tom, do you remember what your answer was?" he asked.

Lund's face took on a sober look. "Yes, of course I knew such a day would come. In fact, I wondered why it had taken so long. Zero and one are numbers just as A, B, C, D, E, F, and G are letters. What differentiates letters from numbers? Nothing really; they're both alphabets and they both form the basis of languages. Your father and I believed the same thing."

"My dad told you that you probably had the swiftest mind in existence," said Caine.

"That's high praise," said Lund. "But undeserved."

"And now," Caine pressed on, "if you will indulge me, I would like to see how swift that mind still is. At this very moment as we sit here, I would like you to think exclusively in terms of numbers, not words, in arriving at your answers. Then, when you have an answer, I would like you to translate those numbers into words. Remember: quick questions, quick answers. Sound okay?"

Tom Lund smiled. "That's how my mind works anyway," he said. "I always translate words into numbers; that's the language I know best."

"Okay, here goes: Does another universe exist aside from ours?"

"Not to my knowledge, but my guess is yes."

"If yes, what might be the distance between them and us?"

"More than any mind can fathom."

"Will there ever come a time when future generations will bridge that distance?"

"Future generations of other creatures and their science might. I don't think it ever was nature's intention for us to do that."

"Why not?"

"Because we were not designed for that journey."

"Why not?"

"The carrying capacity of our home planet will soon be stretched far beyond the point at which our science and the resources of our planet could ever possibly get us there."

"So then what lies ahead for us?"

"Clearly neither our science nor the resources of our planet will get us as far as our imagination promises."

"So, will we blunder our way into extinction?"

"One cannot blunder one's way into the inevitable. Extinction is only as far away as we can manage to keep it."

"What about Matthew Perch? Does he exist?"

"Yes."

"Where might he be as we speak?"

"Everywhere you expect him to be. Presently, he is very much in your head. What you may not know is that he may well be waiting for you to seek him out. It seems to me that among the seven billion people on this planet, you will likely find that a Matthew Perch is not all that rare." Tom Lund began to chuckle, and soon his chuckles became infectious laughter; Caine began laughing, too. Soon, Lund and Caine were both roaring, convulsing in ways that threw each back to a time long before such deliciously unbridled behavior had to be corralled and locked away in now-forgotten trunks of memories.

Finally, the men drifted back toward silence until Montaro spoke. "You've never heard of a woman named Whitney Carson, have you?"

"No," said Lund.

"Franklyn Walker?"

Lund shook his head.

"Soon, they will be having a child; you don't know what will happen then, do you?"

Tom Lund shook his head. "But I do know this," he said. "You're looking for answers. You don't know where to turn and you don't have much time. That, I think, is why you're here. Because you're desperate, you're looking in places you ordinarily wouldn't have thought of: me, Luther, your father. And somewhere in all of this are these people you mention, in particular this Matthew Perch, whoever he is. You've worked your way through conventional thought and are now willing to look at other forces, other realities. Since I don't know this Perch fellow, there isn't much I can offer you in that regard—except that if you do meet him, and I expect you will, you should look him right in the eye and let him see who you really are. He will not be able to see who you are if you do not allow him to; and he will not be able to see you without also letting you see who he is."

Caine stared at Lund, taking the measure of his elder. "My dad was right; you are a wise old duck," he said. "I truly thank you for your counsel."

"It's been my pleasure," Lund said. "By the way, can I have a copy of all those questions and answers from my interviews with your dad? I'd love to read all that flattery. I'd just love to stuff some of it right up some folks' noses." Lund grinned, chuckled to himself, then erupted into another round of full-bodied laughter. Caine tried to resist but was sucked in again. Eventually, their laughter diminished to broad smiles.

The two men stood. Caine hugged the old man, then handed him the folder of interview transcripts. All things considered, Caine thought, he had gotten what he didn't know he had come for: a visit with a father he barely knew. The contents of his father's briefcase had reminded him of words P. L. Caine had often said—that every man must always try to face his troubles, fight his demons, and look both friend and enemy in the eye and, as Tom Lund had said, "let them see who you really are."

Caine started for the door, stopped, turned, then asked, "One more question?"

Lund smiled and beckoned with both hands for Caine to ask whatever he wished. Caine dug into his shoulder bag, fished out one of his dad's old notebooks, then searched through it until he came to a particular page. He read aloud: "What each person sees with his or her eyes is instantly transmitted through highly sensitive regions of one's internal self, across a network of instincts, intuitions, emotions, through countless chambers of our brains, and on into that most private place inside ourselves, the headquarters of our individual existence, the human mind, where a judgment is made as to the importance of what we see, and how what we see might apply to our ongoing struggle to survive as individual human beings."

"Now here comes the question," Montaro said. "Was what I just read your thought or my father's? It isn't clear in his notes."

Lund chuckled. Then, his face turned serious. "Listen, I had it all over your father in mathematics. He was good; I was the genius. But he was the one who saw the world as a philosopher as well as a mathematician. As I've told you, outside of mathematics, I'm not really good at much else."

Caine looked long and hard at Lund. "If you ever come to New York, it would be my pleasure to see you again," he said.

32

EVER SINCE MONTARO CAINE HAD BEEN THRUST PREMATURELY into the world of adult concerns at the age of eight when his father died, he had been conscious of the sensation that he inhabited more than one world at any given time. But in the days that followed his visits to Luther John Doe and Tom Lund, he felt that sensation more profoundly than ever. How many worlds did he actually inhabit? It had become hard for him to keep track. He was Montaro Caine, CEO of Fitzer Corporation, trying to survive a hostile takeover bid that was persisting even as news of the fallout from the Utah mining accident was beginning to recede. He was also Dr. Montaro Caine, the M.I.T.-educated Ph.D., leading an ad hoc team of scientists and medical professionals trying to gain control of two mystery coins that could revolutionize industry, perhaps even prevent disasters such as the one that had taken place in Utah.

He was Montaro Caine of Kansas City and he was Montaro Caine of Westport, Connecticut; he was Montaro Caine of The Carlyle Hotel, and at the same time, he was Montaro Caine, citizen of planet Earth, whose citizens would have to find a new home someday when their sun began to die. And, as Montaro led a meeting in the living room of his Carlyle apartment, where he debriefed Drs. Howard and Elsen Mozelle, Dr. Michael Chasman, and Anna Hilburn about all he had learned from Tom Lund and Luther John Doe, he was soon made aware of another important role he held, one that he realized he had been somewhat neglecting during all this drama; he was also Monty Caine, Cecilia's husband and Priscilla's father.

The meeting in The Carlyle was contentious and highly charged, so much so that Montaro ignored his cell phone each time it rang and didn't even take the time to check to see who was trying so persistently to get hold of him. He was emphasizing to everyone gathered in his living room the need to focus on the most pressing matter at hand—finding Whitney and Franklyn Walker as quickly as possible so that the couple would have their child in Manhattan under Dr. Mozelle's care; Matthew Perch's prophetic words suggested that something magnificent would surely happen upon that occasion. And Luther John Doe's story, no matter how improbable it had sounded, only added to the sense of urgency.

"We must do all we can to have Whitney's child delivered here," Montaro was saying when another chirp from his telephone made him finally shut off his ringer.

Meanwhile, Dr. Chasman, Anna Hilburn, and the Mozelles debated whether or not they should inform government agencies about the coins' existence, and if so, which agencies? NASA? The FBI? The CIA? The Department of Homeland Security? Elsen Mozelle insisted that doing so would be prudent, but her husband remained dubious.

"If those government fellows ask when this 'spaceship' is coming, what do we say?" Mozelle asked. "If they ask where it's going to land, what do we tell them? If they ask what kind of creatures are on board, how do we respond? That there are none? That the ship operates itself? That it roams the galaxy at the speed of light looking for a hospitable planet? That the last ship of those extinct alien creatures will be reborn here so that they can retrieve their entire civilization and culture, which has been preserved in human genes, DNA, and chromosomes, all of which is materialized in the form of coins that were found in the hands of newborn babies? If I were at NASA and someone told me all that, I'd laugh them out of my office; it's too off the wall. Plus, we'd lose control of the coins."

"But we know that the story isn't off the wall," Elsen said, scooting forward from the corner of the couch. "Each element of it has been experienced by one or another of us in this room."

Throughout the meeting, Michael Chasman played the role of skeptic, scoffing at Luther John Doe's words. "A race of creatures so advanced that they possess the technology to survive longer than the sun that gave them life? Nonsensical prattle from an autistic old man." Nevertheless, Chasman admitted that the very existence of the coins suggested profound implications that might lie beyond the scope of human understanding. "Of course, as a scientist, I have to dismiss Luther's mumbo jumbo, but at the same time, I also do have to give serious thought to what Montaro said about the organic nature of the particles," he said. "If what you've told us is right, Montaro, then we are no longer simply in a race with Fritzbrauner and Gabler for possession of both coins. We could be either at a new frontier for science or at a tragic new turn in human error. In the latter case, the risk we run in not sharing what we've learned with the government could be catastrophic. Not only for us but for the entire country."

By meeting's end, Anna Hilburn agreed to help Montaro's investigative team, which had not yet succeeded in tracking down Whitney and Franklyn Walker; Chasman and the Mozelles volunteered to contact the Department of Homeland Security and the office of New York senator Alfonse Alfaro to inform them of all they knew about the coins. At which point, Montaro finally took the time to take out his phone, turn it back on, and look at the message displayed: "You have ten missed calls." When he checked his voice mail, he discovered that all the messages had come from Cecilia.

"We've got to talk about Prissy," Caine's wife said after he called her back. "Your 'friend' Whitcombe called. We're due at the Stockbridge police chief's office tomorrow at one."

33

THE WALLS OF THE OFFICE OF ALBERT MASTERSON, CHIEF OF PO-
lice of Stockbridge, Massachusetts, one hundred and fifty miles
and more than a few light-years away from Fitzer Corporation, were
covered by citations, awards, trophies, and a variety of framed photographs of the chief in familiar poses. There was Masterson in his dress
blues, shaking hands with the former Stockbridge chief; here he was
receiving a commendation from Massachusetts governor Deval Pat-
rick; and there he was standing proudly in pinstripes with his arms
around two star players of the Little League baseball team he coached.

Gordon Whitcombe, already somewhat sweaty and rumpled, was
waiting inside when the desk sergeant showed in Montaro, Cecilia,
and Priscilla, each of their faces displaying varying aspects of uneasiness. At the sight of Whitcombe, Priscilla flinched. When her mother
had told her that she would have to attend this meeting, she had
loudly protested, but after her father informed her that she had no
other option, Priscilla consented—Montaro Caine was CEO of his
family, and unlike at Fitzer Corporation, about which she had been
reading all too much lately, Priscilla knew that there was no chance
for anyone to launch a successful takeover against him, hostile or
otherwise.

"I'm glad we're all able to meet like this, before formal charges are filed and the law takes its usual course," Masterson said after the Caines had sat down in the chairs positioned across from him. "I've found that having a chat with the family is always useful, especially when the lawbreaker is still in her teenage years. Mr. and Mrs. Caine, I appreciate your being here to support Priscilla in light of the seriousness of the allegations. And, Priscilla, I hope you can appreciate the importance of having your parents' support at a time like this. Still, I would be less than candid if I didn't point out that the evidence against you is pretty conclusive. It would help your situation if you would, in turn, be candid with us."

Priscilla prepared herself to do battle, to defend Nick at all costs. But she was disarmed by the sound of a knock at the door. "Come in," Chief Masterson called out. The door opened and the desk sergeant entered, followed by Nick Corcell.

Priscilla's eyes bulged.

"Good afternoon, Chief Masterson." Nick was dressed uncharacteristically in a jacket and tie, and his blond hair was cut short. He looked less like the often shirtless, always smooth-talking, working-class, athletic scholarship jock she knew from campus and more like a wannabe pre-law student toadying up to the partners in some white-shoe firm. But it was unmistakably Nick; even with her eyes closed, Priscilla could have recognized him by the smell of his aftershave.

"Afternoon, Nick, thanks for coming."

"Thanks for asking me, Chief." Nick turned to face Montaro and Cecilia. "You must be Prissy's parents; I'm Nick."

Montaro shook the young man's hand and Nick stared steadily into Montaro's eyes. Montaro stared back, impressed and somewhat alarmed by the young man's composure. Cecilia's response was less cordial; she looked blankly at the hand Nick was offering her.

"So, you are Nick," she said coldly.

"Yes, ma'am."

Nick stepped over to Priscilla, all the while sensing Cecilia Caine's watchful eyes upon him. "Hi, Prissy. How are you?"

"I'm good, Nick."

"Great." He touched her arm gently and Priscilla seemed to take strength from his calmness.

Looking back at Montaro and Cecilia, the young man said, "I've been looking forward to meeting you both, Mr. and Mrs. Caine; Priscilla has told me so much about you. But I'm sorry it has to be under these conditions."

Knowing from the world of business that there was usually little to be gained from rudeness or hostility, Montaro nodded politely. For her part, Cecilia kept her suspicious eyes fixed on the young man as he sat beside Priscilla.

"Nick," Chief Masterson began, "it's obvious to us that you and Priscilla are very close and that you want to do anything you can to help her. We understand that. But we don't want you to bend the truth in any way just because of your feelings for her. All we want is for you to be straightforward and honest."

"That's why I'm here," Nick said.

For the next fifteen minutes, Nick Corcell responded amiably to Chief Masterson's questions. Cecilia Caine was not the least bit convinced by the young man's "Yes, ma'am; No, sir" act, but she did find herself glad that her daughter's friend—she did not let herself think of him as a boyfriend, let alone a lover—was so gifted at glib insincerity. His answers were all crisp and to the point. Taken together, they painted a picture of Priscilla as a young woman too decent, too well brought up, too morally well balanced to consume drugs, let alone distribute them on campus. It was a picture that Cecilia wanted desperately to believe was true and that Montaro knew without question was false. Nick told the chief that he was certain Priscilla was innocent of any wrongdoing and was willing to sign any document attesting to that assertion.

"Sure, there are drugs on campus, Chief," he said. "People pass joints around fairly openly. I have heard of the selling and buying of marijuana on and around campus all the years I've been a student there, and I know more than a handful of people who have occasionally indulged. But, to the best of my knowledge, Priscilla is not one of them."

Whitcombe twisted uneasily in his chair, regretting that he would not have a crack at questioning this slick pretty boy. There was something dangerous about this kid, the lawyer thought, something too cool and smooth, something that someday could cause harm to Priscilla and her family. But for the moment, Nick seemed to be winning over Chief Masterson, and as the Caines' lawyer, that was precisely what Gordon Whitcombe needed the kid to do.

When the chief stopped questioning Nick and turned his attention to Priscilla and her parents, Nick Corcell smiled, proud of himself. He felt suddenly flushed with a sense of his own power. It was the second time that day he'd felt that way. In fact, as far as he was concerned, the most dramatic events of the day had already played out hours earlier. First thing in the morning, he had been cruising west along the Massachusetts Turnpike in his Volkswagen Beetle convertible, gusts of summer wind warm against his bare, suntanned torso. His mind was in high gear, too, moving methodically over the few remaining points that needed to be smoothed out before the business transaction awaiting him could close.

Nick's Volkswagen exited the turnpike and picked up US-20. His left hand was draped lightly on the wheel while his right hand rested on the overnight canvas bag on the passenger seat. He checked the car's clock and saw that he was running ahead of schedule, so he relaxed his speed as a Bruce Springsteen song came blasting from the speakers. Nick changed the station before he could even identify the song; the Boss was his stepfather's favorite, and the only time Nick ever listened to Springsteen music was when he was trying to impress naïve, upper-crust Connecticut girls like Priscilla Caine with his blue-collar street cred. For the remaining fifteen miles of his drive, Nick blasted Eminem.

Nick had grown up in South Boston in a small two-bedroom apartment. He had lived there with his mother, Angeline Corcell, and her husband, Nick's stepfather, Anthony Stavros, who every weekday evening brought home with him the nauseating stench of the fish market where he worked. One time, long before he had begun to shave, Nick spent his entire weekly allowance on aftershave lotion, which he'd splashed around his room to chase away that smell he hated so much.

Nick had been only six when his father left for reasons that Nick still couldn't understand. Piero Corcell had worked in the fish factory, too, but his smell was different; Nick had associated it with a time his family had been together long before Stavros entered the picture. Even now, Nick wore a healthy splash of aftershave lotion every day, even on days when he didn't shave.

When Nick arrived in the parking lot of the Holiday Inn in Great Barrington, Massachusetts, the hotel was busy. A weekend convention of manufacturing associations was being held there, a fact that Nick had taken into account when he had chosen this date and location. The parking lot was nearly full. Nick paid close attention to every vehicle in the lot, making sure that there wasn't a gray Mercedes in sight, eventually guiding his car into one of the few available slots before turning off the motor.

Nick reached into his overnight bag, fished out a T-shirt, and slipped it on before he exited the car, overnight bag in hand. Upon entering the air-conditioned lobby, he checked out everything and everyone. Looking behind the hotel's front desk, he made sure that there was a small white envelope in the key box for Room 371. Then he casually altered his course in the direction of the coffee shop. The place was packed with an early lunch crowd, but he found a seat at a vacant window table, which afforded a perfect view of both the lobby and the lot. When the waitress came by, he ordered a Coke.

From his table, Nick watched the battleship gray Mercedes as it entered the parking lot and cautiously circled the area twice before it came to rest in an empty spot by the hotel entrance. The Mercedes's windows were tinted, so Nick couldn't see inside, but soon his eyes focused upon Millard Wilcox and Norton Lightman, who were emerging from the vehicle. Wilcox was a tall, handsome man in his midthirties, with wavy black hair and a Mediterranean complexion. Though Lightman may have been about the same age, he was a striking contrast to his companion; he had an overhanging gut, an accumulation of fat under his chin, and he wore a preposterous red bow tie.

Nick's eyes tracked the two men into the lobby where they requested the key to Room 371, which was registered to a Mr. MacAllister Brown.

"Right away, Mr. Brown." The smiling clerk turned toward the key boxes where Lightman caught sight of the small white envelope.

When the clerk handed Lightman the envelope, Lightman ripped it open. Inside was an unsigned typewritten note: "Minor changes necessary. No problems. Will explain later. Go to the phone booth across the street from the Main Street CVS. Repeat, no problems."

Nick sipped his Coke as he watched Lightman pass the note to Wilcox before the men left the lobby. They returned to the Mercedes and sped off. Nick paid for his drink, then strolled briskly back to his Volkswagen and started it up. He gunned the car over a familiar back-road shortcut that quickly took him to the rear of the CVS. He entered the store, then walked toward the windows at the front of the store.

When Nick saw the big Mercedes approaching, he waited until it nestled close to the empty phone booth across the street before he dialed a number on his cell phone. Nick watched Lightman leave the car and approach the phone booth; there, the man picked up the receiver, looked at it suspiciously, then answered, "Yeah?"

"I'll see you at the Berkshire Motel. Room 63 is booked under the same name as before, MacAllister Brown. I'll meet you in fifteen minutes."

"What the fuck is up?"

"No problems. Save your questions," Nick replied, then hung up.

The Berkshire was a no-frills establishment, one of the few in the region. A few minutes after Lightman and Wilcox made their way to Room 63 on the motel's second floor, there was a knock on the door. Wilcox sprang from the plastic chair where he had parked his beefy body. He thumped across the room and yanked the door open, revealing Nick Corcell.

"May I come in?" Nick waited until Lightman waved him forward with an impatient gesture. After Nick entered, Wilcox closed the door and moved behind him. Nick stopped a few feet away from Lightman. "You wanted to see me, sir?" he asked.

"What the fuck is this? What's going on?" Lightman whispered.

"What do you mean? Nothing's going on. You said you had something to show me. That's why I'm here, to see what it is."

Lightman gave Nick a long, searching look, then glanced questioningly around the room. "How come we're here instead of the other place?" he asked.

"What other place?" queried Nick.

Lightman's jaw tightened. He centered Nick in the crosshairs of a cold, threatening stare. "Are you crazy? What kind of game is this, kid?"

"Game? I don't know what you're talking about, mister."

A look of understanding flashed in Lightman's eyes. "Oh, he thinks we're wired. Isn't that right, kid?" he asked.

"Son of a bitch," Wilcox said and laughed.

The tension seemed to drain from Lightman. "Relax, kid. If anyone in here is wearing a bug, it's you." Listening to his own words, Lightman seemed to tense up again. "What's in the bag?" he asked.

"No bugs," Nick said with a shrug. He tossed his overnight bag to Lightman. "Take a look."

Lightman caught the canvas bag, looked inside, and found only a change of clothes and a bottle of aftershave. "O.K., kid," he hissed. "Explain. Get to the fucking point."

"There's nothing to explain," Nick said. "May I see what you said you wanted to give me?"

Lightman nodded to Wilcox. The pudgy man laid his briefcase on the bed and opened it to reveal stacks of hundred-dollar bills.

Nick looked down at the money, then up at Lightman. He smiled.

Lightman did not return the smile. "Now, have you got something for us?" he asked.

Nick studied the two men at length before he answered. "I have no idea what you're talking about. I better get outta here." He turned abruptly and headed for the door.

"Hey, wait a fucking minute," said Lightman. Nick opened the door, made as if to step through it, then suddenly stopped. He looked down—there was a package in the doorway. He spun around to face Lightman and Wilcox.

"It looks like a package has been left here for you. Want me to bring it in?"

"Sure," Lightman answered.

Nick picked up the package, closed the door, and reentered the room. He handed the package to Lightman. They held each other's gaze for a moment before Lightman gestured to the money lying on the bed in the open briefcase.

"Why don't you check the package to see if it's exactly what you were expecting."

Lightman and Wilcox huddled over their package to make sure the six pounds of pure cocaine they were paying for was all there. Meanwhile, Nick counted twenty stacks of hundred dollar bills. When he was done counting, Nick dumped the money into his canvas bag.

"Thank you, gentlemen, for being so generous."

Lightman extended his hand to Nick. "You're a pretty strange kid. But I guess a guy can't be too careful, can he?"

Nick took his hand. "Whatever you say, mister. Whatever you say." He turned to the door, slinging the bag over his shoulder.

"Maybe we'll see you again, if the price is right," Lightman called out.

Nick looked back at him. "Maybe," he answered. Then he opened the door and was gone.

In the quiet, empty hallway, Nick could taste his own fear; he could smell it, too. As he started toward the stairwell, his awareness of his surroundings heightened. Entering the stairwell, he began to sweat. When he reached a first floor hallway, he saw a maid carrying linens and towels into an empty room; an elderly couple hobbled past him. Nick continued briskly along the hallway until he reached Room 21. He knocked lightly.

Frankie Naples, a wired and wiry young man in his midtwenties, opened the door just enough to let Nick slide in, then slammed it shut. Inside, Frankie turned from the door to face Nick. "Everything go okay?" he asked.

"Smooth," Nick replied, then moved quickly to the bed.

"Great. Fucking great. You did good, kid." Frankie watched Nick unzip his bag and dump the hundred thousand dollars onto the bed.

"It's all there. I checked it. You check it again; then I'm outta here."

Frankie, a courier for a sophisticated Boston-based narcotics syndicate, grabbed a stack of bills and started counting while Nick glanced at his watch. His job was nearly done. From here, according to the plan, Frankie would take the money to Boston where it would be processed, stored, and eventually shipped out of the country to be washed.

"It's all here," Frankie finally said.

"Good," Nick replied, and the men shook hands.

"See ya." Nick broke for the door.

"Where you heading?" asked Frankie.

"Gonna pass by school, pick up some clothes, then pop down to Manhattan to hang out for a day or two."

"Ain't you graduating this week?"

"Yeah. In three days."

"Then what?"

"College, eventually. Look, Frankie, I gotta split. Don't break the speed limit going back with that stuff."

A half-hour later, at his dorm room, Nick was packing his carryall bag when he heard the hallway phone. A half-minute later, he heard a voice call out: "Nick Corcell, phone for you. Are you in there?"

"Yeah," Nick yelled back. "Who is it?"

"Some guy named Albert Masterson wants to talk to you."

A shiver ran through Nick as he walked down the hallway and picked up the phone. He knew that name. "Hello?" he said in a matter-of-fact tone.

"Hi there, Nick, this is Police Chief Masterson again. Remember me?"

"Yes, sir, of course."

"I'm calling to ask you to come down to our offices. Mr. and Mrs. Caine are coming up from Connecticut with their daughter, Priscilla. The last time we talked, you offered to speak on her behalf. Would you mind?"

"Oh, no, be glad to. What time?"

"Soon as you can. They should be here any minute."

———

The hardest part of the day seemed to be over for Nick. He had already done his part in defending Priscilla, and at this point, most of what he was doing was listening. The chief was continuing to drone on and on as Priscilla reached out to touch Nick's hand. He turned to her. She looked into his eyes and he smiled.

"Mr. Whitcombe," the chief said as he faced the portly lawyer, "would you care to add anything to what's been said here?"

"Well, Chief, as you know, I've known this young lady from the day she was born," he began.

Priscilla scowled. It wouldn't take much more of this bullshit to make her throw up, she thought. She hoped Whitcombe would choke on his words. But Whitcombe's remarks were not the snot-nosed flattery she had anticipated. The lawyer was critical in the same tough, honest way that her father usually was. He ripped her to pieces, but only in those areas where she knew she deserved it.

"Priscilla thinks she knows a great deal more than she, in fact, does. Her parents are somewhat of a disappointment to her, since she's convinced that they don't know nearly as much as she does. It's a typical teenage assessment; she's spoiled, but not rotten. Not yet. There are strong, steady hands on the parental controls still. And they will continue to guide Priscilla with loving concern and with respect. Priscilla is not a bad person, Chief. She's a pain in the butt a lot of the time and a little too selfish and self-centered at other times. My call on Priscilla Caine is that she's a good kid with lots of room for improvement."

"Thank you, Mr. Whitcombe." Chief Masterson rose from his seat. "I thank you all for coming in. We will be in touch when we decide whether we will be going forward with the charges."

Cecilia and Montaro shook hands with Chief Masterson. Then Priscilla stood and did the same. Whitcombe followed her and Nick followed Whitcombe.

The chief pumped Nick's hand firmly. "Where're you parked, Nick?" he asked.

"Out back," Nick said.

"Good. I'll walk you to your car. There's something I'd like to ask you."

"O.K." Nick turned to Priscilla, who was waiting in the doorway, and waved. "I'll talk to you later, Prissy."

Priscilla waved to him, then followed her parents and Whitcombe out of the chief's office. The chief watched them go, then closed the door.

Turning to face Nick, he said, "I wanted to tell you this in private, Nick. You don't need to worry about Priscilla being pregnant. Her parents had her checked. She just missed her period for whatever reason. That's all. No pregnancy. I know you're glad to hear those words."

"I sure am," Nick said sheepishly.

"Come on, we'll go this way to your car."

Chief Masterson led Nick from his office through a rear door that opened into a back hallway. The two men walked until Chief Masterson suddenly stopped in front of a closed door. "Let's just stop in here for a second." He opened the door and gestured for Nick to enter.

When Nick saw who was in the room, he gasped. There, seated at a table before him, were Norton Lightman and Millard Wilcox. Between them was Frankie Naples. Spread out on the table was the hundred thousand dollars he had turned over to Frankie less than an hour and a half earlier.

"I'm sure you know these gentlemen. Business acquaintances of yours, aren't they?" the chief asked Nick.

Nick stared at Lightman's and Wilcox's detective badges, then lowered his eyes to meet those of the young man seated at the table like trapped prey. He saw only panic and resignation in the eyes of the once feisty bundle of energy he knew to be Frankie Naples.

"Sit down, son." Chief Masterson indicated the unoccupied chair beside Frankie and Nick numbly obeyed. When he was seated, the chief continued. "Read him his rights, Joe."

Dazed, Nick Corcell suddenly thought he could see everything clearly. He thought he had been so clever and careful, but it had all been a setup, probably even the words he had spoken on behalf of Priscilla Caine. No one would press any charges against her; society protected rich bitches like that girl, and working class folk like him always paid the price.

Nick listened to Detective Joseph Delconsini, the man Nick knew as Norton Lightman, monotone the familiar words that he had heard so often on TV procedurals—*you have the right to remain silent; anything you say or do can and will be held against you.* When the detective finished, Masterson sighed deeply, then spoke. "So, my babies, with time off for good behavior, each of you will be locked away for no less than ten years. By the time you get out of the slammer, the world will have passed you by." He glanced at Nick. "College will have passed you by, son. You will probably spend the rest of your miserable life on the dung heap of society, eating shit. Which is, as far as I'm concerned, exactly where you belong."

The ring of a wall phone interrupted him. Detective Howard McGraw, who had been known to Nick as Millard Wilcox, stepped over to the phone. "Yeah," he said into the mouthpiece. "Yeah. Right. O.K." He jerked the receiver toward Masterson. "For you, Chief."

Masterson scurried across the room, grabbed the receiver from McGraw's hand, and growled into it. "Yeah? All right, we'll be right there." He hung up, looked at his detectives, and made his way to the door. "We'll be back in a few minutes," Masterson told Nick and Frankie. "Don't get any ideas about walking out the back door. It's locked. As you probably know, you're entitled to one phone call. Think about how you want to use it."

Masterson followed his detectives out of the room, closing the door behind him.

"Bullshit. It's all bullshit," Frankie blurted out when they were gone.

"What is?" Nick asked weakly.

"That phone call. Them leaving the room. It's all bullshit. They want to make a deal. That's what they're fishing for. But they want us to ask for it."

"What kind of deal, man?" Nick asked anxiously.

"They want our guys in Boston," Frankie told him lowering his voice.

Nick noticed that his hands had begun to shake.

"We could do it. We could walk out of here like nothing ever happened," Frankie said. "I can take this money on to Boston just like I'm supposed to."

Nick nodded his head in the direction the cops had gone. "And what do they get?"

"They get you and me, a couple of scratchers, working on the inside for them."

"How do you know?" Nick asked.

"I can smell it. Sometimes you know things without seeing or hearing 'em. Sometimes you gotta rely on your other senses, kid," said Frankie. "The question is how bad do you want to stay out of the warehouse? We've got a shot we play our cards right."

"Our cards?" Nick thought. He considered the Caines and their pretty Westport mansion and he considered his mom and her husband's two-bedroom apartment in South Boston. He thought of Priscilla who would be going off to college in a couple of years, and he thought of himself in prison.

"What would I have to do?" he asked.

———

Montaro Caine was behind the wheel of his Mercedes, speeding along Route 7, joining the rapid flow of vehicles rushing toward Connecticut. Cecilia, who was never comfortable on highways, kept her eyes focused on the speedometer. But she waited until the car was traveling well above the speed limit before she offered a gentle reminder.

"Better late than never, honey. Get us home in one piece, O.K.?"

Caine's foot eased up on the gas pedal as he briefly glanced over to his wife. "Sorry," he said with a distant smile.

Silence fell as Caine found his mind had already drifted many, many miles away from the Berkshires; he was thinking of coins and Fitzer Corporation and Matthew Perch and of all those other roles he had to play when he wasn't being father and husband, responsibilities that he didn't always know how to shoulder properly. As always, he would have to rely on the example set by his grandfather, whose ninety-ninth birthday was rapidly approaching; how much longer could Montaro rely on the wisdom of P. L. Caine, he wondered. At least a few more years, he hoped. So lost in his own thoughts was he that when he paused to glance down at the dashboard clock, he realized that nearly an hour had passed since they had left Stockbridge. He looked up into the rearview mirror and saw his daughter's reflection.

"Priscilla," he said. She lifted her eyes to meet his gaze in the mirror. "That's the last you'll see of Nick Corcell." Her father spoke in the no-nonsense tone Priscilla had learned early in life never to challenge. "I'm sorry. Your mother and I will do everything we can to help you ride this through, but you won't be seeing Nick again."

Tears instantly welled up in Priscilla's eyes. She felt a rage against her parents, wanted to lash out at them. Cecilia half turned in her seat to look at her enraged child and reached out to her, but Priscilla ignored the gesture. "That really sucks, Daddy. I mean that really fucking sucks!" she blurted out, before collapsing into sobs.

Still, as her father drove along the Merritt Parkway and Priscilla was able to dry her eyes and catch her breath, she found herself beginning to develop some small new hope. If the events of the past weeks and the experience of seeing her father's name in the newspapers in association with the mining disaster and the Fitzer takeover rumors had taught her anything, it was that Montaro Caine might not always be as right as his daughter had once thought him to be. Her father had said that she would never see Nick Corcell again, and he seemed sure of himself, but as for Priscilla, she was not so sure that Nick would disappear from their lives quite so easily.

As for Nick himself, he was cruising toward Boston along the Massachusetts Turnpike with what he felt to be a new lease on life. Frankie Naples had left Stockbridge a half hour earlier with the hundred thousand dollars in the trunk of his car. Nick wasn't wearing his confining, fancy suit anymore, and the sunshine had never felt so good against his back. As far as Nick was concerned, the rich Connecticut bitch and her big-time parents were history. Bruce Springsteen was singing "Working on a Dream" on the radio, and Nick didn't even feel moved to shut it off.

In fact, Nick turned the volume of the stereo louder and began singing along up until the moment when he became aware of a black sedan riding close behind him, flashing highway lights at him. Assuming the driver wanted to pass, Nick pulled right, but the car remained behind him. Looking into his rearview mirror, Nick could see that two men were inside the sedan, wearing sunglasses; the man in the passenger seat was waving, gesturing for him to pull off the turnpike.

The men could have been undercover cops from the Stockbridge P.D., friends of Frankie Naples, or members of the Boston outfit—Nick had no idea. The only thing Nick knew for sure was that whoever was in that car was someone he didn't want to talk to. He briefly considered flooring his VW, but he knew that the Beetle could never compete with the eight-cylinder American sedan behind him. Good looks and a polite manner had gotten him through every scrape he'd ever been in; he'd have to hope that would prove true again. Resigned, he signaled a turn into the right lane, then got off at the Newton exit.

Nick parked the car in the first parking space he saw—in front of an upscale coffee shop called Taste—and the sedan pulled in behind him. He got out of his car at the same time as the men in their dark suits and sunglasses.

"How can I help you, officers?" Nick said with a smile as he approached them. They looked like Federal agents or narcs, Nick thought, but when they flashed their business cards at him, he understood that they were neither.

"We're not cops, Nick," said the bulkier of the two men. "My name is Alan Rothman and this is Carlos Wallace. I think you might be able to help us."

34

Despite the best efforts of Montaro Caine and his associates, meetings with government officials to discuss the significance of the coins and the prophecies of Matthew Perch and Luther John Doe yielded no useful results. Alfonse Alfaro, the bald, bespectacled New York senator with his familiarly chubby face and thinning gray hair, quickly agreed to a meeting. But when Caine and Howard Mozelle revealed that they weren't interested in discussing either the senator's reelection campaign or his committee's ability to influence mining safety legislation, he quickly adjourned the meeting and directed one of his secretaries to facilitate an appointment for the men with NASA's chief of staff. The NASA rep informed Caine and Mozelle that he wasn't at liberty to discuss whether he would or wouldn't act upon the information they had given him, after which the men met with the deputy director of Homeland Security, who said that his agency's funding had been slashed, and the men really needed to be talking to the FBI.

Anna Hilburn's efforts to determine the whereabouts of Whitney and Franklyn Walker were proving to be no more successful. Whitney's uncle Frederick and cousins said that Whitney and Franklyn were on vacation, but none of them knew where. Whitney's uncle had sent a letter to the couple, but had received no response. Lawrence

Aikens learned that Cordiss Krinkle was spreading the word that the couple was safely ensconced in some European country, but neither Aikens nor Curly Bennett was able to learn in which country that might be. And, after Aikens met with Montaro, both men agreed that whatever information Cordiss was spreading was probably false anyway. Near the end of a week's worth of fruitless meetings, unproductive phone calls, and unanswered emails, Montaro understood something that P. L. Caine had impressed upon him when he was just a boy—that he would always have to rely on himself.

P. L. Caine's ninety-ninth birthday celebration was held in the retirement community of Seaview Estates in Carmel. During Montaro's childhood, P.L.'s birthday parties were lively and extravagant affairs, where the Canadian Club flowed freely, but now that P.L. had outlived just about all of his contemporaries, this birthday celebration was comparatively subdued—in attendance were a few friends P.L. had met at Seaview as well as Montaro and his family. The red velvet cake with white frosting was barely large enough to accommodate all the candles that Cecilia Caine had placed upon it.

The modest birthday party suited the Caines' needs. Montaro could not recall when he had last spent this much uninterrupted time with his family; most probably it had been before Priscilla had entered boarding school. And, though Priscilla had alternately cried, shouted, and sent furious text messages on her iPhone during the limo ride to the Teterboro Airport, once the Caines had boarded their private jet, she didn't speak, scream, or whisper another word about Nick Corcell. Even after the family had arrived at the Monterey Peninsula Airport, Priscilla didn't even bother to turn her phone back on.

During the waking hours of their three days together, Montaro rarely left his grandfather's side. While walking along the beachfront and chatting in his grandfather's living room, he told P.L. everything about the coins and was surprised to find that his grandfather never doubted any part of his story. The man had seen nearly one hundred years of history and had traveled from the old country of Austria to the United States just a few years before the outbreak of World War II, leaving behind his parents, who had thought it would be safe for them to stay. He had fought in World War II on the American side, had witnessed the advent of motion pictures, computers, cell phones, transoceanic aviation, space travel, and the loss of his wife and only son—if anyone could believe that multiple worlds existed beyond ours, it was P.L.; he had already seen dozens.

"Grandpa, I know you're not a scientist," Montaro said one afternoon when his wife and daughter were out shopping on Ocean Avenue and the two men were alone at the counter in P.L.'s kitchen. "But the more I think about the nature of these coins and the more I become convinced that they can defy gravity, matter, space, and maybe even time, the more I'm beginning to think that there would be no need for the Seventh Ship to land in order to retrieve them. If the ship does land here, it would have to be for reasons other than the coins. But I can't for the life of me figure out what those reasons could be."

Though Montaro had been thinking out loud as much as he had been speaking directly to his grandfather, P. L. Caine listened intently and gave Montaro the same advice he had given him so long ago: "When the time is right, the truth will reveal itself," he said. "Listen to what you can't see, my boy, watch what you can't hear, listen carefully to your inner voice, and trust your instincts. When the time to act arrives, I am sure you will know how to proceed."

The words were simple and familiar, and yet they were all Montaro needed to hear to regain his confidence. For him, his grandfather's voice had always had a magical quality, a healing power. His company was floundering, Richard Davis's takeover bid had not abated, the coins were beyond Montaro's reach, and, for the time being, so were Whitney and Franklyn Walker—and also, it seemed, his daughter. And yet, P. L. Caine's words reminded Montaro of what he already knew—that he had the power to overcome all this; after all, P. L. Caine had lived through far worse and had survived.

The night after he and his family returned from Carmel, Montaro Caine sat alone in his Carlyle apartment, tired to the point of exhaustion. Part of him wanted black coffee, part of him wanted a stiff drink, but when he rose from his couch, he sought neither. Instead, he walked over to his living room desk and removed from the bottom left drawer the small, flannel bag that held the hand-carved model of the Seventh Ship. Ever since meeting Luther John Doe, Caine had often marveled at the mysterious way that nature had invested a master craftsman's skills in the hands of a young black boy with a twisted chin, a withered leg, an unknown background, and a mind that seemed to exist in some universe light-years beyond our own. Caine had explored the surface of the carved object countless times, searching for seams that might reveal a hidden entryway, but he had never found one. And yet he didn't doubt that at the appointed moment, somehow the ship would reveal its mysteries.

On this particular evening, Caine puzzled over the object for nearly an hour before reaching for the flannel bag to return it to his desk drawer, when, suddenly, the object began to vibrate in his hand. Stunned, he dropped it on his desk and stood from his chair. Slowly, the model of the Seventh Ship began to open. Dazzling colors and stunning three-dimensional shapes twirled around inside it. Then they billowed out of the wooden shell into Caine's living room. Everywhere around him, colors and shapes transformed themselves into images of objects and beings that Caine had never seen or ever dreamed existed. There was no sound at all, yet the images seemed to dance to some internal music of their own. Caine felt as if he were actually hearing the colors, seeing the sounds. It was like watching a private display of the aurora borealis. Finally, the colors, shapes, and images all gathered together in a breathtaking formation above the object, at which point they suddenly froze. They remained like that, motionless, for ten seconds or so. Then, as if on cue, they instantly disappeared back into the interior of the object, which, in turn, slowly closed itself. And after the ship had closed and once again resembled nothing more remarkable than a woman's compact, Montaro could still see a lingering image in his mind of a person he had never met and yet immediately recognized.

The time had come, just as Luther John Doe, Matthew Perch, and P. L. Caine had predicted. And it was at this point that Montaro, stunned beyond belief yet armed with new strength, felt as if he knew all that he had ever needed to know. And at this moment, too, he felt that his primary obligation was no longer to his company, or even to his family, but to an unusual man from another place and time named Matthew Perch.

35

THE FOLLOWING MORNING, CAINE GATHERED THE MOZELLES and Anna Hilburn in his living room. He had ordered breakfast for all of them, but as they sat around his table, no one touched the food or coffee. Though none of them had seen the model of the Seventh Ship open to reveal its breathtaking display, each could detect the astonishment Montaro had experienced and the new strength it had given him. He spoke, almost as if possessed.

"Something happened to me last night, something so riveting, so amazing that even I have trouble believing it, and yet I must ask you to understand that every bit of it is true," Montaro said, his voice hushed as he told the story of what he had seen.

"From where I stand at this moment, it appears that the strands of each of our lives are being woven into a destiny still unclear, and as yet untold," he said. "Perhaps we are closer to that destiny than we think. There is no question in my mind that we are already an inseparable part of something unique and astounding. Consider everything we have seen up to this point. Consider the minuscule particles dislodged from the original coin that have reunited with it. How could those particles perform such a feat? How could they escape an airtight cast-iron safe, whisk themselves across thousands of miles of ocean to another continent, and, there, reaffix themselves on the coin exactly where they were originally located, all in what must have been only a matter of seconds, if that long?"

Caine stood, then walked over to the desk phone. "I am going to ask your indulgence in something that might strike you as unethical," he said. "I want you to listen in on a private conversation, if the person I am calling is available. If you're uncomfortable with this, feel free to leave the room."

No one moved, so Caine picked up the phone and dialed. Moments later, a voice came through the speakerphone. "Hello?"

"Is this Kritzman Fritzbrauner?" asked Caine.

"Yes..."

"Montaro Caine, here. Forgive this intrusion."

"No intrusion, Montaro. What can I do for you?"

"Are you in your office as we speak?"

"I am."

"Would you please go to your safe, open it, and tell me if the coin you purchased from Cordiss Krinkle is exactly where you left it?"

In the void of a silent pause, an instant alert to danger could be heard in Fritzbrauner's voice. "Is this some kind of joke? Tell me, why should something in my safe not be where I left it?" he asked.

"Because it's possible that the coin has disappeared, however strange that may sound to you. It is of great importance to both of us that you look. Please, I urge you, check the safe now."

Fritzbrauner chuckled. "You have stumped me, Montaro," he began.

"Let me be clear," Caine interrupted, his voice somber. "Neither you nor I, nor anyone else, can claim outright ownership of either of the coins. We all have a stake in their fate, but ownership is out of the question—no matter what the price. Not even Whitney Carson Walker and her husband, in whose tiny hands the coins first entered this world, can claim outright ownership of them. Now, with the birth of their first child drawing near, I believe that something highly unusual and monumental may be about to take place, something astonishing and historic. But for now, all I'm asking is for you to please check your safe."

After a long pause, Fritzbrauner spoke. "All right, Montaro. I will do it now."

Through the speakerphone, Caine could hear a deep intake of breath, and then an exhalation. In a surprisingly even tone, Fritzbrauner spoke. "It's not there, Montaro. So tell me, where is it?"

Caine chose his words carefully. "As you may recall, during dinner at your home, you asked me a question that I could not answer. You asked me what I made of that fellow Matthew Perch. At the time, I had very little knowledge of the man."

"And now?" asked Fritzbrauner.

"Much has changed."

"I see," Fritzbrauner said. "But what does this Matthew Perch have to do with my safe, or the personal property in it?"

"I don't know for sure. But I've come to believe that Matthew Perch is more than we have imagined. Possibly more than we are capable of imagining. His life, it seems, embodies destinies, miracles, and truths that are inextricably intertwined with your life, my life, and the lives of countless others, in ways that logic and reason cannot explain. Matthew Perch and I have never met, and yet I believe he knows everything he needs to know about me. I also believe he knows all he needs to know about you, about Roland Gabler, about Richard Davis, the Mozelles, Carrie Pittman, and about Cordiss Krinkle. In short, I believe that Matthew Perch knows each of us who has claimed or has sought to exercise control or ownership of the coins. Before a third coin arrives, as I expect it soon will, I believe that the mountain should go to Muhammad."

"Montaro," said Fritzbrauner, his voice snappy, "exactly what are you suggesting?"

"I'm suggesting that you put aside your personal agenda and your judgment and, for once, believe in something other than your money," Caine fired back.

"Well, by my judgment," Fritzbrauner said, "that's a very tall order. What makes you feel that any of those people you mentioned will even be received by this mysterious gentleman, even if he is all that you perceive him to be? By Howard's own records, the man has received only two other human beings in the past twenty-six years: Mozelle's wife and Hattie Sinclair. My take on Perch is that he is no more than an eccentric hermit who wants to be left alone."

"I respectfully disagree," said Caine. "I firmly believe that he is waiting to meet us. And here's something else: I also believe that what you call your 'property,' which by some inexplicable process has left your safe, is now in the possession of Matthew Perch."

"Montaro," Fritzbrauner said. "What you believe is entirely up to you. I need facts, evidence. I paid a price for a piece of property, which has now gone missing. Whatever mystical way you came by your knowledge and believe it to be in the possession of this Perch character is not enough."

"Kritzman, I can explain the 'how' and the 'why' to you, as I understand them. As to the larger and more pressing question of 'to what end,' my guess is that Perch will have to provide that answer. Time is running out. This is an opportunity that may never come again."

"A moment, Montaro," Fritzbrauner said. "By what procedure was my property removed from my safe, and by whom? I would greatly appreciate whatever you can tell me."

"I believe you already know the answer to that question. But you are not yet ready to accept it," said Caine. "The truth is that you can't win this one; but losing could teach each of us more than we ever thought we would know. There are huge, unimagined lessons waiting for us if we join forces and work together. In the end, what you hear may well be worth the money you have paid. I urge you to think about it and call me when you have reached a decision."

Caine hung up the phone, then turned to the others in his living room. "What I've just told Fritzbrauner," he said, "is what I learned last night, not through words, but through the images I saw."

After a moment of silence in which each individual seated in Caine's living room seemed to consider the implications of his statement, Howard Mozelle spoke up. "What about the second coin, the one Gabler has? Has it disappeared as well?"

"We'll find out soon enough, but I'm certain it has," Caine said. "And I'm equally certain that I know where it is."

"And where is that?" Howard Mozelle asked.

"In the hands of Matthew Perch," said Caine.

36

WHEN ANOTHER DAY AND NIGHT PASSED WITHOUT ANY WORD from Fritzbrauner or any progress in determining the whereabouts of Whitney and Franklyn Walker, Montaro summoned Lawrence Aikens and Curly Bennett to his apartment. Aikens appeared at Montaro's door punctually as always, but, ten minutes past the appointed time, Curly, who seemed to be neglecting his duties of late, still had not arrived. Even though Montaro said nothing about Curly's tardiness, Aikens, sitting in a chair opposite Caine, massaged the fingers of his left hand with those of his right, movements that spoke clearly of an unmistakable turmoil within.

Caine took a deep breath. "Let's get to it," he said. "We don't have much time, so hear me well. You've been loyal to me. We've worked well together. I've trusted you. And I still do. I am not altogether sure I can turn Fitzer around, but I'm giving it my best try. If I manage to pull through, I'd like you to stay. If I don't, and you do stay, I'd like to share with you something I learned from my grandfather. Some people don't always mean what they want you to think they mean, but if you listen hard enough, your ears will begin to hear new things. One day you will be able to listen to someone and see their real meaning hidden underneath and between their words. And sometimes you will even find those meanings sitting right on top of their words for all to see, though most people will not see them because they don't know that your eyes can hear the truth and your ears can see it. The other night, I heard truth with my own eyes and I saw it spoken with my own ears. Curly isn't here yet, but I can hear what he is telling us."

"What's that?" Aikens asked.

"Curly's a great assistant," said Caine. "You will not find anyone better. But I believe that you've been driving him away, and that can cause problems for all of us if it hasn't done so already. Do you understand what I'm saying?"

Aikens stared at Caine with a mixture of discomfort and embarrassment. "I'm here for you, Montaro," he said.

"Good," Caine replied with a smile.

When Curly arrived a few minutes later, Caine ushered the men into his office and gestured for them to sit. Then, he took a USB memory stick from a desk drawer and inserted it into one of his computer's portals.

"I want you guys to listen to something," he said.

The first sound to come out of the computer's speaker was a ringing telephone. After the seventh ring, a man was heard to answer the phone.

"Curly Bennett here."

"Hi, Curly Bennett, Gina Lao here. Remember me?"

"Gina Lao, of course."

Caine tapped his keyboard and the recording stopped.

Turning to Curly, he asked, "That was your voice, yes?"

"It was." Curly's face was flushed.

"How close are you and Gina Lao?"

"Not very."

"How many times have you spoken with her by phone?"

"Five or six times in the last few weeks."

"Driven by romantic interest?"

"I think more on my part than hers. She is a girl of remarkably good looks, sir."

Montaro smothered a smile. So did Aikens.

"So, her interests were not the same as yours?" Caine asked.

"No, not really. Her aim was to open me up."

"For?"

"Information."

"About?"

"You and Lawrence."

"What did she want to know about us?"

"We never got that far. Something happened that made her lose interest. I think somehow she was able to find out what she needed without me."

"And what do you think that was?"

"Those two people who visited you in the lab, Freich and Beekman, she wanted to know about them. There were some other names she mentioned, too."

"Did you report any of this to Lawrence?"

"No sir, I didn't."

"Tell me why."

"Because my activities are all assigned to me. And that was not one of my assignments."

"Then, in your view, Gina Lao was strictly extracurricular?"

"You might say that."

"All right, last question. You're a very talented investigator, and you're a pretty sharp guy. I'm sure you could have figured out the relevance of your findings. So, let me ask you, would a pat on the back, from time to time, help you to smile a little more and report back to us when there is information we might actually need to know?"

"I wouldn't put it quite that way, sir," said Curly, his cheeks flushing again.

"See that it happens anyway," Caine told Aikens, then looked at each man in turn. "Now, I need both of you to focus all your attention on Whitney and Franklyn Walker. I don't want you to rest until you've found them. Your loyalties cannot be divided on this matter; it is too important. Do you understand?"

"I do," said Aikens.

"And you, Curly?" asked Caine.

"I do," said Curly. "You have my word on that."

Caine shook hands with both men, then stared directly at Curly Bennett. "By the way," he said. "In case you're wondering, I'm the one who ordered the tap on your phone. Lawrence knew nothing about this." He turned to Aikens and tilted his head apologetically. "It was both necessary and a good idea at the time. But I trust you now and I know you will not disappoint me." He smiled, and added, "Show yourselves out, gentlemen."

37

THE MODEL OF THE SEVENTH SHIP WOULD NOT OPEN A SECOND time. No matter how often Montaro picked up the object, rubbed its surface, or shook it, Luther John Doe's carving remained motionless as it had for nearly half a century. Montaro hoped that somehow it might reveal to him the location of Whitney and Franklyn Walker, teach him how to find Matthew Perch, or at least reward him with another magnificent display of colors and shapes. But there was nothing.

And yet, in some way, the model had already done its work, for it had reminded Montaro of the value of patience, something often sorely lacking in men in his position with the pressures he faced. Luther John Doe's model had taken nearly fifty years to open and reveal its interior; Luther had waited the same amount of time to tell Montaro all he knew that he had kept inside him. How many years had the Seventh Ship traveled? Montaro understood that if he remained focused and determined, if he trusted his instincts as P. L. Caine advised him, he would arrive at a place he wanted to be, even if he didn't yet know where that place was.

Soon enough, even without any apparent action on his part, events began to move forward, as if plans beyond the scope of his own understanding had already been put into motion. Anna Hilburn finally managed to get hold of one of Whitney's cousins, who had actually heard from Whitney in a letter and learned that she claimed to be working for an international nonprofit agency developing health-care clinics in Africa, and also that the baby in her belly had begun kicking harder, as if it, like the images Montaro had seen in Luther's carving, was preparing to emerge and reveal its secrets. Montaro immediately turned this information over to Lawrence Aikens and Curly, advising the investigators to use every means at their disposal to follow up on it.

And one early morning, when Montaro hadn't even made it in to work yet, Larry Buchanan dropped by The Carlyle unannounced with information that he said couldn't wait and that he hadn't wanted to discuss over the phone.

"What is it, Larry?" Montaro asked as he adjusted the knot in his tie in his living room mirror while Larry helped himself to a tall cup of black coffee.

"It's about your pal Fritzbrauner," Larry said.

"What about him?"

"He's coming into town," said Larry. "Old man Hargrove's having him over to dinner at his place in Chappaqua this weekend. Guess who else is coming to dinner?"

"Colette Beekman?" Montaro asked.

Larry leered at his friend. "I know what you're thinking about, Monty. Same thing I'm always thinking about," he said. "Yeah, Beekman'll be there. But you know who else?"

Montaro shrugged.

"Richard Davis, Herman Freich, and Roland Gabler. What does all that tell you?"

Caine didn't pause. "A fact no longer in question, and one I already anticipated." He spoke simply, with an almost Zen sense of calm about him, as if what Larry was telling him had already been predestined. "They're joining forces. It also tells me that one of them will be calling me after they have that dinner."

"Probably so," said Larry, then added, "Here's one more thing for you." There was a painful edge to his voice now as he opened his briefcase and took out a large brown sealed envelope. He passed the envelope to Caine, who understood that the painful edge in Buchanan's voice resulted from the fact that Larry's boss, Julius Hargrove, was using Larry as his messenger boy.

"What is it?" Montaro asked.

"They have a proposal for you."

"For what?"

"They want you to join them."

"Really. How'd they figure that all of a sudden?"

"I suppose they think you could cause trouble for them later down the line and it'd be better for them to have you on their side."

"So, they think they can get me cheap?" Montaro said. *And also maybe if I join them, they think their coins will miraculously reappear*, Montaro thought, but didn't say this out loud.

Larry didn't respond. Caine took a letter opener from his desk, sliced open the envelope, and removed the document, which consisted of two stapled pages on Hargrove, Hastings and Dundas company letterhead. Caine scanned the offer, which detailed ownership stakes in both the coins themselves and in any future coin or coins that might come into being, and also in any profits that might come from exploiting or synthetically reproducing the elements in those coins in the future. The details of the proposal, the percentages, obligations, and everything else that was enumerated in the document's stiff legal language, were not nearly as important to Caine as what the document signified, which was that Kritzman Fritzbrauner had not fully understood or accepted what Caine had tried to tell him. He was still thinking in terms of ownership, even though by now he should have understood that the coins had wills of their own and could not truly be bought, sold, or owned.

Caine folded the proposal and slipped the pages back into the envelope.

It had taken all of Larry's pride and will power to keep himself from peeking at the proposal while Caine had been scanning it. Now he looked Caine straight in the eye. "Good news?" he asked.

"Don't know yet," Caine said, and Larry understood that was all he would get out of his friend. When Montaro's cell phone rang, Montaro draped an arm around Larry's shoulders and walked him to the front door. Montaro stood in his doorway watching Larry until he was finally swallowed by the first available elevator. When Montaro took out his phone to answer, it had already stopped ringing. He called into his voice mail to hear the message, and was met with the sound of Roland Gabler's voice. Gabler didn't even begin with a hello.

"Who stole the coin from my safe?" he asked.

38

OVER THE WEEKEND, WHILE KRITZMAN FRITZBRAUNER WAS apparently dining with Julius Hargrove in Chappaqua, along with Colette, Roland Gabler, and the others, Montaro shut off his cell phone and didn't turn it back on. He didn't return Gabler's message and he didn't respond to the proposal that Larry Buchanan had left with him. He made no contact with the Mozelles, Anna Hilburn, or any members of his investigative team. He left his laptop at his office and went back to Westport, where he didn't answer the home phone except when his grandfather called. He instructed Priscilla and Cecilia to do the same.

He dined out with his family one night and hauled out the barbecue on another, grilling fresh scallops en brochette—Priscilla's favorite. Priscilla now seemed to be in excellent spirits. She had been reinstated at Mt. Herman Academy—the Stockbridge police chief had informed Gordon Whitcombe that he would not be pursuing any charges against her—and she would be returning to boarding school at the end of the summer for her senior year. Montaro hoped that she had not tried to make any contact with Nick Corcell, but he knew better than to ask.

During the late nights and the early mornings, Montaro and Cecilia made love with uncharacteristic frequency and fervor, and Cecilia noted that her husband seemed calmer than he had in months, more so even than he had seemed in Carmel, and certainly more than before the whole fiasco with Fitzer and the Utah mining disaster.

"Then everything must be all right and there's nothing to worry about," Cecilia said hopefully late Saturday night as she rested in the arms of her husband.

"There never was," Montaro said, knowing full well that the one thing his wife always sought was reassurance. He was happy to provide her with it, even though he didn't seek it for himself. He simply knew that neither Gabler nor any of the others would attempt to contact him until their Chappaqua weekend was over, and that even Richard Davis would not make any move until that time. For the weekend, he could wait, be patient, and enjoy his life, knowing that events would unfold at their proper pace in the due course of time.

But when the weekend was over, everything changed as he had understood it would. The moment he arrived back at his office at Fitzer, his email inbox was flooded with messages, and before he even sat down at his desk, the phone began ringing. Montaro assumed that the person calling would be Gabler to ask about his coin or Julius Hargrove demanding a response to the proposal and asking if Montaro would join them, but he was surprised to learn that Kritzman Fritzbrauner was on the phone.

"Montaro, the mountain has finally come to Muhammad," Fritzbrauner said in his usual lofty tone. "What do you say to that?"

"I am nearly speechless, Mr. Mountain, and welcome is what say I," responded Caine, who felt a good deal more fondness for Fritzbrauner than for any of the others plotting against him. Though every bit a competitor, Fritzbrauner was an exceedingly cultured and well-mannered one. "I hope you're here for a while. I owe you a dinner, as I recall," said Montaro.

"I am on my way to Argentina for a few days, with my daughter, to visit her mother. But our plan has called for us to pass through New York, so I think that a dinner might be in order on our return. All's well with you?"

"Depends on the day, Kritzman; but so far so good."

"Glad to hear it. I am looking forward to picking up our last conversation, which was so suddenly interrupted."

"So 'rudely' interrupted would be more to the point," Caine said by way of an apology. "I hope that you have forgiven me for hanging up on you. I humbly ask that you chalk it up to a holdover from my socially impoverished youth. Now, about that dinner."

Caine made tentative plans to meet with Fritzbrauner but knew that he would have to postpone them the moment after Lawrence Aikens dropped by the Fitzer offices out of breath and unable to conceal his enthusiasm. By the look on his face, Caine understood that his chief investigator had important news to relate.

"You got something?" Caine asked.

"Think so." Aikens laid an unsealed envelope on Caine's desk before taking a seat across from him.

"What's in it?" Caine asked, gingerly fingering the envelope.

"A letter."

The letter was addressed to Frederick Carson, Whitney's uncle, but the return address was what caught Montaro's eye. It was a postal box in Alcala de Henarés, Spain. The name above the box number was Whitney C. Walker.

Montaro paused before taking the letter out of the envelope.

"Tampering with the mail is a felony," Caine told Aikens, who blanched, then smiled slightly.

"You're gonna turn Curly in?" asked Aikens. "I thought you told me I should be nicer to him."

Caine smiled slightly, then opened the envelope and took out a letter that Whitney had written to her uncle Fred. The letter, neatly handwritten in black ink, chastised her uncle for failing to respond to her previous letters. Whitney inquired after the health of various friends and family members, and she detailed the weariness she was feeling now that she was in the third trimester of her pregnancy. The letter contained little information of interest to Montaro until the last line: "And please, once again, don't tell anyone where we are. The work we're doing here is supposed to be top secret. Love to all, Whitney."

Caine looked up at Aikens.

"Where the hell is she, man?" Caine barked.

"Alcala de Henarés, Spain," Aikens said.

"Yeah, I can read envelopes, too," said Caine. "Where is that?"

"A small town outside Madrid," said Aikens. "I'm running checks on everything: whether there is or isn't a telephone or computer connection; who other than Whitney and Franklyn might be living there; also the name of the nearest hospital and whether she's been seeing any doctors there. And, of course, we're trying to pinpoint how often Cordiss and Victor fly in from San Remo and how long they stay."

"Well, you can forget about the computer and telephone," Caine said. "If Victor and Cordiss are doing their jobs right in keeping Whitney and Franklyn isolated, there won't be anything like that. They've probably been intercepting Whitney's mail, too; I'll bet that's why she thinks Uncle Frederick hasn't written her back. You'll have to find a way to get her to a telephone outside the house. If Cordiss Krinkle is with her, tell your contact people to be careful. She's very smart, as you well know, and we don't want her to move Whitney anywhere. It is absolutely essential that not even a hint of suspicion surfaces. All right, you better get on it."

"You got it," Lawrence Aikens said.

39

Montaro Caine was back in his Fitzer office, gazing out at the view of Manhattan that was largely shrouded in the fog of the approaching evening when Nancy MacDonald's voice crackled over his intercom: "I have Anna Hilburn on the line for you."

Montaro sprang to attention. Whatever disconnected, anxious thoughts had been coursing through his brain immediately vanished and were replaced by a heightened sense of urgency and duty.

"Put her through," said Montaro. Then, upon hearing the nurse's voice, he asked, "What is it, Anna?" From the sound of Hilburn's excited, out-of-breath voice, Montaro already had a pretty good idea of why she was calling him.

"I've got her on the phone," said Anna.

"Who? Whitney?" Caine asked.

"Yes, she's on now. From Spain. I'm trying to conference the doctor in, too. Are you still there? Are you listening?"

"I'm listening all right."

Apparently, someone had cut the wires to the house in Alcalá de Henares where Whitney and Franklyn were staying. But Lawrence Aikens's men had moved fast and, for the first time since Whitney Carson Walker and her husband had arrived in Europe, they were able to contact the world beyond their little Spanish village. Aikens had made arrangements for a Fitzer-owned jet to fly the Walkers back to New York with a team of doctors on board to monitor Whitney, since she was already well on her way through the third trimester of her pregnancy, when air travel was generally discouraged. But for all that to happen, Anna and Mozelle would have to convince Whitney and Franklyn that Cordiss Krinkle had been deceiving them all along.

Montaro heard a click, then for the first time he heard Whitney's voice—excited yet nervous, as if she hadn't spoken to anyone she knew in a long time. She seemed so young, so trusting, so naïve. She reminded Montaro of his daughter, at least how he had remembered his daughter from before she had gone to Mt. Herman and met Nick Corcell.

As she spoke, Whitney seemed to sense that she wasn't supposed to be speaking on the phone. "Are you still there, Anna?" she was asking.

"Yes, yes, I'm here," Anna said. "I'm just trying to get the doc on the line for you. He's in with a patient, but he'll be out any minute now. But where are you, Whitney? You said Spain? Where in Spain?"

"Outside Madrid," Whitney said. "How are you, Anna? I haven't seen you or heard your voice in so long! I haven't heard anyone's voice in so long. We've had such trouble with these phones and the Internet, too. Nothing works around here. How're you? How's your arthritis?"

"Fine, fine as I can be, Whitney," Anna said. Then, trying to keep Whitney focused on the matter at hand, she asked, "But Spain? What brought you there?"

"It's a long story, and we're alone now, but I don't know how long that will be, so I don't know if I'll have time to tell it."

"That's all right," said Anna. "Here's the doctor for you now. Doctor M? Whitney's on the phone, calling from Spain."

Just then, Montaro heard Howard Mozelle burst in, speaking loud and fast, trying to conceal his own excitement and anxiety. "Whitney? Is that you?" he asked.

"Yes, Dr. Mozelle, it's me."

"My, my, my. Whitney! Whitney! Whitney! For goodness sake! What is this I hear? Spain? What on earth are you doing over there, young lady?"

"I've been working on a project." Whitney sounded tight-lipped and evasive. Mozelle tried to put her at ease; his tone was friendly and paternal. *Gradually*, he and Montaro had told each other when they had planned for how they would handle this phone call; they would try to convince Whitney of the truth *gradually*. "Don't try to accomplish everything in one conversation," Montaro had advised. "Gain her trust." Mozelle knew that this was the right course of action, and yet, he couldn't help wanting to tell her everything he knew now, before the line was cut, or Cordiss showed up, or Whitney was called away.

"Well, we've been very worried about you, Whitney," Mozelle said. "We've been trying to reach you. We called Atlanta, New York, your uncle Fredrick."

"Why were you trying so hard to reach me?" Whitney asked.

"Well, you missed your annual checkup," he said. "So, how's the pregnancy going? Tell me about it—your feelings, your baby, your husband, all of it."

"I'm sorry I haven't stayed in touch, Doctor, but my life these last two years has been a bit of a mess, and almost all of it was my fault. Bad relationships, one right after the other, until—an amazing person came along. And he's right here beside me."

"Tell me, Whitney, how are you feeling at this moment?" Dr. Mozelle continued more pointedly.

"I'm not sure," she said.

"Something wrong?"

"I don't know, Doctor. It's hard to explain. Something just doesn't feel right. The baby's kicking, and, of course, I understand that's normal, yes?"

"Yes, yes, that's very good, in fact."

"But it seems like he's all over the place. And sometimes it hurts on one side, and I get little feelings as if he's trembling. Is that possible? Trembling? How normal is that?"

"Whitney," the doctor said calmly. "It's very hard for me to make any kind of diagnosis over the phone. But it sounds to me like that little person inside you is getting ready to make his entrance."

"This early?" asked Whitney.

"Could be. But I can't really be sure. Are you seeing a doctor over there?"

Whitney paused. A long silence ensued before Dr. Mozelle spoke again.

"You know, I'd really like to see you for an exam to make sure you're being properly taken care of. Are you returning to the States soon?"

Montaro could hear Whitney swallow. Then, he heard her mutter something to Franklyn. Franklyn muttered something back.

"Oh, I don't know," Whitney finally said. "Maybe in three weeks or so."

"And how long will your employment last all in all?"

"Five months, give or take," said Whitney.

"Give or take what?" Mozelle asked. And when Whitney didn't say anything, Mozelle said agitatedly, "You realize that the baby might well arrive before your employment is over."

More muttering on Whitney and Franklyn's end. More silence.

"Well, I certainly hope you are being well compensated for your work," Mozelle couldn't resist adding.

"Fifty thousand dollars, and all expenses paid," Whitney said proudly.

As he listened from the comfort and privacy of his own office, Montaro could understand how easy it had been for Cordiss to deceive Whitney. Montaro had wondered what he and Luther John Doe might have in common with Whitney Walker. Luther had said that they might just have been all honest people who trusted others and had the capacity to believe. That description seemed to fit Whitney Carson Walker almost too well.

"Forgive me," Dr. Mozelle told Whitney, "but I have to tell you something that might come as a shock." He paused again, wondering whether this was the time to reveal the truth; he sensed that this might be his only opportunity. It wouldn't take much effort for Cordiss to move Whitney and Franklyn somewhere else if she knew that Whitney had been in touch with him. Unable to hold back, Mozelle blurted out, "I think you should know that the two people you are working for, Cordiss Krinkle and that boyfriend of hers, that Victor Lambert, have already made millions by stealing something that has been in the care of my wife and myself since you were born. They brought you to Spain under false pretenses; they have misled you."

Whitney said nothing, so Mozelle continued, speaking as quickly as possible.

"Whitney," he said. "I don't believe you're getting proper medical care wherever you happen to be in Spain. Anna and I would like your child to be born in America. We would like to bring your child into this world just as we brought you into this world. Anna and I would like to bring your *son* into this world in the same hospital in which your mother delivered you. I have talked with my friend Montaro Caine, who is listening in on this conversation at this very moment. As soon as you say the word, Montaro will arrange to have a member of his security team meet you. That person will bring you to the airport in Madrid and take you back to America on a private plane with doctors on board. Time is short. So, the moment you understand that what I am telling you is true and that you want to do what I am advising you to do, you call me. Are you okay, Whitney?"

After a pause, Whitney said, stammering slightly. "Yes. Yes, Dr. Mozelle. Okay. But I think we have to get off the phone now."

"The moment you call us to tell us what you want to do, we'll take care of everything else," Mozelle said.

There was another long pause. Whitney didn't speak at first, but Mozelle and Caine could hear her breathing. Then she spoke. "What makes you think I'm having a son?" she asked. "Nobody told us that." But before Mozelle could speak, Whitney said, "I'm so sorry. I really do have to go now." And then she hung up.

"You there, Caine?" Mozelle asked Montaro.

"I sure as hell am here."

"Then you heard it all?"

"Every word."

"I didn't know how else to handle it, it was all so sudden. I lost my cool. I hope I didn't blow it. What do you think? Did I mess up?"

"You did beautifully!"

"I shouldn't have said all that. I shouldn't have gotten so angry. But I couldn't help it."

"Howard, I couldn't have done nearly as well. You hit all the right notes. Between now and tomorrow, both Whitney and Franklyn will have lots to think about. Waiting a day is all right. But tomorrow we must convince Whitney and her husband to return to America immediately. And in the meantime, let's hope that Cordiss Krinkle didn't take their passports."

Just a few minutes later, Whitney and Franklyn called back. Once again, Anna Hilburn answered, then conferenced in Mozelle and Montaro. This time, Franklyn was the one speaking.

"We don't need another day, Dr. Mozelle. We're ready now to do what you say."

"What made you decide so quickly?" asked Mozelle.

"When I heard what you said to Whitney, it was the first time that anybody said anything that made any kind of sense to me," said Franklyn. "From the time this whole thing started, I figured something wasn't right. Something just didn't set right with those two—Cordiss and Victor. And now I know I should have trusted my instincts. Plus, you know, we're still waiting to get our first check."

———

Whitney and Franklyn's departure from Alcala de Henarés went off without a hitch. As Caine had feared, Cordiss had hidden their passports. But Franklyn found them in a locked cabinet that he was able to pry open with a screwdriver. At a nearby gas station, they bought a phone card that allowed them to call Mozelle's office. Neither Cordiss nor Victor was on the scene when a hired car appeared outside the door of the safe house and whisked the Walkers to the Madrid-Barajas Airport. Cordiss and Victor were most probably now in Chappaqua with the rest of the others who were plotting to gain ownership of all the coins; or perhaps they had already learned that Whitney and Franklyn had been discovered, and they had cashed out their bank accounts. The millions they had earned so far would help them to stay out of sight in San Remo, Paris, or any other city they chose for as long a time as they wanted.

On board the Fitzer jet, Whitney experienced a sense of fluttering in her belly, but the baby did not arrive as early as Mozelle had feared it might. By the time she and Franklyn arrived at JFK Airport, Whitney's only symptoms were jet lag, ravenous hunger, and the gnawing ache she felt at being lied to, betrayed, and exploited by someone she'd thought was her friend. She felt afraid, too. She and Franklyn had no job, and they still owed back rent on their Atlanta apartment. Soon there would be a child. Diapers, clothing, food—it was all too overwhelming to consider.

When the Walkers were in the examination room at the Mozelle Women's Health Center, Franklyn looked on lovingly at his wife's belly as Anna Hilburn drew Whitney's blood, took an ultrasound, and checked her heart, arteries, and other internal organs. Whitney felt at ease in Anna and Dr. Mozelle's presence—in Spain, she had been checked by two different doctors, neither of whom spoke much English. Dr. Mozelle declared Whitney to be in excellent health. Her anxieties, in both the doctor and his nurse's view, were the results of life changes that had come galloping her way before the light of her own experience was bright enough to illuminate the pitfalls that lined the roadways of her life. But, Howard Mozelle thought, they might also be the result of something unknown that would surface upon the birth of Whitney's child.

"How much longer do you think it will be?" Whitney asked the doctor as she got up from the examination table.

"About a week, no longer," said the doctor turning to Anna. "Are you of the same opinion?"

"Yes," said Anna. "A week. Probably less."

Whitney Walker hugged her husband tightly.

"Just one week," Whitney said. Tears flowed from her eyes as Franklyn held her close.

40

I T WAS TO BE A STRANGE SORT OF BIRTH, QUITE POSSIBLY THE strangest in the history of Mount Sinai Hospital, where Dr. Howard Mozelle had enjoyed professional privileges in the obstetrics ward for nearly thirty years. During the course of his career, he had overseen hundreds of births in these delivery rooms. He had delivered babies in rooms full of friends and family, and alongside countless midwives and doulas. Yet in his experience, at the very moment of birth, what couples sought more than anything was privacy and solitude and the illusion that the rest of the hospital was empty, that theirs was the only family in the world. Everything else was a needless distraction.

After a child was born, Mozelle tried to send parents home with their new babies as soon as it was medically permissible—not because he wanted to cut down on costs, but because he knew that, no matter how hard he tried, a hospital would always be an unnatural sort of place. He wanted his patients to leave behind the drugs, the machines, and the medical implements, and get on with the business of becoming a stronger family. He deeply believed that a birth was a profound, private event, which should have as little interference as possible from anyone aside from the family members and their doctor. Part of him wished that Whitney Carson Walker could have the same intimate experience with her husband that Whitney's mother had had. And yet he knew all too well that this would be impossible. The birth of Whitney and Franklyn's child was to be a monumental occasion—anything but a private, family affair. Lawyers were involved now, businesspeople, investors. The birth was to be videotaped so that all would be able to see how many coins would be found in the hands of Whitney and Franklyn's child.

With the assistance of Dr. Mozelle, Montaro Caine had arranged to hold a meeting in a conference room in Mount Sinai on the floor below the obstetrics ward. There, he hoped, the issue of ownership of the coins that already existed and those that would soon materialize would be decided once and for all or rendered moot. Though the whereabouts of both coins were still unknown, all parties sensed that they would reappear at some point, and everything needed to be worked out in advance of that occurrence. Nancy MacDonald, on Caine's instructions, had sent invitations to just about everyone associated with the story of the Walkers and the coins—including Luther John Doe and Thomas Lund, Carrie Pittman and Hattie Sinclair; he had even instructed Nancy to send an invitation to a certain Bahamian island in care of Matthew Perch, a man whose dwelling had no known address.

Invitations had been sent to both Caine's allies and his foes. Caine had invited Michael Chasman and Richard Walmeyer, and he had invited Richard Davis and Roland Gabler. He had invited his opponents' lawyer Julius Hargrove, and he had invited his own lawyer Gordon Whitcombe. He had invited those whose allegiances still seemed uncertain to him—Kritzman Fritzbrauner, Colette Beekman, and Herman Freich. Whitney's uncle, the Walkers' only living relative, received an invitation as well, although he was too ill to make the trip from Brooklyn. Along with the invitations that his secretary had sent, Caine had included a letter that expressed how important it was for everyone to work together to solve, or even better, to look beyond the issue of ownership. He had stressed the fact that this birth was a matter far more important than how much money the coins might be worth and who might ultimately be entitled to what. He hoped that the birth could bring all sides together as opposed to driving them further apart. He said in his letter that he wanted everyone to be on hand at the hospital when Whitney and Franklyn's child was born. And just about everyone on Caine's invitation list had said yes with the exception of Whitney's uncle and Matthew Perch, who had not yet responded to Caine's invitation. By the time Whitney's water broke, Caine figured that he would most probably not hear from Perch at all.

Whitney had trusted Dr. Mozelle when he told her of the necessity for all these strangers to be in the hospital on the occasion of her child's birth, while Franklyn remained suspicious. And yet, after Dr. Mozelle had explained the story of the coins to the couple, apologizing that he hadn't told them earlier, both understood that the matter, though nearly impossible for them to fully grasp, was beyond their control. They agreed to the videotaping of the birth and everything else Caine and Mozelle had proposed.

The morning Whitney went into labor, the blinds in Whitney's hospital room were drawn and the light was dim. Red lights from the video cameras that were positioned around the room were visible, yet the cameras made no sounds. Whitney lay in her hospital bed, while Franklyn stood beside it, holding one of her hands as Anna Hilburn held the other. Every so often, a tremor would course through Whitney's body. Whitney would wince at the sudden, rolling pain, but whenever the doctor asked if she wanted medicine, she waved him off and shook her head.

"Breathe easy," Anna Hilburn told her patient. "Breathe."

In the birthing room, there was a sense that something miraculous and otherworldly was taking place, and yet, there was nothing particularly unusual about this. Even after so many years, Anna Hilburn and Howard Mozelle still found every birth to be a miracle, the transporting of a small, living being from one world into another.

Another pain stabbed through Whitney's body and she clutched Franklyn's hand so hard, it seemed to him as if his wedding ring might just break off his finger at the knuckle. Franklyn shut his eyes and clenched his teeth while Whitney cried out, emitting a loud, low sound that seemed to come from deep within her.

"Push, child," Anna said softly to Whitney. "It's almost time."

Anna knew that the baby would be born in moments—she didn't have to look at Whitney to know this. The baby was announcing its entrance, and it didn't have to say a word.

One floor below, the Mt. Sinai conference room was a different world entirely. Everyone at the four conference tables had arranged themselves into configurations that represented their apparent allegiances. At one table sat Kritzman Fritzbrauner, his daughter Colette, Herman Freich, Verna Fontaine, Roland Gabler, and their lawyer Julius Hargrove. Hargrove was a stout, broad-shouldered man with more hair on his knuckles than on his head, and he looked every bit the part of one of New York's most-feared attorneys. At another table sat more attorneys from Hargrove's firm. To Caine, the most conspicuous aspect of that table was not who was sitting at it but who wasn't—his old friend Larry Buchanan, who still wasn't in these lawyers' echelon. At Caine's own table sat his family's lawyer, Gordon Whitcombe, Elsen Mozelle, and four empty chairs, which would have been occupied by Anna Hilburn, Howard Mozelle, and Whitney and Franklyn Walker, had they not been busy on the floor above. And at the last table sat Luther John Doe, his caretaker, Tom Lund, Carrie Pittman, Richard Walmeyer, Michael Chasman, and Hattie Sinclair.

At the center of the room stood Montaro Caine. For him, the road to this day seemed to have begun forty-six years earlier when his father had died, but in fact, it had started even earlier than that, perhaps months before Dr. Robert Caine's arrival in New York, when Luther John Doe had carved a model of a ship for a boy he had never met. Or perhaps it had begun hundreds of thousands of years before that, when the Seventh Ship had journeyed from its dying world into space in search of a planet whose sun would not die so soon. That model that Luther had carved was now in Montaro's jacket pocket.

As an eight-year-old child, Montaro could not have had any idea of the significance Robert Caine's death would have on the world around him, only the impact that tragic death had on his own tiny world and that of his mother and his grandfather. Now he understood that, from the moment Robert Caine had died in that airplane crash outside Kansas City, his father's life and his untimely passing had led everyone in this room to this particular moment, intertwining all of their fates. Even the future of Montaro's company seemed to lie in the hands of two babies born twenty-six years ago, and in the hands of their baby who was busy being born upstairs.

Though at this moment he stood alone, Montaro took strength from those around him, from the living and from the dead. He took strength from the confidence his wife and daughter still had in him; he took strength from the examples his parents had set; and he took strength from the words that P. L. Caine had spoken to him when he was a boy, and again when he was a man: "A man has to stand up to hard times no matter what." No matter how hard these times may have been, Montaro was standing firmly and he felt strong. Not long ago, he might have needed a drink to steady his resolve. Even more recently, he might have felt exhausted and wanted nothing more than a few hours of peaceful sleep. Now, he felt as awake and alert as he ever had.

The conference room was abuzz with nervous anticipation. The lawyers and executives at Julius Hargrove's table were discussing percentages, fees, and technical definitions of ownership. Those at Montaro's table were speculating about what Howard Mozelle might find when Whitney's child was born. One coin? Two? Coins similar to the ones that they had already seen? Different coins entirely? Ones depicting new celestial configurations? Montaro's own mind was swirling with the words he planned to use to address the room. But the moment he cleared his throat and made as if to speak, a deadly quiet took possession of the room. He thought that everybody was looking at him, but in fact, nobody was.

Instead, everyone in the room had turned to focus on the conference room's revolving door, which had begun to turn as if of its own accord. Standing in the doorway, there appeared a tall, lean black man. He seemed to be in his middle years, with a still handsome face and salt-and-pepper hair.

Several audible gasps were heard as the man took a few steps into the room, then looked around, his eyes resting for a moment on each of the four tables. Tears streamed down Hattie Sinclair's and Elsen Mozelle's cheeks, and they caught each other's eyes across the tables. Though decades had passed, the man's face appeared little changed.

Montaro immediately knew who the man was; yes, some things you could know without ever having been told.

For his part, Julius Hargrove looked on suspiciously. Though he had not called the meeting and was not in charge of the agenda, he was used to being in control. Since no one else had spoken to the self-possessed, dark-skinned stranger in their midst, Hargrove stood up and looked around at the other tables, then gestured toward the man and approached him. "Sir," he said, "are you an invited guest, or an employee of the hospital?"

The man took his time before answering. "I believe I have been invited," he finally said. "But no, I'm not an employee. I am here as an observer. I am here to see, to listen, and to remember."

"Are you with the press?" Hargrove asked.

"No, I am not," the man answered, at which point Elsen Mozelle stood.

"Mr. Hargrove," Elsen said as she wiped her eyes. "This gentleman is very well known to me and also to Hattie Sinclair."

"Who is he?" Hargrove asked. "What's your name?"

"Matthew Perch," the man replied.

Hargrove smiled, and yet his smile was neither kind nor welcoming. "Ah, you're the elusive Mr. Perch," he said. "You're the one who cures cancer with bush medicine. We hear that you are a miracle worker in that regard. You are indeed welcome here, Mr. Perch. Your reputation precedes you. My apology to you. Please take a seat."

But Perch remained standing, and then, after surveying the scene, seeming to diagnose it as he would a patient, he turned and began to move toward the revolving door. Hargrove followed Perch through that door and out into the main hallway. For a man of his age, Hargrove moved quickly but not quickly enough. He had to shout to make himself heard: "Mr. Perch, a word or two with you."

Matthew Perch slowed his pace but did not stop.

"Sir," Hargrove said when he had finally caught up to Perch, "my firm is here as part of Mr. Fritzbrauner's, Mr. Davis's, and Mr. Gabler's legal representation. We are here to fashion a fair and just resolution as to who, among the people present today, are the true owners of the items at the center of this complex issue; who, in light of the laws of the United States, are the legal owner, or owners, of the two coins in question. I am sure you are aware of the coins I'm referring to."

But all that Hargrove was saying seemed to sound like inconsequential gibberish to Perch, who stopped for only a moment before raising his hand to silence the lawyer. "I am going to the delivery room," he said. "I don't think it would be wise for you to follow me there."

Hargrove had always known that his success in corporate law was largely attributable to his ability to read both his clients and their opponents in the world of industry. But now, a warning sign rattled within him. He instantly understood that Perch might be a man he could not read.

"No," Hargrove answered, his voice now significantly quieter and less self-assured. "You are right, of course."

"Good," said Perch. "You can raise whatever issues you wish upon my return."

Upstairs, Matthew Perch entered the delivery room unseen. Whitney was pushing hard as her husband held her hand, while Anna Hilburn reached for the baby, whose head of slick black hair was now clearly visible.

"He's crowning," said Anna, and Whitney gave a throaty moan that seemed to make the whole room vibrate. When Whitney closed her eyes tight to fend off the pain, she saw swirling colors and shapes, a spectacular, private display. At the foot of the hospital bed stood Dr. Mozelle, who caught a glimpse of Perch—he stood there as if he had always been there, as if he had never left, as if he was standing where he had always belonged. The men shared a silent nod of recognition as Whitney gave another strong push accompanied by yet another, even louder, deeper moan.

Franklyn gently placed a cool towel on his wife's forehead while Dr. Mozelle moved closer to his patient.

"There you are," said Mozelle as he saw the baby's head. "Whitney, you're almost there."

"Breathe, honey," said Franklyn. He gave his wife his hand again and she squeezed it gently, then harder.

"Ready, honey?" Franklyn asked.

Whitney managed a small smile. Yes, she was ready. She gave another push.

And now, the baby slid out of her body—a slippery boy with a mass of dark curls upon his head. When Franklyn cut the umbilical cord, Whitney trembled and cried, a cry that turned into happy laughter as she watched Anna Hilburn wrap the baby in a clean white towel. Tears appeared in Franklyn's eyes as Anna handed the baby to Franklyn, who brought the baby to his wife. Whitney grasped the bundle and clutched it to her chest.

The new parents beamed at each other, both of them crying now. They had no consciousness of Dr. Mozelle or Anna Hilburn or of Matthew Perch standing before them. They seemed to have forgotten the cameras in the room and the conference room full of people one floor below. Franklyn sat at the edge of the bed with his arm around Whitney. She rested her head on his shoulder. They both smiled at their first child, his tiny eyes closed.

Then, the baby opened his eyes. He squirmed underneath his swaddling blanket, and as he did, Whitney understood that he was trying to do something; he was trying to open his hands.

41

Downstairs in the conference room, the lunch plates had been cleared, coffee was being served, and Julius Hargrove was standing at the podium, speaking of the coins that had disappeared from Kritzman Fritzbrauner's and Roland Gabler's possession. Directing his remarks toward the table where Montaro Caine was seated, Hargrove said he hoped that whoever had removed the coins from the safes would now return them to their rightful owners; then a discussion could begin regarding how an agreement about shared ownership could be reached. Hargrove discussed what Caine's diminished role might consist of in a restructured Fitzer Corporation led by Richard Davis. He emphasized the fact that, despite Montaro's industrial and scientific expertise and his years of leading the company, Davis's extensive experience in management and finance would be indispensable when it came to exploiting the properties of the coins. But midway through that thought, Hargrove noticed that everyone had stopped listening to him. All eyes were focused on the conference room's revolving door.

Hargrove turned to see Howard Mozelle and Matthew Perch re-entering the room. Mozelle, dressed in the suit that he had worn under his scrubs, seemed deep in thought.

"Well, Doctor?" Hargrove asked simply, "How did it go?"

Mozelle stood silent for a moment, then approached Hargrove at the podium. "Exactly as I had hoped," he said, speaking specifically to Hargrove but loudly enough so that the people gathered at the tables could hear. "Mother and child are doing well. Anna's taking care of them."

Hargrove proceeded to interrogate the doctor as Matthew Perch looked on impassively. "Can you tell us if there was anything surprising or unusual about the extremities of the baby—its arms, its legs, its hands?"

"What, in your view, would be surprising or unusual?" asked Mozelle.

"An object in one of the child's hands, for instance, perhaps a coin," said Hargrove.

"Well," replied Mozelle, "then I would say that there was something surprising but nothing unusual."

"What was in the baby's hands?" Hargrove asked.

"Nothing at all," said Mozelle.

Murmurs of disbelief were heard throughout the conference room. Fritzbrauner and Gabler looked at each other, the former puzzled, the latter suspicious. Richard Davis loudly cleared his throat. Colette Beekman appeared to tremble. Several men at one of Hargrove's tables stood up. Surprise registered on just about everyone's face, save for those of Tom Lund, Luther John Doe, and Montaro Caine, who had endured so much in these last months that little could surprise him anymore.

"The baby opened his eyes," said Mozelle. "Then he opened his little hands. I thought one or two coins would fall out, but nothing did."

"Then what in the world was he doing when he opened his hands?" asked Hargrove.

Matthew Perch stepped forward. "He was reaching out to his mother and father," he said. "As any newborn child would."

"It was all filmed as we agreed," said Mozelle. "You'll be able to see for yourself."

"No coins?" Hargrove asked.

"None," said Perch.

"Nothing unusual, you say?"

"Miraculous, yes. But no, nothing unusual."

Hargrove now seemed more curious than combative; even he could not resist the commanding, hypnotic presence of Matthew Perch. "But do you have any idea why?" he asked. "We all assumed...Everybody here, we had all been told..."

"Because there is no need for coins anymore," Perch said, interrupting. "The first coins already did the work they were needed for."

"What work was that?" asked Hargrove.

"They brought Whitney Carson and Franklyn Walker together, and then they brought all of you together," said Perch. "The child is always the miracle, not any object it was or wasn't holding. The first coins were brought here by the remnants of a dying civilization, one many light-years away from this one. The coins could have appeared in the hands of any of a number of human beings, but they appeared to Franklyn and Whitney, who, as they have grown up, have proven why they were chosen—for their honesty, their decency, their openness, their ability to believe. These are among the qualities that allow a species to survive. These coins were given to Whitney and Franklyn to show all of you the way forward. All of you have been waiting for something physical to happen, something you can see with your own eyes, but perhaps the most important thing that the coins have brought is something that's inside of you. The knowledge contained within the coins, if it is used properly, can save this planet's inhabitants from dying out one day too, can keep it from suffering the same fate that the travelers on the Seventh Ship journeyed all this distance to escape."

Silence ensued. Hargrove considered what Perch said, weighing its improbability against the certainty with which it had been said. Now, when Hargrove spoke, his tone was noticeably softer. "What happened to the other coins? The ones Whitney and Franklyn were born holding? The ones my clients purchased?" he asked.

"I believe Montaro Caine can help you answer that question as well as I can," said Perch.

Montaro looked back at Perch, at first uncertain of the man's meaning. When Montaro had first met Tom Lund, he had asked him about Perch. He now remembered Lund's response. Lund had said that he didn't know Perch, but, he added, when Montaro did meet him, he "should look him right in the eye and let him see who it is that you really are. He will not be able to see who you are without letting you see who he is."

As he looked Matthew Perch straight in the eye, as Lund had counseled, Montaro saw a man whose kindness and self-assurance reminded him very much of his own father. And it was at this moment, when Montaro was remembering the smile on his father's face, the gentleness of Robert Caine's touch, the depth of the man's brilliance and his capacity for understanding, that he felt something faintly vibrating in the pocket of his blazer and he began to understand why Perch was staring at him so expectantly. Montaro reached inside and felt the small flannel bag that contained the model Luther John Doe had carved of the Seventh Ship. He took the bag out of his pocket, and when he looked up, he saw that Luther was staring straight back at him. Caine turned to Matthew Perch, who in turn looked to Luther.

Caine walked toward the podium. "If you please," he said. "There is someone here I'd like all of you to meet. Some of you here are familiar with him and his story. His name is Luther John Doe. Luther, would you mind joining me up here?"

Luther nodded cautiously. He stood and moved slowly toward the front of the room, accompanied by the bullish and somewhat stocky orderly who had accompanied him on the trip to Manhattan. Luther's physical condition seemed to have deteriorated even since Caine had seen him. The severe deformity of his hip and right leg made it all but impossible for him to maintain even the slightest degree of balance without his aide's help. When Luther had taken his place beside Caine, he rested one hand upon the podium, using it for support.

"Do you know why you're here, Luther?" Caine asked.

Bewilderment gathered on Luther's face and a touch of panic seemed to seize his body. "I'm here because you and Dr. Mozelle sent me an invitation. You know that," he said.

"That's true enough," said Montaro with a gentle smile. "Well, then tell me this. How do you feel about being here?"

A long pause held while Luther appeared to examine his feelings.

"I guess I feel important being here, with all these important people," he finally said.

"Surprised?" Caine asked.

Luther shook his head. "No, not surprised. I always imagined I'd wind up in a place like this."

"You foresaw it?"

"I guess you could say that."

"Well, do you think anything in particular now that you're in this place and you look around and see yourself in the midst of all these important folks?"

Luther surveyed the crowd. "Well," he said, "I think everyone in this room must have done something in their lives that has led them to this particular place on this particular day. That's what I think. I also think that this may be the end of the line for some of us. I know that's true for me. I've lived with some pretty strange experiences, but I don't think I can carry them around with me very much further. I've done my part, served my purpose."

"What was that purpose, Luther?"

"To carve the model of the Seventh Ship out of the vision I saw, and to send it to you, Mr. Caine, by way of your father. To this day, I can't tell you why I carved it, or how I knew to give it to your father. Or even how I knew that your father had a son. I just knew that I was supposed to do it. And I knew that a day would come when others would seek me out. I couldn't have carved it without the help of my friend Tom Lund—he's sitting right there. He's the one who taught me about the sun, the solar system, galaxies, the universe, all that I could see in my mind when I pictured the Seventh Ship and how it traveled through space to get here."

Montaro opened his hand to reveal the bag that contained the model of the Seventh Ship. He slipped out the model and held it in the palm of his hand where it continued to vibrate.

"This is what you carved for me?" Caine asked. "When I was just a boy?"

"That's the one," said Luther. "I gave it to your father. I made it for his son."

"Thank you, Luther," said Caine. He held out his hand to Luther and the two men embraced before Luther and his caretaker headed back to sit by Tom Lund.

The vibrations from the Seventh Ship were growing more intense and Caine, like Luther, could also sense that he had been led to this moment, that whatever his purpose was in life, it had something to do with holding this wooden model that Luther had carved. He could see Perch moving toward him, one hand extended. As if he already knew what to do and what was expected of him, Caine passed the model to Perch, who then walked over to Luther. The two men stared at each other, and as they did, they seemed to share an understanding. Perch smiled. Luther smiled back and his eyelids fluttered slightly. "Soon, it will be time," Perch said softly.

Luther nodded. His smile widened. "Yes, I know," he said.

Perch held the model in the palm of his left hand, then walked around the tables, showing it to everyone seated in the room. Gradually, the object began to quiver. Perch placed the carving of the Seventh Ship gently on the table in front of Richard Davis.

The carving of the Seventh Ship continued its low vibration. Then Colette, whose face thus far had been a mask of conflicting emotions and allegiances, shouted "Oh! *Mon dieu! Regard ça!*" The carving slowly began to open, almost as though it were about to give birth. Colette drew back, while her father, Roland Gabler, and the others at her table leaned in for a better view. Hargrove walked over to observe as well. The carving's vibrations continued to intensify, causing the object to float upward in a swirling motion, first in one direction, then in another. It hovered in midair for several seconds, then gently descended to a different place on the surface of the table, where it continued to open. Inside the model were the two coins, lying in spaces that appeared to have been designed specifically to receive them. Shock registered on the faces of both Fritzbrauner and Gabler. Colette's face was pale. Hargrove, agitated, was the first to speak.

"What's the meaning of this, Caine? Have you gathered us here for some kind of laser light show? What kind of trick is this?"

"Not a trick," Caine said, speaking almost in a whisper. "This is not magic. This is not make-believe. This is real. This is what I experienced myself. I do believe that this man, Matthew Perch, and these coins are in touch with a reality far beyond our understanding. I believe that these coins represent a level of science completely unknown to us. And after listening to what Matthew Perch has said, I believe that they contain a message. A warning? A friendly gesture? An opportunity? I can't say for sure, but I feel that within these coins are answers to questions that humans have been posing ever since we had the capacity to ask them: How many other civilizations are out there? How advanced are they? Are there so many that they cannot be counted? Or are we the only ones left in this vast galaxy, this big universe with billions of galaxies?

"One day, perhaps soon, perhaps in a far distant time, our science will come to understand the mysteries embedded in these coins. In them might very well be the history of a civilization, a culture, a language, a people—all waiting in limbo, while the majestic results of their science roam this awesome galaxy in search of a solar system that might contain one planet that will allow them to survive.

"It is my opinion," he continued, now directing his remarks specifically to Julius Hargrove, "that we are not here to negotiate; we are here to learn, regardless of property rights, ego, or greed. May I suggest that all of you put aside your suspicions and open your mind to possibilities?"

As soon as Montaro Caine stopped speaking, the others in the room began talking, interrupting each other, speaking louder to make themselves heard.

"First of all, I'm interested in learning how my property could have possibly left my vault and wound up in that thing," said Roland Gabler.

"I would like to know that as well," Fritzbrauner chimed in.

"You're the sorcerer here, Mr. Perch. You're the man with all the answers, right?" Julius Hargrove said.

Hattie Sinclair rose to her feet. "How dare you?" she demanded as Elsen Mozelle came over and took the woman's hand in hers. "You don't even know this man. This man saved my life. He saved hers, too. When you insult him, you insult me. And I won't have it."

"Neither will I," said Elsen Mozelle, whereupon Carrie Pittman stood.

"I know babies. I've brought hundreds of them into this world," Pittman said, pointing to the coins resting in the Seventh Ship. "I brought one of those into this world in the hand of one of my babies. That was God's work, God's doing."

"It is destiny that has brought us together. *Destiny,*" Caine said, trying to regain control of the meeting. "The Seventh Ship, the coins, all of us. That's what Matthew Perch has told us. It's our responsibility to explore what lies before us, to honor that destiny. The coins belong to no one. Not to me, not to you, not to anybody. There is no boundary that can hold them if they decide not to be held. Kritzman's vault couldn't hold them, Roland Gabler's vault couldn't hold them either."

When the confusion and the arguments finally subsided, fading into mutters, then silence, Julius Hargrove turned his attention to Matthew Perch; once again, he was an attorney, questioning a witness as if before a packed courtroom. "Mr. Perch," he said. "Who, in your opinion, owns these coins?"

Perch did not pause before he answered. "No one does," he said.

"No one?" asked Hargrove.

"That is the truth," said Perch. "And truth is all there is."

"Then who will determine their fate?"

"Those who helped to bring them into this world."

"Are you speaking of yourself, Mr. Perch?" Hargrove asked.

"No," said Perch. "I speak of Whitney and Franklyn Walker. Nothing can be decided in their absence."

Perch cast his eyes upward, almost as if he could see through the ceiling into the delivery room on the floor above where the Walkers were resting with their newborn child. And then he looked down again and reached out a hand to Luther John Doe, who took a deep breath and rose to his feet. Though Perch said nothing, his meaning seemed clear—in the room above, one being had entered this world; here in this room, one being was preparing to leave it. No one was looking at the model of the Seventh Ship as its doors began to close.

42

A WEEK LATER, MONTARO CAINE HOSTED A DINNER IN A PRIVATE room at the back of the Beaumont restaurant. Only Tom Lund, Luther John Doe, and Luther's caretaker were missing from the group that had gathered in the hospital for the baby's birth. The Beaumont was a dining establishment so opulent that when Franklyn Walker entered the room of gilded frames and glittering chandeliers with his wife and their sleeping, as yet unnamed, newborn son, whom Whitney was wheeling in a carriage, he muttered that he felt as if he were entering the Palace of Versailles.

Julius Hargrove and his team of attorneys were seated at one table with Kritzman Fritzbrauner, Colette Beekman, Richard Davis, Verna Fontaine, and Roland Gabler. At Montaro's table sat Howard and Elsen Mozelle, Anna Hilburn, Gordon Whitcombe, and Franklyn and Whitney Walker. The only individual who did not sit at either table was Matthew Perch. Dressed in a clean but simple white shirt and dark pants, he sat alone in a corner, observing the proceedings. He ate nothing and drank only ice water. In his pocket, the two coins were wrapped in gauze, awaiting their final destination.

In hosting the dinner, Montaro was finally making good on the promise he had made to Kritzman Fritzbrauner—that he would treat him to a dining experience that would match the one he had enjoyed at Fritzbrauner's Swiss estate. And, to Montaro's mind, this was the loveliest restaurant in all of Manhattan, one where he had celebrated just about every important occasion with his family—his appointment to the position of CEO at Fitzer; his wedding anniversaries; his daughter's eighth-grade graduation; P. L. Caine's eighty-fifth, ninetieth, and ninety-fifth birthdays. Perhaps his one-hundredth would be celebrated here next year. The Beaumont's chefs had prepared a twelve-course meal, but food was hardly the most important item on the menu. After the final course, negotiations that could well determine the fate of the coins and Fitzer Corporation were set to begin.

As they sat in the Beaumont dining room, still dazed by all that had happened and all they had learned over the past weeks, Whitney and Franklyn understood that they now had a vital role to play in deciding the fate of the coins. The responsibility was great, yet perhaps hardly greater than the responsibility they now felt toward the baby they had just brought into the world. Whitney felt overwhelmed, while Franklyn still remained skeptical.

Toward the end of the magnificent meal, Montaro stood to propose a toast. "Kritzman Fritzbrauner, I raise my glass to you," he said, holding his wineglass aloft. He gestured to Howard to hold up his glass as well. "Howard and I greatly enjoyed the sumptuous dinner at your home, and this setting is as close as we can come to replicating its elegance. We each raise our glass to you and to the better self you see in the mirror of your mind. Know that our toast comes from the better selves we all see ourselves to be in the mirrors of our own minds. We salute you and your beautiful daughter, Colette."

Colette Beekman Fritzbrauner's face flushed and she felt the same familiar yet indefinable rush of emotion she seemed to sense whenever she was in the same room as Montaro. Kritzman Fritzbrauner looked proudly upon his daughter, but she did not meet his gaze before he stood and extended his glass toward Caine and Mozelle.

"Montaro," Fritzbrauner said, "thank you for those very kind words. Montaro and Howard's presence at my house made for a most enlightening evening. I invited a number of erudite friends who were steeped in science, philosophy, and history and had more than a passing familiarity with cosmology. They all tried their best to stump

Montaro, only to discover how truly well rounded he is, not only in the corporate world, but also in the arts and sciences. You will not be forgotten by those guys anytime soon, Montaro. I drink to your health as well."

As Fritzbrauner sat and Montaro prepared to continue his speech, a tuxedoed and somewhat flustered maître d' entered the dining room and approached Montaro.

"Mr. Caine," the maître d' said in a hushed voice. "I am sorry to interrupt, but there are some people who wish to join your party."

"By all means, show them in," Montaro said; he had, in fact, instructed the Beaumont's staff to tell him when Tom Lund and Luther John Doe arrived, and he was pleased that Luther, whom he had arranged to have stay in a nearby hotel with Tom, was feeling well enough to attend. But when the maître d' reentered the room, he was accompanied by Cordiss Krinkle and Victor Lambert. Montaro had never seen Cordiss or Victor before and, from the descriptions he had been given, he would not have recognized them—they wore dark, conservative clothes and Cordiss's hair was pulled back in a severe bun. But from the reactions on the faces of those who knew Cordiss and Victor, Montaro understood exactly who they were.

Whitney's hands reflexively flew up to cover her face; a cry emerged from her lips as she remembered the time that she and Franklyn had spent in Alcala de Henarés, essentially imprisoned there. Franklyn felt a surge of anger when he saw the look on his wife's face. Everyone remained still as they watched Cordiss and Victor move to the center of the room.

Julius Hargrove addressed his remarks to Cordiss; he alone seemed unsurprised by her appearance. "You have something you wish to say?" he asked, prodding her to speak. Cordiss nodded uncertainly, then moved forward a few hesitant paces. As Victor held her hand, she cleared her throat; when she spoke, her voice barely rose above a whisper. She did not seem to be pissing ice water now.

"We apologize for interrupting your dinner," she said haltingly. "We only wish to say something to all of you, and then we will be on our way."

Cordiss looked to Hargrove, then to Montaro. But as she looked to the Walkers and tried to catch Whitney's eye, she saw only Franklyn's stern and unforgiving glare. Cordiss took a deep breath.

"We have wronged some of you," she said. "We have stolen from some of you and sold what we stole to others in this room. We are here to try to make restitution, to the extent that we can. For having wronged you and broken your trust, we apologize. We will pay back every penny of the money we received. We know who the coins truly belong to. I stole the first coin from Dr. Mozelle's office; that one rightfully belonged to you, Whitney."

Whitney could not bring herself to look at Cordiss, whose voice buckled as her eyes drifted downward. Cordiss made as if to speak further, but her voice caught in her throat. She turned to Victor, who finished her thought.

"The second act of theft was my doing. It was not my first, but I hope it will be my last," said Victor. "The victim was that lady sitting there." He pointed to Carrie Pittman. "We took advantage of you, Miss Pittman. I'm sorry and ashamed. We are both deeply ashamed for what we have done. From this moment on, we will try to make it right."

Cordiss and Victor stood quietly; they seemed to be expecting punishment or forgiveness, but neither came immediately. For her part, Carrie Pittman assumed that Victor and Cordiss must have heard the voice of God urging them to mend their ways. Some of Hargrove, Hastings and Dundas's attorneys figured that Victor and Cordiss were merely being practical and trying to avoid criminal charges. Montaro briefly considered whether some otherworldly event had occurred, something akin to the display he had witnessed when the model of the Seventh Ship opened and caused him to view the world and his place in it in a different light. But when Montaro looked to Matthew Perch for confirmation, Perch showed no reaction. Franklyn remained dubious; he refused to be conned again.

Hargrove stepped toward Cordiss. "I think I speak for everyone when I say that I thank you for those remarks, Ms. Krinkle," he said. "But may I be so bold as to ask what has led to you to this, shall we say, sudden conversion?"

"You can," said Cordiss slowly, as if trying to regain her composure. "But I don't think that many of you will believe me, or that you will forgive me. After all, I still have not been able to forgive myself."

Again, Cordiss looked to Whitney, but Whitney was still looking down; her husband's arms were wrapped around her.

"Well, what is it?" Hargrove asked Cordiss. "What miraculous event has happened?"

Cordiss squeezed Victor's hand tightly, but when she spoke, her voice was so soft that Hargrove had to ask her to repeat herself.

"What's that?" Hargrove asked. "What did you say?"

"I'm pregnant," Cordiss said, speaking through her tears, "and I couldn't bear the idea of raising a child who would profit from our crimes and our dishonesty. Neither of us wants that to be our child's inheritance."

At first, no one spoke. Everyone remained seated, almost frozen in their positions. Then, Whitney rose from her chair.

"Oh, Cordiss." Whitney's voice trembled. Whitney made as if to walk forward. But Franklyn grabbed her hand and eased her back down into her chair.

"No," he said kindly but firmly to his wife. "Not again." He would not allow Cordiss to abuse his and Whitney's trust anymore. He wasn't certain of Cordiss's motivations—whether she was working for Hargrove or for some other men in the room, or whether, as usual, she was merely out for herself. Whatever the case may have been, he didn't buy Cordiss's remorse or the story of her pregnancy. It seemed too convenient. His instincts told him that her speech had been staged for his and Whitney's benefit, to win their favor and somehow gain control of their lives—and the coins—again. When Cordiss and Victor humbly excused themselves from the room and Hargrove moved to the center of the room as if on cue to take their place, Franklyn felt certain that his suspicions had been correct.

"Well," said Hargrove, facing the Walkers as if he were wrapping up a case, "let me get to the crux of this matter. My clients have instructed me to make you an offer on their behalf—five million dollars for each of the items that you, Mr. and Mrs. Walker, are presumed to have legal rights to. We urge you to consider this offer."

Whitney and Franklyn looked at each other, hardly able to comprehend the amount of money that was being discussed. Franklyn turned to Gordon Whitcombe, who was sitting beside him. "What the hell does all this mean?" he asked.

Whitcombe stared back at Franklyn. "I don't know what it means, Frank, but, it's sure as hell an offer," he said. Whitney and Franklyn turned back to look at each other again; they both thought of the small town in Spain where they had already been sold a bill of goods.

Hargrove moved toward the Walkers, then took a seat across from them. He leaned forward, plaiting and unplaiting his fingers. "Whitney," he said slowly and clearly, "you have heard the offer my clients are making. Our interest is genuine. In a matter of days, this money will be yours to spend as you see fit. Please take some time to discuss the offer we are making."

Hargrove got up and returned to join Fritzbrauner, Gabler, Richard Davis, and the others at his table. Franklyn smirked slightly, then shook his head in disbelief before leaning in toward Whitcombe. "You mind if I ask you something?" he said.

Whitcombe nodded. "No, go right ahead."

"If we take the money," said Franklyn, "then these guys own the coins, am I correct?"

"If the coins can, in fact, be owned, that is correct," said Whitcombe. "Montaro has filled me in on the coins' unusual properties."

"Tell me about these guys. How rich are they?"

"Very."

"All that money probably wouldn't make much of a dent in their assets, right?"

"That's a reasonable assessment."

"But if they own the coins, in a sense they'll also own a part of my wife and me?"

"You could put it that way," said Whitcombe.

"What other way could you put it?" Franklyn asked, then looked up to pose a more general question. "Where are the coins right now?" he asked to the room at large.

Matthew Perch spoke up. "In my possession," he said.

Franklyn looked at Perch, then looked at his wife, who smiled at him.

"What do you think?" Whitney asked Franklyn.

Franklyn whispered something to Whitney, who whispered something back to him before Franklyn addressed a question to Kritzman Fritzbrauner.

"Mr. Fritzbrauner," he said. "Millions of men and women are inspired by the accomplishments of individuals such as yourself and the other men at your table. People hold you in high regard. You're known for your generous contributions to worthy causes. You and your families live, as do my wife, my child, and I, on planet Earth. Our ongoing survival depends totally on this particular planet. This is our only home. Let me ask you this—why do you and Mr. Gabler seek to own the coins?"

"Well, Mr. Walker," Hargrove began.

"Forgive me," Franklyn interrupted—his manner was polite, but his voice was firm. "I would like to hear what Mr. Fritzbrauner has to say."

A swift glance passed between Fritzbrauner and Hargrove before Fritzbrauner spoke. "Because they are rare, Mr. Walker," Fritzbrauner said, "and I collect rare objects. It would be a great honor for me to have them, or even one of them, in my collection. It's as simple as that. No mystery. No hidden agenda."

"The same goes for you, Mr. Gabler?" asked Franklyn.

"Same," said Gabler.

"Now, let me ask you this," Franklyn continued. "You have offered us a great deal of money for these coins, more money than I ever thought I would see in my life. And yet, from what we have learned, these coins seem to have their own minds. Say we sell these coins to you and they once again disappear. Would you then ask us to repay you?"

Fritzbrauner had no immediate answer to this question. Briefly, Hargrove huddled with Gabler and Fritzbrauner. "The risk will belong entirely to my clients," Hargrove finally told Franklyn. "Once the sale is made, that will be the end of the matter from your perspective."

Franklyn whispered something to his wife, then gestured to Montaro, asking him to join them. For some minutes, they spoke in confidence with Gordon Whitcombe. When they were done, Franklyn nodded to Montaro, who stood and walked toward the center of the room. He moved as if in a trance, thinking back over the events of the past months—the difficulties with Fitzer; his daughter's precarious situation; the strange appearance of the coins, which had brought him to this private room in an elegant restaurant with an odd assortment of people he was now connected to in ways he could not even explain. He thought of the model of the Seventh Ship that had hovered before him, filling his room and vision with breathtaking, colorful images.

Montaro knew that he had to speak, but he still did not know what he would say. *Speak what is inside you,* he heard his grandfather's voice telling him. *You have been listening as best you have been able, with your inner ear, with all your senses. You have opened yourself to the world and the people around you. You have been paying attention, hearing the words beneath the words, hearing the words unspoken.* And then, as he listened to the voice of his grandfather inside, Montaro found his own voice.

"Franklyn and Whitney reject your offer," he said. "But we would like you to join us in a major endeavor—one that, we believe, will prove rewarding not only for myself or my company but for everyone in this room and for those beyond this room as well." Not a flicker of a reaction appeared on the faces of Hargrove or his associates and clients; their confident smiles remained frozen on their faces.

Spreading his arms wide, as if to embrace everyone present, Caine continued. "Each of us has experienced the state of tranquillity, a peaceful state of being that comes at times of its own choosing. Very often it comes when we are most in need. It calms our thoughts and nurtures our body for a time—then passes on. We also know turmoil. We are frequently distressed by it, very often ravaged by it. Tranquillity and turmoil are, fundamentally, opposites, but in some configurations, they are as close as next-door neighbors. Though they can be light-years apart, they very often dwell in the same house.

"On this little planet we call home, we struggle for survival among an astonishing variety of other life-forms, among which we perceive ourselves to be the preeminent force—the force in charge. Is that not the way it is for us? We live here. We die here. Are we alone in this galaxy? In this universe? In this solar system, we seem to be the only human beings. But in the galaxy, in the universe itself, I believe there may well be countless other forms of life. Among us here today are signs suggesting that we are not alone in our galaxy. In fact, some of these life-forms might even be similar to ourselves. In a distant future, a thousand generations from now, if we are lucky enough to still exist, our science will provide the children of the future with answers to profound questions that have not yet been formulated by the greatest thinkers of our own time. Science must bear witness on our behalf; it must question our greatest thinkers, listen to them, challenge them, support them, and, most of all, demand answers from them. Science and education are the only forces that can, one day, take us to places not yet dreamed of. Under no circumstances should these coins be shut away in the dark reaches of steel vaults and iron safes, or on the shelves of museums or private collections before we have had a chance to uncover the purpose behind their existence. That is, of course, if they allow us to examine them.

"Here, now, is our offer to you, Hargrove, and to those you represent. Let us create a foundation to which the coins will be entrusted. If Kritzman, Richard, and Roland choose, they may all be on the board of that foundation, and so may Franklyn and Whitney. The board's purpose will be to support the growth of science and education. Why science? None of us in this room knows for sure whether we human creatures are, or are not, alone in the universe. Only science can lead us to such answers. Only science, over time, will be able to take us to the nearest sun, point us toward the center of the galaxy, guide us within safe range of a black hole. If, on the other hand, we discover that we are alone in the galaxy, then science will be our best tool as well for learning how to cope and survive.

"As human beings, we are imperfect creatures who will spend our lives reaching for that better self we so often see in the mirrors of our minds. We are unable to accept the fact that the real self and the better self together are who we really are. We are unending opposites, made up of both good and evil; capable of love and hatred, kindness and cruelty. With the help of our better selves, we can invigorate the strength of this great country and, in turn, the world at large."

Caine stopped speaking and a long silence prevailed. All eyes were on Hargrove and those at his table. Suddenly, a roar of laughter came rumbling out of the lawyer. "Not only have you rejected our offer, you've come with a proposal of your own," he said. He turned to Matthew Perch, who was standing near the door.

"Mr. Perch," Hargrove said. "Unlike the rest of us, you are perceived to be an extraordinary human being by some who are present here. Before we respond, would you care to offer your thoughts on the issues we've been discussing?"

"My thoughts?" Perch asked, then said simply, "They echo Mr. Caine's." The room fell quiet once again as Hargrove and Perch stared at each other.

Kritzman Fritzbrauner spoke up. "Mr. Perch," he said, "may I ask you a question?"

"You may," said Perch.

"Some weeks ago," Fritzbrauner began, "Montaro called and asked me to check my safe to see whether or not the coin I had purchased from Cordiss Krinkle was still in my vault. When I looked, I discovered that it had vanished. I'd like to know, did you, in any way, have any influence in the removal of that coin from my safe?"

"I did not."

"Did Montaro, to your knowledge, have any connection with that coin's disappearance?"

"Not to my knowledge," said Perch. "But he's here, so you may ask him directly."

"I would," Fritzbrauner replied, "but he has said such nice things about me tonight that I don't dare accuse him." Spontaneous laughter quickly bubbled at Fritzbrauner's remark, then just as quickly disappeared when the Beaumont's maître d' returned. This time, the maître d' was accompanied by Tom Lund and Luther John Doe's caretaker.

"Once again, please excuse this intrusion, gentlemen," the maître d' said, "but, I believe these were the people you have been waiting for."

"Yes, we were," Caine replied. "But where's Luther?"

"He died this morning," the caretaker said.

A ripple of disbelief coursed through the room before the caretaker spoke again. "He died peacefully. But before he did, he asked me to give you these." She reached into her shoulder bag and withdrew a batch of sealed envelopes.

"And what are those?" Hargrove asked.

"Letters. From Luther. He woke me up early this morning and asked for my help in writing some letters. He seldom wrote anything, but when he did, he would dictate it to me. I wrote down what he said word for word. When we were finished with the letters, he seemed exhausted and confused. Then he looked up at me and said, 'Promise me you will see to it that my letters are read. Then take me home so I can rest.' He died five minutes later. His last request was that each letter be read aloud."

The letters were addressed to each of the Walkers, Matthew Perch, Colette Fritzbrauner, and Montaro.

Caine rose to take his letter. Though he had not yet read a word, his eyes were already wet, thinking of the strange, crippled man who was one of the last people to see his father alive.

Montaro read aloud from the letter Luther had written him while Luther's caretaker and Tom Lund distributed the rest of the letters to their intended recipients. "The gift I carved for you those many years ago, I had seen it in my dreams. Everything I told you and Dr. Mozelle, when you finally came to see me, was true. I never lied," Luther had written. "We will meet again. And when we do, it will be in a world far away, one that will be waiting to greet us."

Caine sat back down and rested his head on his hand as he contemplated the words he had read. The room was utterly silent. Then Matthew Perch opened his letter. "You will wander through the twilight of times past and those yet to come," he read with quiet solemnity. "Prepare yourself for journeys without end. You will come to know many more of Heaven's endless secrets, and observe the majesty of their designs."

Next, Colette Beekman Fritzbrauner read aloud what Luther John Doe had dictated in his letter to her. "You wonder what your purpose is," she read, surprised to find her voice wavering. "What is your destiny? You have questions but no answers. In the search for answers to life's questions, purpose and destiny reveal themselves in a variety of subtle, complex signs and hints, not all of which are easily under-stood. Put your questions to whoever you feel is obliged to provide you with such answers as you seek. Do not hesitate. Upon some lucky occasions, you will find that the person who has the answers to your questions is none other than yourself."

When she had finished reading, Colette continued standing, star-ing down, her watery eyes still fixed on the page. She thought of what her "purpose" and her "destiny" might be, and how these words that touched her so deeply could have been written by a dying man who barely knew her. Then, Colette slowly raised her head and stared at Matthew Perch. Looking directly at him, she asked, "Do you believe what Luther John Doe said? That our individual destinies have led each of us to gather here?"

"I do," Perch said.

Colette pressed on. "The little model we all saw last week, the one that lifted itself off the table—did it have the ability to choose for it-self how best to protect itself when there seemed to be danger? Was that carving doing its own thinking when it seemed to be looking for a safe place to land?"

"That is my interpretation," Perch said.

"And the materials in the coins that we are fighting over," Colette continued. "Can those elements, and will those elements—as some at this table have stated—be of considerable advantage to humans in the years ahead?"

"I believe this is so. Yes," Perch said.

As Colette spoke, the dynamics in the room seemed to shift. Her-man Freich and Kritzman Fritzbrauner appeared surprised, much the way Colette had looked surprised when reading the words contained in Luther's letter. As Colette looked through her gathering tears at Montaro Caine, she recognized what it was that drew her to him, not so much a physical attraction but a quality of his that had been miss-ing from her life, one she longed to embody—a truth, an honesty, the same sort of quality she saw manifested by some of the others who were in the room with her—the Walkers, the Mozelles, Anna Hil-burn, Carrie Pittman, and Matthew Perch.

"Do you know what my destiny is, my purpose?" Colette asked Perch.

"I do not," said Perch. "But I, like Luther, believe that if you look hard enough within yourself, you may find your answer there." Kritzman Fritzbrauner saw his daughter's tears and he immediately understood her turmoil—Montaro had spoken truthfully, he thought, for turmoil and tranquillity could indeed live in the same house. A deep understanding passed between the man and his daughter, an understanding that did not need words to make itself known. Fritzbrauner turned from his daughter and spoke directly to Franklyn. "We hear what you are saying—in more ways than you might think," he said. "You and your wife have honorable values; we all recognize that. We do understand." He then nodded to Julius Hargrove as if relaying some signal. Hargrove leaned forward, focused on Franklyn, and said, speaking in the spirit of conciliation, "Our wants and needs may be different, Franklyn, but they are not necessarily incompatible. I sincerely believe that we can resolve this issue in a manner acceptable to both sides. Our position on Montaro's proposal for a foundation is that we will remain flexible as long as joint ownership continues to be a viable possibility. As long as it can work its way through the channels of honest give-and-take, your foundation will have our blessing, but not our participation, not yet. That decision will ultimately be up to you."

Franklyn nodded and considered. Hargrove's answer was a good one, and yet, he sensed, not quite good enough. Holding the two remaining letters in his hands, Franklyn hesitated, gazed around the table, then opened the letter that bore his name. "Your destiny and that of your wife and child are written," he read aloud. "And so they will remain. What will be will be. Matthew Perch will be gone soon, and so will I. Mr. Perch's obligations await him elsewhere. In my case, my days are done, and my final sleep is near." Franklyn then opened the last letter, which was addressed to his wife. He handed it to her and she read its one brief line aloud. "Only you and the universe know for sure what the destiny of your son will be."

Franklyn took his letter and his wife's, folded them, and slipped them into a pocket of his jacket. Then he spoke, as if the contents of Luther's letters had revealed all that he needed to know. "I believe that by now, we have all had enough time to consider our situation," said Franklyn. "And I think we all agree that despite the financial transactions that have taken place, the coins rightfully belong to my wife and me. At the same time, it is clear by now that they really belong to no one but themselves. If we can put them to use for the greater good of humanity, and if they don't first whisk themselves away to some place where perhaps they will be needed or appreciated more, that is what my wife and I believe we must do. Kritzman, Roland—I am truly sorry about your financial loss; Cordiss and Victor took you for a ride. They took us for a ride, too, and Howard and Anna and Carrie Pittman as well. But your loss has no bearing on the decisions we must make now. It is true that my wife and I could use even a small part of the money you have offered us—especially now that we have a son. But we have been presented with a unique opportunity. If we have been chosen for some higher purpose, surely we must have faith that we will find ways to take care of our more mundane needs.

"My child is only one week old," he continued. "Leaving him a planet with no investment in its future would be a betrayal. Here I am, almost thirty years older than my son. Yes, I am fairly well educated, reasonably well informed. Yes, I try as hard as I can to stay abreast of what makes the world go around. My wife and I want future generations to remember we were once a part of an historic moment in time and that we made the right decision.

"Whitney and I have no intention of taking your money, my friends. If your sole object is ownership, then there will be no need for any further discussion. But I trust Montaro, and I hope you will be able to join us in discovering the next step in this extraordinary journey. What lies ahead is a mystery.

"But," Franklyn concluded. "If there is anyone who can enlighten us about these mysteries, he is with us in this room." He turned to Matthew Perch. "Before you leave, Mr. Perch, would you be willing to share some of your wisdom with us?"

Perch looked at Franklyn, then upon the faces of each and every person in the room with the same intense understanding with which he had studied the faces of Hattie Sinclair and Elsen Mozelle many years before. Then Perch spoke. "The places I will go, you cannot," he said. "If you could, you would not. Your destiny is not mine. Your home is here. And your home is endangered. Consequently, so are you. Without this home, you or perhaps your children or grandchildren will die. Clearly, your destiny now rests in your own hands. But as Franklyn and Montaro have both told you, the seeds of a solution are already in your hands. The longer you do not act, the weaker the better self in each of you becomes, and the harder your struggle grows against the relentless pulls of greed, selfishness, and the addictive lust for power, which breeds wars and indifference to the sufferings of fellow human beings. Montaro is correct—science and education are the seeds that will blossom into the answers you seek. If you succeed, one day your efforts will have helped to forge new worlds in far-off civilizations in the distant reaches of our galaxy.

"It is not my place to tell you how to preserve the wisdom embodied in the coins, and perhaps the wisdom is not to be found in the coins, but in yourselves—you, after all, must learn how to use the knowledge and experience that lies within them. The man who has been handed that wisdom, in the form of a spaceship carved for him by a young boy, is here with us. Follow him and you will know how to proceed."

With this last statement, Perch's eyes focused on Montaro Caine.

Caine nodded and smiled. He felt both gratitude and a sense of responsibility, for he understood the faith and trust that both Matthew Perch and the Walkers were placing in him. He shook hands with Franklyn, then with Whitney. He smiled as he regarded the baby, still asleep in his carriage. He approached Hargrove's table, where he noticed that Colette's eyes were still moist. He offered his hand to her and she surprised him by giving him a warm embrace. Montaro turned to thank Perch and wish him well, but the man had already disappeared into the New York night.

Epilogue

THE BABY WAS HEALTHY—EIGHT AND A HALF POUNDS, WITH HIS mother's trusting brown eyes and just a hint of his father's suspicious smile. His parents had named him Luther John Walker—a tribute to the strange, gifted orphan who had helped to bring them together. Now, a boy named Luther John would have a last name and would grow up knowing who his parents were. Luther John Walker's hearing had been checked, his breathing was normal, and he already knew how to nurse from his mother. As he lay in Whitney Walker's arms, the boy's little fists were clenched tightly, but nothing was inside them.

Matthew Perch stood in the conference room of Howard Mozelle's clinic, the two coins still in his pocket wrapped in gauze. Mozelle had just given Whitney and her baby one last checkup before their trip back home to Georgia and was handing Franklyn a list of pediatricians in Atlanta. Anna Hilburn was finishing the day's paperwork and preparing to shut down the office for the evening. Still seated around Mozelle's conference table were Elsen, Montaro, Kritzman, Colette, and also Julius Hargrove and Gordon Whitcombe.

This would probably be the last time that all of these people would be gathered together in the same room. Later that night, Franklyn, Whitney, and their baby—with Dr. Mozelle's permission—would be flying back home to Atlanta on a private jet provided by Caine. In the morning, Kritzman and Colette would board a plane to Buenos Aires to see Colette's mother, after which they would travel back home to Switzerland. Montaro was due back home in Westport. And soon, Matthew Perch would be leaving too, although his destination was unknown to the others.

The details had not yet been worked out, but the basic framework for an arrangement had been agreed upon by all parties—the coins would be entrusted to a foundation whose board would include Montaro, the Walkers, the Mozelles, Kritzman Fritzbrauner and his daughter, as well as Richard Davis, Verna Fontaine, and Roland Gabler. Tom Lund would help to oversee the foundation's finances. Fitzer Corporation would provide the seed money for the foundation's initial endeavors. On Montaro's insistence, his friend Larry Buchanan would serve on the foundation board as well. However, if the foundation decided to develop and exploit the knowledge contained within the coins, the money gained from any endeavor would be used to support science and education. The agreement had not been easy to reach—Roland Gabler and Verna Fontaine had both argued that board members should receive greater compensation for their participation; Julius Hargrove had advised his clients to take more time before arriving at their decision. But Fritzbrauner had been firm and, eventually, everyone had come around to his idea of accepting the agreement both for the good of humanity and for that of their own egos. For Davis and Gabler, especially, the idea of being remembered for generations to come as men who had helped to develop the properties of the coins ultimately proved to be more important than the idea of owning the coins or profiting from them.

Now, with an open hand and a solemn expression, Perch passed the gauze-wrapped package to Franklyn, who passed it to his wife.

"Here," Perch said. "Here are the objects that brought all of us together."

Whitney gently unfolded the layers of gauze. As she stared at the coins for the first time, her lips quivered, and her eyes moistened. She made as if to speak but remained silent. She passed the coins to her husband, who likewise remained speechless as his tears began to flow.

The Walkers couldn't say for certain what impressed them more—the beauty of the craftsmanship that had gone into the smattering of stars that appeared on the faces of each coin, the fact that two and a half decades ago their hands had been as small as their son's were now and had clutched these very coins, or the understanding that these coins had brought the two of them together. Whitney handed the coins to Colette, while her father peered over her shoulder.

As father and daughter looked at the coins, they knew that in addition to the mystical tale of their arrival, the coins had demonstrated other great powers; they had brought Kritzman and Colette closer together. Colette looked to Matthew Perch, who nodded at the Walkers, and Colette handed the coins back to Franklyn.

"We're entrusting these to you," Franklyn said to Montaro.

But as Franklyn held his hand out to Montaro, Perch shook his head. "Keep them with you," he told Franklyn. "They will find their proper destination when it is time." Franklyn covered the coins with the gauze and placed them in his pocket. Perch nodded his approval.

Matthew Perch seemed as though he was getting ready to leave. He was gazing at the office door, or perhaps through that door to the world that lay beyond it. But before he could leave, Kritzman Fritzbrauner spoke.

"May I offer just a few words of thanks before you go, Mr. Perch?" Fritzbrauner asked.

Perch nodded.

"I don't really know who you are, or where you come from," said Fritzbrauner. "We met only a few days ago. But from what I've seen of you, I'm glad to have met you. You're a gentleman, the likes of which I've seldom seen. Somehow, you have taught me more about myself than just about anyone else ever has.

"Who are we?" Fritzbrauner asked, looking around as if to search the faces of the others in the room. "Who am I? I have always thought that I was hot stuff. I now realize I'm not." He pointed a finger at Perch. "You are hot stuff," he said. "That old black man Luther, he was hot stuff. He took with him to his grave a history of two worlds—one we know, the other so technologically advanced that we still can't comprehend it. What he knows will lie with him forever. What remains is still contained in the carving he made for Montaro.

"I admit that at first I didn't get it," Fritzbrauner said. "It's taken me this long to sense that something monumental has been happening. It's all around us, right in front of us. You, Mr. Perch, have opened my eyes. Being here with you feels like the beginning of the end of a monstrous darkness. I agree with Montaro. If we can all work together, despite our egos and our greed, despite whatever faults we might have, we may be able to see our way through the darkness to the light. Our journey may often feel like the steps of a baby being led to a place it does not understand. But if our choices are good and our motives are pure, we may trust that we will be led to the right place."

He reached for his daughter's hand and grasped it tightly. Colette smiled, and Matthew Perch offered a slight smile as well. Perch then gently placed a hand on Fritzbrauner's shoulder.

"You are right, of course," Perch said. "You do not know all the answers you seek to know yet; you shouldn't expect to. But you are beginning to ask the right questions, and that is what is most important. Too often, questions take the shape of one's doubts, and those doubts strive to weaken the better selves inside of us. Only by the constant strengthening of our better selves can we win against those doubts. There are doorways everywhere, leading everywhere. Let your better selves guide you and, who knows, one day, somewhere in a place far away, in this world or another, we may meet again."

Matthew Perch then turned to Montaro. "Allow me to tell you that, in my opinion, your company will heal and revitalize itself until it stands, once again, as strong as ever it did," he said. "Mind you, this will not happen without challenges, both for yourself and for your family. But if you trust your instincts, if you trust the paths that your father and grandfather and those before them made for you, you will see your way through."

Hargrove and Fritzbrauner each made as if to speak, but Perch held out his hand.

"Now, I truly must go," said Perch, "But all of you, remember that when the passage of time commingles with worthy efforts, the universe never fails to take notice and reward you in ways you are seldom aware of. If you remember nothing else, remember this."

Moments later, Matthew Perch was gone.

———

A glorious night was falling and the skies were clear as Montaro Caine stood in front of Howard Mozelle's clinic, waiting for the parking lot attendant to bring him his car. He had said good-bye to Kritzman Fritzbrauner and to Colette; he had wished the Walkers good luck, and he had told the rest of the members of the soon-to-be-formed foundation board that they would all be in touch, once Julius Hargrove and Gordon Whitcombe had worked out the details.

The worst of the after-work traffic had passed, and Montaro was anticipating a quick ride back to Westport. He was eager to get home to Cecilia and Priscilla—though he knew that he had had good reasons for spending as much time away from them as he had of late, he regretted all the nights he had spent alone at his apartment in The Carlyle. Yet he was a stronger man now—he was no longer a man of restless, sleepless nights, for whom a strong drink helped keep his terrors at bay. For all the time he had spent away from Cecilia and Priscilla, these two women would be granted a more thoughtful and considerate husband and father; in some way, the coins could be credited for creating this small miracle too.

Montaro had been standing alone on Park Avenue for some minutes when he heard the sound of a car slowing as it approached him. He reached for his money clip so that he could pay the garage attendant when he realized that this wasn't his car; it was a newer model Mercedes, navy blue, not black. Montaro was surprised when the Mercedes pulled up alongside him. The two passenger-side doors opened, and from the car emerged Carlos Wallace and Alan Rothman. The men wore ties and dark suits that almost seemed to match each other's; if Montaro had not known these men, he might have mistaken them for federal agents.

"Good evening," Montaro said warily as the men nodded at him, then shook his hand. Rothman stood close to Montaro, while Wallace stood in front of the rear door of the car, blocking Montaro's view of what was inside. "To what do I owe the pleasure?"

"We're here to offer our congratulations," said Rothman. "We've heard all about the foundation. It sounds like a worthy endeavor." But from Rothman and Wallace's stiff postures and pained smiles, Montaro knew that they had not sought him out in the spirit of cooperation.

"Thank you," Montaro said, then waited for the men to reveal their purpose.

"We understand that everything has been settled," said Rothman. "At least as far as the coins are concerned." He took a breath. "Business at Fitzer is, of course, another matter."

"I think you're mistaken there," said Montaro. "I've been meeting with your colleagues and your representatives. I've spoken with Davis, Hargrove, and everyone else. And at this point, I believe that everyone's needs have been satisfied."

"Perhaps. But we also have needs, and they have not been satisfied," said Rothman. "I do wish you luck with your foundation. But if your plan is to remain at the helm of Fitzer, that might not happen quite so easily. There could be complications."

Montaro's eyes narrowed. "Exactly what sort of complications are you referring to?" he asked.

Rothman stared directly into Montaro's eyes. "Put it this way," he said. "Certain information has come to our attention that might make it difficult for you to maintain your position."

"Really," Montaro said. "And where does this information come from?"

At this point, Carlos Wallace moved aside to reveal a person sitting in the backseat of the Mercedes.

Rothman opened the car door. "Step out here a minute, Nick," he said.

Nick Corcell was wearing a good suit and gleaming black shoes; apparently, he was being paid well. He looked cocky as he got out of the car.

Montaro felt his anxieties returning. Rothman did not need to say anything more for Montaro to understand what he and Wallace had in mind. This wasn't the end of the Fitzer story, far from it; Montaro had already known that this would be true even before Matthew Perch had told him that great challenges lay ahead. How often had P. L. Caine taught his grandson that there would always be hard times, and that a man had to stand up to them no matter what? The way forward wouldn't be any easier than the way here had been. Rothman and Wallace wouldn't give up their quest for power, and surely, Cordiss Krinkle and Victor Lambert wouldn't either. Most probably, Rothman and Wallace were planning to blackmail Montaro into resigning; they knew that he had used his influence so that the Stockbridge Police Department would stop pursuing charges against his daughter. And once again Montaro would be forced to weigh the importance of his career against the importance of his family, the public concerns he faced at his job against the private ones he faced at home.

As Montaro searched for the right words to speak, he felt a slight vibration inside the pocket of his sport jacket, and that vibration eased his doubts. He knew, without even needing to open the model of the Seventh Ship that Luther John Doe had carved, that the coins were once again inside it; they had arrived at their chosen destination. Many years ago, Perch had prophesised that someday the "son" would hold the coins. Not until this moment did Montaro understand that he was the son of whom Perch had been speaking, and that the coins would be in his care.

When Montaro's Mercedes emerged from the garage and the attendant stepped out from the driver's side of the car, Montaro stared Rothman and then Wallace straight in the eye. And then, remembering something, he smiled.

"You know," Montaro said, "a man who is far more intelligent than you or I can ever hope to be once told me that in order to see who a man truly is, you need to look him in the eye. Looking in your eyes, I can see exactly what you men are. I should feel hate for what you would like to do to me and to my family, but in my heart, I have only pity."

"Pity?" Rothman asked sneering.

"Yes. Pity," said Caine. "Over these past few months, I've learned that there are multitudes of worlds beyond our own. I feel sorry that you will never be able to see beyond this one."

"Is that some kind of threat?" asked Rothman.

Caine shook his head, then recalling something Matthew Perch had said, he responded. "It is simply truth," he said. "Truth is all there is. I hope you enjoy your day at Fitzer Corporation tomorrow. Understand that it will be your last." Then, Montaro paid the attendant, got into his car, and began his drive home.

Traffic clogged the highway when Montaro approached the Triborough Bridge en route to I-278. With his car stalled behind the line of cars in front of him, he took a moment to look up at the sky. The lights from the city cast a haze across the darkened firmament, but nevertheless a configuration of stars was visible. The stars were arranged in a recognizable pattern, save for one extra star that was passing through. Montaro knew it was nothing more than a meteor, or a shooting star, and yet it brought to mind the star or moon he had seen on the coin that he had examined many years ago and that was now inside the model of the Seventh Ship that was in his pocket. And as he saw that star making its way across the sky, almost as if leaving one world for another, he felt a profound surge of optimism. The car in front of him began to move forward and Montaro put his foot on the gas pedal; he headed home, ready for what awaited him.

———

Whitney and Franklyn Walker saw the shooting star, too. They were on board the jet bound for Atlanta when they saw it traveling across the sky. Their son, Luther John, had been sleeping in Whitney's arms since the moment of takeoff; the lights in the cabin were off, and aside from the pilots and a physician, they were the only ones on the plane.

Whitney and Franklyn did not know the names of the stars they were seeing out their window, but they both felt that when they saw the shooting star, someone or something was heading toward home, just as they, too, were heading home. They were not surprised to find, when Franklyn took the gauze out of his pocket, that it was empty;

after a long journey, the coins were on their way home now, too. The coins had traveled through so many worlds to bring Franklyn and Whitney Walker together and guide them through this world. As the Walkers looked down to watch Luther John sleep, they knew that their love would be strong enough to guide their son through this one.

Acknowledgments

M Y LIFE HAS HELD AN ENCHANTING FASCINATION WITH THE universe. As a young boy, as young as four or five, I was often drawn to the dense sprinkling of lights in the sky and I would wonder how so many such lights could be everywhere at night and disappear so completely by morning. The seed for this book was planted in that young boy's fascination.

No book is ever the work of one individual. Such is the case with this one, for without Cindy Spiegel, *Montaro Caine* would have remained an arresting idea instead of maturing into a truly stirring adventure. Her unrelenting instincts were so keen that she recognized each and every emotional heartbeat that pounded in the chest of every character in this book. Hers is a challenging profession, but she manages to unearth the humanity at the heart of every manuscript she chooses to publish, with a work ethic that is unyielding in bringing out the best there is in each author she represents.

To my editor, Adam Langer, who has as firm a grasp on the English language as ever there was—he has heard language spoken on a multitude of cultural levels that define class, educational levels, and social standings, all of which speak of the who that we are and the who that we aspire to become. He is a wordsmith of extraordinary talent and swift execution, and I thank him for his professional approach and insight.

To Susan Garrison, gifted, talented in countless areas. Her sharp eyes and her many talents are eagerly awaiting her decision to set her sails toward the stars.

To Sherrie Brooks, my right-hand "man," a hard and experienced worker adroit in so many areas—all of which she seemingly effortlessly calls upon as she manages the day-to-day keeping of the office and details of my many obligations running flawlessly.

Carl Sagan, a good friend, no longer here and sorely missed. He has left behind his many books, his many thoughts of who he was and what he has done—what he has really done.

And to my family, for none of this would have been remotely possible without their love and support, especially that of my rock, the love of my life, Joanna.

ABOUT THE AUTHOR

The author of three bestselling autobiographical books, *This Life* (1980), *The Measure of a Man: A Spiritual Autobiography* (2000), and *Life Beyond Measure: Letters to My Great-Granddaughter* (2008), Sidney Poitier is an actor, film director, author, and diplomat. In 1963, Poitier won an Academy Award for Best Actor for his role in *Lilies of the Field*, and has starred in films including *To Sir, with Love; In the Heat of the Night;* and *Guess Who's Coming to Dinner*. The movies he has directed include *Uptown Saturday Night, Let's Do It Again, A Piece of the Action,* and *Stir Crazy.* In 1999, the American Film Institute named Poitier among the Greatest Male Stars of All Time, and in 2002, Poitier was chosen by the Academy of Motion Picture Arts and Sciences to receive an Honorary Oscar for "his remarkable accomplishments as an artist and as a human being." He was the Bahamian ambassador to Japan from 1997 to 2007. And in 2009, was awarded the Presidential Medal of Freedom, the United States' highest civilian honor, by President Barack Obama. Mr. Poitier was born in Miami, Florida, but spent his first fifteen years growing up in the Bahamas, on Cat Island and later in Nassau. Mr. Poitier currently lives in Beverly Hills, California, with his wife of forty-four years, Joanna Shimkus Poitier.

ABOUT THE TYPE

The text of this book was set in Janson, a misnamed typeface designed in about 1690 by Nicholas Kis, a Hungarian in Amsterdam. In 1919 the matrices became the property of the Stempel Foundry in Frankfurt. It is an old-style book face of excellent clarity and sharpness. Janson serifs are concave and splayed; the contrast between thick and thin stokes is marked.